REALM ONLINE

OATHBREAKER

STUART THAMAN

NEF HOUSE PUBLISHING

Realm Online: Oathbreaker

Copyright © 2019 Stuart Thaman
Nef House Publishing
www.stuartthamanbooks.com

ISBN: 978-1-937979-52-2

Cover by J Caleb Clark (www.jcalebdesign.com)
Interior layout by Bodie D Dykstra (www.bdediting.com)

ALSO BY STUART THAMAN

The Goblin Wars Series
The Minotaur King
Siege of Talonrend
Death of a King
Rebirth of a God

The Umbral Blade Series
Shadowlith
Mournstead

Killstreak Series
Respawn
Heavy Armor
Kingsgate

Forsaken Talents Series
A Dark Path
A Black Soul
A Ruined World

Realm Online Series
Oathbreaker
Citadel Deathgaze

Chronicles of Estria
Blood and Ash

Short Story Collections
Unsheathed
Against All Odds

For my cats. They don't really help me write, and they barely even acknowledge that I'm alive, but I love them nonetheless.

CHAPTER 1

"How many more pigs could you possibly need?" Jaerth exclaimed. He watched his master, a raven-haired woman named Bokta, slaughter a pen full of pigs and dump their innards into a boiling vat. The woman wasn't preparing the pigs to be eaten, as evinced by the hexagonal star drawn with salt on the ground beneath the pot.

Bokta shot Jaerth a crooked glance. "Summoning requires great patience and great sacrifice," she told him for what felt like the hundredth time.

"Yes, but have you ever been successful?" the insolent boy asked. He was only fifteen, and he had not yet learned his place.

Bokta laughed, her youthful voice displaying all the arrogance her status as a blood witch afforded her. "It will work, little one," she scolded, though she was only seven years older than her assistant. "Just wait. In due time, I will have the demon in my grasp, enslaved to my will, and he will obey my every command."

"As long as I get paid," Jaerth muttered. He herded another pair of small pigs into the room from their pen outside. He felt bad for them, but a job was a job, and he didn't often complain. Needlessly killing a few pigs was pretty far from the worst act he had seen the self-proclaimed blood witch perform in her constant pursuit of some demon or other equally crazed machination.

"Bring my scrying mirror," Bokta commanded, and the boy complied at once. The mirror was covered in many layers of filth and grime, with only the very center left clean enough to function.

Bokta sprinkled a few grains of powdered sulfur over the surface, bringing it to life. In the center of the crusted mirror, she saw her target—the demon she would summon into the world and then bind. His name was Maxkrannar, and he was mighty indeed. Bokta had been watching the demons in their realm ever since she had learned how to scry with her mirror, and they fascinated her day in and day out. She knew all of their adventures, all of their heroic tales, and most of all, she knew which demons could command the others. Maxkrannar was one of the most highly respected beings she had ever deigned to follow. His exploits were known throughout the demon realm, bringing reverence and obedience with them in droves.

"When will you be able to summon the demon?" Jaerth dared to ask.

Bokta brushed a strand of black hair from her face. "You will know when I am ready," she answered. "For now, we must continue to prepare for the demon's coming. The components take a long time to make ready."

"What does the demon eat?" the boy wondered aloud. "I bet he'll be hungry when he gets here."

Bokta put a thoughtful finger to her chin. "I have only seen him eat one thing, a dry biscuit," she said, an expression of curiosity coming over her face.

The image on her scrying mirror swirled and manifested before her eyes. Maxkrannar was at the center of a great battle, slaying strange lizards and massive hornets with impunity. He wielded a mighty war cleaver and wore what looked to be hundreds of pounds of gleaming, golden plate protecting his body. Sometimes, if Bokta was lucky, she would get to see the demon use his own magic. Maxkrannar could throw great thunderbolts through the air to strike his foes, but she had only seen him do it on a few occasions.

The blood witch stared on with rapt intensity as Maxkrannar slaughtered wave after wave of vicious beasts. She tilted her mirror to get a look at where the demon was going, but she already knew the goal of his quest. There was a powerful queen at the top of a temple in the distance—a hideous being with six arms and two heads who could spit acid strong enough to melt armor. Bokta had watched the demon kill the six-armed woman dozens of times. The method of the six-armed woman's revival still eluded the witch, though she was confident her demonic champion would put an end to the wretched beast once and for all.

She watched as Maxkrannar commanded his four companions into position, heroic warrior demons in their own right, and the group gained a foothold into their adversary's sacred temple. Beams of fire shot down on the group from enchanted lanterns suspended from towers, adding a warm red haze to the entire scene. As he had done many times before, Maxkrannar called out a command, and one member of his team began to glow with a pale blue aura that extinguished the flames.

Bokta's heart caught in her throat when a new development, one she had not seen before, appeared in the scrying mirror. In the midst of combat, another group of demons charged in, and they seemed determined to bring Maxkrannar to his knees. The newcomers were similarly clothed, but they carried different banners attached to their armor. Bokta knew their sigil. She had seen it before, but only once, and never when her beloved Maxkrannar was on such an important mission.

The two groups fought, and spells flew through the air, accenting the constant ring of metal on metal. After the briefest of moments, the clash was resolved. Two of Maxkrannar's companions were dead, and the unexpected attackers had all been routed. The three remaining demons stood still for a long time at the entrance to the temple. They stood in such fashion often, sometimes not moving for hours, and Bokta had a theory about why. *They must communicate without speech*, she surmised, though if that were true, she knew she would have a much more difficult time controlling the powerful demon when she finally summoned it.

Eventually, some half an hour later, the three remaining demons faded away into nothing. Bokta watched a moment longer before she tilted the mirror vertically and dumped the sulfur onto the ground. The image swirled away, leaving behind a sour smell in the air that matched Bokta's ruined mood.

"More pigs!" the woman barked.

Jaerth brought three of the animals into the small room and led them to side of the cauldron. "These are all that are left," the boy said.

"Fine," Bokta spat. "It will be enough. Slit their throats and drop them into the mixture."

Jaerth shuddered in disgust, but he picked up the knife anyways. "What exactly does this accomplish?" he asked.

The blood witch whirled on him. "It is a demon I am summoning, not some basket full of kittens!" she yelled. "The demon will require lubricant to make it through the rift between our worlds! He will expect to be welcomed with a shower of blood and gore!"

"Fine, fine," Jaerth relented. He slid the knife across another pig's neck and then threw the carcass into the boiling pot.

"Tomorrow," Bokta said with a hiss. "I'll summon the mighty demon tomorrow . . ."

CHAPTER 2

"Fuck it . . . I'm gonna be late," I mumbled. My keys were *always* never where I left them. In fact, nothing in my shitty apartment ever seemed to stay right where I left it. I pushed aside a few empty beer cans that had been building up on the only counter space in the room and heard my keys jingle against aluminum on their way down to the floor. Apparently, one of the beer cans had still been half full as well.

"I'm never getting the deposit back on this place," I needlessly reminded myself. I flicked the switch to turn off the lights on my way out the door and nearly tripped over a package waiting in the hallway. It had probably been there since yesterday. I checked the label to make sure the box held my new gaming headphones, then tossed it through the door behind me.

My car, a beat-up '06 Ford Taurus with dents in all four doors, was parked just slightly over the line in the garage next to my apartment. As it turned out, that was good enough to earn my seventh parking ticket in the past two months. Ratchet-ass bitches always giving me fines . . . I crumpled the ticket and threw it in my cluttered back seat with all the others. My car didn't really 'peel out,' but it certainly squeaked as I mashed on the gas to get to work.

As predicted, I arrived at Hefner, Deen, and Anderson Accounting, LLC, exactly twenty-one minutes after I was supposed to. And yes, I knew my accounting firm was named after three porn stars. The old guys that founded the place had totally mundane names themselves, and they thought it some huge joke to slap a risqué trio of monikers on the front of the business. Unfortunately, most of our clients were old ladies who had inherited their money from their late husbands, so none of them ever got the raunchy innuendo. Such a waste of a mediocre joke.

"You're late," my boss, a short and portly man named Jim, droned in my ear. He stood next to my cubicle like a little gnome, a sly grin on his face and an overly large coffee mug in his hand.

"Yeah, sorry, I'll stay until six tonight," I told him.

Jim let out a comically long sigh for effect. "I believe we have now reached your third instance of tardiness this week, Steven," he chided.

"It's just 'Steve,'" I told him again. How many times would he refuse to use my name? Only my parents called me Steven, and they had basically stopped calling altogether after I quit repaying the student loans I had taken out in their names back in undergrad. That was reasonable, I supposed, but it still sucked.

"I'm not sure how much longer Mr. Barnes is going to want your kind here," Jim said cryptically as he walked off, inexplicably humming some annoying tune into the rim of his coffee mug. What the hell was 'my kind' supposed to mean? Underachieving white males? Sorry, buddy—that's about ninety percent of the accounting workforce.

"Hey," my only friend in the office said, peeking his face around the corner of my little prison. His name was Brayden, a name I despised, but he was actually a cool guy most of the time.

"What's up?"

"You're not staying until six tonight, right?" he asked.

"Fuck no," I replied. "We're raiding tonight."

Brayden stuck out his fist for me to bump, just another one of the wildly 'bro-ish' things he did to live up to his frat-boy name. "There's my man!" he said with a laugh. "We can't expect to stop the spectral invasion without our fearless raid leader!"

"Yeah, yeah," I said. "Just help me get my audit report typed up so I don't get fired. Realm of Crafted War isn't free you know, and neither is my rent."

"Dude, Realm is only thirty a month! You could make that begging for change on the street," he said. I wasn't sure if he was serious or not. Brayden often concocted some of the world's dumbest ideas.

"What about my rent?" I asked. To be honest, the prospect of never returning to my little hell hole of a job was somewhat intriguing. Maybe I would just keep buying lottery tickets . . . The infamous tax on the poor paid off for some people, right?

Brayden's face lit up like I had just suggested the best thing he had ever heard. "Dude, come live with me!" he basically shouted. "You can crash in my basement!"

"You mean your parents' basement?" I clarified with a sigh.

"Yeah, man, Bill and Nancy would love you. You're right

up their alley," he went on, completely uncaring that he was a thirty-year-old with a full-time job still living at home.

"Right up their alley?" I repeated. "What, am I joining their sex club?"

"Eww, man," Brayden said with mock disgust. "Get outta here with that shit."

I turned back to my work and pressed the power button on my monitor. "Just type half the report for me," I told him. "If you get it done before lunch, I'll give you an extra loot roll tonight."

I could practically hear Brayden's fist pump from his cubicle. "Yeah, man, if those magic regen shoulders drop, I'm totally rolling on them," he said. Brayden had been playing Realm since even before I joined, and he always bragged about knowing every single piece of gear the devs had ever made, including the stuff not yet released. He'd played in the beta, and according to him, that made him some sort of self-proclaimed Realm of Crafted War deity. Whatever.

"So get typing," I commanded. I grabbed a manila portfolio from a plastic tray on my desk and tossed it over the cheap barrier separating our computers.

Five o'clock didn't roll around soon enough. It never did. The time just ticked slowly away, taking my will to live with it. Finally, after several coffee breaks, several bathroom breaks that took far longer than necessary, and a twenty-minute foray to the vending machine that resulted in absolutely nothing since I had no cash, most of the office began to leave. I waited for Jim to appear fully engrossed in whatever graph was displayed on the massive monitor in his corner office, then ducked out a side door that led down to an emergency exit.

Back at the Pineview Terrace Apartments, I threw some nasty pre-cooked meat pocket thing into the microwave and fired up my computer. My desktop computer was the only thing of value I owned in the world. I had built it myself, and I was damn proud of it. My computer launched faster than most people would even be able to find the power button—which was discreetly hidden behind a white, unlabeled panel. Pretty bitchin', I know.

The microwave beeped, and I grabbed the hot paper plate from the little rotating tray inside and sat down to raid. The login screen took a painfully long time, but I used the wait to unbox my new headphones. They weren't the best, and the mic wasn't even fully mobile, but they would work, and they were cheap. Plus, they had a good bit more red LED lighting than my last pair, just in case an errant female happened to wander into my room and be impressed by a slightly overweight nerd with pretty lights over his ears. It hadn't happened yet, but I never gave up hope. I was an optimistic kind of guy.

"Welcome to Realm," a voice I knew all too well chimed. For whatever reason, Snowstorm Entertainment had updated literally everything about the game over the last ten years, but the soft, female intro voice had never changed. I had even made it my ringtone once, but that was back when I had been in a rather dark place. I'd prefer not to delve into the details.

As always, I took a minute to admire my character on the selection screen. I had hundreds of different characters spread across multiple servers, but Maxkrannar was my pride and joy. He was my first character, the epicenter of my online addiction, and I'd probably die in real life if his data ever got cleared somehow from the server. He stood tall amidst a generic city of ruin, his two huge swords held easily in his muscled hands. He had horns that spiraled up from his forehead and marked him as an Oathbreaker, a class of fallen paladins that used to defend the Realm but now sought to destroy it. Oathbreakers were hard to play, and some said they were overpowered, but I had picked it for the lore. If I was going to sink thousands of hours of my life into something, I wanted that something to be thoroughly badass. Some people had cars they worked on every night, other people shot heroin into their bodies until they died. I had Realm.

I clicked the 'Enter' button which started another loading screen displaying images of the great battle that had been raging ever since the last patch came out. No matter which battle scene the game randomly chose to show, the words 'Created by Tom Arnold' were always printed across the top in semi-transparent letters. As for the battles themselves, the Oathbreakers had finally established a beachhead at Citadel Deathgaze, and enemies had been pouring out to meet us every day. That was the area the game had randomly decided to display on the loading screen, and it was also the destination we had in mind for the raid.

My voice-over interface sounded, and I clicked the little green phone icon that spliced me into the team chat. "Hey, guys," I said, accepting the instantaneous party invite on-screen as well.

"Sup."

"Hey, man."

"How's it going?"

"We gonna finish tonight?"

"I finished your mom last night."

"Guys," I interjected, getting my four closest friends back on track. "Are you ready? We need more potions than last time. Hey, Cro, did you get any more herbs? I'll need, like . . . six of those regeneration pots."

"Yeah, man," Cro answered. He opened a trade window with me and handed over a stack of red potions. "Let's just hope we don't get ganked like we did yesterday. That was bullshit."

"Yeah," everyone agreed over top of each other.

"Did anyone check the message boards last night?" I asked. "I bet it was one of those lame guilds from New Zealand that's always posting gank videos online."

"Yeah, I checked," Cro said. "If it was them, they haven't uploaded anything yet."

Our characters mounted up on various beasts of burden to head toward Citadel Deathgaze, but my attention was momentarily stolen by a strange smell in my apartment that made me look around for its origin. "Ugh, it smells like ass in my place," I said over chat. "Give me a minute, guys, it smells like I left the stove on or something. It reeks."

I gently laid down my new headset on the side of my desk. The stove wasn't on, and nothing was backed up in the bathroom, not that either option would have been a surprise. I made sure my only window was shut and locked, though it always was. I thought it might actually have been painted shut. I glanced up at the smoke detector in my small kitchen. A little red light slowly blinked on the front, and I guessed that was a good sign. Hell if I knew.

"What's carbon monoxide smell like?" I asked once I had my headset back over my ears.

"It doesn't have a smell, dipshit," Brayden graciously answered. His character, 'Strongwarrior43,' had a little speech bubble over its head. He emoted, making his character bend over in digital laughter. His character was decked out in obsidian armor, the most expensive thing anyone in the party owned, and I had been jealous of it since the day he'd won the roll for the drop.

"No, it smells like almonds. I saw it once in a movie," Cro added.

"Then why would you need a detector for it in your house?" Brayden countered. He had a point.

"Because almonds smell good, you jackass!" Cro fired back. "Who's gonna walk home, smell fresh almonds in their kitchen, and bail out? Everyone likes almonds. They're gonna stay, and then they're gonna die."

I had to admit, Cro had a point as well. "I'll look it up later," I told them. "But if I suddenly disappear during the raid, you'll know it was carbon monoxide. And, Brayden, I'm leaving you nothing in my will. All I own goes to King Halfthor, the mighty leader of the Oathbreakers!"

"You're so lame," Brayden said. Again, he had a point.

We reached the base of Citadel Deathgaze, and then everything went quiet. A few low-level Oathbreakers were fighting boars a ways behind us in the noob area, but other than them, no one was nearby. "Looks like it's just us, boys," I told my party.

"Woot!" Cro said. "More loot for me!"

"Alright, let's get the buffs rolling. I can't be late again to work tomorrow, so I need some sleep tonight. We have to be finished by two, two-thirty at the latest," I said.

The smell grew stronger in my apartment. I tried to wave it away, but it clung to the stagnant air. I didn't have a ceiling fan or I would have turned it on. Maybe it was time to open the window.

"One second, guys," I said, my frustration starting to

grow. "I've gotta figure out what the hell this smell is. It's driving me nuts."

I checked the bathroom again and flicked on the fan, leaving the door open to hopefully vent the place. It took the efforts of two different kitchen knives, but I managed to get the old window near my couch to slide up a few inches before it abruptly stopped for no reason at all. The outside air was fresh and clean smelling, unlike every single object in my apartment. Sadly, there wasn't enough airflow to get the wretched scent out of my beloved raid space.

"Whatever," I said, defeated. "I guess just call the cops if I die."

My raid mates laughed, and it looked like we were ready to begin our assault. Strongwarrior43 issued a magical shout, granting us each a power buff for the next eight minutes. It wasn't enough time, but if we planned it correctly, the two minutes of downtime while the skill was still on cooldown would come right during a lull in the fighting.

I was just about to click an aura on my skill bar when something in my chest made me take my hands off the keyboard for a moment. "Guys, for real, I think I might have been poisoned," I said into the mic.

"Cleanse incoming," Cro replied automatically. A blue haze washed over my character, clearing away any negative magical effects, of which there had been none.

"I'm talking about real life," I said, and the group chat got a little quiet. We cleared a wave of trash monsters in front of the citadel and stopped. "No, seriously, I think there's carbon monoxide in my apartment."

"Dude, you alright?" Brayden asked.

"I—I don't know."

A crushing sensation developed on my ribcage like

some invisible hand had begun throwing rocks into my bones. I tried to stand, but it was like a thousand-pound weight had been strapped to my chest. I couldn't move. "Guys, this is fucked up. Something's . . . Something's wrong." I could barely breathe.

"Uh, should we call the cops?" Cro asked, his voice ringing with concern, though I couldn't tell if he was being sincere or not.

"It fucking hurts!" I yelled through gritted teeth. The fake leather of my cheap office chair squealed in protest as I was pulled down toward the ground. The little pressure latch that kept the chair up to desk height crumpled, and the whole seat dropped about ten inches.

"What the fuck is happening?" I yelled, thankful that my headset was still on. I couldn't move my hands away from the armrests on the chair, and I couldn't even stretch out my fingers. All the blood in my body was being sucked into my center. I felt like I was about to crash through the floor.

"Dude, Steve, come on, man, what the hell are you doing?" Brayden shouted.

"Come on, Steve, let's just do the fight," Cro added. Apparently, that loser didn't believe me.

"Guys . . ." I struggled to speak. "Call the cops. I'm . . . gonna die."

The invisible weight increased, and the rest of the chair beneath me shattered in a violent spray of cheap plastic. I had a few extra pounds around my waist to be sure, but I wasn't even close to the ponderous size of some of my coworkers at the accounting firm, and I used the same chair in my apartment that we had at work! I knew it was *exactly* the same, mainly because I had stolen it from an empty cubicle a few months ago.

Lying on the floor, I could barely think. The headset had fallen from my ears when I had hit the carpet, but I could still hear my party talking frantically through the speakers. It sounded like one of them was in the process of calling the police.

Good. I didn't want to die in such a shitty, smelly apartment. Not before I finished my endgame build on Maxkrannar, at least. I still had some sick-ass loot to acquire. Lofty goals, I know.

I tried to lift my head from the dirty floorboard, but my neck snapped painfully back down, holding me rigidly in place. Then the floor began to crack as well. The wood splintered all around my body, and then everything went black.

CHAPTER 3

Holy shit.

Wherever I was, it smelled like a slaughterhouse full of guts that had been cooking in the hot sun for a decade or two. A few years ago my little nephew had thrown up at some family barbeque while I had been holding him, and a little bit of the kid's vomit had made it into my open mouth. That had been a rough day. Today was far worse.

I opened my eyes, and that was an *immediate* mistake. Whatever was putting off such a putrid smell also seemed to be covering my face, and my eyes burned like they were on fire. But hey, I was alive. That was the important part, though I'd probably be dead once my landlord saw the damage to his floor. My deposit would cover the spilled beer on the carpet, but the actual flooring was probably expensive. I was fucked.

Luckily, my arms were still capable of movement, so I pulled myself up to my elbows.

"It worked!" a female voice shrieked in happiness from somewhere to my left. "It worked! I summoned the demon!"

The fuck?

Her accent was hard to place, like a mixture of Australian and something I didn't know. And what was that business about a demon? If there was a demon in my apartment, I was going to go apeshit. There was no way in *hell* my deposit was going to cover that kind of nonsense.

I brushed most of the vile substance from my face, thankfully able to see once more.

I wasn't in my apartment.

I was in a hut—like a straw hut from a documentary about sub-Saharan Africa—and that wasn't a good sign. A woman, the owner of the strange voice, stood a few feet in front of me with her hands clasped over her chest in anticipation. Her broad smile quickly turned into a frown. "Who are you?" she asked.

"Who am I?" I tossed back at her incredulously. "What the fuck just happened? Where am I? Who are you? Why am I covered in . . . pig guts?" Everything about my surroundings felt like some kind of sick dream. But I knew what had happened in my apartment had been real. You couldn't feel pain or smell stuff in a dream, right?

"Where is the demon?" the woman questioned. She wasn't upset, but I could easily read the disappointment in her voice. It wasn't the first time a woman had been disappointed upon seeing my homely visage. I had tried online dating once. Let's just say my profile had been a little doctored up, kind of like the resume I had used to get my shitty job.

"Why the hell are you going on about a demon?" I shouted.

The woman took a slow step backward. "The demon," she said again in her strange accent. "You are not him?"

I shook my head. "What in the actual hell are you talking about?" I got up from the pile of gore and shook the bigger chunks from my clothes. It was hard not to vomit. For whatever reason, the wild transformation of my entire world did a decent job distracting my mind from the nausea growing in my stomach.

I noticed a boy standing near the room's only door and looking terrified. Maybe he had some answers. "Where the hell am I?" I demanded, facing the cowering boy. His eyes were wide, and he didn't respond. In the silence, my heart rate slowed a bit, and I finally realized what the two loons in front of me were wearing. The woman was dressed mostly in woven grasses with a few bits of leather showing here and there. She was young, maybe my age, and *damn* was she hot. I mean, she was *really* attractive. Her weird, pre-civilization outfit barely covered her ample features, and it was about that time that I realized I had been staring. Did I mention that I wasn't great with the ladies?

"Uh, you're in Tamernil," the boy finally said, his weak voice barely audible. He was dressed in a similar fashion to the woman—all leaves, grass, and animal hide—and to be honest, it didn't look as good on him as it did on her.

"Where the hell is Tamernil?" I asked. I was never great when it came to learning geography. Maybe I was dreaming about being trapped in a strange documentary. "Are we in Africa?"

The woman's confused expression told me my theory was wrong. She also wasn't black, more olive-skinned I guessed, but that hadn't really crossed my mind until I had asked the question. Fine. I was used to being wrong.

"South America?" I asked, but the woman spoke English.

Her accent was weird even though I understood her words. And the only thing I knew besides English were maybe six different colors in Spanish, eight ways to order slightly different tacos and burritos at fast-food places, and maybe forty words in Finnish I had memorized off the back of a beer bottle at a classy European bar Brayden had dragged me to a few weeks ago. I hated those snotty bars where everything tasted almost sour and was twice the price of a regular beer.

"What is . . . South America?" the woman asked, clearly confused.

"Oh man. We have a long way to go," I told her. "I'm guessing this is some village somewhere in just the absolute dumbest part of the world. Somewhere without maps or the internet. Are we in Tennessee? Maybe Alabama? Arkansas? Has Bill Clinton ever been the governor here? That would explain at least half of this kooky shit."

The woman only looked more confused. Maybe she was a Democrat and I had hit a chord she hadn't expected. "Tamernil," she repeated. "That's where you are. But I summoned a demon!"

Back to the demon shit. Maybe we were both talking about Bill Clinton and we just hadn't realized it yet. "So Tamernil is a city in Arkansas?" I asked.

"What is Arkansas?" she asked, only slightly botching the pronunciation.

Damn. That was what, strike ten? And I hadn't begun to fathom how I had gotten to such a wretched place, or what I was doing covered in blood and intestines. "Just let me use your shower, or a bucket of water, or whatever you have out here in the sticks, and then I'll call someone," I told her. Thoughts of getting back to my raid flashed through my head, but I didn't really have the time to give them any consideration. Judging by the woman's clothes, finding a computer would probably be tricky.

Again, confusion was the only response.

"A bucket of water? They do have buckets in Arkansas, right?"

The boy across the room hurried to a corner, rummaged through some things, and then handed me a wooden bucket that looked like one of the cheeky decorations you saw in a Midwestern restaurant that tried to trick its customers into thinking they were in the Old West.

"Can you fill it with water?" I asked the kid. He ran out the door, presumably to a pump or something outside. "I swear, if I have to shit in an outhouse, I'm going to leave a bad review online for whatever teleportation device brought me here." That would teach them.

"You aren't the demon," the woman said again, still questioning my presence in overt disbelief.

"Right, so about the demon you were summoning," I said. "How did you do it? How did I get here? Was I kidnapped? Chloroform?"

The woman pointed to a stone tablet behind me. It was hanging on the wall, kind of like a television at a sports-themed restaurant would be, but it was comically not a television. The smooth stone surface had what appeared to be blood smeared across it. I looked around more and realized I was standing in some sort of poorly drawn shape made of salt.

"Great, so you're a witch," I concluded. "Just perfect." *I'll wake up any minute now*, I thought. I remembered a teacher in high school talking about sleep paralysis. *Must be it. The world's most vivid sleep paralysis. But the smell . . . You can't smell in a dream! I'm sure of it!*

I pinched my arm, really grabbing the skin and twisting

hard. It hurt, but I didn't wake up. That wasn't a good sign. At that moment I decided to make a second account just to give the shitty teleporter two bad reviews instead of only one. But hell, that technology didn't exist! Perhaps I had watched too many sci-fi movies.

The woman's face seemed to light up. She pointed to her buxom chest with a smile. "Blood Witch!" she said excitedly. "I'm a Blood Witch!"

"I don't know how to interpret that," I told her honestly. The last person I had met who had claimed to use magic was some crazy woman at a comic convention who had supposedly 'healed my aura' with voodoo juice from a plastic bottle. She had said she was a witch, and she had even worn an edgy pentagram necklace I knew for a fact had come from a shitty mall store marketed directly to pre-teen angst.

"I'm a Blood Witch. I tried to summon a demon, but I got you instead," the gorgeous tribal woman carried on. She was animated when she spoke about her claimed profession, and her vibrant arm movements made some of the grass slip from her breasts. I didn't mind. In fact, it felt like something I should encourage. You know, to help her self-esteem.

"So can you cast a spell for me? Maybe send me back to my apartment that you trashed?" I asked politely, hoping in the darker parts of my mind to add to her budding happiness.

My plan worked. The self-proclaimed Blood Witch gyrated as she began what looked to be a very stereotypical round of spell casting, and her primitive brassiere continued to slip farther and farther down her toned chest.

Then she cast a spell. She just did it.

There wasn't a big fireball or some loud explosion as

lightning came crashing down outside, but rather a cute little luminescent butterfly escaped from the palm of her hand. I was pretty impressed. But I had seen magic shows in the past. I had never been to Vegas for one of the big production value events, but I had seen plenty of them on the internet. Maybe she'd had the butterfly tucked away in her hand all along, just waiting. Highly unlikely, but possible. And it seemed a weak explanation was all that my stunned mind wanted to consider.

"Hello," the butterfly said, its little insect mouth barely capable of forming the word.

"What?"

"Hello, I'm Quonlononololope," the tiny creature told me.

"I just call her Qu," the Blood Witch cheerfully added. She snapped her fingers, and then Qu vanished in a spectacular display of vibrant colors.

"So this place is wherever Peter Pan goes when he trips on too much acid," I stated, scratching the stubble on my chin.

Unfortunately, the witch hiked her garments back up to their original places. Maybe she had seen me staring. The prettiest girls always did.

"Do you believe me now?" she asked.

She wore a bit of a frustrated expression, so I decided not to push the fact that magic wasn't real. I figured I'd save that doozie for another time, preferably a moment in which I wasn't covered in guts. "Yeah, sure," I told her. "You have a name?"

Just then the boy returned with the bucket, though the water inside it was clearly leaking from a myriad of gaps in the wooden planking that formed the sides. I quickly grabbed it from him before too much of the water could escape, then promptly shoved it right back into his arms. There was plenty of dirt, a small minnow, several tadpoles, and some green algae in the bucket along with the water.

"Yeah, I'm good," I told the boy who looked like he might cry. "I'm just gonna look around on my own now, if that's alright." Honestly, I needed some time and some space to figure out exactly what the hell was going on. If it was a dream, I'd wake up. If it was a crazed delusion brought on by carbon monoxide poisoning, I'd die pretty soon. Either way, I'd get some answers.

"My name is Bokta," the strange witch informed me. She followed me outside into what I presumed was the Arkansas wilderness, though it didn't really look like anywhere in the United States. In fact, the wilderness around the small hut didn't really look like any place on Earth. I pinched myself again. Nothing happened.

"So, Bokta," I started, "you said this place is called Tamernil?" She nodded. "And where is everyone else?"

"I'm an outcast," she said sullenly. "I'm an Oathbreaker."

Wait. Pump the goddamned brakes.

Some of it started to click, but not in any way that made much sense. "The demon you were trying to summon . . ." I said slowly.

"Yes," she went on, her fan girl enthusiasm returning. "He is an Oathbreaker as well! That is why I've been watching him!"

"And his name is Maxkrannar, isn't it?" No one else in my party had played an Oathbreaker.

"Yes!" she shouted in my face. "The demon! Maxkrannar will save me and the other Oathbreakers from the Dread King!"

"Oh shit."

"Do you know him?" Bokta asked. "Do you know the demon Maxkrannar?"

"Well..." The moment of truth had arrived. Should I come right out and tell her she tried to summon my Realm character? Should I tell her that she's fucked if the best she could do was summon a portly accountant who was bad at math and worse with a weapon? Honesty would certainly be the best way to go. Maybe she would send me back—assuming she could.

"Maxkrannar is the most skilled, courageous, and powerful demon I have ever seen," the witch said with a touch of awe in her lovely eyes. Yeah, she was a fully-fledged Maxkrannar fan girl—the nutty kind that would cosplay as a character and travel across the country to meet the voice actor.

Skilled. Courageous. I could get used to that.

"Yup, that's me, Maxkrannar, the mighty level-ninety demon Oathbreaker, at your service," I announced with an exaggerated bow.

"Oh, I knew it was you!" Bokta exclaimed like a dramatically fainting woman from an old silent movie. She fell against my torso in similar fashion, and I couldn't keep the ridiculous smile from my face.

I had certainly been hugged by a few well-endowed women in my day, but none that had ever actually wanted me to hug them back. It was a nice feeling.

"Yeah, so, in this form . . . I mean, when I look like a human and not like a demon . . . I mean, when I'm not in my demon form with the horns and all, you can just call me Steve."

CHAPTER 4

I spent most of the day outside trying to wrap my head around . . . well, everything. Bokta didn't live near anyone, and the solitude was kind of nice. She finally came out to see what I was doing sometime after nightfall.

"Maxkrannar?" she whispered. The boy had left her hut a few hours ago, and I was thankful for it. Not that I thought the privacy would lead to anything with the woman . . . but the thought *had* crossed my mind.

"Just Steve," I reminded the strange woman who likely was an actual witch, a fact my mind was still struggling to fully understand.

"Have you had enough time to think?" she asked.

Would I ever? It hadn't taken me very long to come to terms with the fact that I was here, and maybe that was a sign of my poor mental state. The way I saw it was simple: either I would wake up after the longest dream in recorded history, or what the woman said was simply true. She had tried to summon my Realm character, but she had gotten me instead. Maybe I hadn't paid enough attention during physics in high school, but I was fairly certain that cross-planet summoning—or whatever had happened—wasn't actually possible. Then again . . . here I stood.

"I don't know," I told her honestly. She sat down beside me on the hard-packed dirt and stared up toward the sky.

"Tamernil isn't too bad, you know," she said quietly. Good to hear she felt a little twinge of guilt when it came to upending my entire life. She still had a fan girl kind of look in her eyes.

"Well, it doesn't sound too great, either, what with the Dread King running around killing people," I replied.

Bokta shook her head. "He doesn't kill people, and he certainly doesn't run around," she laughed.

That wasn't the answer I was expecting. "So, what makes him so dreadful?" I asked.

The Blood Witch let out a sigh like she couldn't even believe I would ask such an obvious question. "The taxes, mostly," she said. "But there are so many other reasons. We used to elect our mayor here in Tamernil. Then the Dread King took over. He sent our mayor away and installed his own. None of the tax money goes to public improvements anymore, either."

Wow. So the Dread King was a bureaucrat. I guess that made him pretty dreadful. "His real name isn't George the Third, is it?" I asked her. She hadn't shown any recognition when I mentioned Bill Clinton earlier, but maybe Tamernil was in just a slightly earlier time period. Or perhaps the town existed in the colonial days.

"No one knows his real name," Bokta answered mysteriously. So King George was still an option. I made a mental note.

"What's the name of the whole region?" I asked her. "Tamernil just refers to the nearby city, right?" I didn't want to just sit down and pump the woman for info—I'd never remember it all in any case—but I needed to get my bearings.

She nodded. "Tamernil is only a few miles in that direction," she said, pointing over her shoulder. Nothing could be seen in that direction except trees. "The province is called Rowane."

"And the entire kingdom?"

"We call it the Realm," she answered.

Well shit. Was I inside some kind of ultra-advanced virtual reality simulation? I looked in the top-right corner of my vision where the mini-map would be on the display in Realm. There was nothing. Normally, I would have a row of abilities across the bottom of my vision that I could activate with the press of a button. I tried the air in front of me where I thought the '1' key should have been. In Realm, Maxkrannar would have charged forward and regenerated exactly one and a half percent of his health.

In the physical, tangible place called Realm, my body didn't move when I pushed where the buttons should have been. I just looked like a lunatic slapping the air at nothing. Still, I couldn't let the notion drop after only a single trial. I tried to push the other buttons at the top of my non-existent keyboard and sadly, none of them worked. Maybe they needed to upload a patch. Maybe I wasn't a high enough level yet. Characters didn't start getting their good skills until level ten online. Maybe I was just in a test realm for a new virtual reality project, and I would need to level up before I could use my skills. Guess I had missed the email invite to the beta server. Ha, Brayden would be jealous as hell if he could see me right now.

If even half of the theories swirling around in my head were true, one thing was certain: I needed a quest. Grinding boars didn't sound like too much fun. And from the looks of the interior of Bokta's hut, someone had been doing just that already, and I didn't know what the respawn timers were like. If I was going to get powerful enough to start using skills—assuming skills existed like that—a quest would have to be priority number one.

"So, Bokta," I continued, "have you always been here?"

She looked confused. Bad programming? "I was born in Rowane, but not here in Tamernil," she answered.

"You remember your childhood?" I pressed on, working another theory around in my head.

She smiled. "Of course. My parents were always kind to me, though they threw me out when I started to learn blood magic," she explained.

So she wasn't a scripted projection of my consciousness, unless the programmers had given her memories too. The thought felt a bit extreme, but it wasn't impossible.

"Can you show me your demon form?" Bokta asked, her eyes wide with expectation, before I had a moment to fully wrap my head around the virtual reality theory. Needless to say, her question caught me a bit off guard.

"Uh, not right now," I told her. I needed to deflect, but she looked up at me with her big brown eyes so full of expectation. I didn't want to let her down. I was also not a demon from a video game. What an impasse. "I need to get stronger," I finally said, hoping to figure out my first quest soon.

"What do you mean?" she asked.

"You know, like whatever people around here do to get better . . . at whatever it is they do," I tried awkwardly to explain. How do you tell someone who may or may not be in a video game that you need to power level to the endgame content if you're going to be some mighty savior?

Bokta smiled with recognition. "You mean the challenge board in the center of Tamernil!" she exclaimed happily.

Perfect. Part of me expected jackpot lights to start flashing like I'd just hit big money in a cheap casino. A quest station conveniently located in the center of the village was exactly what I needed. If Tamernil was a starter zone for the next expansion of Realm, I should be able to fly through it in no time.

Level zero. Maybe level one would have been a better assessment, but I knew better. Relying on only my human skills would certainly warrant level zero. But I had a mission. A quest. Or ... I would have one soon enough. As long as I wasn't slaughtering boars, I'd be happy.

Bokta's hut only had one bed, so I had no choice but to sleep under the stars. Luckily, my parents had forced me into Boy Scouts for an entire year back in the day, during which I had learned nothing. The night in Realm wasn't too cold, which was perfect since I hadn't been summoned while holding a blanket. I did, however, get pulled into Tamernil while wearing my undershirt from work, a pair of dark pants, and somewhat uncomfortable dress shoes that I've owned since high school. That would need to change. If everyone dressed like Bokta, I would stick out like a sore thumb. However, truth be told, I had never understood the expression. How often did people notice wounded thumbs?

When morning arrived, I was already awake. Sleeping in a foreign place without walls or a roof was just as hard as anyone would imagine. My neck hurt and I still smelled like absolute shit. After taking a leak, I waited for Bokta to emerge while occupying my time with a healthy dose of pacing. I spotted a pond not far behind the hut, and it must have been the same one the weird boy had used to fill the bucket the previous day. The entire top of the pond was one unbroken layer of smelly algae. No shower for me.

I tried to push some of the algae away to take a drink, but I just couldn't bring myself to drink pure giardia. Maybe I was selfish.

Backing away from the pond, I decided to wait for some cleaner water. If it got bad enough, I had watched a few survival shows where guys bragged about drinking their own piss, so I filed that notion away in the back of my head as a last resort. The bucket of disease might be better, or maybe I could mix the two and be dead in a week.

The Blood Witch came out of her hut about half an hour after sunrise, somehow looking even better than she had the day before. She wore a slightly different outfit of reeds, grass, and leather, and I didn't mind inspecting it for every single difference.

"Can we go to Tamernil?" I asked when my eyes had experienced enough. "Also, I'd love to get some clean water."

Thankfully, it turned out Bokta had a collection barrel for rainwater on the other side of the hut. She let me take a few big drinks before resealing the top and giving me a stern look. "Rainwater is expensive," she scolded.

"It doesn't rain often here?" I asked her.

"Every ten days," she said. So, my programming theory got a tick stronger. Real planets and real continents did not have rain schedules. Virtual worlds might.

"You cannot go to Tamernil looking like that," Bokta added, stealing my attention back from my own ponderings.

I wasn't sure I wanted to wear a bunch of leaves. "What else do you have?" I asked.

She looked me over once, then went back inside her hut. A moment later she emerged holding a decent-looking leather vest and what I could only describe as a straw hula skirt. "I'll take the vest, but that skirt isn't going on my body," I told her plainly.

"People will think you're rich if you wear those," Bokta explained. "Only the noblemen own stitched pants. You were a noble back in your home world, right? A noble among the Oathbreakers?"

Was I going too deep into the lie? Yeah, probably.

"You bet I was," I told her. "I had more gold than anyone could count, all the finest silks and robes, and a thousand slaves living in my palace waiting to do my bidding."

Bokta seemed impressed. "Perhaps you could take me to your world someday," she said.

"Speaking of which, do you know any way to send me back?" I asked. Finally, the question that had been weighing on my mind came to the surface.

"Why would you want to leave?"

"What if I need to get something from my world?" I replied. "I might need some special demon weapons."

"I don't know," Bokta said. Not the answer I had been hoping for. "I've never sent anything back."

"I'm the only person you've ever summoned, aren't I?"

Bokta nodded sheepishly, her fan girl bravado temporarily stymied.

"Well, shit." So there wasn't any going back. Tamernil was my life now. It was who I was. I couldn't help but smirk when I thought about my landlord furiously trying to find me for rent and all the damage to his floors. I felt a little bad about leaving my parents without telling them, but eh . . . they would make it.

"Can you teach me magic?" I asked her, thinking of all the crazy shit that must be possible in a place like Realm. Needless to say, I had dreamt of living in fantasy worlds for years, desperate for some escape from corporate America and the brutal grind of everyday life.

"My blood magic is strictly outlawed," she laughed. "Teaching it to you could get us both killed."

I'm wasn't sure I believed her. "You're still alive," I pointed out.

She smiled, and I couldn't keep my mind from trying to come up with ways to seduce her. Granted, my methods had never really worked before unless my prey had been particularly intoxicated, but it wasn't too late to find out if Realm had any booze.

"If you know who to please, who to pay off, and who to avoid, you can survive as a witch," Bokta said devilishly. I guess Tamernil wasn't *that* much different than back home.

The walk to the city wasn't too bad. I was pretty out of shape, something I blamed entirely on my desk job behind a computer, but the fresh air actually felt good. Moving my legs a little helped me take my mind off of the dizzying reality that was slowly permeating my consciousness. We didn't talk much on the walk, either. I had a hundred more questions about the technology of the world, the Dread King she seemed to fear so much, and a million other things, but I really didn't want to get overwhelmed. If I took it all one step at a time, I would survive. Which gave me another idea.

"Hey, Bokta," I said, pulling her attention back from whatever it was in her palm that she was watching. "When people die here, is there any way to bring them back?" It felt like useful information.

She looked at me strangely. "No. Do they come back to life where you're from?"

"Ah, nope. So, people stay dead. No respawn."

"What does that mean?" she asked.

How could I explain respawning in a video game to a woman who had never seen electricity? "Don't worry about it," I said. Besides, we had just arrived at Tamernil. I still needed to learn about magic, and that would have to be a somewhat high priority task, but there would be time.

CHAPTER 5

T he village was pretty much exactly what I had expected. There were a few multi-story buildings, but almost everything was low to the ground. A handful of people milled about, selling wares and gossiping on the corners. The center of the little town was dominated by a somewhat large building that showed signs of clear upkeep, which the other structures tended to lack. There weren't many windows on the largest building, and it wasn't built in the half-timbered style of the others. In fact, the central building was the only brick establishment in the village.

"That one looks important," I said, stating the painfully obvious. I noticed a few passersby staring at my stitched pants, but none of them said anything I could hear.

"That's the mayor's office," Bokta explained, recapturing my attention. "The challenge board is there on the side." She pointed out a tall pegboard with a few notices nailed to it.

"Awesome," I said, excited to see if I could get my first quest. If the village really was a virtual reality, next-gen server for Realm, I was determined to be the best. No one crushed low-level quests like Maxkrannar. And any quest they'd offer would be better than running numbers on spreadsheets for managers who didn't give two shits about me.

There was just a slight problem.

Every single posting on the board was written in an alphabet I couldn't decipher. It looked kind of like a mix between Russian and Old Norse runes, though the script was in a circular pattern that made absolutely no sense. I stared at the circular postings for a while before Bokta recognized my confusion and mercifully stepped in to help.

"This one is looking for recruits for the army, but it is always here," she said. She waved her hand dismissively over a poster with two large circles of writing. "The flier here calls for farmhands for the harvest. Here's one from McCallister, the man who owns the tavern. It says he needs help."

Perfect. I had made enough characters in Realm to know every starter quest by heart. I would probably have to lend a hand with some menial task in the tavern and then be rewarded with a dagger or a cape of some kind for my minimal troubles. Or better yet, doing a starter quest might unlock some kind of tutorial. Maybe a bucket of XP would flash in front of my vision.

"That building is the tavern, right?" I asked. There was a painted sign hanging just above the doorway with a frothing mug nearly identical to the ones marking every such establishment in Realm. Another idea crossed my mind. "Also . . . are there any brothels here? Is prostitution legal?"

Judging by her expression, Bokta wasn't happy. Her fan

girl had been kicked down a notch to somewhere around 'moderately enthused disciple.'

Damn.

"Oh, nevermind," I said, casually playing it off. I walked into the tavern and found just what I had hoped to find. An older man played some kind of lute or whatever in the corner while singing about a buxom wench, and said buxom wench carried around tankards of foaming ale in a traditional German-style outfit that perfectly accentuated her pleasantly voluptuous nature.

There were a good dozen or more patrons, and a few of them turned to stare at us, the newcomers. I didn't pay them much attention, except for the lone girl who looked my age sitting in a corner with two men who appeared as if they could each break my neck with a single hand. Let's just say I didn't pay attention to her for long.

"Yeah?" the bartender offered when I approached. I checked my back pocket for my wallet. It was still there, so I had a few bucks. If only I hadn't removed my phone from my wallet before I'd been summoned . . . But hell, it probably would have been useless.

I took out a ten and slapped it down on the bar like they did in old western movies. "I'll take a pint," I cheerfully told the bearded man across from me.

He picked up the bill from the counter and looked at both sides. "The hell is this?" he asked, tossing it back in my face.

"Well . . ." I hadn't thought it through. How about changing the subject? That sounded easier than explaining fiat currency to a grumpy bartender from the middle ages. "I saw your post on the challenge board. You need some help?" I tried to palm the bill inconspicuously from the counter back into my pocket, but my sleight-of-hand skills were pretty terrible. In the end, I just made it awkward.

The man looked me over with a disapproving smile. If only he had been the father of someone I was taking to a high school dance, the situation would have been so familiar I would have been able to breeze right through.

"You strong enough to fight?" he asked. I knew what he expected me to say.

"I might be," I told him with all the confidence I could muster. "Depends on the job. What do you need?" Perfect. Awkwardness aside, I was about to receive a starter quest. Fighting probably meant clearing out vermin from an attic. Every game had starter quests, and Tamernil was no different.

I tried not to think about the man's tree-sized arms on the off chance that the fight he wanted was going to be against him an arena. And then another tidbit decided to tickle my mind: whatever was too strong for him to handle was likely so far beyond my skill and athleticism that I'd die within seconds of accepting the quest. Regardless, I felt like I should at least hear him out.

"Rats in my cellar—"

"I'm the man for the job!" I interrupted. A few rats? Maybe the big muscle-man was just afraid of the little critters like almost every other human alive. Luckily for me, I had owned a pet rat in the second grade named Patchwork. I had been able to kill Patchwork in a couple weeks without even trying. I should be able to slaughter hundreds of them if I really put my mind to it.

"Rats in my cellar the size of boars," the man clarified with a sly, knowing grin.

Alright, maybe I had rushed into things. I looked at Bokta next to me, and her expression was hopeful. I was also standing close enough to her to get a glimpse down her straw-made shirt. There was no way I was going to chicken out on my first quest in front of a girl like that. It just wasn't something people did. If there were dialog options in my new version of Realm, the choice to back out like a little bitch would have been displayed in red, maybe with a skull and crossbones or a little down arrow next to it.

"I'm on it," I declared, slamming my fist down onto the bar top for dramatic effect.

Sadly, the bartender just kind of scoffed. "The cellar is around back," he said, sliding a key my way. "Get rid of every last rat, and I'll pay you when you return."

I snatched the key from the bar and slid my arm confidently around Bokta's waist to pull her along with me. Surprisingly, she didn't resist my subtle advance. In fact—and maybe I was seeing more of what I *wanted* to see than what was actually there—she seemed happy about the contact. "Come on," I said, "let's go kill some rats!"

We got to the cellar entrance behind the tavern in no time. Perhaps I was a bit too eager to start earning experience points and getting my greedy hands on some hot new gear, but I didn't care. The entrance wasn't locked, so I threw it wide open, tucked the key into my pocket, and led the way down into the darkness. And by darkness, I mean it was really dark. There wasn't any light at all. I wasn't wearing a watch when I had been summoned, and my phone had been sitting to the left of my keyboard, so I didn't have that, either.

"Uh, do you have a torch or something?" I asked. Dungeons were usually full of ambient light in Realm and all the other games I had ever played. Sometimes the programmers had placed little torches on the walls, but no one cared enough to look for them. The game had always been about combat and leveling, not scenery.

Bokta laughed at me. "I'll ask the bartender for one," she said with a shake of her head. Whatever progress into Bokta's panties I had made evaporated with her smile, and I was left to stand there awkwardly as my beautiful guide went back inside to remedy my foolhardy mistake. Luckily, she came back only a minute or so later with a lit torch held in her hand.

"Here," she said, holding it out to me. I took the torch and lifted it up to illuminate the stone stairs. They were old, but they looked solid, and there was plenty of room to go down into the darkness without hitting my head on the bottom of the building above.

We reached the bottom of the stairs, and nothing seemed out of the ordinary. There were a bunch of shelves holding all sorts of typical stuff you always saw during starter quests. Only casually inspecting the wares, we moved through the shelves toward the back of the room and came to an old wooden door with a section missing at the bottom. It looked like the planks had been chewed away.

Summoning all my bravado, I pushed the door inward on its squeaky hinges. It took a bit of force to move it, but the thing finally gave way and swung open. The other side was outrageously large for a simple tavern's root cellar, and I couldn't help but compare it in my mind to all the other cellar-based dungeons I had explored in the games I had played. The sizes of the underground complexes never matched what would actually have been feasible with medieval technology. Standing at my side, Bokta didn't look surprised.

There was a long hallway before us, and a bunch of paintings and other trinkets lined the walls on rusty hooks. Past a few doors that led off to either side, a large one stood at the end of the hallway. "Shall we?" I asked, flashing my most charming smile.

Bokta nodded to urge me onward. "Ratlings have been moving through the area since the Dread King had them driven out of Mara to the north. They're mostly peaceful, but they'll fight if they have to."

In all honesty, I was terrified. The only rodent other than Patchwork I had ever killed had been a raccoon. I had hit the creature with a rock by accident when I had thought there was a burglar trying to get into my house. I think I had scored a lucky shot back then, or else the raccoon had been close to dead to begin with. Either way, the animal had died, and then I had cried for a week. I wasn't a great beacon of moral righteousness by any means, but I also wasn't a murderer. Especially not an animal killer.

We walked slowly down the tight corridor, Bokta's warm breath fluttering through the shaggy brown hair that covered my ears. The door at the end of the hallway was about as ominous as a door could get. There were thin strips of iron running horizontally across it, and I could hear chittering from the other side. Lots of chittering.

"Does everyone have a cellar this large?" I asked Bokta.

"I haven't been in everyone's cellar," she snarkily replied.

"Whatever." I put my hand against the door and pushed, finding it also unlocked. The heavy chunk of wood took its time to move inward, but the hinges were a lot quieter than the ones on the first door. It made me think the door was used a lot more often than the other one, but I couldn't imagine for what. In video games, the creepy doors underneath innocuous taverns were always home to human sacrifice, torture chambers, demonic cults, and all manner of cannibals. Or maybe I had played some weird games.

Regardless of my preconceptions, the other side of the heavy door revealed exactly what I had been looking for: about a hundred rats swarming back and forth like a herd of vicious cats chasing a laser pointer. "Oh man . . ." I muttered. "You can do magic, right?"

Bokta stared at me through the flickering torchlight. "It is illegal, remember?" she said quietly. "I could be found, and they would kill us both."

I didn't even have a club. And when the man upstairs had said the rats would be the size of much larger animals, he had meant it. They came up to just below my knees. "So . . . what do we do?" I stupidly asked. I could basically feel the woman's admiration waning with every passing second. If I was going to make the best of things and get laid while I was here, I'd need to do something big to step up my game before I ruined my chances altogether.

Bokta kept staring at me with an expression I hated. "You're a demon and an Oathbreaker. I've seen you kill hundreds of winged harpies and other monsters without breaking a sweat!" she reminded me.

Well, what would Maxrannar do? What would I do in Realm if I were to be confronted by a mob that was just beyond my level? Call in reinforcements over voice chat? Ask my guild for help? Get some better gear? Ha, no way.

"Leeeroy! Jeenkiiins!" I yelled at the top of my lungs, just a split second before I remembered that you couldn't respawn in real life, even though the entire idea was based on the presumption that Tamernil *was* real life. Who knew? Maybe I could respawn, and no one knew exactly where. That would make some sense. Some.

I charged through the swarm of rats like a madman. I kicked my legs hard in front of me and swung the torch as I moved, but I quickly got bogged down. I wasn't sure there was a single dead rat to be seen before I had lost all my momentum and come to a halt. At the very least, I knew I had wounded a few, but I was only a third of the way through the room. And by wounded I basically meant inconvenienced.

Then the rats seemed to realize I was standing there, panting in their midst. The nearest beasts leapt up from the ground in a flurry of claws and teeth. Their little attacks didn't hurt much since their mouths were so comically small, but there were just so many of them! It didn't take long before I was running back toward Bokta with lines of blood all over my lower half. So much for nice expensive pants. But had the rats' jaws been as large as their bodies likely dictated, I would have been killed.

When I reached the Blood Witch, she looked more confused than ever, but she grabbed me by the arm and hauled me back into the previous passage.

"Was that a spell?" she asked once I was safe again from the horde. Her admission meant it was possible—perhaps plausible or even expected—for me to learn magic. Figuring out some magic jumped up a notch on my list of priorities.

"Ha," I laughed. "Not exactly." A particularly painful bite mark oozed a good amount of blood down my right leg. Yup, the pants were completely ruined.

"What are you going to do?" she asked.

I needed a weapon. Some armor wouldn't hurt. "You don't have a sword, do you?" I wondered.

She shook her head. "Swords are expensive," she remarked.

"Good ones always are, but there has to be some junk I can use until I can buy a better weapon," I mused.

Bokta looked around the little hallway, but there wasn't anything there. "Maybe there's something you can use back in the other room?" she offered.

We went back into the first chamber of the large cellar to search around for some sort of weapon. There wasn't much. After about twenty minutes of searching, the best I had was a cask of sweet red wine and a hammer that was too small to be of much use. It would have to work.

I headed back to the heavy door with all the clawing and screeching on the other side, the small cask under my arm and the hammer through a loop on my tattered pants. There was enough of a gap between the bottom of the door and the dirt floor that my plan might just work.

I wrenched the stopper off the wine cask and tipped it over, letting it run under the door to the angry critters on the other side. At least from what I could hear, the rats liked it. I let them feast for a long time, probably more than an hour, while Bokta and I sat with our backs against the wall making small talk. It turned out she wasn't keen divulging all of her Oathbreaker secrets, and she was less enthusiastic about giving a lecture on Blood Magic. Beyond her reluctance, it turned out her specific brand of sorcery was gender specific, so I'd have to find something else anyways. Still level zero.

The torch didn't have much life left in it by the time the wine was fully gone and the rats sounded like they had quieted down on the other side.

I inched the door open. To my surprise, there weren't any rats up against the door near the stained dirt. A few of the animals were asleep not far off, and the rest had resumed their incessant scurrying in every direction.

Luckily, they didn't seem to remember that I had just been there trying to kill them. Or maybe my first attack had been so lame that they didn't consider me a threat. Hammer in hand, I moved over to the nearest sleeping rat. The white-furred creature's mouth was stained with red wine. I lifted the hammer high, closed my eyes, then brought it down sharply on the thing's narrow head.

Killing a huge, sleeping rat wasn't fun. In fact, it was rather far from fun. I didn't like it at all, and my stomach liked it less. Despite not having eaten in some time, my body still found the strength to vomit all over the ground. When I recovered, I flicked the majority of the blood and brains from the hammer and slid the tool back into my belt loop.

"That's not going to work," I told myself. Even if I could get every single rat drunk enough to pass out, there was no way I could walk up to each one and bash it to death. Since none of the living rats appeared to be in a killing mood, I decided to have a look through the room to see what else was there before doing anything rash. Much slower than the first time, I pushed my way through the herd of overgrown rats to the back of the room. There was another door that I hadn't seen before. I thanked my lucky stars that the rats didn't appear to value their individual members' lives too highly.

Leaning close to the door, I couldn't hear much from the other side. I could just barely make out the sound of a single voice. It wasn't human, but it was certainly speaking a language. Or maybe it *was* human, and I just didn't recognize the accent. So far, the three people I had spoken with had been easy enough to understand. Perhaps whoever it was on the other side was from a different continent in Realm. Maybe they were from one of the other expansion packs.

The door opened before I could really comprehend what was happening, and out hobbled a little person in a ragged set of clothing that looked worse than mine. Actually . . . it wasn't a human. It wasn't a little person at all. The bipedal humanoid scuttling through the crowd of rats, completely oblivious to my presence at the side of the door, was what I could only describe as an inverse-lizard-centaur-thing. The bottom half of the creature was certainly human, with pale legs and bare feet that looked like a child's, but the top half resembled a gecko. Needless to say, I was a bit taken aback.

"Uh," I stammered.

The thing turned back to me with surprised eyes. It spat out a line of words that had enough pattern to be a language, but they were completely unknown to me.

"Do you speak English?" I asked. What a stupid question. I hadn't even figured out if the people here called the language 'English' or not. For all I knew, they might refer to it as C++ or some other programmer's language.

"Yes," the goofy lizard amalgamation croaked out in a tiny voice that was a mix of old-timey British and a komodo dragon being run over by a tour bus. Go ahead and try to imagine what that sounds like. It could not be done. The accent had to be heard in person to ever be comprehended.

"So, these are your rats?" I awkwardly asked. What else was I supposed to say?

The short creature stamped his little foot. "Pray tell, why have you ventured into my lair? And at such an hour, no less . . ." the thing demanded in the most polite way possible.

"Let's just say I'm lost," I weakly offered, "and are these your rats?"

The lizard guy then did what everyone else in Tamernil

had done after they had talked to me. He looked totally confused.

"So . . . The rats . . ." I tried to lead him on.

Finally, the lizard man nodded his head.

"Hey, some progress!" I couldn't help but exclaim. "What are you doing with them?"

The lizard man looked down at a few of his oversized vermin with a loving smile. Hopefully he didn't see the one I had splattered all over the floor. I counted it lucky that the other rats were moving around so much that the corpse was hard to spot. "They're my pets," the lizard answered with his strange accent. "I breed them here. You're in my home, intruder!"

I took a step back with my hands raised to show the weirdo rat breeder that I didn't mean any harm. "What's your plan, though?" I asked. "You can't just stay down here forever, right?"

That seemed to give the little guy a bit to think about.

"Well, I will need more room once the herd numbers over two hundred," he mused after a moment of contemplation, hopefully forgetting about my whole intrusion. Maybe half-rat, half-lizard things had poor memories. I got the notion that the creature was the gambling and bargaining type, kind of like the stereotypical portrayal of goblins and gnomes in fantasy games.

"Any idea when that would be?" I asked. Maybe my quest would be easier than I was trying to make it.

"Perhaps in another thirty or forty weeks," the creature answered. "But why are you here?"

Okay, I just needed to dodge his nosy question a little longer. "What would it take to get you to move along a little ahead of schedule? What would you need to move out tonight?" I asked. I also noticed he was not wearing any shoes, and my mass-produced semi-dress sneakers were probably the best articles of footwear anywhere in the world, even if they were a tad uncomfortable for my taste.

He thought for a little longer, then took the bait. "What do you have to offer?" he demanded, sticking out a scaly finger at my chest.

"Well, I heard that the mayor is rounding up a bunch of guys to come down here and kill you," I told him.

"Nonsense!" the lizard shouted. "The mayor is a good friend of my brother! She would never do such a thing!"

Well, that plan didn't work. Time for the shoes. I hoped he liked forty-dollar knock-offs I had bought back in high school. "Alright, alright," I told him. "Now how about a fine pair of new shoes?" I pointed down to my worn sneakers with a used-car-salesman-esque grin. "You *know* how expensive a good pair of leather boots is—these are a steal!"

The lizard put a hand to his scaly chin, so I kept up the pitch. I felt like my original assessment had been correct. The little guy liked to wheel and deal.

"These are name-brand shoes, the best in all the Realm!" I carried on.

His eyebrows, if reptiles even had eyebrows, seemed to rise a little. "And which cobbler made such strange attire?" he wanted to know.

Which cobbler . . .? Oh yeah, a cobbler was who made shoes in the old days. "Why, good sir, I'm glad you asked," I announced. "These happen to be made by the *master* cobbler Nike, the goddess of victory herself, in a far-off land called China, where the sun is hot, the rivers sometimes catch on fire, and a giant wall surrounds the land for thousands of miles! Just getting something past the wall is a feat worthy of song! And the goddess Nike does not part with her shoes without a fight!"

Damn if my pitch wasn't effective. The dude had never seen modern footwear, of course, so he was wildly enthralled. My embellishments had only been icing on the cake. Lacking any semblance of a poker face, the lizard nodded. I slipped off my right shoe and handed it over for him to check out.

"Yes, yes," he hissed after only a cursory examination, his reptilian tongue darting around the edges of his mouth. "Give me the goddess's shoes!"

I took off the second shoe, but held it back. "You have to move all your rat pets first!" I reminded him. "Then you get the second shoe!"

He thought for a while, then finally nodded. Got him. I should have gone into sales instead of accounting. I was a natural. I half expected a bit of experience to flash before my eyes and increase the charisma stat on my character sheet, but I didn't have any such luck.

The lizard guy issued a sharp whistle with his fingers in the corners of his mouth just like a coach at a little league game. The rats sat up on their haunches at once. "To the tunnels!" the lizard commanded, and the rats instantly scattered into a dozen or more little openings in the walls.

Without the herd moving around, the dead rat was painfully obvious. "The mayor already killed one!" I shouted in mock terror, turning my body to try and hide the hammer.

The lizard eyed me suspiciously. I tossed the second shoe at him to pull his attention away from the rat corpse before he had second thoughts. "Alright, so all your rats are gone. I'll need you to join them promptly," I said. I'd seen enough episodes of *Cops* to know how to act like I had a lot more authority that I actually did.

I breathed a sigh of relief as the lizard scampered back

into the hovel whence it had come. It gathered up an old battered trunk, slipped on my shoes, and ran out of the room through the wall. Mission accomplished. Sure, I'd lost my only two valuable possessions in my shoes and my pants, but I would figure that out later.

CHAPTER 6

I emerged victorious from the cellar, a dead rat in my hand, a hammer in my belt loop, and Bokta at my side. The loose stones and dirt under my socks were a bit painful to walk across. Whatever my reward was, I hoped it would cover a pair of boots, preferably enchanted ones. I couldn't imagine getting something legendary from a first quest in a starter zone, but magic boots to give me a little extra speed? That sounded reasonable.

We headed back to the tavern owner, and I slapped the dead rat down on his bar like Perseus presenting the head of Medusa to Athena. "They're all gone," I declared. "Every last rat is gone."

"You killed them?" the gruff bartender asked.

Well, not really, but how would he know the difference? "You bet I did. Killed them all," I stated.

The bartender looked skeptical, but my myriad of mostly minor cuts and scrapes seemed to put his mind at ease. "Bessie!" he called over his shoulder. A burly woman that looked to be his daughter came out of a back room to answer his call. "Go down and see if the rat problem has been taken care of, lass!"

The woman hurried off toward the back of the tavern after a short curtsy. She came back only a moment later, and she was empty-handed. "They're all gone, Father," she said before returning to the back room.

"My reward?" I asked, holding out my hand with a smug expression on my face.

He dropped a single silver coin into the palm of my hand before turning his attention back to another patron.

"Just one?"

Bokta smiled and led me out of the tavern just as I was beginning to protest. "I'm sure you're used to vast sums of wealth, but what he gave you is fair," she said once we were outside.

The coin was small, maybe the size of a quarter, and had a strange face etched into one side that looked like a cross between a sphinx and a dragon. The reverse of the coin was blank and smooth.

"Can I get some shoes or some boots?" I asked. My socks wouldn't hold up long on the stone-ridden paths of Tamernil.

"There aren't any cobblers that live here in Tamernil," Bokta said. "But I can probably make you some sandals."

She could make me straw sandals? Anything for Max-krannar the demon Oathbreaker, I guess. No expense would be spared.

"How about a sword?"

Bokta pointed me in the direction of a forge a little way down the road. "You don't have enough money for a sword, but you might be able to get a dagger or something small," she explained. I couldn't imagine what a full set of endgame gear would run. I'd have to genocide entire species for that level of cash.

"What are the other challenges?" I asked her. "If I'm going to help you get rid of the Dread King, I'll need more equipment. And probably an army. And maybe a tank."

Sadly, nothing new had come up while I had dealt with the ratlings, so the only other challenges posted on the board were to join the military or to become a farmhand. Both were far from ideal.

The inside of the blacksmith shop looked a bit like a cheap weapons dealer at a Renaissance Faire. There were a few swords, most of which were too large to be practical, and a couple long-handled axes resting in one corner. Unlike the shop, the blacksmith wasn't at all what I had expected. She was tall, with muscled arms and a thick torso like a Swedish power lifter.

There were a few racks of smaller implements behind the woman, and one of the weapons looked like a Roman gladius. "Hey," I started awkwardly, not sure what the typical protocol was. "How much are the swords?"

The big blacksmith laughed at me. She picked up a piece of unformed iron that probably weighed over a hundred pounds and tossed it on top of a nearby anvil. "What you need sword?" she bellowed in broken English, further reinforcing the Swedish stereotype in my mind.

"I'd like to buy one," I told her slowly. I held out my single silver coin.

The woman rearranged a few things on the anvil before looking into my hand. She shook her head. "No sword," she stated flatly. "Six gibs, sword. One gib, knife."

I guessed the currency was called a gib, but who knew? I would have to clarify it with Bokta later.

The blacksmith grabbed a knife from one of the shelves and handed it to me by the handle. The knife was about the size of a plastic one you'd get with a fast food breakfast, and the blade wasn't much sharper. There was a rock on the shelf behind her that might serve me better if I just put it in the bottom of my sock and whirled it around. I was fairly sure I'd seen a sap like that before in a prison show, except with batteries or soap instead of a rock.

"How much for the rock back there?" I asked, giving her back the knife.

She plucked the rock from the shelf and dropped it into my hand. "Whetstone, half gib," she stated.

"I'll take it," I said with a smile. The rock had a worked edge that wasn't flat. It was far from perfect, but I might be able to use it to file down a stick into a spearhead. Better than nothing . . . barely . . .

The blacksmith took my silver gib, set it down on her anvil, and then smashed it in half with a single strike from one of her hammers.

All in all, I left the blacksmith with a little progress made. I had half a silver gib, a small hammer, a heavy whetstone, and a smoking-hot Blood Witch standing by my side. Not too bad. It certainly beat going back to work in my cubicle of boredom and death. I still didn't have the slightest clue how I could beat the Dread King fellow, but that could wait. I was still level zero and a long way from the endgame cap.

We headed back into Tamernil the next day. Not surprisingly, there wasn't much to do at Bokta's hut, and she seemed intent on getting me to use my 'demon form,' which she thought would require me to just get stronger as a human. Whatever. If I was stuck here, which wasn't necessarily a terrible place to be stuck, I would appreciate the chance to explore a bit and figure things out. Oh, and it turned out Bokta didn't really know how to fight. She could cast a few pretty cool spells, but the constant fear of being caught kept her magic essentially silent. And only a single one of her spells had anything to do with fantasy combat. Or at least that was what she told me. I got the sneaking suspicion that she didn't quite trust me yet—a reasonable assessment—despite her status as a fan girl.

The challenge board in the village didn't have anything new. That was quite a shame. But really, I was still a bit sore from the previous day. Bokta had fed me a bit of pork last night, though my belly rumbled with hunger. I needed some more water too. She, being all lithe and fit, was used to subsisting on the minimum. I, on the other hand, was American. Rumbling stomach on my mind, I went to Mc-Callister's tavern to grab something to eat, curious to know how far my half a silver gib might take me.

I had my socks doubled up with the whetstone inside them like a sap, and I had tested it earlier against a tree with pretty impressive results. The socks wouldn't last long, but I could figure that out when the time came. I had also managed to use the stone to carve and bash a long, somewhat straight branch into a spear. The weapon was about as tall as I was, which was about five feet five inches, and I used some of the torn cloth from my pants to wrap a handle on it. Plus, now I had shorts.

The shoes Bokta had made for me were certainly lacking. They kind of fit, but there was nothing to tighten on them, so they kept slipping around as we walked. Maybe I would get used to them, maybe not. Regardless, the bottoms were hard enough to protect me from the stones on the road, so they would have to work for now.

"What kind of food do you have?" I asked the bartender. I assumed his name was McCallister.

He recognized me from yesterday and grinned. It seemed I had made a friend. "We have stew, and we have sausage. What'll it be?" he asked.

Bokta sat down next to me in a fashion somewhat reminiscent of a lost puppy. She still had a bit of pork she had brought with her, so she didn't order anything. "How about the sausage," I told the man behind the counter. I placed my half a gib on the bar, but the man pushed it back toward me.

"The rats didn't come back—you can eat on the house," he said. I had no way of knowing if he was being generous or if the food was simply worth very little. Either way, I didn't care. Free meals were free meals.

"Awesome! Thanks," I replied, slipping the broken coin back into my pocket.

McCallister yelled something into the back room, and a moment later his daughter emerged with a big plate of sizzling sausages that she sat down in front of me. They looked like bratwurst, and that was plenty fine by me. Before she left, the woman poured about half a pint of dark beer from one of the kegs behind the bar onto my food. That was a bit different. Perhaps a sterilization method? Would beer be strong enough to kill bacteria and whatnot? I wasn't a scientist, but it seemed plausible.

I was easily hungry enough to rip into the sausage without much consideration for the strange topping. Surprisingly, the beer added a unique flavor, something I had never tasted before, and I had to admit that the combination worked damn well. It didn't take long for the plate of food to vanish and my belly to be quite full.

"Hey," I said to get the bartender's attention once more. He glanced my way from the end of the bar. "Tell me something. How out-of-place do I look? Can you tell I'm not from here?"

The bartender looked me up and down with a knowing smirk. "Are you from the Realm across the sea?" he asked with an eyebrow raised.

That was some news. There was more than one Realm. Maybe each continent would be a different expansion pack? Maybe a different server? Perhaps Maxkrannar actually lived on one of the others, constantly struggling against hordes of enemies in search of the perfect loot build.

"Yeah," I answered casually. Being from across the sea seemed good enough for now. "I stick out, don't I?"

The bartender nodded. "You'd fit in better in a big city. Lots of people come from all over and end up in Mara. Maybe you'll find whatever it is you're looking for there," he explained.

"How far is it to Mara?" I asked. A big city sounded like it would have a ton more quests. More quests meant more progression and some leveling. I could basically feel my fingers begging to hold a mouse and keyboard again.

The bartender thought for a moment. "Twenty miles? Maybe thirty?"

I was certainly glad they used imperial units. The only metric conversion I knew was that a marathon was twenty-six miles, which was forty-two kilometers, which was entirely too far for any human to run in less than eight months' time.

Now if only I could call an Uber to take me there. No way was I walking in Bokta's straw-leather-reed-cloth slipper things. "Are there any wagons or horses that go there regularly?" I asked.

"My daughter will be taking a wagon full of empty barrels back to a cooperage in Mara tomorrow afternoon," he said. "You can ride with her if you like. But be warned: she doesn't talk much, and don't piss her off. She's broken men twice your size."

"When you say 'broken'... never mind," I muttered. Best to leave the cryptic warnings unexplained. "What time is she leaving?"

"Afternoon," he repeated. "I told you."

Oh, right. The quantification of time and all. Clocks probably didn't exist, at least not out in the starter zone.

"So I should just meet her here?" I asked.

He nodded. "She'll be loading up right out front. You won't miss her."

Awesome. So I had one more day left in Tamernil before I got to see the big city. Hopefully there would be better quests on the challenge boards in Mara. Until then, I needed something to do, and Bokta hadn't seemed too sure about the presence of a brothel . . . so I needed *something else* to do.

"Whatever happened to that little kid that was in the hut when I arrived?" I asked her. We were both standing out in the morning sun once more, and the heat was pretty noticeable. A hat would not have been a bad thing to acquire. I was pale enough to get sunburned easily.

"Jaerth helps me every now and then," Bokta explained. "He lives here, but I have not had need of him since you arrived. He did his job."

"And he won't tell people that a Blood Witch lives in their village?" I asked. A little kid as a helper to a demonic summoning felt like a needless liability.

"He will not," Bokta said with quick confidence. "If he does, I will kill him."

That settled that. The threat of death had always held my lips shut without complaint, and I was sure it worked just fine on the kid.

"We should get ready for the trip tomorrow," I offered. I wasn't exactly sure what we would need to get ready, but *something* should be done in preparation. We might not be able to throw our junk into mom's minivan, but there must have been a medieval equivalent.

"I have food for the journey," Bokta said. "How long do you plan on staying in Mara?"

"Do we have to come back here?"

The Blood Witch thought for a while before answering. "You're right," she said after a minute. "If we are to overthrow the Dread King, we don't need to be meddling around in the village. The sooner you can assume your demon form, the better."

"Are there any other Oathbreakers in Tamernil?" I asked. Meeting more of her rebel group might prove to be a good thing.

"Not in Tamernil," she said. "But there are many of us in Mara. That is where I'm from."

Maybe the other Oathbreakers could help me attain my 'demon form,' though unless they had a computer, I didn't think it was going to happen. "I need to try out my spear," I told Bokta, hoping to get some combat experience before we left the village.

"The recruiter should have some practice dummies," she explained. She pointed down the main street toward a building marked by red pennants fluttering in the warm breeze, and we started off at once.

The army recruiter's office was pretty close to what I

had expected. There was only one room, and it had all sorts of military equipment lining the walls, along with a few posters oddly reminiscent of the Uncle Sam 'I Want You' fliers, except Uncle Sam had been replaced by some odd-looking guy in a suit of armor. "Is that the Dread King?" I asked quietly.

Bokta noded.

A blonde man in his thirties with a scraggly beard ran up to make a quick introduction before I could ask any more questions. "Looking for glory, son?" he cheerfully asked, slapping my shoulder like we were old friends. "Here to join the king's best? Ready to go out and slay monsters, make your fortune, eh?"

The guy reminded me of the National Guard sergeant that used to hang out around my high school looking for the lowlife kids who couldn't get accepted into college. "Nah, I'm good, man," I told him, refusing to make eye contact. "I'm just hoping to get some swings in on a practice dummy, if you have that kind of thing."

The recruiter beamed his fake, cheesy smile, following his script perfectly. "Right this way, bucko!" he basically yelled in my ear. I let him lead me out a door in the back that opened up to a large training pavilion containing a few other men my age busy with short swords and clubs.

"This fine lad wants a go at the spar!" the recruiter happily announced. That was most certainly not what I wanted to hear.

"No, I just want a training dummy," I tried to correct, but the man didn't pay me any attention. He grabbed one of the other guys and positioned him across from me in the blink of an eye. Shit, maybe sparring was an unskippable tutorial.

My opponent had a wooden sword with a huge cross

piece in his hands. He was wearing padded leather clothing that looked like it had been designed specifically for combat training. I could hear Bokta chuckle under her breath behind me. Her confidence was a lot less comforting than her fan girl idolization.

"Um," I hesitated, "this spear is real." I showed my instructor the point of my makeshift weapon. Killing a huge rat had made me puke. Hurting a human by accident would probably do a number on my psychological state. Again, I wasn't a murderer. I couldn't help but think of all the thousands and thousands of people Maxkrannar had killed in Realm. But in a video game, you knew their death screams weren't real. You could turn it off, go to bed, and head to work the next day to be miserable like always. If I killed someone with my own hands, I would need years of therapy. Expensive therapy. I didn't have the gibs for that.

The recruiter deftly snatched the spear from my hands without much resistance. He set the end over his knee, drew a sword from a scabbard at his side, and hacked off the point I had spent so long trying to make.

"There you go, son," he said as though he had just done me some great favor.

"Fantastic."

Before I could even think about getting myself prepared for the trial ahead, the man in front of me rushed in with his wooden sword held high above his head. I had a pretty good reaction time, but only with a keyboard and mouse. My mind knew exactly what to do—and my body suffered a painful hit to the top of the head as a result of my inaction.

"Hey, that hurt," I whined, rubbing my scalp.

The man jumped backward on the balls of his feet with a little victory shout. I tried to catch him off balance and swung in hard for his chest with my stick, but he dodged the attack almost effortlessly by skipping to the side. I moved the staff back in the other direction, effectively keeping the man at bay, but not scoring a hit.

Then he rolled under my stick and came up with his wooden sword lodged in my gut. Thank god it didn't break the skin. I couldn't imagine what healthcare was like under the Dread King, and I hadn't brought my insurance card from back home—not that my coverage was that great anyways.

The sword tip hurt like a bitch. Thankfully, the man realized I was in pain and dropped his weapon down to his side as he clambered back to his feet—which was perfect, because it didn't hurt as badly as I had let on, and I brought my stick down hard on my opponent's back. The wood cracked loudly across his spine, and he fell prone like a sack of potatoes.

I hit him two more times as he tried to get his footing. When he finally did, I could tell he hurt more than I did. Bokta clapped, which was all the encouragement I needed to swing again with all my might. The man deflected my baseball bat-esque weapon with his own sword, and then my momentum carried the stick up the length of his wooden blade where it released, catching the poor guy fully in the teeth.

Okay, I felt bad about that one.

I stepped back to let the recruiter come to the man's rescue, to see if he was alright, but the wannabe soldier surprised us all. He charged across the few feet separating us on all fours like a dog, performing a tackle that would have made Ray Lewis proud.

I hit the ground hard. All the air rushed out of my lungs, and I immediately felt a little dizzy. Somewhere in the tussle, I lost my stick and was left with only my hands. I got in a good block on the first strike, but the guy's second punch crashed into my jaw. I felt like a UFC fighter on my back struggling to survive without brain damage against some enraged fiend raining down blow after blow on my poor face.

Thankfully, the barrage only lasted another ten seconds or so before Bokta rushed to my aid. She threw her body into the man, knocking him to the ground. It was nice to have someone around that thought you were some powerful demon lord who needed protecting at all costs. She was my devoted fan club, and I was a hapless celebrity.

We all stood, and I was a little shaky on my feet. At least my mouth wasn't gushing blood like the other guy's.

"Not too bad," the recruiter said with his usual cheerfulness. He tossed my stick back to me and motioned for the two of us to square off again.

"Uh, I think I've had enough," I said. I didn't want to wimp out, but I also didn't want to die. Sometimes discretion was the better part of valor, right? I was pretty sure some famous general had said that, or maybe a president. Maybe I had read it on a video game loading screen. Plus, I hadn't received any experience points yet. But again, the whole concept of experience being measured in a nominal sense was still a wild guess.

"Nonsense!" the cheery recruiter shouted.

"Well, can you just teach me some technique?" I asked, trying to make it sound like I wasn't begging. Maybe that was the key to leveling: acquiring new skills.

The recruiter sighed, which I took as a good thing, and then slapped me on the shoulder. "Alright, son, step over here," he said.

Finally. Some real training.

He led me to a practice dummy made of straw, sticks, and little bits of cloth here and there. The man stood behind the dummy, which felt like a dangerous place to be, though I didn't question it. He hooked his arm under the dummy's wooden appendage and held his sword straight up.

"The first thing you have to learn is to not die," he began.

"Yeah, I agree. That sounds pretty useful."

"So, when someone is coming at you and all you have is a spear, you need to disarm them and prevent them from getting close," he explained. "Try to knock my sword away."

That made sense. Hunters in Realm sometimes used spears, and their most annoying ability was to disarm their opponent and then scurry backward to use their bows. I should have thought of that myself.

I jabbed my stick forward and then swept it to the side where it clattered against the sword, but completely failed to disarm the recruiter.

"No, not like that," he said sternly. "Stab for my hand. Fingers hurt when they get smashed, right? Try to smash my fingers against the hilt. *Then* pull to the side to rip the weapon away."

That made more sense. I struck forward for the man's hand, connected pretty solidly, then hooked the end of my stick beneath his cross piece and wrenched it upward. It worked! His sword flew a few feet through the air before landing with a thud on the ground. Achievement unlocked! You've earned the Riposte skill! The words didn't flash themselves into existence before my eyes, not in a literal sense, but in a very real way I felt I had progressed to level one.

"Hey, not bad!" the recruiter said with a nod of approval. He plucked his weapon from the ground and turned, suddenly coming at me with a snarl on his face.

I jabbed out again, aiming directly for his hand, but I wasn't quick enough. He closed the distance between us in an instant, then bonked me on the top of my head with the pommel of his weapon. It hurt like a bitch.

I staggered backward, and the recruiter relented. "Any chance I could get a helmet?" I asked him.

He smiled, and I got the sinking feeling that I had just fallen into a blatant recruitment trap.

"Why, certainly!" he exclaimed. "All new recruits get a free set of practice armor and a sparring sword! So what do you say, ready to join the ranks, soldier?"

Oh, a free set of armor? A worthy quest indeed! "Yeah, I'll take it!" I told him. "Can I sign up today and then come back tomorrow to start my training?"

The recruiter looked like he loved my idea. "Let's get the papers signed," he said, again slapping me on the back.

I followed him into the small office where he pulled out a rolled parchment from a desk drawer and smoothed it with his palms. He took a feather pen, dipped it in ink, and handed it over. "Sign right here," he said, brimming with joy.

In my best, most swoopy handwriting, I applied my signature. Well, not mine. I signed it as *Donald J. Trump*, but the man didn't give it a second look.

"And my armor?" I asked.

"Right this way!" He had taken me for a gullible fool, but I had played him better. A bonus charisma point would certainly have been in order.

He took me into another room where he helped me grab a leather breastplate, some properly fitting boots, a belt, and a pair of leather bracers that looked oddly like the cheap ones I had seen for sale at live action role-play shops. Everything fit pretty well, and the recruiter was all too happy to have me aboard. I bet he got a good commission for each sucker he sent to their death.

"Alright, well, I'll be back tomorrow around noon. I can't wait to join the army!" I told him, inching toward the door.

"I can't wait to have you along, Donald," the man cheerfully replied.

Perfect. Free armor was the best kind of armor. Sure, I'd essentially faked my way into the military which would probably piss off more than a few people up the chain of command, but how would they find me? A medieval world wouldn't have the resources to stage a manhunt for a petty criminal like me, so if I never returned to Tamernil, I would be fine.

CHAPTER 7

T he next afternoon, McCallister's daughter was in front of the pub just as expected, busily loading empty barrels into an oxcart. There wasn't much room left for people, but I didn't mind being crammed on top of Bokta for a long journey. In fact, such an ample bosom sounded like a nice place to rest my head. The tavern keeper's daughter, a stark and homely contrast to the Blood Witch, was stoically silent as we helped her finish loading. She kind of creeped me out. When we were all set to go, her father came out to see her off, and that was that.

Goodbye, Tamernil. Goodbye, military.

The journey was far from a smooth one. The roads of Realm were about as bad as the highways in Michigan after a heavy winter, which was to say that they might as well not have existed. The cart jostled along down the dirt path at a modest pace, constantly threatening to throw the empty barrels over the sides with every jump and turn.

Luckily, the distance between the two cities wasn't large. After about an hour and a half, Mara appeared as a little speck on the horizon. Most of the landscape between Mara and Tamernil was just farmland, basically no different than driving through Indiana or Ohio. I had done that trip enough in my day, so the time spent on the bumpy wagon passed fairly quickly.

As we got closer, I was pretty astounded by the sheer size of the city. It rose up from the farmland like an oasis in the desert, an oasis made of stone walls, half-timbered buildings three and four stories tall, and circular guard towers that lined the path on either side. Banners streamed from the windows of the towers, and the foot traffic beneath them was substantial.

"Why did you ever leave this place?" I asked in wonder. Mara looked incredible. The city spanned at least a few square miles, though I wasn't a cartographer by any means. By comparison, Mara was New York City, and Tamernil was made up of the bad parts of Gary, Indiana, which is to say it was the entire city of Gary, Indiana.

Bokta smiled at me. "My magic is illegal here," she whispered, keeping an eye on our driver to make sure she didn't overhear. "I'm an Oathbreaker. If I'm caught, my head is worth ten thousand gibs."

"And we're just waltzing back into the city?"

She laughed. "I don't look exactly the same as I did when I became a wanted woman," she said. "But we must still remain inconspicuous. Don't let down your guard."

"What do you mean?"

We passed beneath a stone archway flanked on both sides by circular towers. Mean-looking archers peered down at us from either side, but no one came out to stop or even inspect the ox cart.

"I used to be a bit bigger," she said with a hint of a laugh in her melodic voice. "There's a baker on the east end of Mara that makes sweet cream cakes. Let's just say he used to sell out by noon whenever I was around."

"I'll have to try one," I casually remarked before realizing that I had basically just told a recovering alcoholic that I was looking forward to hitting the local bar. "S-Sorry," I stammered. "I didn't mean it like that."

"No, I'm past that now." She laughed like I was a complete idiot. Which I was, of course. Social interaction had never been my strongest quality. "It's all about lifestyle changes. Just the little things, over a long enough span of time, and now I look like this!"

Shit. So she knew she was gorgeous. For whatever reason, those were always the hardest girls to sway. I felt whatever slim chance I thought I had slipping out between my chubby fingers. Though if my aunt on Facebook was to be believed, Bokta's story must have been a lie—weight was all genetics, right? Ha! Bullshit.

We rolled on through the city, down a cobblestone path that was somehow bumpier than the road outside of the city. I tried to think up something witty to say to break the uneasy tension I had inadvertently created between us, but nothing came to mind.

Finally, the ox cart came to a stop outside a huge brewery that could entice a swarm of hipsters from miles around if it had been back in my hometown. Big copper stills poked up through the shingle roof in a square pattern. Our driver hopped off the front bench and got to work without giving either Bokta or myself so much as a cursory glance. I jumped over the side of the cart first and offered my hand for the Blood Witch to take. She ignored it, further adding to my awkwardness, and landed gracefully by my side.

"So," I began, "where's the first stop? Are we going to meet the other Oat—"

She covered my mouth forcefully with her hand, her eyes darting around nervously. Surprisingly, her hand smelled like lavender. But maybe I should have been worrying about more important things.

"Don't say it," she kind of growled, her voice restrained yet clearly conveying her seriousness.

I nodded sheepishly.

"We need to meet someone," she said, most of the kindness back in her sweet voice. "Get your gear, and I'll take you there."

I felt kind of bad leaving McCallister's daughter to move all of her barrels by herself, but she didn't seem to mind the solo work, so I followed along behind Bokta. It took a while to process the sheer enormity of the medieval city. I was a little depressed that there wasn't a big castle in the center of the town with huge curtain walls and knights in shining armor, but I guessed I would get to see one of those before long. There weren't any church steeples, either, which I supposed made sense, but it felt weird to look at an old-style city and not see them. I made a mental note to ask Bokta about the religion of her Realm when I got the chance. In the online version I knew so well, there were cults that worshipped the eight different Underlords, and Oathbreakers acknowledged only one: the Desecrator. I kind of hoped the religion would be the same here, if only so that I could watch one of their cult rituals like I had during the cinematic cut-scenes of Realm Online.

Bokta led me through a few streets, around several corners, and past a bustling market full of traders and eager customers. The smells hanging in the air were too many to identify, though I *knew* there were roasted almonds somewhere just out of view. I nearly bowled over a little kid who was chasing a cat through the street, and I had to use another passerby to catch my balance.

"Sorry," I mumbled, pushing forward to catch up to my lithe guide.

We came to a place that looked like a biergarten, and Bokta pushed through a pair of saloon-style doors. The inside didn't look much different than the outside. The roof was just a woven set of thin wooden slats, like a garden trellis turned on its side, and it let the afternoon light through in dappled patches to scatter over the many tables full of patrons. Bokta walked up to a young woman filling glass mugs with foamy beer and whispered something in her ear. A short moment later, the woman nodded toward a door and silently departed.

The door at the side of the hall wasn't locked, and Bokta pushed through it without any hesitation. There was a short staircase that we quickly descended, and someone shut the door behind us almost at once. Everything was eerily dark.

"Uh—"

"Shhh," Bokta silenced me.

I followed her footsteps around a tight corner, ducking my head under the low ceiling. She knocked on what I assumed was another wooden door similar to the first, then we waited for a painfully long time.

"Yeah?" a gruff voice finally called from the other side.

"Sixteen red penguins," Bokta replied with a confidence that didn't fit her erratic words. "Only one of them wears a hat."

The door swung open, flooding the cramped tunnel with torchlight.

"That's a goofy-ass password," I said under my breath.

Bokta shot me the briefest glare before stepping into the next room. My own password to log in to the Realm servers was 'TrickyDick74'—an obvious homage to the one and only Richard Nixon—so I couldn't judge too much.

Two men stood guard on either side of the door like statues—statues with huge axes in their meaty hands. The one on the right was needlessly shirtless, making me feel a little bad about the pudge around my own waist.

Only a handful of other people were there, and one of them was the same race as the strange lizard creature I had encountered beneath the tavern in Tamernil. I wanted to talk to the little guy, but he was deep in conversation with a woman who looked remarkably like a high-class prostitute. I decided to leave the little lizard bugger to his own business and followed Bokta to an area similar to a fancy nightclub's VIP section. Not that I had ever been in one in real life . . . but I had seen a ton of movies. It looked like one of those.

Two more bouncers were there, both thankfully with shirts on, and both holding weapons. Behind them, a single woman lounged on a stack of velvety pillows with a drink in her hand. She wasn't dressed like a crime boss with a fat cigar and all pinstripes, but it was certainly the vibe she gave off. Granted, I have never met a crime boss, either. Everything I knew came from movies and games, which basically meant I'd be golden.

The woman recognized Bokta, and she waved the two of us up onto her crowded pillow pavilion. Lying on a bed of velvet cushions with two attractive women was something I had always dreamt of doing, but the situation felt a little less than desirable. It felt dangerous. The low roof overhead didn't help. And I typically wasn't a claustrophobic kind of guy.

"This is Amethyst," Bokta said with an air of reverence. "She organizes the Oathbreakers. Most of the others live outside Mara, and Amethyst helps keep everyone in contact. She also has leverage with most of the jailors and council members. That's how we stay hidden, for the most part."

"But she has a stripper name."

Both of them began scowling at me, which was weird, especially because I hadn't said anything . . .

They kept scowling. Amethyst took a sip of her drink, her eyes sending daggers my way.

Oh hell. I said that out loud. I called the leader of their underground rebellion a stripper. Fuck me. "Uh, no, I didn't really mean that . . ." I tried painfully to recover. It didn't work. "I just . . . In my world, only certain types of people have names like that—gemstone names."

Bokta let out a disappointed sigh. "I summoned him only two days ago," she said quietly. "He's a demon, an Oathbreaker like us, but he hasn't yet figured out how to take his true form."

It was not the most ringing endorsement, but it got Amethyst to relax a bit. And that was good enough for me.

"Sorry," I muttered.

"Right," Amethyst stated behind her drink.

Thankfully, Bokta charged ahead with a new topic of discussion. "Have there been any developments lately?" she asked.

Amethyst finally pulled her eyes away from me, and I could practically taste their lingering judgment. "There have," she replied, "and I'm going to need your expertise. Taros was captured several days ago. We need to free him."

"Taros? How did they know?" Bokta asked.

"We think someone reported him to the council,"

Amethyst answered. "They picked him up before we could move him out of Mara."

"Shit." Bokta shook her head, a strange motion for someone lying down. "Where are they holding him?"

"One of ours saw them take him into the municipal dungeon, so that's an advantage," she explained.

The municipal dungeon? That sounded awfully formal. "How many dungeons are there?" I asked.

"Six," Amethyst said. "The municipal dungeon has the lowest level of security. Breaking in to retrieve Taros should not be very difficult."

Perfect. Looked like quest number two in Realm would be a jail break. "How many of these have you pulled off before?" I asked. I just hoped to god we weren't going to try to go in totally blind. Even if the municipal dungeon was the lowest level of dungeon, it sounded at least a little risky. Rushing into my first quest had been nearly catastrophic.

"We've had to rescue a few of our comrades," Amethyst said cryptically. Her answer was vague enough to make me think there was a good chance she was lying. Bokta didn't add anything, so I guessed I just had to believe her.

"When do you want to move?" the Blood Witch asked.

Amethyst smiled. "We go tomorrow at dawn. You two can stay in one of the auxiliaries tonight and for the next few days. We'll be ready an hour before sunrise."

"And the reward?" I asked. There was always loot after a dungeon run. *Always*.

I saw a twinkle in Amethyst's eye that told me it should be pretty nice. "I take care of my own," she said, again being as cryptic as possible. I wasn't sure if she meant turning these pillows into the brothel I had been seeking or giving me some gear, though honestly I was fine with either. Or maybe even both. Both sounded pretty good.

CHAPTER 8

It was hard to sleep in the underground rebel complex set only a few feet beneath a noisy beer hall. There weren't many rooms in the auxiliary, but there also weren't many people. Perhaps it was the prospect of my second quest that kept me up tossing and turning most of the night. Regardless of the reason, I was awake well before everyone else.

Sadly, there was no food in the Oathbreaker bunker.

When Amethyst emerged from a different auxiliary, she was dressed for battle. She had a leather harness over her chest, and unsheathed swords dangled from either side of her hips. They were loosely balanced in a bit of chain, some sort of system that looked far too complex for me to ever pull off. In the online Realm, there wasn't much of a scabbard and sheath set-up. Maxkrannar carried his weapons *somehow*, and that process was never actually explained, nor was it terribly important. Whenever

I hit 'Z' on the keyboard, he would draw his swords and axes. Simple. What Amethyst was wearing was about as far from simple as it could possibly get.

Bokta arrived in the main chamber a little while later, and two of the brutish guys acting as bouncers followed her. I guessed they were the ones who had to empty all the chamber pots, and I didn't envy their job in the least. As far as I could tell, the Oathbreakers appeared to be structured in a matriarchal way, though I wasn't sure exactly how much power Amethyst wielded beyond our walls. She could be a low-level organizer, ultimately answering to some higher power somewhere else within the organization. Or she could be the head honcho.

When we were all ready to go, Amethyst led our little party up the cramped stairs to the beer hall above. Thankfully, the staff had a decent spread of food waiting for us, though we weren't given much time to enjoy it.

Sunlight was just starting to appear when I finished my last bit of biscuit and fell into line. I was able to whittle a decent point back on my stick, transforming it once more into a shoddy spear, though it felt wholly inadequate. Bokta had no visible weapon, and the two goons each carried huge nightstick-style clubs. I was betting they could each bash in my head with a single strike.

I leaned next to Bokta so only she could hear. "Are we going to kill people?" I asked tentatively. Images of the dog-like rat flashed through my mind.

"Only if we have to," she answered. That didn't help in the least.

"Do you think we'll have to?"

Bokta's expression was stern. "Oathbreakers leave no witnesses," she stated flatly. "We can't let them know the rest of us exist."

If only ski masks had been invented back in medieval times . . . They didn't exist in the version of the game I knew, either, but some programmer somewhere should have made an invisibility cloak or something. No class in Realm had a true stealth ability, though I would have loved to see one in action. Popping out from stealth as an Oathbreaker would have been totally badass. The practical applications were basically limitless.

Mara was relatively quiet in the early morning hours. Noise came from a few different shops on either side of the street, but there was no crowd of people to push through like the day before.

The municipal dungeon looked a bit like an old-time jail. The walls were all stone, it was only one story, and there was a painted wooden placard above the door showing a pair of manacles. We stopped a block or so away, our team leaning up against a wooden building that served some arcane purpose I couldn't deduce from its sign.

I felt like I should have at least had a hood or something pulled over my face. Standing more or less out in the open felt preposterously careless. Maybe my little crew of Oathbreakers was a bit amateur. Although, to be fair, I was only in the second town. If everything really was some sort of game, the first handful of locations were bound to be thoroughly lame. I wouldn't find competent allies until at least the third or fourth area. Being level one sucked.

A guard walked out of the front door of the municipal dungeon, rubbed the sleep from his eyes, and then turned to lock the door behind him. He strolled down the street, and I presumed his shift was over. Everyone in my group fell deathly silent.

Amethyst held a finger over her lips, making eye contact with everyone in the party, then scampered forward to the door. She pulled a key from her pocket, slipped it in the door, and pushed her way inside. The rest of us ran across the street to follow her and ducked into the dungeon.

The inside of the building was a bit different than the county jail I had visited in the fifth grade on a school field trip. There was no desk, no cozy little break room for a bunch of bawdy detectives to eat donuts and drink coffee, and, most strikingly, there were no windows. Instead, the only thing in the room was a staircase down. I could tell the architects—or programmers—who had designed Mara enjoyed basements.

Amethyst took the lead, and I filtered to the very back, letting the two goons take the spots right after their leader. "He's on level three," the woman whispered to the rest of us. Everyone tensed up.

We passed the first subterranean level without stopping. No guard was there to accost us, either, just a heavy iron door. It felt like a pretty substantial measure to build such a complex for what was considered the weakest-level dungeon in the city. Maybe I had left Tamernil a bit too early. No one liked to play through *every* quest in the tutorial, right?

Voices came up from the second tier, and they didn't sound friendly. Then again, we were in a dungeon, so there were bound to be some rather unsavory fellows contained below. Quietly prowling on the balls of her feet, Amethyst held up a fist to stop us. I couldn't help but feel like I was in a live-action episode of *Cops*. My heart pounded in my chest, and my hands started to perspire.

Before I could fully gather my wits and whatever inside me that counted as nerve, Amethyst dropped down to the second-tier landing with a thud, her two weapons suddenly in her hands. Almost at once, a fight broke out.

Shouts rang at me from all sides, and I couldn't see enough to tell who was winning and losing. The battle was pure chaos, and it had taken less than the space of a heartbeat to develop. No prep time with the guild leader going over buffs and tactics. Hell, not even time to catch my breath.

Then it ended. Almost as quickly as it had begun, everything went quiet except for the heavy breathing of the two grunts. I could just barely see over Bokta's shoulder, spotting someone, presumably a jailor, motionless on the ground.

And now, just a few days into my new life, I was an accomplice to murder. Unjustifiable murder. We were the bad guys breaking a criminal out of jail. Back home, the worst I'd ever done as far as the law was concerned had resulted in a pair of speeding tickets. Sure, the fines had been pretty ridiculous—at least for a broke nobody like me—but it just didn't compare. Speeding and killing another human being weren't even close to the same category of offense. I tried to push down the vile sensation growing in my stomach and slowly creeping up the back of my throat. Suddenly, I regretted eating so much at breakfast.

Summoning as much courage as I dared, I stole a glance at the body as we filed down to the third section of the municipal dungeon. I was fairly confident the man on the ground was still breathing, but I was far from a doctor, and I might just have been seeing what I wanted to see. A shudder ran down my spine. I knew what we'd done.

The third floor had no guard waiting outside the heavy iron door. That was welcome, but I also knew for a fact there were guards on the other side. The voices of men, two by my judgment, came through the door as low mumbles.

Amethyst held up a hand again, not that any of us were moving—there was nowhere left to go, no fourth floor below us. Gingerly, like a cautious parent not wanting to wake a sleeping child, she tried her key in the lock, and it didn't work. Then it made a painfully loud clicking noise that halted the conversation on the other side of the door.

"Gary?" a voice called through the metal.

Great. Adding a name to the guy my party may or may not have just killed made it about a thousand times worse. Gary was probably a wonderful guy. I bet he had kids out there in the city, too, and they were depending on his paycheck. Terrific. Sorry, Gary. Sorry, Gary's kids.

A jingling of keys came from the other side of the door. The guards were coming out.

Amethyst backed the rest of us up a few steps with a wave of her hand, then motioned for Bokta to come forward. "I'll take the first one," our leader whispered. "You and the demon handle the second. I want to see what he's capable of."

Oh *hell* no.

"I—"

The door opened, and a wide-eyed guard stood there with keys in his hand and a sword at his side. The second man, standing a few paces behind the first, shouted and drew his weapon.

Amethyst grabbed the first jailor by his shirt and pulled, dropping down dexterously into a squat with one foot out that tripped the man as he tumbled forward. At nearly the same time, Bokta yanked me along by the wrist and charged forward.

She dragged me with her over the first guard and through the doorway. That was when I saw two more guards at the other end of the hallway who were running toward us full speed with weapons drawn. That pair hadn't been part of the plan. We still had the numbers, five against four, but that was only true if I actually counted for a full one. Luckily, the Blood Witch at my side didn't seem to mind the odds. Bokta slammed her shoulder into the soldier right in front of her, separating us in the process.

My shitty spear felt like a bad joke in my hands, especially when compared to the metal armor and swords we were up against. The guards weren't encased in steel like stereotypical knights from video games, but I was sure my weak weapon wouldn't do much against even the lowest quality metal breastplate. The nearest guard took a swing for Bokta's head, and I winced in anticipation of the blow. When the man's sword connected with the side of her head, she sparked to life with magical energy that repelled the attack.

The man staggered backward, but he was quick to recover. Bokta ducked under another swing, then threw her hands forward like an anime character about to shoot a giant laser beam from her palms. I desperately prayed she had suddenly gone all super-Saiyan and was about to loose some Earth-shattering death beam of glory that would end the fight in the blink of an eye.

Instead of a laser or some other apocalyptic conjuring, an anticlimactic bit of black smoke issued from the woman's hands and wrapped itself around the man's chest. He swung again, and it looked like his sword was going to split Bokta's head in half. I lunged out with my piece-of-shit spear to put the wood between her skull and the steel edge of the weapon, desperate to avoid watching Bokta's brains splatter the ground. I got there in time—which shocked me more than it should have—and I stopped the sword, though the momentum of the swing forced my spear to crash into Bokta's head. The man's blade lodged in the spear's shaft, so I yanked it back to my body. The recruiter in Tamernil would have been proud—I had successfully disarmed an opponent. I was only level one, but I was already using my solitary ability to save lives!

Bokta fell back painfully on her ass, probably reeling from a concussion. At least she was alive. And hey, I *had* kind of saved her life. Sadly, I didn't get much time to relish my little victory because the final pair of guards was nearly on top of me.

I wasn't sure what I screamed, but something high-pitched came out of my mouth pretty quickly. I held my spear as tightly as possible and dropped to the ground like a beaten dog. A wild battle clashed right over my head. Peeking through my fingers like a kid at a horror movie, I saw the two goons from the beer hall fully engaged in battle right above me, their legs knocking into my back as I cowered.

I half-crawled, half-threw myself to the side to get out of the way. A few seconds later, everything was finished. One of our brutes had a nasty gash on his side, and all of the other guards were dead or in the process of dying. There was more blood than I had ever seen in my life, save for the one time I had attempted to donate at the Red Cross and had passed out before the needle had broken skin.

Bokta didn't look so good. She was wobbly, and she hadn't taken her hand from the top of her head. I bet she'd have a killer headache the rest of the day, assuming my maneuver hadn't given her irreversible brain damage and turned her into a vegetable. That would've been rough. Arrive in Tamernil, make a single ally I could trust, and promptly render her useless for the rest of her life.

Looking even worse, the man she had fought was still on the ground, a bit of smoke twirling slowly above his chest. "What did you do to him?" I asked when the realization of what had taken place fully sank in past the adrenaline clouding my thoughts. The magic was even more terrifying than all the blood. No insane number of hours spent on Realm, of which I had logged thousands, could have ever prepared me for the weight of seeing real magic used in combat. Even if the spell had been visually lackluster, it was incredible at the same time. It was *magic*, and not just a colorful butterfly.

Bokta groaned. "He's just stunned," she muttered. "He'll be up . . . in a couple minutes . . ."

Amethyst walked over to the prone guard and casually waved away the smoke with her hand. With an air of indifference, she drew a thin stiletto dagger from one boot, knelt, and pushed it through the side of the man's throat.

"No witnesses," she declared.

That pushed my nausea over the limit. I puked, narrowly avoiding everyone's feet, and my stomach clenched so hard I felt like my ribs were going to break. A second wave hit shortly after the first, and there was no stopping it.

When I finally stopped retching, everyone was staring at me. "A demon, eh?" Amethyst scoffed. Guess I failed her test . . .

So, I wasn't great at first impressions when it came to executing prison guards in cold blood. Mutual combat aside, what I had seen felt like murder—no different than the guard in the hallway by the stairs. We were still the ones breaking into a government facility to kill people and rescue a convict. That was kind of hard to swallow. Similar to the contents of my stomach. Was I ready to be evil? Could I actually do it? Sure, that's what I had played online . . . but in real life, I had been a malcontent at worst. Some— my parents chief among them—would undoubtedly have called me a lazy degenerate. But murder? *Murder?*

Even Bokta recovered faster than I did. She reached a hand down to lift me from the ground, which I was grateful for, though I still didn't really know what I was going to do. More than ever, thoughts of getting back home flooded through my mind.

"Come on, we don't have much time," Amethyst said once I was on my feet again. There were about thirty different jail cells lining either side of the dismal hallway. Like above, smoky torches in iron sconces were the only sources of light.

The woman didn't know which cell held her companion, so she went up to the metal doors of each one and slid the little window plates in the center to the side. It only took her a second or two at each door to determine that Taros wasn't there. Finally, when she was nearly at the end of the hallway, she found him.

"Give us a minute, Taros," she said through the small window. One of the brutes had all the keys from the guards, and Amethyst stepped aside to let him try them one at a time. The clicking noises they made filled the narrow stone corridor with an eerie echo.

It took a full minute, and then the door swung open on noisy, un-oiled hinges. Much to my surprise, Taros stepped out completely naked. He appeared bewildered, perhaps a bit unbelieving, but he had a stupidly large smile on his face nonetheless.

Amethyst wrapped him in a quick embrace as she welcomed him back to the fold.

"Do you know that guy?" I asked Bokta. He had a shaggy beard and a bunch of fresh lacerations all over his body. He looked kind of like a stereotypical biker asshole, except for the naked part.

"He used to be one of the leaders of the Oathbreakers,"

she explained. "His kid was killed during a raid once, and he left after that."

"That seems fair," I said, more to myself than her. But then again, the Oathbreakers felt closer to a crime family than a political movement. You couldn't just leave crime families, even when your kid got killed—everyone knew that.

"What's going to happen to him now?" I asked, suddenly fearing the answer. If they really were operating like the mob, and one of their own had been pinched . . .

I felt like Bokta could read my mind. She was a witch, though, so maybe she really could. "No witnesses, remember?" she whispered through a sinister smile.

If she was just trolling, she was a master. If she wasn't, I was about to get sick all over again.

"Amethyst is going to kill him?"

She laughed, unable to keep up her ruse any longer. "He knows too much," she snickered, "but he's still an Oathbreaker, retired or not. We don't kill our own unless we really have to."

At least I wouldn't have to watch Amethyst ram her dagger through his flesh. That was mildly comforting.

Naked prisoner in tow, we made our way back to the stairs at the end of the hall, and I picked up one of the soldier's swords as we passed. The weapon was far better than my spear, so I just tossed the wooden thing down to the ground. The thought of my forensic evidence being traced back to me briefly crossed my mind, and then I remembered that CSI wasn't a thing in Realm. If they had the knowledge and technology to trace my fingerprints or DNA and then hunt me down, so be it. I would be impressed.

Sadly, we were moving back to the surface too quickly

for me to stop and loot some armor from any of the corpses, and the inner power-gamer in me cried a little bit at the missed opportunity. I would never have left a corpse untouched online, even the low-level ones from beginner dungeons.

All at once, sounds from the top floor stopped me in my tracks.

People were waiting for us. They sounded angry. Amethyst halted our little troop with another upraised fist. I counted five separate voices from the other side of the door. There were six of us, but I didn't offer much in a fight, and I was pretty sure Bokta needed an MRI to confirm which parts of her brain had turned to soup. And Taros was stark naked without any weapons. As far as strength was concerned, we were basically at three and a half.

Amethyst stood unmoving—presumably concocting a fool-proof plan to see us through the other side—for all of a couple seconds, then positioned the two brutes at the very front. One of them was still a bit beat up. She whispered something to them, then turned and spoke to Bokta. After a curt nod, Bokta then whispered to me, like we were playing some big game of telephone except the message involved killing and the strong possibility of death. I didn't remember that version from kindergarten.

"When the door opens, we split left," the Blood Witch said in my ear. She noticed how badly the sword in my hands was shaking. "Just hold the handle against your stomach, then ram the pointy end into their gut." That was comforting. But hey, that level of advice had worked well enough in *Game of Thrones*, so it might as well work for me. I was stronger and smarter than a little girl on a TV show, right? Ha, probably not.

I was in the middle of remembering my favorite

episodes from the series when one of the brutes shoul-
dered open the door and charged. In an instant, everyone except me exploded into action. Honestly, our group
looked rather impressive . . . for about three seconds. Then
the very first brute got himself skewered by three points of
a sharp palisade angled directly at chest height.

The second of our tanks managed to twist his way to the
side of the bloody corpse that used to be his comrade, and
we were two and a half against five. One of the five had a
crossbow. What a nice little surprise. Without that joyous
addition, the fight would have just been too lopsided to be
fair!

The crossbow clicked and thrummed, and we were
down to one and a half against five. Amethyst was still
whirling at full strength, and I figured Bokta, Taros, and
myself all combined for a solid half. And we hadn't struck
a single blow.

A bit of blood spurted onto my face from the second
brute's fatal neck wound. Maybe six feet away, the crossbowman dropped his weapon to his boot to begin the
arduous process of reloading his deadly, and altogether
overpowered, weapon.

Bokta rushed left, and Amethyst broke to her right.
That left me exposed right in the center, wide-eyed and
terrified. Fantastic . . .

I ran left like the plan had originally called for, hoping
that the quick deaths of our two tanks weren't going to ruin
it all, though I knew they likely would. Bokta summoned
up another burst of smoke to her fingertips and flung it out
in a wide arc. The smoke latched itself onto the eyes of the
nearest soldiers, making them stagger back and shriek in
surprise. Picking the easiest target, I went straight for the
crossbowman.

With two of them blinded, there was an opening that let me get right up in the face of my intended prey without meeting any resistance. Then I just kind of looked at him. We were both terrified. Clearly, I had never killed anyone. Judging by the look in the other guy's eyes, I didn't think he had killed anyone, either. Well, no one other than one of our brutes a few seconds ago.

He was shaking just as badly as I was, and his crossbow dry-fired in his hands before he had the chance to load a bolt into it. That was probably for the best, because he would have shot himself in the foot had there been a bolt on the track.

For whatever reason, the sword in my hand felt exceedingly heavy. I lifted it up by my side, then lowered it back down again. I could see a bit of snot glistening on the soldier's upper lip. I had read plenty of fantasy books in my day, and whenever the main hero killed a couple dozen goblins up close and personal, the author had never stopped to describe how utterly soul-crushing the act was for the hero. Unless the hero was a callous bastard—and I'd read a few of those, too—the hero had to feel the weight of all that slaughtering bearing down on his very existence. Was I a callous bastard?

The soldier's crossbow dropped noisily to the ground. Or maybe I was the only one who could hear it, lost as I was in my own thoughts amidst the roaring clash of battle all around me. The guy drew a knife from his belt. He pointed it at my gut, apparently following the exact advice Bokta had given me.

Everything happened in slow motion. I brought my stolen sword to my body and angled it downward, pressing the hilt tightly into my own abdomen. The two of us awkwardly stepped forward. No one was eager to kill. My sword was probably three times the length of his knife, though, so my blade hit his chest long before I had to actually worry about his.

The man's eyes went wide, probably wider than my own. My sword didn't go too deep, maybe an inch into the fat of his belly beneath his shirt, but it was enough. He took a step backward, pulling my weapon out of his gut as he moved. Blood poured from his body. So much blood.

"Oh, shit, I-I'm sorry . . ." I stammered awkwardly. I put my hands up like I was on some medieval police show and my carriage had just been pulled over for an expired horse registration. The sword clattered to the ground between us. I knew I should have picked it up, but I just couldn't force my muscles to move. Not even my eyes wanted to move. No, they were content to stare at the destruction I had wrought.

Another soldier fell to the ground between me and the moderately wounded crossbowman. I looked and saw Bokta thrashing about to my right with her hands held out like claws. She had one of the blinded soldiers on the ropes, and Amethyst was making pretty decent work of the remaining guard off to the side. The man at my feet was dead. He had dark smoke twirling over his eyes, and his Adam's apple was gruesomely missing. Fortunately, there was nothing left in my stomach to vomit out onto the floor.

It took me a couple seconds to realize that my sword was now underneath a corpse, and I had no intention of rolling the guy over to get it. Not yet, at least.

Thankfully, the crossbowman collapsed to the ground with his back against the wall a few paces away from the action. I grabbed his crossbow from the ground and mimicked his motion with my foot through the big loop on the front. I'd never loaded a crossbow before, but I'd seen it done in plenty of movies, and crossbows weren't terribly complex to begin with. The thing required a considerable amount of strength to span, but I got the string locked in tight. The only bolt I could see was the one lodged in our brute's neck. I shuddered, but I took a step toward the corpse.

The bolt slid out of the guy's shredded neck with a sickening sound. Blood oozed over my fingers, further twisting my stomach into the world's most complex knot. I set the bloody quarrel onto the track in the center of the crossbow and snugged the end up against the string.

I have to say, it felt a little poetic to kill a soldier with his own weapon. I aimed the crossbow at the sitting man's chest. The only gun I had ever fired in my life was a friend's SKS, a heavy rifle from the Cold War that made a boom like a cannon and had nearly dislocated my shoulder. The crossbow's lever-like trigger took a lot more force to pull, but the recoil wasn't nearly as bad.

The bolt disappeared into my target's upper chest, and the man stopped groaning. Just like that.

Once you've killed a man, you can never really go back to being the same person you were before. If Tamernil really was an alternate or advanced version of Realm, my title had just gone from Steve the Accountant to Steve the Murderer. Or maybe it would be Steve the Little Bitch. Perhaps Steve of the Shattered Psyche.

Emotional trauma aside, there was no possible way I could go back to reality. I was officially in too deep. Even if I found a teleporter to drop me off in front of the Pineview Terrace Apartments, I wouldn't take it. Mara was my home, and I knew it without a doubt in that single instant.

CHAPTER 9

Back at Oathbreaker headquarters, or whatever the complex beneath the biergarten really was, I just sort of collapsed onto the floor. No one else appeared at all bothered by the events of the day, and I was starting to get the impression that human life wasn't very highly valued among the people of Realm. Though when I thought about it, life wasn't valued at all in a video game, either. In a way, it made sense. Wanton slaughter was part of any good RPG, so why would it be different here? Still, it was hard to see some of our own so mercilessly killed.

The two brutes we had taken with us were both dead, but three more who looked strikingly similar to the first two awaited our arrival. Then it finally clicked in my head. The beefy soldier types were just that. Red shirts. NPCs. Fodder for the enemy so the real heroes didn't get cut to ribbons. My 'enhanced virtual reality video game' theory picked up a bit more weight. And if they weren't *real* in the way Bokta, Amethyst, and myself were *real*, it helped dull the sting of their deaths quite a bit. Still, there wasn't much rationalization that would help me cope with the fact that one of the NPCs had been slain by my hand. I tried to ignore it.

Completely at home in his birthday suit and unfazed by the killing, Taros stretched his back and let out a long sigh. "You haven't heard from Crow, have you?" he asked Amethyst.

The woman took off her swords and threw them down near her pillows. "Not for several days," she responded.

Taros shook his head. "Then they got him as well."

Everyone in the room went silent. Apparently, Crow was some sort of big deal—much more important than the brutes. "You're positive?" Amethyst asked after a moment.

"Heard them talking about it," Taros added solemnly. "Some of the guards said they knew where he was hiding. That was three or four days ago."

"Shit," Amethyst cursed under her breath. "They won't take him into the city, he's too important."

"You're assuming they want to capture him alive," Bokta said from the side, still rubbing her head. "They've probably already killed him."

Everyone was quiet again. It felt like as good a time as any to at least figure out who the guy was. "So, Crow is a big shot Oathbreaker, right?" I asked.

They turned to me, but none of them looked too upset that I had interrupted. "He used to be the mayor of Mara before the Dread King tossed him out and installed one of his corrupt puppets," Amethyst explained. "Now he's one of us."

Bokta pulled the attention of everyone in the room back to her with a frustrated sigh. "If he's still alive, we have

to save him," she stated. Everyone nodded. "We'll need information. They might take him to Essence for a public
execution, and we cannot allow that to happen."

Everyone seemed on board with the plan, though it
sounded like a pretty significant increase in difficulty from
the first mission. If Crow was the deposed mayor, they
would probably have a ton of soldiers guarding him, and
not just basic enemies, either. There was bound to be a
boss fight involved somewhere. That sounded exactly like
the kind of fight I'd prefer to avoid.

"So what else needs to be done?" I asked. "Anything not
so dangerous?

Amethyst thought for a moment with a finger on her
chin, her expression a mixture of confusion and disappointment. "We'll need someone to find his records," the
woman said.

"Perfect," I jumped in. "Bokta and I will take care of it.
You guys can handle the next jailbreak."

She paused like she was rethinking her words, then
nodded, a grin spreading across her lips. "Good, but Bokta
must go with us. Her skills are invaluable. Besides, a little
larceny is a one-person job. Harder to get caught that way,
right?"

Aww, shit. That was not what I wanted to hear—a solo
mission. And I had certainly watched enough action movies to know that I wasn't cut out to be a ninja or secret agent.

"And where are the records stored?" I asked, trying to
sound as courageous as I knew everyone expected me to
be. Sadly, I didn't think there was going to be a big server
room with a rudimentary password that I could get into
in a couple minutes with a laptop and a Wi-Fi connection.

"You need to get inside the Municipal Court of Documentation and Regulation," Amethyst said as though

I should have known the name of the building all along. "Come, I'll give you something. You can leave in an hour or so." She waved her hand and turned, summoning me like an obedient golden retriever.

Though my pride wanted me to defy her and stay obstinately immobile until I got a proper invitation, I didn't really have much of a choice. Plus, the idea of new gear was undeniably enticing.

Down the dark corridors, Amethyst led me into a small side room housing three treasure chests, each about the size of a few shoe boxes stacked into a cube. Memories of RPGs flickered through my brain as my heart was so overrun by anticipation that it nearly stopped beating.

My reverie only lasted the briefest of moments before Amethyst pulled out a key and slipped it into the chest on the far right. No cool soundtrack rang out overhead. No Zelda-style theme played to let me know that I was about to get some sick loot. Hell, the tumblers in the lock barely made any noise as they moved. The whole experience was very underwhelming. It almost made me want to turn back and leave whatever reward was there. *Almost.*

Amethyst took a small leather pouch from the chest and closed it, quickly returning the key to her pocket before I could get a good look at all the other loot I was sure was inside. She handed over the pouch, and it felt like a bunch of heavy rods were wrapped within the folds.

"Lockpicks," she said with a smile. "The Court of Documentation is *always* locked."

Well, that was just wonderful. According to the movies, lock picking was a simple skill that required no time, no prior knowledge, could be applied to any lock or safe, and only took about four seconds as long as the protagonist was wearing a snazzy suit and sneaking around the back of a dinner party. I should be just fine. Ha, I would be fine if I could locate a tailor to make me a three-piece suit. And I would likely need a ball or masquerade with some sort of ambassador to be going on nearby. I was basically already James Bond, come to think of it. Not bad for only having been here a few days.

"So is there any other reward for helping to spring Taros?" I asked, feeling a little more than disappointed that my only loot came in the form of the requirements for the next mission. It was like a teacher promising a reward, forgetting halfway through class, then assigning extra homework.

Amethyst smiled, and I couldn't tell if it was playful or condescending. I was pretty bad at reading people.

"I could use some proper armor and a weapon," I told her. My stolen sword was decent, but it was certainly a beginner weapon. Nothing special or magical about it at all.

Amethyst fished out a couple coins from one of her tight pockets and dropped them into my palm. "Four gibs," she said happily. "You did well today. Now bring me those records before nightfall, and I'll have four more gibs waiting for you."

Up to four and a half gibs felt pretty solid. I wasn't sure what I could buy, but I knew I could get *something* decent, especially in a larger town with lots of vendors to drive competition.

"Hey," I said, catching Amethyst's attention as she led me out of the room. "I'm not sure I can read," I told her.

. . . and that sounded way worse than I had intended. Ever the charismatic one, I was.

Amethyst raised an inquisitive eyebrow.

"Well, that's . . . no, I didn't mean it like *that*," I stammered, my face red. "I *can* read, but I can only read

English. Like, everyone speaks the same language as I do, but where I'm from we write it differently."

Amethyst walked me back to the main room where she produced a few sheets of thick paper from a chest of drawers along with a feather pen and ink. "Here," she said, handing everything to me. "Show me how you write."

I had no idea what to put down on the paper, so I signed my fake name as I had done for the recruiter back in Tamernil. *Donald J. Trump.* The recruiter had been able to read it well enough, and I had never stopped to figure that out.

"Donald J. Trump," Amethyst slowly repeated.

"So you *can* read my writing," I said, clearly confused.

Amethyst took the pen from my hand and began scribing something in a circular pattern directly beneath my forged signature. "This says Donald J. Trump also, but in our writing," she explained.

I couldn't read her swoopy circle bullshit in the least. It looked like a drunken Russian man had tried to write a bunch of Cyrillic letters, but someone had spun his page around as he wrote and he had been too inebriated to notice. "I can't make sense out of that at all," I said honestly. "But how can you read my writing? Why did you learn my style?"

Amethyst stifled a laugh. "We learn to write like that when we're just children," she said. Pointing to her own writing, she went on, "This is much more sophisticated. It explains more with fewer characters, plus it looks neater."

It did look pretty cool. She was right about that part. "Yeah, but I can't read it," I reminded her. "How will I find the right files?"

She drew several more circles on the bottom of the paper and then tore it off. "It would take too long to teach you, so just match the file name to this one," she said, pointing to the first circle she had drawn. It all looked like a bunch of gibberish.

Folding the paper and handing it to me, Amethyst gave me a somewhat demeaning pat on the shoulder like I was some sort of insolent child who had just been scolded by an underground crime boss. "Match the symbols on the files. If Crow was taken recently, his file should be out somewhere and easy to find, probably on a desk or something," she said.

Yeah, that sounded *super* easy. "Also, not to be a huge burden or anything, but I don't know how to pick a lock."

Amethyst let out a very disappointed sigh. I knew she was judging me, and I was failing. I guessed Bokta's status as my sole fan was going a long way toward keeping me around with the Oathbreakers.

Still wearing her judging face, Amethyst took me by the wrist and walked over to the door leading down from the beer hall above and knelt, holding open her hand for the lock picks. I dropped the pouch into her palm and crouched down to learn. Acquiring new skills in Realm Online was a hell of a lot easier than actually watching someone do something and then trying to repeat the action. I wondered in the back of my mind if there would be some sort of skill vendor in Mara who would take my gibs, snap his fingers, and suddenly I'd be able to do some cool shit. It didn't sound likely, but hey, that was essentially what they had done in *The Matrix*, so it was possible, right?

The woman took a slender pick from the leather pouch and slid it into the lock. Following the pick, she inserted a bent piece of unadorned metal into the bottom of the cylinder and put the slightest amount of weight on it from the hand still holding the pick. Grabbing my fingers with her free hand, she used me as an extension of herself to jiggle the lock's internal components until I felt the pick meet resistance. Then she turned my hand, added some more weight to the tension wrench, and the whole thing unlocked. It was actually pretty simple.

"Damn," I muttered in disbelief. "No way would it have been that easy on a real lock back home."

Amethyst handed the picks back to me so I could try a few more rounds. I knew the locking mechanism was extremely rudimentary when I was able to unlock it again on only my second try. I was starting to wonder if the pick kit was even necessary, or if I could have just used a stick or something else equally slender.

When I figured I had the process more or less memorized, I stood back up and brushed the dirt from my knees. Bokta was lying down on the cushions not far away, a wet rag draped over her forehead.

"Sorry about that," I apologized meekly, coming up to her side.

She smiled, keeping her eyes closed. "You saved my life," she reminded me, and a little flutter of appreciation tingled its way through my stomach.

"Y-Yeah," I slurred, "just doing my part, I guess. You should really get some proper medical care. My spear hit you pretty damn hard. You . . . probably have a concussion."

The Blood Witch nodded slowly, and I realized I didn't have a clue what 'proper medical care' would actually entail. "I'll be fine," she said quietly.

It was clear the adrenaline of the day had worn off, and Bokta was feeling every ounce of the heavy blow her head had taken. Truth be told, I was kinda surprised her skull hadn't fractured. The mere fact that she had survived was nothing short of amazing luck, at least by my standards.

Still standing awkwardly to the side in the underground lair, Amethyst cleared her throat to grab my attention. "The Municipal Court you're looking for is to the east. Ten blocks, maybe eleven. I don't remember exactly," she said firmly. "You best be on your way if you want to make it back before dark."

I had originally planned on spending some time grilling Bokta about her magic and how to advance through the world—though I figured a hallucinogenic character sheet suddenly appearing wouldn't be too unlikely—but it seemed I had no time. Always on the go.

I put my tired feet in motion toward the exit with a resigned sigh. When I emerged into the daylight, lockpicks and a handful of gibs in my pocket, the reality of what I was about to do began to take hold fully in my mind. I was going to break into a government records archive. If I was caught, an infraction like that didn't feel like a misdemeanor. I wouldn't be paying a fine and skulking back to the Oathbreaker hovel. They'd kill me. Probably without a trial.

First things first, I pushed the gruesome images of my death at the hands of some Realm official as far from my head as possible. I could deal with that later. There was still a decent amount of daylight left, and that meant the markets would be open and bustling. If I didn't have time to learn more about the world from my Oathbreaker companions, I could at least gather some info from the locals.

Finding a decently sized market wasn't difficult, but reading the signs above the stalls and shops was impossible. None of them were written in my version of English. Only swoopy circles of drunken Cyrillic script. Even so, the gear merchants were obvious. Their stalls were all next to each other on the side of a broad avenue full of customers, and their tables nearly overflowed with merchandise. There were swords, daggers, maces, armor of all makes and qualities, and row after row of glass bottles containing liquids of every color I could imagine.

I approached the first vendor and gave his wares what I thought was a discerning eye. Bearing an uncanny resemblance to the street merchant in *Aladdin*, the man behind the booth lifted a long scimitar in my direction, offering it hilt-first with a huge grin on his face. "The best swords in all of Mara, mark my words! And for you, hearty traveller, a deal! A discount! My best offer of the day. A curved blade to add flair to your side and cuts to your enemies, and a steal at only thirty gibs! My absolute bottom price for you, sir!"

Ha, no sword for me. "I'm uh . . . just looking right now," I said, politely declining to touch the merchandize.

Undaunted, the merchant somehow managed an even wider grin. "You wound me, fair master! But for you, only twenty-four gibs, yes? An absolute offense to my honor to accept so little!"

I started walking away, and the man kept pace behind his little stall, still holding the scimitar out for me to take. "I will lose money without a doubt, though I cannot see a fine man so unarmed. Twenty gibs! A mere twenty, and you'll be slashing your way across the city in no time!" he nearly yelled.

I waved and looked away, quickly heading to a different stall—any stall—far enough to be out of the merchant's focus. In a few seconds, the overzealous pitch came to an end, and I was free once more to inspect the various goods being bought and sold.

A wooden stall draped in green and red silk caught my eye. The merchant was a young woman, dressed similarly to her wares, and she didn't appear nearly as forthcoming as the sword merchant had been. In fact, she looked a little bored as she casually wrapped a strand of her deep black hair around a finger.

Underneath her silks were several rows of carved dice of every shape and color. Of all the things I had expected to see in Mara's trade district, dice certainly hadn't made the list. Not even close. Though my first thoughts as to the use of the dice drifted toward the myriad of Dungeons and Dragons campaigns I had played throughout the years, I had to admit that the idea of people living in a fantasy world sitting down to play a tabletop game was a bit odd. What would they roleplay when magic was real? What was left? To fantasize about being *normal* felt out of the question. *Hey, I'm Steve, a level twelve Accountant multiclassed with crippling depression! Just fifty more XP until I can learn a new ability: Cry Myself to Sleep!*

Outside my thoughts, I couldn't help but smile. Sure, I was still level one, but I had sort of acquired a new skill. Once I had the chance to prove my lock picking for real, I'd essentially be level two. Not bad.

The woman behind the booth must have seen me staring, lost in my own thoughts as I was. "Interested in any?" she asked for what more than likely was not the first time.

"Yeah," I answered, snapping back to reality. Ha. *Reality* was certainly a finicky term. "What . . . What are they for?"

The woman smiled a little, not like a salesman trying too hard to close a deal, but a genuine smile that made me think she wouldn't launch right into a scripted sales pitch. "Well, the first three rows of dice are made from either wood or stone, so they're perfect for games. The next two rows are enchanted—not weighted or cheated, mind you— and they're useful for all sorts of things," she explained.

"Enchanted?" I repeated, my mind awash with the most ludicrous possibilities it could conjure. "Enchanted dice?"

"That's right," the woman said. She still wore her smile, and her hands were behind her back like a professional. That's when I noticed a bit of the sun reflecting off a fearsome black dagger tucked into her leather belt.

"What do they do?" It felt like the obvious question. Or maybe enchanted dice were so commonplace in Mara that I had just given myself away as a foreigner.

The woman spread her arms over the enchanted dice, pointing to a group of red eight-siders. "Small enchantments, as I'm sure you know, hold best on ivory and scrimshaw. The reds are all whale bone, fresh from the Essant Sea, and they help with physical activities—if you're lucky." She moved to the next group, a section of pale yellow die with twelve sides each. "If you're after fortune, the ivory-golds will help every last gib in your purse look as appealing as it can."

"And the blue die?" I asked. I tried not to get my hopes up that my measly sum of coins would be able to purchase even a single one, but it was impossible. Showing enchanted die to a gamer was like handing Rick James a bag of crack.

She waved her hand over a collection of blue six-siders in the back row. "The ivory-blues are special, custom pieces. They'll help you out in almost any situation. Just think of what it is you need, give one a roll, and hope for a six!"

"And if someone rolls a one?" I recalled summonings based on thoughts going poorly for the Ghostbusters.

The woman's smile turned into something more sinister, yet still upbeat and playful at the same time, like the devious grin of a politician who knows they're about to win but still has to maintain decorum. "Don't roll a one, and you'll never find out," she said, her voice barely above a whisper.

The last group of dice was a handful of four-siders, crystal white and vaguely translucent. "And those?" I asked.

"Ah, you have a fine eye. The Euclidian Pyramids activate on two through four, so you only have one bad side." She carefully picked one up and placed it in the palm of her hand, letting the reflection fly all around the silks covering the stall.

"But what does it do?" I nearly demanded. Suddenly, I felt like I had fallen into a thoroughly conceived plot. She had me wrapped around her finger, and I hadn't even realized that I was holding all my gibs in my left hand so tightly my knuckles were soon to match the color of the die.

Another quiet, subtle laugh escaped her lips. "Euclidian Pyramids can save your life, if you don't roll a one," she said. "And at four thousand gibs, they're in hot demand."

So that's how much a life was worth, then. Four grand could fetch a seventy-five percent chance of *not dying*, assuming the woman was telling the truth. After all, I hadn't seen any of the dice in action.

"Alright," I said, casually slipping my gibs back into my pocket to not appear so poor or desperate. "Could I see one used? Not a Pyramid, of course, but one of the lesser die? I'd love to see how they work."

Nodding as though she had expected exactly such a request, the woman picked up a red eight-sider and folded her fingers around it. With her other hand, she reached below her table and grabbed a wicker basket full of rocks. Holding it out at arm's length, it didn't take long for her muscle to show signs of fatigue and begin to shake. Then, after maybe ten seconds, she couldn't hold it any longer, and she dropped the basket to the ground with a loud thump.

"Now," she said, giving the die in her hand a good shake, "let's hope we don't get a one, shall we?" She tossed the die into a small wooden tray at the back of her table, and it landed on five. A little burst of red light flickered out of the object's surface and vanished into the woman's torso.

"Ready?" she asked, though I wasn't really sure how I couldn't be. I nodded.

She bent down and grabbed the basket, then hoisted it easily into the air, her arm straight out from her side. Even after twenty seconds had elapsed, the basket didn't waver. "See?" she said with a smile. "It was only a five, not a full eight, so it won't last long. Maybe another ten seconds." Finally, she let the basket drop to the ground.

"That's amazing," was all I could think to say. "I need one."

Returning the red eight-sider to its place on the table, the merchant glanced up and said, "Twelve gibs for a red. They aren't strong, but they're the cheapest I have."

A heavy sigh came unbidden from my mouth. I had meant to adopt as much of a poker face as I knew how to try to haggle her down to a number I could afford, but I had ruined any chance of fruitful negotiations almost before they began. Resigned to suck up my pride and let her know I was dirt poor, I figured asking at least couldn't hurt. "I have four and half gibs. That's it. There's no way you'd take that little, right?"

A new gleam appeared in the woman's eyes. "Actually . . ." She ducked under her table for a second, then came up with a silk pouch the size of a tuck case from a deck of playing cards. There was a single die inside, and she bade me hold out my palm to catch it from the bag. What tumbled out was beautiful. A six-sider, shiny black, and the pips were tiny little carved skulls.

"Black tourmaline from across the Essant Sea," she said, folding the silk bag and setting it in the little wooden dish where she had made her demonstration.

"What's this one do?" I asked. I couldn't keep the fascination from my voice in the least. I was Rick James, and the woman had just handed me a *monstrous* bag of crack.

"I've never rolled it myself," she explained, "but . . . certain cults favor the black tourmaline in their rituals . . . if you understand."

"The Desec—"

"Shhh," she interrupted, a stern countenance coming over her visage. "Do not speak such a name in an open place as this."

"Sorry, I . . . I didn't know . . ."

Glancing side to side, the woman waited for a moment before speaking again. "Black tourmaline will bring a certain intercession. Simply do *not* roll a one. Not on that die. Not ever."

Summoning the Desecrator's intercession? The bag of crack just became a fresh kilo from South America, uncut and ready to enslave me to its addiction. "And it only costs four and a half gibs?" I muttered, barely aware that I was even speaking aloud. The little skulls in my hand danced in the light, and I could practically *feel* the magic emanating from them, though of course I had no idea what anything like that was supposed to feel like.

"Four and a half gibs," the woman replied, holding out her hand. I mindlessly let my coins jingle down onto her palm, and then she handed me the silk bag—transaction complete.

"Remember," she said. "Don't roll a one. And only use it when you really need it. Black tourmaline isn't something to be trifled with."

Honestly, I didn't really hear the words coming from her mouth. I ripped my gaze from the die and slid it into the silk bag, clutching it tightly in case it accidentally fell out. A thousand other questions rushed through my mind once the intoxicating trance of my first magic item finally waned, but the woman was already with another customer. I'd have to figure it out on my own.

CHAPTER 10

Before I made it all the way to the Municipal Court of Documentation and Regulation, I wanted to get one more thing straight in my head. I knew that Mara and Tamernil existed somewhere—somehow—inside the online game that had ruled my life for the past half a decade. That much was finally crystal clear. There was no chance that whatever realm this was, it wouldn't be a version of Realm of Crafted War. The Oathbreakers, the Desecrator . . . it was too much coincidence to be able to write off any longer.

If everything here was based on the game, or however it actually had been created, that meant there should be eight different Underlords, each with their own cult, and most with their own meeting places or houses of worship. As an Oathbreaker in the online game, there had never been much need for me to get too wrapped up in all the aspects of the religion, but I knew the general story fairly well.

The most common cult, the one almost every new player in Realm elected to follow, was directly opposed to the Desecrator: Valiance, Protector of the Light Most Holy. All the Valiance players were essentially paladins and priests and other do-gooders. If they existed, they'd be easy to find. Sure enough, rounding the corner from the market to the next street presented a fine view of Mara's Valiance temple, a gleaming lighthouse made from white marble with a huge, reflected torch at the summit. I'd probably mistaken it for a guard tower upon entering the city, or maybe I'd been too distracted by Bokta's chest to have noticed. But there it was, standing tall.

The leaders of Valiance were Torch Bearers and Librarians, tasked with protecting their sacred flame and following a bunch of other ridiculous rules designed to make kids who wanted to play as shiny knights feel some sort of connection to 'higher principles' or some shit. The temple in Mara was a brilliant, exceedingly tall monstrosity that exuded all the right vibes of justice and purity.

It made me sick.

Knowing I had a little bit of the Desecrator in my pocket made me want to walk up to the front door and roll the die right then. But I had a task to accomplish, and Amethyst didn't seem like the kind of woman who took disappointment lightly.

As the in-game story went, Oathbreakers were all descendants of an offshoot sect of Valiance worshippers—paladins who were fed up taking orders from a crusty old Torch Bearer or withered Librarian and had struck out on their own to follow a different Underlord. They broke their oath to Valiance sometime between the first and second expansion packs, and the Oathbreaker class had been the result. The overpowered and cool-as-shit, badass result.

A few of the other cults weren't too bad either, but none of them were as steeped in epic-ness as the Oathbreakers. Druids and other nature-types always favored the Progenitor, a horse god whose emblem presided over all the races in the larger towns. Sacrificial shrines, basically Mayan pyramids with stone altars at the tops devoted to the Shipwright, could be found near any large body of water, and all the sea-faring captains of the world were the Shipwright's sworn priests. They didn't do much, no ongoing war like Valiance and the Desecrator, but their temples were always pretty cool and full of loot.

Perhaps the most boring of all the Underlords was Baron Archidemas the Wise, patron of governmental affairs, civilization, and other bureaucratic bullshit no one had the patience to understand fully. The Baron didn't have any temples or other structures, just parliaments, town halls, and other civic structures bearing her seal. The Municipal Court of Documentation and Regulation would most certainly have her likeness plastered on its walls.

Another common choice for online characters to follow—probably because it offered one of the coolest quest lines with some of the sickest gear at the end—was the cult of Miasmara, the war goddess. Her followers were hardcore soldier types, declaring every battlefield to be a temple, and they formed small mercenary armies of highly trained fighters called Crimson Centuries: always a hundred soldiers led by a single female captain. The entire organization was run by a Shieldmaiden, and I'd never played a character deep enough into Miasmara's quest line to know much else.

Perhaps the most mysterious of all the Underlord cults was the Unsworn Mask. Played characters in Realm couldn't choose to join, only NPCs, and no one ever knew their identities. They showed up at funerals, warzones, catastrophes, and other events full of death to usher the souls of the fallen to . . . somewhere.

Of all the eight Underlords, well, there were actually nine in total. The eighth cult followed Catsi and Funen, two sibling cats said to be the propagators of unexplained mischief. They had no formal organizations, no outspoken followers or priests, and no shrines other than the occasional cave filled with riddles and vermin bones that NPCs would claim were made by the cats. Catsi, as the common belief told, was a black cat whose only marking was a single white spot on her chest. Funen, her brother, was supposed to be a golden lynx. The online version of Realm had a few achievements and vanity titles related to the cat pair, but no specific quest lines or progressions. Every now and then, if you adventured in some of the lesser known areas, your character would come across one of their little caves. They'd be marked by a few rodent skeletons leading to an alcove, and there would always be a riddle written in coal on the walls. Solving the riddle would summon one of the cats to bestow a reward of loot, but the gear was never that good, so most people didn't care to finish their quests.

The Valiance temple at the end of the wide boulevard looked exactly like all the temples in the major cities online. No banners, no flags—just a huge lighthouse topped by sacred flame. Online, the game would never permit an Oathbreaker to enter a Valiance temple. It simply wasn't possible. An invisible barrier would stop you, and a dialogue popup would tell you to get lost.

Naturally, I had to try it. I wasn't *exactly* an Oathbreaker yet . . .

No one on the street really paid me any attention as I strolled down the lane looking inconspicuous with my hands in my pockets. The temple's entrance was a plain wooden door, painted red, with a curved top. No guards stood to either side to keep Oathbreakers back, so I tested the handle and then walked inside. So far so good. No eruption of fire, no invisible hand pushing me back into the street.

The interior of the temple, something I'd never seen much of online, was actually rather interesting. There were statues and other holy relics, or so I assumed, and a few of their members were busy with various tasks. Interestingly enough, a handful of the men and women inside were working with hammers and other tools on a long set of iron chains. Maybe an anchor chain for a ship? I had no idea.

"Are you looking for the Librarian?" a middle-aged man asked, seemingly coming from nowhere.

"No . . . I'm just looking around, if that's cool," I answered.

The man nodded solemnly and stayed at my side. "If there's anything I can help you with, please do not hesitate to ask. And of course," he went on, his voice droning, "the Torch Bearer is not currently accepting visitors as he prepares for the campaign."

"Right on, man," I said. "What campaign?"

The man looked as shocked as I figured he was capable of feeling, which meant a single eyebrow on his forehead lifted up about two millimeters. "You have not heard of the Glorious Charge?"

"Nah, I'm new in town," I told him honestly, still watching the people working on their large, odd chain.

The man placed a stiff hand on my back and turned me toward a painting next to the door that I hadn't noticed yet. "The Glorious Charge," he said with a bit of awe in his voice. "Every six years the followers of Valiance set out on the Glorious Charge, hunting Oathbreakers and demons, and bringing their heads back to Mara to burn in holy fire atop the temple. This year's Glorious Charge should be one of the best in recent memory! The Torch Bearer and Librarian have located a den of vile beasts, more than we've slain in the past, and not far from the city!"

That didn't sound great for my cause. Although . . . Ambushing a Valiance raid was exactly what Maxkrannar would have done online. It might not be a bad idea.

"Well, good luck!" I told the man, turning to leave and find my courthouse.

He bowed ever so slightly at the neck. "May the everlast—"

"Yeah, yeah, all the blessings of whoever upon your shoulders, too," I cut him off.

Back in the street, it took me a little while to find the proper municipal court. It was a squat, stone building with cloth overhangs keeping the sun from the only door on the front side. No one was coming or going, but there were plenty of people about nearby who would see me if I tried to pick the lock in the afternoon light. Moving slowly to try not to draw attention to myself, I walked down the alley between the court and whatever building—it looked like a bank or counting house—was next to it. A single door faced the alleyway, and it was barred with iron just like the windows on either side of it.

Luckily, no one was in the alley. Figuring they had plenty of drunks in Mara just like back home, I stumbled down the tight corridor until I was across from the door, then strategically lurched my body into the iron bars, testing whether or not the door was locked. Heh. It was. Of course it was.

Still keeping up the façade of drunkenness, I slumped

back against the building opposite the door to wait. I figured I'd give it a while as the sun descended. If anyone came out, it would give me a chance to see the inside a little. If not, well, that'd be a good thing, right? If the door wasn't used often, it would reduce my chance of getting caught . . . hopefully.

CHAPTER 11

A few hours of sheer boredom passed by, and all I could really think about was rolling the die. It stayed in my pocket through the long wait, but my fingers never left its surface. I kept tracing over the pips, feeling the little indentations of the carved skulls, and relishing the cool touch of the tourmaline against my skin. No matter how much I fondled the thing, it always stayed cool. If only I could find a pillow made of the same stuff.

Then, when the sun had long since set, I was confident the Municipal Court was empty. People had come and gone, not regularly by any means, throughout most of the day, and it had been quiet for what felt like about thirty minutes. Or maybe it was like twelve minutes. Honestly, I still had no idea if Mara had discovered the quantification of time yet. I was leaning toward huge clocks or sundials existing somewhere, especially if they had such an extensive bureaucracy to run, but I hadn't seen one yet.

Just another thing to add to the long list of stuff I needed to ask about when I got back to the Oathbreaker compound.

Once I had determined it was more or less safe to approach the door and test my newly acquired lock-picking skills, I set to work with my back toward the main thoroughfare, still trying to keep up my drunken image to anyone who might get a little too curious. I slid the pick and tension wrench into the bottom of the lock just like Amethyst had shown me, and damn—it worked on the third try. Not bad! Again, I had to chalk it up to medieval-style locks being far from secure. Even though I knew my skill wasn't actually all that great, I still felt a little bit like an absolute ninja as I gently pushed open the door. And I was a level two ninja, I decided. Knowing how to riposte and pick some basic locks was cool and all, but I also needed some magic before I'd really consider myself to be progressing. At the end of the day, level two was pretty lackluster.

The inside of the court wasn't terribly exciting. There were some wooden desks, a few chairs, some extinguished candles, two barred windows letting in a little bit of light, and several floor-to-ceiling shelves which held stacks of paper files. No metal filing cabinets had been invented yet, and that was a relief. One less lock to pick. I pulled the paper Amethyst had given me out of my pocket and moved to the first desk.

Holding the paper next to what appeared to be file names on the desk, I moved it slowly, taking my time to see if anything would line up. Nothing on the first desk matched well enough for me to bother taking it, so I moved to the second, angling my body to prevent blocking the light from coming in through the nearest window. Again, I moved the paper along, shuffling the files spread out on the desk to get a better look at their titles. One of them appeared close. It wasn't exactly the same, but it could have been Amethyst's handwriting that made it look different. Or it could be the wrong file. Still, I scooped it up and grabbed the three files under it as well—just in case. Maybe the others would be relevant to Crow's file, or maybe they'd be useless. No way to find out until I made it back to Oathbreaker HQ.

A smile on my face, I turned toward the door I had come in, but a noise caught my attention. There was another door in the back of the building, presumably leading deeper into the court, right next to a big oil painting of Baron Archidemas the Wise. From behind the door came a soft scratching sound. Looking at the portrait of the fat woman dressed like she just came from a Shakespearean cosplay convention, it occurred to me that the Baron would likely be better named as a Baroness, and that was a little strange. Whatever. The Baron was the Baron, same as the online version of Realm: rotund, pompous, and stuffy.

More scratching came from behind the door. I gave Archidemas one last glance before moving to the door and testing the knob. It was unlocked. Silently, I turned the knob all the way until I felt the door come free of the frame. Whatever was scratching at the bottom of it was adding a little bit of weight, pushing back against the force I was applying from the other side. It wasn't much, like the strength of a small child.

Slowly and as quietly as I could, I eased the door inward, my knuckles white on the knob. When it was about eight inches open, I discovered what had been making all the scratches on the other side of the wood. A cat! A small orange and white cat with cute splotches of brown mixed throughout its fur lazily walked from the next room, brushing up against my legs as it went. It stopped about foot from me, looked up with its yellow eyes, and meowed.

Of all the things I had expected to come from the other side of the door—zombies, enemy soldiers, prisoners, or even one of the court's clerks—a cat had not even been on my list. And it was absolutely adorable! I wasn't much of a cat or a dog person back on Earth, probably because I wasn't responsible enough to own a pet, nor did I have the permission it would have required from my landlord, but I knew I was instantly attached.

Even worse, the cat kept staring at me and meowing like it wanted to tell me something. Unless cats in Mara were different than those I had known back home, it was probably just hungry. I shut the door and knelt down, offering the cat my hand, and it brushed the fur of its neck up against my fingers. It was soft. Then it licked the back of my hand with its rough tongue, sending shivers up my spine.

"What's your name?" I asked the fluffy creature. Then I remembered I was supposed to be on a stealth mission, and I shut my mouth. The cat, on the other hand, was anything but quiet, constantly purring against my legs.

Outside, the night's darkness had set in, and there was barely anything coming in through the windows to illuminate the interior of the court. I quietly made it to the door I had come in on the balls of my feet, then poked my head out just long enough to see if there was a platoon of armed guards on the other side waiting to paint the alley with my intestines. Luckily, there was only darkness.

I slipped out the door, and the cat was so fast I didn't even have to hold the door for it as it scampered between my feet. When the court was closed once more behind me, I escaped the dark clutches of the alleyway as quickly as I could, then immediately slowed down to a normal pace on the street, trying my best to look like everyone else.

As I walked back toward the market and past the Valiance lighthouse, the cat kept pace at my side. By the time I reached the biergarten above the Oathbreaker compound, I had already come up with a name for the little bugger: I'd call him Mr. Patches. Or perhaps Ms. Patches would be more appropriate, but I had no idea how to tell if a cat was male or female. Besides, the way he walked made him look like a cool dude, all fur and confidence. Mr. Patches it was!

The two of us strode through the front entry of the biergarten and toward the Oathbreaker entrance. I had the stack of files from the court under my arm, a set of lock picks in one pocket and a jet black tourmaline die in the other, and a cat at my feet. All in all, I was really starting to enjoy life in Mara. It was just so much more . . . carefree, I guessed, compared to life at home.

On Earth, I worried about so much every single day. Work was an eternal pain in my ass, coming up with rent money wasn't always a sure thing each month, and I basically only had five or so real friends. I'd used Realm as a way to escape from all of that . . . Now, there really wasn't anything I needed to escape from—other than a swift execution should I ever be caught and exposed as an Oathbreaker, of course. Even with the specter of death hanging over me at every turn, it still felt nice. I liked it here. A lot.

Amethyst and Bokta had apparently finished their mission more quickly than I had completed mine, and they were waiting in one of the pillowed areas when Mr. Patches and I returned home.

"You brought a cat?" the sexy Blood Witch asked, her eyebrows raised.

The little guy darted up onto one of the pillows,

completely unafraid of the two women, and sat on his hind legs. He licked one of his paws, and his claws flexed outward like Wolverine.

"Yeah, he sort of followed me here, I guess," I said. Then I remembered the files under my arm and tossed them down in front of Amethyst. "Hope I got the right stuff."

She looked through a few of the files, pushed some of them away, glanced once at Mr. Patches, then found the one she had been after. "Very well done, Steve," she said with a smile. Mr. Patches issued a loud meow before switching paws to clean.

"Did I get all of it? I grabbed the nearest couple files, too. I wasn't sure what all would be relevant."

Amethyst nodded. "Everything's here. Exactly what we needed." She handed a couple pieces of thick paper to Bokta, then leaned back into her pillows as she watched Mr. Patches diligently taking care of his hygiene.

"Oh," I said, pulling the black silk bag from my pocket. "I bought an enchanted die."

I was about to hand the die to Bokta for her to see, but her face was screwed up in an expression of horrid fear, her eyes locked on the little bit of carved tourmaline in my palm.

". . . What is it?" I asked.

"You *bought* that?" the woman said, her voice barely above a whisper and full of what I could only think was disgust.

"Yeah? Supposed to be blessed by the Desecrator, according to the woman at the market," I explained.

I held the die toward Bokta, and she recoiled as though I had just presented a venomous snake instead of a harmless bit of sculptured rock.

Finally, Amethyst spoke up, and I noticed she had

scooted a few feet farther away from me on her pillows. "Black tourmaline—the Eye of the Desecrator himself—is an unholy relic. I've . . . I've heard of them existing, nine of them to be exact, but I never thought I'd see one with my own eyes . . ."

"Oh, come on, you two are just trolling," I said, casually tossing the die a few inches off my palm and catching it again. "There's no way an 'unholy relic' only cost me four and a half gibs, right?" Still, the way they were acting made me wonder . . . They seemed genuine. *Really fucking genuine.*

"Well," Bokta began, shooting a sidelong glance to the other woman, "if you paid real gibs for it, it's yours now. You couldn't get rid of it if you wanted to."

"What do you mean?" The die suddenly felt heavy in my hand. I wanted to throw it, to pitch it clear across the room just to show I wasn't cursed by it or whatever, but the merchant's warning of rolling a one echoed clearly in my mind.

Bokta let out a long sigh. "You didn't know. It wasn't your fault—"

"Like hell! He bought it!" Amethyst cut her off.

They shared another look, then Bokta continued. "The black tourmaline, an Eye of the Desecrator, is a cursed object. When the first Oathbreaker was killed, his nine eyes were taken to nine different Valiance temples and locked away by their most powerful Librarians, for they could not be destroyed. No matter what the Librarians tried, they could not shatter the tourmaline. Then, hundreds of years ago, a group of Oathbreakers stole the eyes. All nine were stolen in a single night. A scrimshander turned them into dice, and then they were lost to the ages."

"But one thing is known for sure," Amethyst said, "the

only way to pass on a cursed relic of the Desecrator is to sell it to someone else. It doesn't matter the price, but the buyer must be willing, and they must know *exactly* what they're buying, or the little bastard shows up again in the seller's pocket the next day. And you were so stupid that you bought one. Just like that." She snapped her fingers, and Mr. Patches jumped a bit at the sudden noise.

I slipped the die into its black silk pouch. "What's so bad about owning one?" I asked, though I wasn't really sure I wanted to know what the answer was. I thought of Indiana Jones and all the other movies featuring cursed relics that I had seen. In most of those, the person who owned the object usually had horribly bad luck. Or maybe it would be like *Lord of the Rings*, and I'd now have to go on an epic quest to throw into a poorly named volcano before it corrupted me and turned me evil. Though . . . invisibility was certainly a perk . . . and I was already an Oathbreaker which was basically evil . . . No, Frodo had taught me enough about messing with that kind of stuff. If it was like the ring, there would be ring wraiths and other nonsense chasing me down to kill me.

Bokta's face had gone pale. "Isn't it obvious?" she said, scooping Mr. Patches up in her arms.

Of all the things . . . that wasn't what I had expected. If harmless little Mr. Patches was my curse, I could live with that. Money well spent. "Cats? You're saying Mr. Patches is my horrible, deadly curse?"

Bokta nodded. "He followed you all the way home without straying, didn't he?"

"Yeah . . ."

"They won't stop. The cats. They'll keep coming. The cats will find you wherever you are, and they'll be relentless. The legends say that while the Desecrator made his eyes, of course, it was the Underlords Catsi and Funen who actually cursed the dice," the Blood Witch grimly told me.

"And being the cat guy is super bad?" I asked. Maybe a fraction of a *fraction* of a second after the words left my mouth, I realized the answer. Of course being the cat guy would suck. You can't run into combat with a herd of cats tailing your every move. You couldn't pick locks in alleyways or sneak about rooftops in the dead of night with thirty purring, meowing little fur balls at your feet, either.

"It draws some attention," Amethyst remarked, her voice full of earned arrogance.

"I get it," I snapped back, images flashing through my mind of trying to find an armorer and a handful of trainers to make a cat army and put the critters to some use. Impractical? Sure, but awesome nonetheless.

The woman sat forward and looked me in the eyes. "You need to get rid of the die, Steve," she said with an air of seriousness so heavy it made me look away.

Bokta nodded, her eyes just as piercing. "Get rid of it. Everyone knows what a hoard of cats means. Once the city guards get wind of it, Valiance will send their spies, and you won't be hard to find."

All the elation I had felt, all the buildup and excitement, was gone. I had been fooled by a pretty girl in a silk booth full of gaming paraphernalia. I hadn't even been in the world for a full week, and I'd already fallen into ridiculous trap. "Of course an enchanted die wouldn't have cost four and a half gibs . . . I should have seen the woman's ploy. I'm sorry."

Bokta got to her feet and wrapped an arm around me. Her touch was a warm counterpart to Amethyst's icy persona. "Don't let it drive you mad. That's a curse in itself, you know? Just try to think of some way to sell it again.

Preferably before tomorrow. Before more cats start show-ing up."

Ha, fat chance of that happening. I wouldn't even be-gin to know how to sell it. Come to think of it, I had to wonder if the woman selling dice in the market hadn't taken up the profession simply to get rid of a single die. Maybe all the others on the table had been fakes, and she had been patiently waiting, day in and day out in the marketplace, for some lame-ass sucker to come along and fall right into the palm of her hand. But where were her cats? I tried to think back and remember everything I could about her stall, but all I had really focused on had been her and the dice. In short, I had failed my percep-tion check. Failed it hard.

When my thoughts finally returned to the present, Am-ethyst was gone. But there was Mr. Patches sitting on his haunches and licking a little spot on the pillows. I shud-dered to think what sort of stain he was removing. "Will the cats need to eat?" I asked. The prospect of becoming the Cat King of Mara would be even worse if the Cat King had to buy food and water for all his obedient subjects. And hell, they wouldn't even pay taxes like properly sub-jugated peasants.

Bokta shook her head as she stepped away from my shoulder. "I don't know," she said. "I've never actually seen someone with an Eye before. We always . . . spoke about the relics like myth or legend, just stories twisted by the long passage of time since the first Oathbreaker. I didn't really believe the thing about the cats until I saw that one."

"His name is Mr. Patches," I told her, holding out my hand for the cat promptly to ignore.

"Don't get too attached, and please, don't name every cat that shows up," Bokta replied. "If the stories are true, the number of cats living in our cellar here will grow quickly, and you'll never remember all of their names."

Something still didn't add up quite right in my head. "You know, I found the cat in the closet at the court. Or I think it was a closet, I didn't really check. I opened a door, and it just kind of wandered out and started rubbing up against my legs. Maybe it wasn't the die that attracted it, maybe it was just a stray cat locked in a closet by accident, and Mr. Patches likes me because I rescued him."

Again, Bokta shook her head. "You'll start finding cats in odd places, I'd bet. But tell me more about the closet. I've not heard of the Municipal Court of Documentation and Regulation having anything but the main floor and a vault. What closet?"

Oh, great. I had inadvertently broken into the court's vault, and all I got was a silly cat. "Yeah," I said with a sigh. "It was the only door in the building other than the two exits. Right in the back."

Bokta thought for a moment with her hand on her chin, her hair falling playfully at the sides of her face. "Catsi and Funen wanted you to have Mr. Patches, so they unlocked the vault. It has to be! What did you see inside? We've been dreaming of the day we'd crack the vault and steal the government's secrets . . ."

"Just the cat, actually," I admitted. "That's it. I took the cat and left. Sorry."

All the excitement drained from Bokta's face. "Perhaps next time . . ." she said.

CHAPTER 12

I kept my cursed die tucked tightly into its silken bag all night. Part of me was afraid to let it out of my sight for fear of it accidentally being rolled and bringing about some catastrophe, but the other part of my mind understood that the little fleck of black would always find me. The more I thought about the object, the more I simply *understood* that Bokta and Amethyst had been telling the truth. The damned thing felt cursed. I knew there was a strong possibility that my mind—like a really detailed and powerful placebo effect—had concocted the entire sensation of the curse, but that wasn't the case. The die contained weight that should have been impossible for such a small, plain object. Part of that weight was purely psychological.

I was lying on my cramped cot with the tourmaline pressed tightly into my palm, a thousand different scenarios running through my head, when an alarm sounded in the Oathbreaker headquarters. It wasn't a real alarm from a radio or a phone, of course, but shouts of panic and anger. Tons of them.

Amethyst's voice was the loudest. She thundered through the narrow passageways, a torch swinging in her hand. I couldn't tell for sure by any means, though it felt like an hour or two past midnight. Maybe it was even later. I made a mental note to sit down and invent the clock whenever I had a few spare moments and stumbled upon a quaint Swiss workshop stocked full of gears and springs and buxom mountain lasses.

"Everyone to the tunnels!" the Oathbreaker leader's voice boomed, shattering my clockwork contemplation. "Now! Move! To the tunnels!"

I scrambled out of my cot, attired myself as best I could in a rush, and ran for the main room. Somewhere behind me, I heard the pitter patter of little feet reminding me of Mr. Patches' eternal companionship. It seemed the cat was just as keen to be out of the barracks as I was, and he kept pace without complaint. At least the cat wouldn't slow me down.

The central chamber of the underground lair was alive with commotion. Whatever sleep had been lingering behind my eyes vanished in the face of all that chaos. Every Oathbreaker in the complex was running around, most with crates or sacks on their shoulders, and rushed commands were issued out in tight little bursts by the leadership. Then, all at once, a huge noise came from above. The headquarters fell deathly silent in an instant.

"They're here somewhere!" came a shout from the biergarten.

"Spread out!"

More stomping and furniture being thrown about. "There! Behind that door, Sergeant!"

A few heavy, muffled booms shook a layer of dirt from the ceiling. "Make way for the ram! Move, soldier, move!" Whoever was in charge had an accent, some fragment of a drawl, and they sounded pissed. Really pissed. Kind of how I imagined Viking berserkers would have been when their commanders whipped them into a frenzy before a raid.

Amethyst brought all the eyes in the room back to her with a clenched fist raised toward the roof—a pre-established signal, no doubt. That's when I noticed what she was wearing. She had her unorthodox sword harness like before, but underneath was only a thin blue garment that I guessed functioned as a nightshirt. It wasn't quite thick enough to mask the protrusions of her nipples. On her shapely lower half, she wore only a dark red skirt and black leather boots. The skirt, crimped and pressed to furl outward at the bottom, was maybe ten inches long. *Maybe.*

". . . regroup at the southern point, then wait for my signal before moving again. Understood?" the curvy woman stated. Silent nods were her answer, and then everyone was moving again.

Shit. I'd been so lost in the intricate details of the woman's revealing outfit that I'd missed the entire evacuation plan. I had ignored the whole damn order like a muster drill on the first day of a cruise when everyone just wants to hit the martini bar and get slammed on espresso vodka so they don't feel like they wasted money on the premium drink package.

Luckily, every other person in the chamber had been a dutiful sailor, so it wasn't too hard to simply follow the press of Oathbreakers surging down a dark corridor. Somewhere in the press, I filtered my way to Bokta's side.

"What's the plan?" I asked, leaning close to be heard over the din.

Behind us, it sounded like the soldiers finally had their ram in place against our door. They'd only need three or so strikes to take it down, judging by the amount of splintering that had sounded after the first weighty slam. "There are two tunnels out of here," the Blood Witch explained between breaths. "We'll take Forecastle Pass. Then, once we're outside, there are a couple safe houses, assuming they haven't also been compromised."

"And if the soldiers catch us in the tunnels?" I asked.

Bokta's eyes were grim in the nearly lightless tunnel. "They'll smoke us. If they can trap us inside, they'll fill the tunnels with smoke until we're dead." That sounded absolutely lovely. And unless the tunnels got a lot wider somewhere up ahead, smoking us out wouldn't take long at all. We'd be dead in minutes.

After another fifty yards or so, the tunnel we had been racing through split into two smaller passageways. To the left, the dark passage sloped gently upward, and the floor was slick with nasty smelling water. The tunnel on the right, which I had to assume was Forecastle Pass, angled downward. It was so dark that I couldn't see more than a few yards inside. For whatever reason, most of the Oathbreakers were taking the path on the left. In fact, only three of us poked our heads inside Forecastle Pass.

"Why is everyone else going the other way?" I asked Bokta, following closely behind her in the dark. I had to duck to keep from splattering my brains all over the jagged ceiling. I had probably missed that part of the plan on account of my wandering eyes.

We turned a tight corner, and the two women pulled to a stop. Amethyst, a smile across her shadowed face, was the first to speak. "Get some light in here, Bokta," she whispered, her mouth close enough for me to feel the gentle heat of her breath against my skin.

Without a word, the Blood Witch moved her hands and summoned her luminescent butterfly companion. The creature didn't offer much, but it was enough to see. And damn, I did *not* mind the view.

"Forecastle Pass is much safer," Amethyst said, finally turning to me. Her swords squeaked in their leather holsters. Sadly, it looked like her two weapons were the only ones we had other than Bokta's magic. Well, Mr. Patches had his claws, but I didn't think he'd fight on command for me. At least not yet.

All the noise from the other tunnel died down. I felt like everyone had effectively escaped, but there was no way to really be sure. "Why doesn't everyone take this route if the other tunnel isn't as safe?" I asked.

Bokta moved her butterfly to the front of our little group. The tunnel narrowed about five feet ahead, transforming from something that would have been uncomfortably passable to something altogether hellish. "Forecastle Pass is for the leaders only. Too many people in here, and we'd be so slow that we'd never make it. Plus, most of the stronger men wouldn't fit," she said with half a laugh.

I wasn't sure if the strong guy bit was meant as a jab at my soft and cuddly belly, and even if it was, I didn't care. Nightmarish scenes of becoming stuck in the tight twists and turns of the cavern thoroughfare consumed my thoughts. I remembered reading about a guy who had gotten stuck in an unmapped cave out west once. He had been there so long—trapped upside down in a dead end too tight for him to wiggle his way out—that the rescue crew didn't have any options. If they had pulled him out by force, it would have broken his legs, and he'd have died from the shock. Still, that way sounded at least marginally better than meeting death upside down in a stone coffin.

The very first squeeze not ten feet in front of me looked tight enough to become my rocky prison.

Bokta and Amethyst moved up next to it without any hint of trepidation. Amethyst, her short red skirt flapping—*teasing*—at the bottom edge of her toned ass, was the first to hoist herself up into the crevasse.

Just like that, she shimmied her way through, and then she was gone.

"Are you ready?" Bokta asked, grabbing the sides of the narrow tunnel with practiced ease.

"No," I answered, shaking my head. "Not even close. I'll never fit!"

She looked me over, her devious smile fading just a bit, then nodded. "You'll make it. There are a few tight spots, but I've seen larger men than you make it through Forecastle Pass. Come on. Let's go."

"By larger, you mean stronger, right?" I replied.

Bokta laughed, but cut herself short, and her voice echoed for a second back the way we had come. "Yes, stronger men than you, Maxkrannar," she whispered in the fluttering darkness. Turning her face to the right, she scraped her way through the narrow tunnel, filling my head with unwanted images of an adult woman squeezing her way through a birth canal. When she was gone as well, the light she had made with her butterfly lingered behind near the ceiling, illuminating the path I had to take.

"Well ... fuck it," I muttered, getting a foot up on the bottom of the ledge. The space was maybe two feet wide, and there was no physical way to get my hips through without turning, so turn I did. I tried to mimic Bokta's movements as closely as possible. She had slid through almost easily, so I figured it had to work. Where Bokta's ample, forward-facing carriage had bumped and scraped against the stone wall, my gut was basically tortured. I couldn't turn my head down at all to see if there was any blood, but I knew my leather shirt—the armor I had tricked from the recruiter in Tamernil—was being shredded. I could only hope my intestines weren't meeting a similar fate.

Sometime a minute or so into the first of what I knew would likely end up being dozens of hellish trials, a gentle hand reached out and grabbed my forearm. "Here, slide yourself up," Bokta said at my side.

Honestly, I didn't really know what she meant. My head was turned right just like hers had been, and that meant my eyes were facing backward instead of forward. It didn't help that the magical light had drifted on ahead of me, either. I felt the top of my head brush against the stone above. It was only the very first squeeze, and I was nearly stuck. Still, my torso had maybe an inch of space on either side, so I knew I'd make it. With Bokta's hand guiding my arm up and over another little rise, I eventually emerged into a space roughly the size of an average elevator compartment. Amethyst was there as well, and she had both of her swords slung on the same side of her body instead of on each hip.

When our light drifted toward the next obstacle, I understood why Amethyst had rearranged her weapons. We had come to what I could only describe as a shelf. It was wide, huge even, but only in that one direction. From top to bottom, the shelf rose up to the height of Bokta's knees, and she wasn't very tall.

"You can either crawl forward or sideways, it does not matter," the Blood Witch explained. Both the women dropped to their knees and began shimmying forward. Amethyst took the head-on crawling approach, and Bokta spread herself out horizontally, scooting her body sideways like a stretched out crab. When her entire torso was deep enough to be out of view, she waved for me to follow.

"This is insane . . ." I muttered, dropping to the ground alongside her. Flat on my belly, I was just barely thin enough to fit into the shelf. Once my body was fully under the overhanging stone, the totality of the tightness finally sank in, eliciting a cruel wave of nauseating terror from the pit of my stomach. There wasn't enough room to breathe. I could open my mouth all the way since I was looking sideways, but I couldn't fill my lungs to more than a third of their capacity. Anything more made my chest hitch painfully against the stone, halting any progress I hoped to make.

"You two . . . do this . . . often?" I asked between shallow gasps. The air tasted like pure sweat.

I didn't know if Bokta was taking it slower than usual in order to show me the way or if she was just as encumbered and slow moving as I was, but she stayed within arm's reach. "Every couple months," she whispered back. "We practice. Never know when we'll need to flee."

My knees and back clattered into the rocks, a painful tax paid for every foot stolen from the shelf.

"How . . . much longer?" I asked. A bit of silty dirt fell into my mouth from above. I tried to get my arm up to scrape my tongue, but it was just out of reach. I had to settle for spitting a few times. Then I realized that I'd be crawling right over my own spit. Not like I had much of a choice.

"Not much more," Bokta said after she pushed through a particularly narrow span of a dozen or so feet. I had to

shimmy upward—or maybe it was actually to my right . . .
a strange direction to consider in the dramatically horizontal environment—to avoid the extra pinch. Following
directly behind Bokta would have offered a superior view,
but I knew I would have been hopelessly stuck there for
eternity. Still, not a wretched way to go if it meant Bokta's fine ass would have filled my vision for days as I dehy-
drated to death.

Finally, the end of the shelf came beautifully into the
sight. The next level of the passage looked open, at least by
comparison, and Amethyst was already waiting there, her
short red skirt caked in grime.

When all three of us were past the shelf, Bokta did
something to brighten her magical buddy, and the room
lit up with thousands of different colors. The cavern we
were in wasn't immense, but that was certainly the feeling
it gave off, kind of like standing in a big stadium or theater
with no one else inside. Up above, the highest reaches of
the chamber were lined with colored flecks of stone and
crystal. The dazzling display continued forward and to the
sides for quite some distance.

"How far does it all go?" I asked in wonder. Funny how
all the fear and claustrophobia that had swamped my
thoughts a few short moments ago had evaporated.

Amethyst appeared just as awed by the sights as I was.
"Miles and miles, but we don't know for sure," she answered. "No one has ever mapped it out, and we've only
found a couple places where the tunnels come up to the
surface."

"How many of the city officials know about the caves?"
I had wandered a little bit from the two women, my neck
straining upward to take in all the radiant colors, and the
soldiers hunting our little band of rebels felt like years ago.

"Everyone knows about the caves," Bokta answered curtly.

"Well . . . that kind of sucks," I said. I tried to listen for any footsteps coming from either above us or back in the shelf, but I heard nothing.

The Blood Witch moved her magical butterfly forward a bit, beckoning us along deeper into the cavern. "Most people don't come down here. They say the caves are haunted."

"Haunt—"

"A pack of ghosts came out of one of the tunnels a couple years ago," Amethyst cut in. "That's when we decided to start learning the routes and exploring. Oathbreakers aren't afraid of ghosts. Not like everyone else."

"When you say a pack of ghosts . . ." I imagined a horde of silvery, incorporeal hands grasping up through the ground like zombies unleashed from a graveyard in a cheesy horror flick.

"Come on," Bokta said, now pretty far ahead of me, her hair shimmering under the multi-colored light. "We shouldn't leave the rest of the Oathbreakers waiting at the rendezvous point." She clambered over a series of several stalagmites to a point where the cavern narrowed once again into something resembling a distinct passageway.

Amethyst pushed me from behind, and I set my feet in motion to follow. Most of the next passage was easily traversable, reminding me of the tourist parts of Mammoth Cave that I had visited once when I was younger. There weren't any handrails or metal light fixtures in Mara's subterranean complex, but they wouldn't have looked too out of place had they been there. Then we reached another part of the tunnel—and it made the shelf look like child's play.

"No way in hell am I going to fit through that . . ." I said. Bokta was the first one to hop up on the little ledge, and even her lithe frame struggled for purchase.

"Hubbard's Climb is the quickest way to the surface," she replied. She had her right foot wedged in a little crook of the wall, and the left half of her body was precariously balanced between two cylindrical stalactites hanging down from overhead. Hubbard's Climb, so it seemed, was basically a chimney. A narrow, dangerously tight, horribly dark chimney.

Amethyst was busy stretching her arms and legs at my side. "Guys," I said, "seriously. I don't think I'll make it up that."

"The next closest exit is several miles away, and it is watched by city guard day and night," the Oathbreaker leader stated, a bit of sharp attitude in her voice. "Hubbard's Climb is the only way."

Like the shelf before, I really didn't have a choice. Mr. Patches meowed at my side as he looked up at the stone chimney as well. At least I had a buddy who would be trekking along at my heels—assuming I even made it to the shaft's entrance.

Bokta gave me a weak smile, sent her glowing friend on ahead of her up the chimney, and then disappeared.

I stepped aside to allow Amethyst to go next. "Watch where I place my feet, then follow quickly. If you need a hand up, just say so. Better to ask for help than fall and break your neck."

"Got it," I answered. Easy rules to follow.

Amethyst planted a foot, wrapped the fingers of her right hand around a protrusion in the stone, and hoisted herself into the beginning of the vertical chute. After a brief moment, she readjusted her feet on a slightly higher notch and pulled herself higher. "Give me a boost," she called down, her voice a little muffled and distorted by the tight stone walls around her upper body.

"Uh . . ." I grabbed on to the stone in a fashion I thought was nearly identical to what Amethyst had done herself, then pushed off with a leg to bring my body a solid four feet off the cavern floor. Amethyst was only about two or three feet higher than me, and her muscled legs ran right down in front of my face.

"A boost?" she said again.

There was nowhere to put my hands to help lift her. Well, there was exactly one place.

I'd never been a veteran of women's bodies at any point in my life. I wasn't a virgin—and that was about where my carnal knowledge came to a grinding halt. Most of my friends had peaked in college, going to frat parties on the weekends and bringing home different chicks almost every Friday night. Part of me had envied that lifestyle, though I had never let it really get me down. After all, there had always been Realm of Crafted War waiting patiently for me to return—alone—from the pubs.

"Hey," came Amethyst's voice. "Where's that boost?"

I wasn't really sure what to say. "You, uh . . . you want me to give you a boost . . . from behind?" I stumbled through, my eyes glued on the woman's incredible ass barely hidden behind her gloriously short red skirt. Then, ever so slightly, she shook her hips right in front of my face. Maybe I just imagined it. Maybe not. I couldn't really think straight.

"Just give me a fucking boost before my arms fall off!" she yelled.

Sucking in a huge breath to try and steady my nerves, I placed my left hand firmly on Amethyst's rear and shoved upward with all the strength of my body that hadn't fled toward my groin. Up the woman ascended, issuing a slight grunt, and then she was gone from my sight around curve.

"Holy shit . . ." I muttered as quietly as I physically could. Placing my hands as close to the positions that Amethyst had used seconds before, I hauled my body into the chimney, then quickly lost part of my balance and had to lunge to keep from falling back to the ground. Once I was in Hubbard's Climb, the only way to go was up.

Surprisingly, it didn't take too much effort to continue the claustrophobic ascent. Perhaps it was a hidden advantage of my relative girth compared to the ladies, but I was able to push hard against the surface in front of me, gain a few feet in altitude, then lean the opposite direction to repeat the action, steadily moving upward like an inchworm.

I caught up to Amethyst after what felt like about fifty feet or so of climbing. She was facing downward, seated, her legs hanging over the lip of a slight ledge where the tunnel changed direction. The back of her skirt was hiked up on a bit of protruding stone. Had there been more light . . .

Amethyst reached down and grabbed my arm, then hauled me up to the ledge with her. There wasn't enough room for me to sit like she was, so I had to settle for awkwardly leaning against the rough wall across from her, my head tilted down to keep from hitting my scalp on the rocks. With the magical light behind the woman, I couldn't see her face enough to read her expression. For a moment, I realized I was trapped. The only way down would be too difficult to manage without falling, and the way forward was blocked by a woman who possessed not one but two swords. If she was pissed at me for the tactic I had employed while boosting her, she could easily kill me. Hell, she could even make it look like an accident.

"The next section of Hubbard's Climb is the most difficult," she said, not a drop of malice lurking behind her words. Thank god for that.

I tried to look over her shoulder, but I couldn't see anything. "How much more difficult?" I asked.

Amethyst turned herself around on the small ledge, one of her legs extending to my section of wall in order to keep her balance. Her leather boot slid along the inside of my thigh as she planted herself horizontally. When she was flat against the floor of the next passage, I realized that it wasn't the darkness that had blocked my vision over her shoulder. It was simply that there wasn't anything to see. The tunnel shrank down to an oval-shaped opening oddly reminiscent of a fish's mouth and about as large as a small duffle bag.

"It goes for about ten feet," the woman said without looking back. She had both of her swords in her hand in front of her and her harness turned to her chest as well. "When you get in, push as far forward as possible. You'll get stuck."

"Wh—"

"Once you know you can't go another inch, exhale. Force all the wind from your lungs and suck in your stomach. That'll give you enough room."

"And what if it doesn't?" I asked. Every warm feeling Amethyst's marvelous ass had imparted upon my very soul was replaced by icy fingers. I felt nauseous and seasick, like I was going to vomit and shit at the same time. Hell, maybe evacuating my intestines would make me that much smaller. It wasn't a bad idea.

Amethyst began shimmying her body forward into the hole. "Once you get stuck, exhale," she repeated. "Make yourself as small as possible, and you'll get through. See you on the other side."

"But what if I still can't fit!" I basically shouted. I attempted to keep the panic from my voice, but my words cracked as they came out, making me sound like a terrified little kid—an apt description.

"Then you'll die in Hubbard's Climb. You wouldn't be the first," Amethyst said. She wriggled forward again, and I heard her audibly exhale. Then her legs flexed, her body wriggled side to side, and she claimed another foot of the tunnel.

I stood transfixed, wedged into the rough stone opposite the fish-mouth opening, watching in horror. Amethyst was smaller than I was. Well, her chest was *a lot* larger than mine, but the rest of her body was toned and sleek like a dancer's.

The last bit of Amethyst's boots disappeared into the darkness. A little sliver of glowing magic made its way back to my position, though it was barely enough to illuminate anything at all.

"I'm through," came a soft female voice. "Your turn."

Great. I pushed off from my cramped section of wall and climbed up the little ledge leading to the fish mouth.

Holy. Fucking. Shit. The opening was beyond tight. There was barely enough room to fit my head inside and turn it around. There was no way the rest of me would make it.

"Did you start?" Amethyst asked from the other side. Slowly, the magical light began to grow, and then I saw the little floating butterfly weaving its way through the darkness to guide me. I was thankful to have the light, but seeing what I was about to shove myself through actually made it a bit worse. The floor of the tunnel wasn't smooth. There were jagged knobs and ridges in the stone waiting to shred my chest. I took off my leather and dropped it back down Hubbard's Climb. It was torn anyways, and every single fraction of an inch I could shave off my size would be worth it. My cotton undershirt went next. I shuddered to think of what the rocks would do to my exposed skin. So be it.

I looked down at my pants. Shedding those would give me some more room. I sighed and figured I would keep them on, if only to save myself the embarrassment of dying naked.

"Steve?" Amethyst's voice drifted down.

"Yeah," I answered, inching closer to the opening. "I'm on my way."

The first couple feet weren't as bad as I had anticipated. It was tight, but it wasn't horrendous. Not yet. I crawled another foot, and one of the uneven rises started crushing my guts against my ribs. It hurt like a bitch. I pushed forward again, and I felt the rock scraping off the top few layers of my skin. Whenever we finally emerged from Mara's underground hell, I'd need an entire new outfit. Preferably a set of armor and some high quality bandages to go underneath for a few days.

After about ten feet, I found the part Amethyst had described. I simply stopped moving. Like crawling into a funnel made of implacable stone, the passage had narrowed to an impossible width. "Guys . . ." I half-gasped, trying to project my weakened voice forward.

"Exhale, remember?" came Amethyst's voice. The little creature of light was right in front of my face, almost painfully close.

"Hello," the cheerful butterfly said with her magical, sing-song voice. "Come along now."

I clenched my eyes and tried to calm my breathing. It didn't help.

"Turn your right shoulder to the side and inch forward a bit," the woman at the end of the tunnel told me.

I moved a little, lifting my shoulder and turning into a human inchworm once more. The top part of the tunnel bit into my collarbone. I had to struggle to keep from yelping, instead chomping down on my lower lip and clenching my fists. Slowly, the tactic worked, and I gained another six inches.

I tried to do the same thing on my left, but there wasn't any room. The tunnel was only a few inches from top to bottom, and my left shoulder was jammed into the gap like a piece of soft plywood stuck in a vice.

"Exhale," Amethyst told me.

There wasn't anything left in my lungs to force out. I held my lips together, my eyes still clenched shut, and dug in my toes. Levering myself forward from the ankles, I pushed. My body refused to move.

"Is he stuck?" one of the women, I couldn't tell which, asked in a hushed whisper.

"Fuuuck," I growled.

I dug in my toes again, pushed out another miniscule iota of air from my burning lungs, and flexed my legs as hard as they would possibly go. The right side of my body moved about an inch. My left shoulder was still pinned, and the awkward half-movement was creating *a lot* of painful torque. Instead of a new set of clothes and armor, I wondered if I'd need a prosthetic arm by time I made it out.

If I made it out.

A woman's fingers laced through the hair on the top of my head. "Almost there," one of them said gently. Then the fingers clenched, and whoever it was yanked hard on my scalp.

I didn't want to waste the opportunity. My cheeks red and my head swimming from the lack of air, I pushed again with my feet. Finally, something on my left gave way. I moved another half a foot forward, and I could feel a bit of new coolness touching the skin of my face and neck.

A second hand wrapped around my right shoulder.

"Wait," I barely muttered. I needed a minute to summon my strength before trying to push again. The problem, though, was that I still couldn't fully breathe.

I think it was Bokta who spoke. "There isn't much time. You'll pass out soon," she said.

My shoulder was pulled forward, and I gave whatever strength I had left to one final push. A nasty, wet, popping sound echoed in my left ear, but the top half of my body emerged from the tunnel nonetheless. My legs came somewhat quickly after my arms, and I felt a bit of warm blood lubricating them as I fell in a heap on the stone floor.

The women stood over me, but I didn't have the strength to look up.

"His arm is dislocated," one of them said. From the unforgiving tone, I assumed it was Amethyst.

"Push it back in," came the quick response.

"Can you stun him so he won't feel the pain?" That sounded like a wonderful idea.

There was a pause. "No, we need him to be able to walk, maybe run, if the hideout has been compromised."

Shit. Before I had time to protest or even look around to get my bearings, two hands were on my wrist, and then everything exploded in pain.

"There," Amethyst said, hauling me to my feet at the same time.

I was so dizzy I could barely stand. Thankfully, I didn't

have to worry about hitting my head. "Are we . . . are we close?" I asked.

"You made it through Hubbard's Climb," Bokta announced, as cheery as ever. "All downhill from here. We'll be back on the surface in no time."

Amethyst slapped me on my uninjured shoulder. "Bokta and I would race through Hubbard's Climb when we were younger. Not together, of course, but one after another. You did well for your first time. I'm impressed."

I had to take a couple minutes just to fully process what the woman was saying, clouded as my mind was with pain. "You . . . you two come here often?" I asked.

"Actually, I made a run last week to drop off some fresh supplies at the hideout. Not bad exercise, eh?" she answered.

Bokta was back at the front of our little crew, and she had Qu floating above her head like a quest giver with a new notification. What was left of the cavern even had a bit of natural light filtering in from up ahead. I thought I could hear wind as well, but it could have simply been a heavy dose of throbbing pain filling my ears.

"Wait," I wondered aloud. "If you run this tunnel for fun . . . there's no way you needed a boost."

It was hard to see Amethyst's face in the shifting, advancing light. She turned to me, and I swore she winked, but she didn't say a word. Right before we exited the tunnel, I heard the soft meow of a cat. Mr. Patches had made it through Hubbard's Climb as well.

CHAPTER 13

The Oathbreaker safe house was actually pretty cool. On the outside, the small group of wooden buildings looked like a standard farmstead that would have matched perfectly in any stretch of Pennsylvania countryside. They had some of the land around it set up as a working farm, and there was even a field fenced off with a pair of horses and a paddock. Everything about the farm was completely innocuous.

On the inside, the hideout was nothing short of a fortified rebel stronghold. The walls and door had been reinforced with flat iron bars bolted directly into the studs. Racks and racks of equipment were stationed around the main room, and a staircase expertly hidden behind a false bookshelf led to a basement where we had emerged from Hubbard's Climb. One of the outbuildings which looked like a typical barn actually contained a sparring ring lined with bales of hay. The whole complex was about a mile outside of Mara, and I realized I must have passed it on the way to the city from Tamernil.

The most striking feature of the entire safe house was a portrait of the Desecrator. Framed in twisting black iron, the oiled canvas Underlord stood next to the fake bookcase with a scowl on his face. As the legend went, the Desecrator had been human, a follower of Valiance and a completely normal person. Then, after years of taking orders and being treated more or less like a dog, the Desecrator had forsaken his oath. At first, a Torch Bearer had tried to chastise the Desecrator, but a fight had ensued. The Desecrator had emerged victorious from the fight, and slaying a Torch Bearer brought dark consequences. Librarians from every lighthouse in Realm had—for that expansion, at least—summoned their paladins and knights in search of the Desecrator.

Other Valiance factions forsook their oaths, and a full scale war broke out in a matter of months. It was said that a stray god, a cast out of the Realm pantheon whose name had been lost to history, had taken a liking to the Desecrator. The problem was, the stray god had been cast out for a reason.

The Desecrator then took a new oath—one sworn in blood and souls.

The dark visage hanging on the wall portrayed the end result of that unhallowed pact. Far from human, the Desecrator was a nothing short of an unholy abomination. The man's face had been blackened by hellfire, his eyes had been sewn shut by heavy leather cord, and his ears had been shorn off until the sides of his face were completely smooth.

Only partially represented on the oil portrait was the Desecrator's lower half. The former follower of Valiance, as part of his ghastly bargain, had given up his human legs. In their stead was a trio of slime-ridden tentacles akin to a kraken's arms drawn at the edge of the world on an old map.

While the Desecrator was certainly more than capable of wielding an impressive array of spells in combat, his weapon of choice was as dark as his countenance. In his hands was Screwgore, a bent and corrupted rectangle of metal that supposedly had been ripped from the top of a Valiance lighthouse. The Desecrator had never sharpened Screwgore, though a demon-god standing well over thirty feet tall didn't need his weapons to serve as cutting instruments. The twisted, corkscrewing beam of scorched metal was more than enough to raze a building with a single swing.

All in all, the likeness hanging on the wall was horrifying.

Seeing it in person, up close and staring me right in the face, made me finally realize just what kind of people had summoned me. Blood Witches were evil. I wasn't sure what class Amethyst technically was, but 'assassin' felt like a solid guess. And Valiance, as frilly and lame as they were online, was the good guys' cult. They *helped* people. The Desecrator . . . desecrated.

Somewhat surprisingly, the tenants of the Desecrator's cult weren't *exclusively* evil, though. Most of the cult was focused on poorly understood ideas related to extreme individual freedom. No rules, no laws, no government. Just freedom to carry on as one pleased. The problems with such lack of regulation were obvious: chaos and anarchy. In the midst of that anarchy, the Desecrator's cults sought to run things like old Viking warlords—survival of the absolute strongest.

I thought back to Bokta's purpose when she had

summoned me. The Dread King, essentially an overreaching bureaucrat, was running Mara with his fingers clutched a little too tightly around the city. It was a classic Oathbreaker quest line from the Realm I knew and loved. A town would be oppressed, and the Oathbreakers would always be the first to show up and resist government authority. Their cause would attract new followers, their numbers would swell, and their strength would grow. Then, once the mantle of tyranny was cast aside, every Valiance lighthouse in the city would be cast out, and the Valiance followers would be put to the sword. Such slaughter would inevitably incur the ire of other Torch Bearers and Librarians, and thus an entire expansion had been born in a new war, sucking in millions of online players on release day alone.

Truth be told, I hadn't really cared much about the cause. Maxrannar had been an Oathbreaker because playing a demon was fucking epic. And online, being the 'bad guy' was a refreshing change of pace, especially in MMOs where everyone is typically railroaded into playing a knight and saving poor villagers from guys like Maxrannar.

Now, whether I was truly stuck in a game world or not, I was a bad guy. A really, really bad guy. Fucking evil. The demon-god painting on the wall was a pretty damn clear reminder of what the Oathbreakers fought for. Sure, overthrowing the Dread King was probably an objectively 'good' thing to be doing, but what would come after that would be hell. A slaughter would follow quickly after the revolution, and that purge would spark a war. I'd played the same quest line a half-dozen times. I wasn't really sure I wanted to live it.

Mr. Patches meowed gently as he followed me to the sparring circle hidden away in the barn behind the farmhouse. It was just after breakfast, and I was scheduled for a little demonstration of sorts. All my clothes had to be tossed after my escapade through Hubbard's Climb. Luckily, the Oathbreaker safe house had some clothes stored away, though they weren't anything fancy. Serviceable at best. My tunic was just a little too large for my shoulders, but the pants weren't too bad. All of it was held together by a simple leather belt. For shoes, I had a pair of stiff leather boots. The tall sides rubbed painfully against my ankles with every step, moving me closer and closer to the training ring that would inevitably show everyone what an idiot I truly was.

"So, time to see what you can do," Amethyst said with a smile as I entered the ring. She was outfitted once more in her usual garb with her swords hanging from their harness at her sides. My shoulder still ached and throbbed despite the linen bandage helping to hold it in place. That bandage continued down over my chest as well. Most of that part sported a deep red sheen of blood. Still, the rapid exodus from the biergarten headquarters meant time was running short—the government's soldiers were on our heels. Without the luxury of time, I had to prove my worth, or else I wasn't worth the bread and meat they were graciously allowing into my belly.

Bokta and Amethyst stood on one of the hay bales to the side of the little arena. They both wore subtle glowers, adding to their muscular and imposing image. At least Bokta, I knew, would go to bat for me. No matter how badly I screwed up, I felt like she would always be a fan girl. She had, after all, been the one to summon me, and that initial infatuation hadn't waned much.

Depressingly, all I could think to show the two women was the sloppy disarm I had learned back in the village. And the rest of the Oathbreakers had still not arrived, so it was only the three of us in the practice area. Two other Oathbreakers, full-timers stationed at the hideout, were still back in the main building. Looked like I'd be sparring with one of the ladies. Fantastic.

"I'm not really great with any of these weapons," I offered. The rack nearest me held a bunch of conventional implements like swords, spears, maces, and shields. A few of them had been worn smooth, their hafts darkened by excessive use.

"I've seen you fight thousands of times," Bokta said, a gleam in her eye. She moved to one of the racks and grabbed a wooden axe and matching practice sword. She tossed them down to me with a little flourish of her hand.

Gracelessly, I managed to snatch the axe—by its wooden blade—out of the air, but the sword smacked me hard across the chin before clattering to the ground. I wasn't even sure I wanted to invite the shame of bending down to pick it up. "Seriously, Bokta, you saw me train with the recruiter back in the village. I'm not any good."

Amethyst didn't care. "Bokta spent a lot of Oathbreaker resources and risked everything bringing you to our plane. Her assurances have kept you alive, but I've seen you fight as well, so there might still be some way you can aid our cause. Show us."

Bokta grabbed a wooden baton with a flared head and jumped down to the ground across from me, her feet instantly set in a fighter's pose.

"Magic," I suddenly stated, grasping at straws. I couldn't take another beating. My shoulder was still wrecked, and any more damage doled out upon it would probably result in serious, permanent injury. And there probably weren't any decent physical therapists nearby to fix it.

"You can do magic?" Amethyst asked. Bokta looked just as surprised. She took a step back.

Well, Maxrannar could cast a few pretty impressive spells. Without a keyboard, I wasn't so sure. "I . . . need time," I said.

Amethyst crossed her arms. "You have all of today. We will wait."

Bokta set down her training baton and scooted backward, sitting down against one of the hay bales. Apparently they were keen to wait right where they were.

I had to figure out something. Preferably quick. "Casting spells is different where I come from. Bokta, what do you do when you cast a spell?"

The woman ran her tongue over her teeth as she thought. "First, you have to know the name of the spell. Not any fancy name, but the spell's true name. Once you know that, you have to visualize the spell happening where you want to cast it, and then you kind of . . . *feel it*, you know?"

That didn't really help. *Feeling* a spell sounded complicated. And that was all predicated on the spell names from Realm being *true* names, whatever that really meant. "Can anyone cast spells? Assuming they know the name and all that, is it something anyone can do?" I asked. Might as well begin with the absolute basics. The Blood Witch shook her head. "You have to do something first to gain access to magic," she explained. With a sigh, she continued, "I swore a blood oath to the Desecrator.

That's probably the easiest way to unlock magic. Well, not easiest, but the quickest. The most common method is to study for years and years under the tutelage of a practiced mage or at one of the magically inclined cults. Or, if you're incredibly lucky, you could find a magic relic. Those let anyone cast, but they're incredibly dangerous."

Alright, I didn't have years to waste in a tower somewhere, and I didn't possess any item other than my cursed tourmaline. Speaking of which, Mr. Patches was busy cleaning himself on one of the hay bales. So far, no other cats had shown up to pester me for eternity.

Although . . . maybe Mr. Patches *was* the magic item I needed. If Catsi and Funen had really been the ones to curse the die, there was a chance the cat was magical, right? I scooped up the little guy in my arms and thought of some of the spells I had been able to use online. I didn't want to try any of the really high-end abilities for fear of blowing up the entire compound, so I settled on attempting to cast Blood Shot, one of the lower-level, beginning spells that all Oathbreakers knew right from the start.

The spell, low level as it was, actually had a pretty cool effect. A hook and chain made purely from blood would shoot out of Maxkrannar's chest like a grapple, travel twenty feet, and latch onto whatever they hit. Then, if the grappled object was heavier than Maxkrannar, the character would be pulled forward to it at a rapid pace. If the target was lighter, it worked in the opposite direction. Either way, Blood Shot was an incredibly useful ability. Dodging and jumping around the battlefield was indispensable.

I imagined the spell, closed my eyes and visualized a gout of blood leaping from my chest, and *really* tried to *feel* it. I figured I probably looked constipated.

Nothing happened.

I wasn't really surprised. Digging my fingers a little deeper into Mr. Patches' fur, I tried again. For a really long time. Still, no blood burst out of my chest, and nothing else of note occurred. Mr. Patches licked the back of my hand. That was about it.

"I don't think the cat is a magic relic. Not like that," Bokta said, offering a weak laugh.

"Could you two give me a day or so to figure it out? The system is new to me." I didn't want to admit defeat, but I had no other choice.

It was pretty easy to see what Amethyst's answer was going to be before she ever opened her mouth. "No," was all she offered.

"Fine." I had to come up with something. Maybe if I had a light or a phone, I could at least fake having magic abilities. For a few silent—unbearably awkward—moments, I just stood there trying to come up with a plan. Nothing really came to mind.

Amethyst began tapping her foot on the hay. I let Mr. Patches wriggle out of my arms. Bokta had her arms crossed, the wooden training baton resting at her feet.

Finally, after a sweltering eternity, at least I had a shred of an idea flitting about between my ears. It was a stupid idea, though. One I kind of hated. And the only thing I had.

"Bokta, give me the blood oath. I want to be a Blood Witch like you."

CHAPTER 14

"I t . . . it doesn't really work quite like that," Bokta said.

At least my proclamation managed to get a rise out of one of Amethyst's eyebrows. I didn't know if the movement was a good thing or a bad thing, but I'd take it. Mr. Patches, on the other hand, appeared entirely unfazed.

"How does it work?" I asked. My stomach was doing somersaults at the prospect of signing up with the Desecrator. Being aligned with an evil deity in a game was one thing, and the world of Mara and Tamernil felt a lot different. But then again, maybe none of it actually was real.

The Blood Witch shook her head. "First of all, only a woman can become a Blood Witch. It takes a certain anatomy . . . oh, never mind that. Male adherents to the Desecrator go a different path."

I didn't want to start tossing around ideas about which part of Bokta's lovely *anatomy* had been required for service in her oath. "Which paths can a man take?" I asked.

Amethyst, smirking, let out a snarky chortle. "You think you're strong enough to take a blood oath?" she tossed at me, flicking her hair behind her shoulder.

"Technically, I *have* done it before. More than once, actually," I proudly stated. Though it had been online, I had gone through the entire cinematic of the blood oath a few times. You couldn't skip it, and the visuals were actually pretty sweet, so it was one of the ones worth sitting through. In the version of Realm I knew and loved, the blood oath ceremony depended on race. For Maxkrannar, a demon like the Desecrator himself, it had been a rather bloody affair involving tusks, captive slaves, and lots of alcohol derived from a fermented mixture of deer blood and mare's milk. Thank god I hadn't had to drink that shit in real life.

But that's exactly what I had just asked Bokta to cook up for me, wasn't it? Shit.

The Blood Witch wore a smile as she explained the two blood-sworn classes that existed. "First," she began, "there's a martial practice. Males can become what we call a Soul Taker, something similar to the Librarians at Valiance temples. You'd need to find an appropriate sacrifice to begin the oath, but it isn't impossible. The truly magical discipline of the Desecrator is called a Sovereign Magus, and they're not all that different from Valiance Torch Bearers. Have you heard of those followers back on your world?"

Hell no I hadn't. Online, Oathbreakers were Oathbreakers. There weren't any super cool subdivisions within the class, though Oathbreakers themselves *were* the coolest anyways.

"Alright, what does it take to become a Sovereign Magus?" The class sounded absolutely wicked—in more than one way.

Bokta looked to Amethyst as though seeking permission, and the leader nodded. "It will require an offering. You'll need something magical, the more powerful the better, and it will have to be stolen from a Valiance lighthouse. There is no other way."

Ah, why did everything have to be so damned difficult! Choosing a class online was a simple button press right before the screen where you got to design your face and haircut. "So, how do I steal a magical object from the lighthouse?" I asked.

Still smiling, Amethyst hopped down from her hay bale and sauntered over. "You still have the lock picks, right?" she said quietly. "You did well enough at the courthouse. Maybe one of your cat friends could help."

She dragged a finger down the side of my chest—the injured side—as she walked away, not waiting for my response. At least she seemed to be allowing me to live.

"No," I said once she was gone. "I actually don't have the lock picks. I left them behind."

"Don't worry. We'll find a way." Bokta moved back to her wooden baton and kicked it up off the ground and to her hand in one clean, fluid motion. "Now, no matter what, you still need to learn how to fight. We've never had a single Sovereign Magus or Soul Taker in Mara, at least that I know of. Becoming one will be difficult. It may take you quite some time."

"Hey, you never said what class you are. Is it just called a Blood Witch? And what about Amethyst?" I asked, bending to grab my two practice weapons from the ground. My shoulder hurt as I moved.

She smiled again. "Yes, Steve, I'm a Blood Witch. And Amethyst chose the other path for female Oathbreakers. She's a Siren. Her specialties are martial while mine are

magical. Every cult which has a strong tenant of combat has four specializations. Was it not the same on your
world?"

"No, not really," I answered. "It was similar, but not really
the same. We had Torch Bearers and Librarians, though."
I didn't know how to explain to her that those classes had
been NPCs, not played characters.

"Well, those are only half of Valiance's leadership. Torch
Bearers, of course, are male. They're magical. Librarians
are all female, and they're martial, though they can usually
cast some spells as well, just not very many. The male martial specialization hasn't been seen in hundreds of years.
Some say Valiance doesn't have one. They're just called
Monks, or at least that's what people say. And the female
spell casters are known as Lightborn Ladies. There aren't
any of those in Mara, either. Just a single Torch Bearer
and a single Librarian stationed at each lighthouse. All the
others get sent off to some convent or whatever up in the
mountains." Bokta had moved closer as she spoke, and it
was clear from her posture that she still intended to spar,
history lesson or not.

She took a swing, and I didn't bother asking any more
questions.

Two hours later, I was sitting in the safe house with a
fresh bandage wrapped around my right knee, two more
bandages on the table waiting to be applied to my shoulder, and a splitting headache. Training sucked. I was terrible at it. Bokta had showed me a couple basic techniques
that hadn't taken me too long to get the hang of, and I had

managed to disarm her a couple times using what the recruiter had taught me, but that was it. The rest of the training session had made me feel like a miserable, bruised failure. As I struggled to change the dressing on my shoulder, Mr. Patches saw fit to give me a nice wet lick on the ear. What a dick.

About an hour after we finished dinner, my headache finally subsided. Or maybe it had simply transferred into Amethyst's skull. The woman was pacing back and forth, frequently checking both the hidden passageway behind the bookcase and the front door.

"What is it?" I asked Bokta who was busy stretching her muscles on the floor. She, unlike myself, had gone for a nice long run after lunch while I had been left to lick my wounds all by my lonesome. The two full-timers had been sent off on a mission of their own.

"The other Oathbreakers should have returned by now," she explained. "If they're gone this long, especially without having at least sent a messenger, it means something went wrong."

"Oh, shit. What do you think happened?"

"Someone sold us out," Bokta went on quietly. "It might have been Taros, but he would have told us when we rescued him. It has to have been Crow."

"If he was the former mayor, they probably tortured him," I concluded aloud.

She nodded. "Of course they tortured him. And he knew where our headquarters was."

"Did he know about this place?" I asked, my voice squeaking. I imagined regiments of soldiers, all trained and well-armed, surrounding the house as we spoke.

Again, the Blood Witch nodded. "If he gave up the safe house, we'll all be dead before sunrise."

"Maybe we should sleep in the tunnels . . ." I didn't understand how the woman could be so cool and casual when speaking about our potentially impending doom. I was pretty close to pissing myself just considering the possibility of already being surrounded.

"If the soldiers haven't come yet, they probably won't," she explained.

"Yeah, *probably*," I repeated.

Finally, Amethyst stopped her pacing. She turned back toward the table where I had just about finished re-bandaging my shoulder. "They've been compromised," she stated. "Tomorrow, at dawn, we have to go into Mara and find them. Every Oathbreaker from the biergarten knows where we are right now. If they've been taken, it is only a matter of time before hordes of soldiers come knock down our walls and drag us into that wretched lighthouse for interrogation. We need information."

Bokta nodded and moved toward one of the other backrooms. "I'll have disguises ready. We'll leave at dawn," she confirmed.

Then Amethyst's fiery gaze fell on me. "You," she said, "come help me. In my room."

That didn't sound good. Her tone was all fire and brimstone, and I knew I had fucked up earlier in the training arena. "What do you need?" I attempted to ask. My heart sank when Bokta disappeared behind another door, leaving the two of us alone. With her at least nearby, I felt marginally more confident that Amethyst wouldn't kill me.

"Just do what I say," she answered. She held open a door to what I assumed was her quarters as it was the farmhouse's largest bedroom, and she was the leader.

God, following her felt like a death trap. I had displeased the matriarch and my hour of reckoning had come. "I'm sure I can help in the morning, right? My shoulder is still pretty banged up. I should get some rest."

Amethyst moved through her doorway and looked back over her shoulder, her long hair cascading down her back. "You have five seconds to come in here and give me a boost so I can reach this shelf, or that opportunity will never again present itself. Your choice."

What . . .

Then it clicked. I don't actually think I'd ever gotten up from a table faster in my life. My shoulder protested every rapid movement I made, but in that moment, the pain was meaningless.

The first thing I noticed when I entered Amethyst's room was a distinct lack of shelves.

Dawn came far too quickly. Another ten hours of sleep would have been greatly appreciated, especially since I had only slept for a couple hours at the most. As it turned out, Amethyst had rather enjoyed ordering me around for a few hours, and my shoulder was paying the price, though I wasn't complaining. Thankfully, she had awakened at least an hour before dawn and left the room, presumably to prepare for the mission into Mara, and those final moments alone before sunrise were pretty wonderful.

But sunrise came as it always did, and I could hear the two women chatting and making preparations—including breakfast—in the main room, so I pushed myself off the bed, found my clothes, and stumbled out the door.

Bokta gave me a sidelong glance for all of a quarter second before returning her gaze to a heavy iron pan and a slab of frying meat. Amethyst, going through a rawhide pack on the table, wasn't nearly as bashful.

"Did you sleep well?" the Siren asked.

"Yeah, I guess," I answered. The mattress had been pretty weak, basically just a six-inch pad stuffed with straw, feathers, and strips of old cotton.

Amethyst wrapped a woolen shawl around her shoulders and over her hair, then popped open a tattered parasol. "What do you think? Will anyone recognize me?"

Bokta turned to give her a once over. "It should be fine," she said curtly. She finished frying the meat and slid it onto a large platter, then poured a little bit of dark, syrupy liquid onto it from a small clay pitcher. The whole concoction smelled amazing, like sweet roasted meat mixed with candied nuts.

When the meat made its way to the table, Amethyst dropped the rest of the disguises to the floor, then ripped a sizeable chunk off the roast with her hand. I followed suit, and Bokta did the same. Awkwardly, the three of us sat in silence as we ate, and I made a point to avoid eye contact with either of them. I didn't know any of the social protocols, though it was pretty obvious that emerging from Amethyst's room had created a palpable layer of tension. Fan girls at comic conventions never enjoyed meeting their crush's wives, after all. Not that Amethyst and I had made any kind of promises whatsoever, but the implications were still there.

Finally, breakfast concluded, and it was time to sneak into Mara. No one had the slightest clue who I was, so I didn't need a disguise. Amethyst seemed at ease with just a shawl hiding her hair and most of her rather recognizable torso. Bokta opted for a more thorough disguise complete with a false beard and a cane.

The safe house wasn't far from Mara's gate, perhaps half a mile, and we made the trek quickly, arriving just after sunrise. From the very moment we arrived, it was obvious that something was going on. Something important. Banners and streamers in all different colors fluttered in the gentle breeze, and they hadn't been there before.

"Some sort of festival?" I asked Bokta.

She shook her head.

We made our way toward the town square, Mr. Patches following dutifully behind. For as early as it was, a huge throng of people were all going in the same direction as we were. Something was about to happen in the town square.

The three of us—well, four if you counted the cat—rounded a corner from one of the market streets and finally saw what the commotion was all about. Right in front of an official-looking building was a long row of scaffolds. The scaffolding held nine gallows, all lined up in a neat little row of death. Behind the gallows were nine Oathbreakers.

"That's the Dread King himself," Bokta whispered in my ear. "He only comes out in public for executions."

"And there's going to be a lot of them . . ." I muttered to myself.

Amethyst grabbed me by the sleeve of my tunic and pressed forward, parting the mess of gathered townsfolk like a ship pushing through ice. She stopped when we were somewhere close to the macabre stage. We were in shouting distance, but not close enough to draw attention to our merry little band.

"You," Amethyst said to me, her voice full of fire once more. "If you're going to steal a relic from Valiance, do it now. Most of their followers should be here in the square. Go." She looked to Bokta, a hand on the woman's shoulder. "We need to figure out how to get them down."

If the two Oathbreaker women were going to put some sort of epic plan into action, it looked like they only had a few minutes. Nine hooded executioners were making their way up a short set of stairs at one end of the scaffolding. Without any better plan jumping out and smacking me in the face, I began pushing my way through the crowd of onlookers toward the Valiance lighthouse two streets away. There really wasn't anything else I could do.

It felt weird to move against the sea of people flocking toward the executions. A few of them gave me some strange looks, and more than one person I passed offered a comment aimed at Mr. Patches, though none of them were clued in to the cursed nature of the adorable feline.

The Valiance lighthouse towered above its shorter neighbors along the street. Like my previous visit, I couldn't tell anything about the interior without going inside. Luckily, the front door was still unlocked.

"May I help you?" an older man said at once. He had been sitting in a chair directly across from the door with a little square of carved marble in his hands. It looked like he'd been playing a game I didn't recognize.

"Hey . . . uh, I'm looking for something," I said. I hadn't expected to be greeted so instantly, and I hadn't made a plan on the short walk from the square. Then I heard a little bit of scratching—Mr. Patches must not have made it through the front door before it closed—and I got an idea. "You see a cat come in here recently?"

The old man raised an eyebrow. "A cat? In the lighthouse?"

I moved toward the staircase with an expression I hoped conveyed confidence, like I knew where I was supposed to be and what I was doing. "Yeah, my cat slipped in here when everyone went to the square," I said.

The man's eyes returned to his marble game. He moved a pair of small pieces from one side to the other, a hint of a smile on his face. "The Torch Bearer has not yet departed for the day's festivities. He should still be in his study on the second floor. If your lost cat is here, he will know of it."

I started up the stairs, praying the Torch Bearer's study wouldn't be located first thing on level two, but the building was not that large around. There probably wasn't more than one room on each floor. That meant I was screwed. "Thanks," I offered weakly, most of my fake confidence gone.

The stairs creaked under my feet as I ascended. I took my time, still trying desperately to formulate some sort of plan that wouldn't end with my neck being the tenth one wrapped in rope on the scaffolds. At least I was fairly confident that none of my peasant clothes could be identified as having come from an Oathbreaker outpost. Hell, as nervous as I was, it probably wouldn't be too hard to figure out I was at least some place I should not have been. Guessing that I was a bad guy was only the next step.

I reached the top of the stairs, and an aroma of chocolaty coffee hit my nostrils. It was pleasant, warm and inviting, like the open door of a small-town café drifting tasty vapors into the morning air. Above all else, it was unexpected.

I didn't know if I was supposed to knock or not. After a moment of silently enjoying the scent, I figured knocking would only help if the Torch Bearer was behind the door, so I rapped my fist against the smooth panel above the handle.

A few seconds later, a voice came from the other side. "Come in," it said.

I turned the knob and pushed through. The coffee scent practically doubled. The room, cozily illuminated by a half-shuttered window on the left wall, was not all that dis-similar from a modern coffee shop, sans metallic machin-ery, of course. There was coffee, several pounds of whole beans in two wooden crates, sitting on the floor next to a large polished desk.

The man behind the desk—the Torch Bearer—was a shining example of a classic armor-clad knight. He was missing the cape, but other than that single detail, every-thing about him said 'crusader' about as loudly as possi-ble. For a magical class, the Torch Bearer certainly looked ready for a melee. Or an outright war to reclaim the holy land from the Saracens. He was gruff and bearded, prob-ably in his forties, and a heavy steel helm sat on the desk next to a pair of scalloped gauntlets.

"Yes? I haven't much time. Out with it," he said. His eyes didn't bother to flick up more than once as he pre-pared to depart. Before I thought of an answer, the Torch Bearer slid back his chair and rose with a clanking of metal against metal. I'd seen armored knights at fairs and festi-vals before, and I knew how much the steel plates must have weighed. The tassets alone were probably close to fifty pounds. The grizzled man moved like they were silk or cotton, barely even noticeable.

I stepped to the side to let the man get to the door, his helmet and gauntlets carried easily beneath one arm. "I was interested in following Valiance," I finally told him, thinking that whatever training or initiation rituals they might have would get me close to a magical relic.

The man stopped at the door, regarded me for a few moments, then pulled it open with a sigh. "Enrollment isn't for another two months, son," the Torch Bearer said. A huge, heavy sword strapped to his side clanged against my knee as he passed out of the door. Sadly, he stopped a few steps down and waved for me to follow. I wouldn't get a free pass to roam around the rest of the lighthouse, it seemed.

Back in the main room, the old man had left, presumably to go watch the executions as well. The Torch Bearer pulled on his gauntlets and tightened the straps around his wrist. "Come back in two months if you want to join," he stated, pulling open the door.

Mr. Patches darted in between his legs, hissing loudly and scraping his sharp claws against the wooden floor. The Torch Bearer watched the cat for a brief second, frowned, and stepped into the street, holding the door for me to accompany him.

I saw my chance, slim as it was. "Come back here!" I shouted at Mr. Patches, though the cat hadn't gone far at all. The Torch Bearer was too far outside to see exactly where the little critter had gone, so pretending to chase him was my best bet. "I'll get him out of here. Just give me a minute!"

A heavy sigh came from the open door. Scooping up the cat in my arms, I ran up the stairs two at a time. "Almost got you!" I shouted to maintain the illusion.

The hinges of the upstairs office squeaked a little as I opened them. I hoped the Torch Bearer would assume the noise had been made by the feisty cat. My heart pounding in my chest, I ran to the other side of the desk and started ripping open drawers. The first two held parchment filled with swoopy, circular writing. The third contained a dagger resting on top of a couple other trinkets. Sadly, the pants I had been given at the farmhouse didn't have any pockets. Anything I stole would have to fit in the palm of my hand.

Pushing aside the dagger and a large ink well, a bit of glinting metal caught my eye. It was a circular medallion, kind of like the metal seals hikers could get at national parks and attach to their wooden walking sticks. The front of the coin was etched with fire, and I didn't bother rolling it over to check the back. Mr. Patches tucked neatly against my chest, I palmed the object against his fur, rather effectively concealing it.

As I made my hasty retreat, I noticed a few coils of the heavy chains I had seen before from the foyer. I guessed they had been finished, and they looked thick enough to moor a decent sized boat—out of place in the well-appointed office. I made a mental note to ask Bokta and Amethyst what they were for, and then I was down the stairs once again.

Mr. Patches licked my fingers. "Got him!" I announced.

The Torch Bearer shut the door behind me and locked it with an iron key he produced from a silk line under his breastplate. "You're going to the execution?" he asked, turning toward the square.

"Yes, sir," I answered. "Who are the people being hung?"

"You haven't heard?" the man replied, eyeing me from the corner of his vision. "My knights and the city guard routed a den of Oathbreakers last night. They'll hang soon, if we aren't already too late."

"That was a damn fast trial," I said with a bit of surprise.

The Torch Bearer shook his head. "Oathbreakers are afforded no trial. Where are you from?"

Shit. I had given myself away. I decided a bit of misdirection was in order. "How far across the Essant Sea have you gone?" I asked him. I made sure to pick up my pace a little. The square wasn't far, and I figured that when we reached it the Torch Bearer would have some important, official business to tend to, and he'd leave me alone.

"I have been to many cities along the Shimmering Coast, from Essence all the way to—"

"Thanks!" I loudly interrupted. "I need to catch up with my three brothers. I'll be back in a couple months to learn more!"

I pushed into the crowd as we turned the corner to the town square. In all the Torch Bearer's armor, the man couldn't ever hope to follow me, though I got the impression that he was happy to be rid of me. When I was sufficiently into the crowd to consider myself lost to the man's sight, I dropped Mr. Patches to the ground and began searching for Bokta and Amethyst.

The two women, disguised as they were, took me some time to locate. All the while, an important sounding bureaucrat droned on from the scaffolding, probably reading a litany of charges or something similar. Bokta and Amethyst were near the far edge of the crowd, leaning against a cart full of produce that had been stopped by the crowd on its way to the market.

"What's the plan?" I asked. I turned over the little coin in my hand. Opposite the side etched with fire was one bearing a book design. It made sense: fire for Torch Bearers and a book for Librarians. I had probably stolen a simple commemorative token, nothing more, but there was always a chance it was enchanted.

Bokta shook her head. "There is no plan."

"What?"

The nine prisoners were now naked, and half of them sported fresh lacerations down their backs. A hooded figure holding a whip paced back and forth behind them. Each man had a noose around his neck.

"Amethyst tried using some of her Siren abilities to seduce away a handful of the guards, but it turns out the one in charge of the lot isn't interested in her feminine charms," Bokta said with a sigh. "Either way, it doesn't matter. There's no time. Too many witnesses. Too many guards."

"We gave it a try. Now we must pray for the Desecrator to look upon their deaths with favor," Amethyst said, her arms crossed tightly over her chest. Her hood was pulled back just enough to let some of her hair fall out of it.

At the far end of the gallows, the Torch Bearer clanked his way up a short set of stairs, and the crowd applauded like crazy. They went wild. It was like the first time a singer stepped on stage at a huge concert—even though everyone in the audience knew exactly what they'd get, they still foamed at the mouth when it all began.

Lifting his hands into the air, the Torch Bearer quieted the crowd. He took off his helm, which he had only been wearing a couple seconds at most since he had walked all the way to the square before donning it, and the crowd went nuts again. Once more, the man lifted an arm, and the gathered mass quelled their furor.

"Is it always so rowdy?" I asked. Yelling and screaming at an execution felt a bit out of place, but then the people of Mara probably had very little in the way of cheap entertainment.

Bokta nodded. "When they're hanging one of us, it is always a raucous affair."

Something about the casual tone the woman used made me wonder about my choice of cult affiliation. "And how often are Oathbreakers hung in Mara?" I dared to ask.

"Not terribly often. Maybe one a year. But the knights like to pin the title on common thieves and outlaws to make themselves look more righteous. At least half of the people they claim are Oathbreakers are just regular criminals," she answered.

"Still . . . one a year feels like a lot," I said.

Bokta turned her attention back to the scaffold. The Torch Bearer was standing directly behind one of the condemned inmates. He gave the naked man a shove, and down he fell. The Oathbreaker appeared again underneath the scaffolding. His body didn't move.

One of the other men on the platform let out a scream, and that earned him two brutal lashes from the hooded fellow with the whip. Then another Oathbreaker fell. There was a snap, and the man was dead. I was *seriously* beginning to rethink my choice of gang. But I had seen too much of Oathbreaker society—I knew their secrets. Amethyst ran a crime family, small as it was rapidly dwindling, and soldiers were never afforded the luxury of leaving the mob at their leisure.

I made it through the first four hangings before turning my gaze. Instead of the queasy, nauseous feeling I'd experienced during and after the fights in the dungeon when we rescued Taros, all I felt was empty. Absolutely soulless. It was hard to tell, but the last man in line looked a bit like the crazy fighter we had sprung.

"Is Taros up there?" I asked quietly.

"Well, he's down now," the Blood Witch answered.

Again, all I felt was empty. A man I had sort of known and risked my life to save was dead not thirty feet in front of me.

The Torchbearer finally came to the last naked, quivering Oathbreaker. The crowd was in a deafening frenzy, eager for more death. A bunch of the people in the closest rows had been hurling all sorts of random objects at the prisoners as well. Part of a crumbled brick hit the last Oathbreaker in the chest, making the man scream in pain. That earned him another lash.

Finally, the armored leader of the lighthouse gave the

Oathbreaker a shove, and the spectacle came to a merciless end. Almost as eager to get on with their days as they had been to witness the executions, the crowd started to disperse. There was no ceremony. No decorum. No shred of humanity.

I had to remind myself that I was a bad guy. To them—to the people of Mara—they just watched their holy protector excise a scourge from their midst. Had I not been directly involved, I probably would have smiled too. I don't think I would have cheered and thrown things, but the dead men certainly would not have weighed heavily on my conscience.

"Well," Amethyst said, sounding defeated for the very first time. "Did you at least steal an enchanted relic?"

Mr. Patches climbed up the side of the merchant's cart to get out of the throng of moving boots exiting the square.

I turned my back to block the crowd's view, then showed the Siren my prize. She took the little coin in her hand, turned it over once, then tossed it back. "Well done! A Torch Bearer's seal of office is not something easily pilfered. And rest assured, it *is* enchanted, though barely."

Nice! For once I had managed not to fuck up the mission, though I had the sneaking suspicion that the woman was being sarcastic. "What's the enchantment?" I asked.

Bokta, looking over the other woman's shoulder, held her head in her hands. "The Torch Bearer always knows where it is. That's the magic. Now we're all going to die."

I reared back to chuck the token into the crowd as quickly as I could, but the Torch Bearer was only twenty or so feet away, moving slowly and clanking with every step. He knew I had stolen it. Hell, he'd probably known the moment I had come down the stairs, and he had just waited to get me to expose my allies.

Amethyst and Bokta started hurrying off in the opposite direction of the gallows, back toward the gatehouses where we had entered Mara. "You really fucked us now, Steve," Amethyst growled under her breath.

I could hear the Torch Bearer's armor clattering behind us. He was steady, implacable, and gaining ground as the three of us got bogged down in the crowd. About fifty feet ahead we came to a wider area, and most of the press of commoners headed toward the shops and other places, leaving the center of the street comparatively open.

"If we make our last stand, we have to do it here," I heard Amethyst say under her breath. Bokta nodded. Her hands were clenched tightly at her sides.

The Siren moved her brown robe aside to reveal her swords, both sheathed on the same hip.

"He's slower than we are," I practically pleaded. I barely had anything to weigh me down, not even a weapon, and the two women were athletic specimens. "Surely we can run!"

Bokta placed a heavy hand on my shoulder. "From a Librarian, you'd be right," she said.

"Torch Bearers excel at prison-like magic. We'll be snared in place the moment the battle begins. Trust me," Amethyst cut in.

I stole a glance back over my shoulder. Padding along about five paces behind us, Mr. Patches didn't appear to mind the impending slaughter. In fact, he bounced along rather cheerfully, his whiskers twitching side to side as he took in all the sights and smells of Mara's busy morning.

Behind Mr. Patches, three other armor-clad knights had fallen into step with their leader. The Torch Bearer had returned his helm to his head, and his huge sword had left its sheath. He walked with comfortable poise. The glint of his blade told me the three of us wouldn't be offered a short, minimally painful trip on a rope for our crimes.

"S-should we split up?" I asked. My voice quavered in my throat.

Bokta nodded, but she held four fingers up in front of her chest so the Valiance soldiers behind couldn't see. She ticked off a finger, and my heart rate accelerated rapidly.

Another finger went down but a moment later.

And another. Down to one. One second before all hell broke loose in the middle of the street. My heart throbbed so forcefully behind my ribs that any more stress would mean the Torch Bearer wouldn't have the honor of taking my life—I'd fall dead in the dirt.

Bokta made a fist. She was in the middle of our little trio, so she kept moving forward, though she sprang into a full sprint. Amethyst broke out left, also running full speed, and I scrambled to the right, pushing past a surprised woman carrying several loaves of steaming bread.

We didn't make it more than ten feet before the street came alive with magical yellow light. All at once I was rooted to the ground by golden shackles. I looked left, my eyes wide with panic. Bokta and Amethyst were both similarly caught.

The Torch Bearer motioned for his lackeys to spread out, forming a crescent of steel and death. It didn't take long for every civilian on the street to race for cover. Interested in more imminent bloodshed, they cowered behind wagons and underneath carts, fearing for their own safety only as much as they could maintain a decent view.

Amethyst let her robe fall to the ground and brought her two swords up in front of her. "Torch Bearer," she called. "Come closer. Let me get a better look at your face, would you?"

I felt my own feet lurch against my ethereal snares. There was magic behind the Siren's voice. Lots of it. One of the men to the Torch Bearer's side took a staggering step forward like a drunk attempting to follow a prostitute to an upper room. Unfortunately for us, his was the only step taken. The rest of the knights were steadfast, and the Torch Bearer himself stood still like a statute carved from granite.

"Ah, a Siren?" the leader called behind his metal helmet. He raised the visor. Maybe that was a good sign that the magic was working. Maybe it meant nothing.

Amethyst let her tunic fall gracefully off her left shoulder. She turned a little, still held fast by the shackles, and bit her lower lip. "Such a rugged man," she cooed. "Don't you want to go somewhere private? Somewhere discreet? I know a place . . ."

The Valiance soldier who had stumbled forward before came on again, and the Torch Bearer slapped him hard across his face with a gauntleted hand. The man winced, then stood erect at once, all the slavering lust gone from his posture.

Whatever magic Amethyst was weaving, it clearly had no effect on the hardened fighters.

Catsi, I thought, desperately offering a prayer, *Funen, if you'd like to play a trick, now would be the time*.

The soldiers began advancing. Just to be moving so effortlessly in so much heavy armor spoke volumes of the men's training and experience. We didn't stand a chance.

I clenched my fists in frustration. I didn't even have a sword or a dagger! I was the standing definition of helplessness.

Although . . .

My pants didn't have pockets, and I had left my cursed tourmaline die back at the farmhouse. But that's not how the curse worked, was it? The die had followed me. Just like Bokta had explained, the Eye of the Desecrator had made the journey into Mara on its own. I patted the top of my thigh, and there it was. The silk bag had been tucked neatly into the top of my pants, held in place by my belt.

I pulled the little tourmaline from its pouch and knelt down to the ground.

"Come on, you rat bastard," I whispered to the skull-etched faces, blowing on it for good luck like a craps player in a movie.

Staring Mr. Patches directly in his cute, narrow eyes, I gave the Eye of the Desecrator a roll.

CHAPTER 15

Five.

Five tiny, glistening skulls reflected the morning light in their black tourmaline shroud.

"Hell yes," I yelled, my feet still thoroughly planted in golden shackles. Five *had* to be a good result.

Bokta, the closest to me, stared in horror at the little bit of glistening stone. Her eyes were so wide they threatened to leap from her face. "What have you done?" she muttered.

"Don't worry, I didn't roll a one."

In the center of the street between the crescent of armored soldiers and us, their prey, Mr. Patches started to twitch. At first it wasn't anything unusual for a cat to be doing, just twitching his head side to side like he was following the flight of a bug he planned on snatching from the sky. But the twitching continued to grow and exaggerate. Soon Mr. Patches was swaying side to side, nearly spinning an entire circle with every movement. All the knights stopped their advance, their eyes fixated on the strange spectacle in front of them.

Mr. Patches began to grow. His brightly colored fur sloughed off in scraggly clumps, making him look more and more like his name until he was completely hairless. Before long, the once normal-sized house cat stood to the height of a mountain lion, and his transformation was not yet complete.

Popping and sizzling sounds filled the street. Mr. Patches continued to expand, rising up to a bipedal stature somewhat akin to a werewolf, but maybe a were . . . cat? His claws extended like those of a bear, then beyond that to a size completely unnatural. When he finally stopped growing, the hairless beast resembled half a giant cat and half a demon, sprouting huge horns from the top of its head. Most notably above all, Mr. Patches' face was twisted and contorted, and his eyes were sewn shut with heavy, blood splattered strips of leather thread.

"For Valiance!" the Torch Bearer shouted at the top of his lungs, though I could hear just a hint of fear in the man's voice. The rest of the soldiers had lowered their weapons.

Whatever the beast had become, it turned and looked at me. Right into my eyes.

"Uh . . . Attack!" I shouted, pointing at the Valiance soldiers closing in. Finally, the magical shackles holding me in place dissipated. I took a few steps back.

The beast-creature-thing followed me. "No!" I yelled at it. "Valiance! Bad! Attack them, not me!"

Mr. Patches cocked his head to the side.

"Come on! I rolled a five! I'm on your team!" If the thing took another step forward, I'd have to book it. But Mr. Patches was huge. His long, sinewy legs would outpace my untrained physique like Usain Bolt in a race against . . . well, in a race against me. I didn't stand a chance.

Slowly, his ragged tongue darting out of his torn and bloody mouth, Mr. Patches turned toward the Torch Bearer. He hissed. The sound was guttural and piercing at the same time as though it had come from two different throats.

Then Mr. Patches obeyed.

The creature lunged forward, skipping off its front paws before rearing back like a bear, and the battle erupted all at once. Everyone still left in the street began screaming, myself included.

One of the knights dove in front of the Torch Bearer and caught the full brunt of Mr. Patches' scything claws and goring horns. Metal screeched against whatever the demon-cat's protrusions were made of, and the knight fell. Watching the sudden outburst of such a thorough killing, I honestly felt bad for the poor knight. He'd been shorn in two, and it hadn't gone cleanly. Somehow, for some ungodly reason, the man continued to moan as his broken torso spouted blood all over the street. His legs were about ten feet away. Well, one of them was. The other was a bit farther than that.

Lifting his heavy sword high into the air, the Torch Bearer began casting, and an eruption of blinding light descended from the sky.

"Look away!" Amethyst yelled. She and Bokta both leapt toward the side, covering their faces with their hands.

The powerful blaze stung my eyes for a split second as I turned and dove. I hit the ground hard on my elbows. It felt like one of them had broken, but I had no way of knowing. All I could tell for certain was that it hurt. I wouldn't be fighting, not that I had planned on it in the first place.

The magical light was so bright and hot that it managed to sting the skin of my back through my shirt. It was like a roaring forge had been opened in the very center of the street, and the Torch Bearer's armor had been slid inside for recasting. I guessed that was how the class had earned their name. It made sense, after all.

More screeching ensued, and the light's intensity diminished greatly. I stole a glance over my shoulder. Mr. Patches had made quick work of a second Valiance man. The only remaining knight was the Torch Bearer himself, his sword still glowing and pulsing with violent magic, though not nearly as much as before. The last remaining knight must have fled. Good for him. Perhaps he'd live.

Offering a deep war cry, the stoic man swung and cleaved at Mr. Patches, but the visionless beast—completely unarmored and unencumbered—was faster. The cat-demon jaunted and spun, thrashing out with his claws, ripping chunks of steel from the Torch Bearer's body.

Another spell cascaded down from the heavens. A blanket of golden light carpeted the entire street, catching everyone within thirty feet of the Torch Bearer in a stinging, burning net. I had managed to scrabble away, but not far enough. The edge of the net caught my legs and feet. It burned. Hell, did it burn. Bokta wasn't so lucky. She was caught fully under the spell, and she shrieked in pain.

Amethyst ran to Bokta's side, a sword in her hand, and began hacking at the golden net. In the center of the street, Mr. Patches didn't have much trouble extricating himself. His horns and fangs tore through the magical material without slowing. The spell had given the Torch Bearer a handful of seconds, and in that time the man seemed to regain a good measure of his formidable composure.

Another spell issued forth from the Torch Bearer's

mouth. The man's sword erupted in dazzling light, and what remained of his heavy armor instantly turned deep red. Using two hands on his hilt, the Torch Bearer started swinging his weapon in huge, devastating arcs, marching forward after every sweep like an inexorable tide. He caught Mr. Patches' left haunch. The beast screamed, again with two juxtaposed voices, and stumbled backward as the net around its feet vanished.

"Oh, shit," I said, scrambling farther away down the street. Amethyst had Bokta on her feet, but the woman was barely supporting her own weight. Her back and legs had been badly burned. I could smell it lingering in the street.

"Run!" Amethyst shouted.

Yes, please. I ran as quickly as my battered body could move, my elbow throbbing with every step. Then a new howl joined the cacophony at my back. I turned for just a second—but I was clumsy. I crashed into a merchant's stall and fell over the terrified man cowering behind the counter.

Mr. Patches had loosed a bit of his own magic. A swarm of darkness—I couldn't tell if it was fog, a cloud of insects, or something else entirely—rose up from the cobblestones. It wrapped around the Torch Bearer, coalescing and oozing, coating the man's steel in inky black. Much to my dismay, the ink didn't last long. Whatever it was started to slip off almost as quickly as it had attached.

No, it wasn't slipping off . . . the Torch Bearer was lifting up from the ground. Like a helicopter steadily gaining altitude, the man continued to rise until I could see the bottoms of his leather boots beneath his steel greaves. Somewhat comically, Mr. Patches had to jump and leap to swipe at the man's feet. He managed to catch one of his claws into the side of the Torch Bearer's right greave, and then the two of them were slowly rising together.

"Holy shit . . ." was all I managed to mutter. The scene was beyond anything I'd ever imagined. Brilliant light drove down from above, connecting with the Torch Bearer's sword, and cascaded onto Mr. Patches' bald head. The light plunged through the magical darkness below, casting it aside with ease.

The cat-demon struggled to hold on. It looked bad for Mr. Patches. It looked really bad. But the Torch Bearer was losing a ton of blood as well. The man's breastplate had been shredded, and those long, nasty claws had shorn more than just metal. They had laid open the chest beneath. Given enough time, the wound would no doubt prove to be fatal. Sadly, it didn't appear that the Torch Bearer would succumb soon enough.

The knight's red armor flashed, and a halo of lightning swirled into existence above his head.

"He's ascending," Amethyst said. She and Bokta had stumbled over to the stall where I hid in order to use the counter to help support the Blood Witch's weight. Below us, the merchant just sobbed and wailed.

"What does that mean?" I shouted.

The Torch Bearer cleaved his sword down below his feet, and Mr. Patches fell to the ground. The cat-demon hadn't been torn clean apart like the knights scattered around the street, but the garish wound was close to going straight through from one shoulder to the next. I didn't know if some sort of unholy Desecrator magic would keep the beast alive or if that was it—the battle's conclusion.

Amethyst readjusted Bokta's weight and began shuffling away. "If he ascends quickly, he'll be gone forever. The Desecrator may still carry the day."

Victory felt about as unlikely as the Desecrator appearing in the flesh to finish the fight himself. Although, whatever Mr. Patches had become *was* pretty close, so maybe there was a chance?

The last shred of my hope vanished as the Torch Bearer cast again, flicking his sword from on high to produce a shower of devastating fire and lightning. Mr. Patches didn't get back up. Perhaps it was my connection to the little guy that cued me in. I knew he was dead. It was over.

We lost.

"Hurry," Amethyst bade. I followed behind her without complaint. "Hopefully he ascends quickly. He can't chase us if he's gone."

It sounded like good logic to me. We made it past another handful of merchant stalls and cowering civilians before another noise, a loud thundering rhythm, made us stop and turn.

The Torch Bearer was thirty feet above the ground, sheathed in glorious, translucent light. Honestly, the sight was so powerful that I instantly understood why so many online players had always chosen to become knights of Valiance. It made sense. The Desecrator had cool cut scenes, dramatic events at the end of quest chains, and over-the-top spell animations . . . but it all paled in comparison. The epic display hovering above the street was more than enough to make me stop in my tracks.

Then I saw what had created the thumping sound. A quartet of armored knights had arrived with some sort of machine. It worked on gears, and the heavy chain I had seen in the lighthouse was coiled on a huge, horizontal cog in the dead center. "What the . . ."

I didn't have time to ask any questions before their plan flickered to life in my mind. Two of the knights worked a long handle, and the chain shot outward into the sky. The end draped over the Torch Bearer's shoulder. Then a second chain took a similar flight, landing on the Torch Bearer's other shoulder, forming an X over the man's chest. Another pair of knights ran from the machine to the center of the street and used long poles to grab the ends of the chain.

"They're . . ." Amethyst gasped.

I finished her thought. "Chaining him to the ground. They won't let him ascend. They'll use him to hunt us. And kill us."

"We need to hurry," the woman growled.

I looped an arm around Bokta's back to take her left side, ignoring the brutal pain shooting up and down my own bones. I lifted, Bokta came off her feet, and we ran. We ran hard.

Behind us, the wheels and gears of the chain thrower, the ascending Torch Bearer's anchor to the very world, began to creak as they moved.

"For Valiance!" one of the knights bellowed.

The Torch Bearer's voice thundered from the sky: "Valiance! Scorch the impure from your world! Turn their bones to ash! Cleanse our world of sin!"

CHAPTER 16

I t felt like a miracle when we stumbled through the door of the safe house with no one on our tail. No giant, flying, magic-throwing Torch Bearer right on our heels. The cart and chain setup they had used to prevent the ascension had taken too long to get moving, and the Valiance soldiers had been keen on making sure their fallen brethren made it back to their lighthouse, letting us give them the slip in Mara's busy morning streets. Still, I knew for a fact it wouldn't be long before we saw them again. We had to get moving.

"So what the hell happened back there?" I asked. I was panting as I lowered Bokta to a seated position on one of the farmhouse chairs.

Amethyst grabbed a bottle from one of the cabinets and forced the Blood Witch to drink it. They had healing potions. Good to know.

"All of the Valiance leaders, all their best Torch Bearers,

Librarians, Monks, and Lightborn Ladies seek to achieve ascendance. If they kill enough followers of the Desecrator, their Underlord will lift them to the sky, and they'll be gone, presumably to join the Light Most Holy. I'd never seen it happen before . . ." the Siren explained. When Bokta had consumed the entire potion, it appeared as though she went to sleep, her sides and back more or less healed.

Amethyst collapsed into one of the other chairs and began untying her boots.

"And all the chains?" I asked. "What the hell was that?"

The woman looked forlorn. Actually, her face showed hopelessness more than anything else. "There is an old legend here . . ." she softly began. "An ancient, terrible legend. Valiance and Oathbreakers have always been enemies, right?"

Since that one expansion a couple years ago, sure. "Yeah, I get it."

"Well, the story goes that the Desecrator was the first Oathbreaker, originally a human. You know as much already. But what turned the Desecrator into a demon?" She pointed to the painting hanging on the wall.

"Huh. I don't know. I'd never thought about it before," I answered.

"The Oathbreaker rebelled against Valiance, and then *something* turned him into a demon. Something sewed shut his eyes. Something gave him horns." The woman's expression turned from sorrow to a new one I did not recognize. Hope? Disbelief? I wasn't sure.

"What does the legend say?" I prodded. I knew there was more to the story, even if it was just a myth after all.

Amethyst's eyes glossed over, and a bit of a smile played at the edges of her lips. "When the Desecrator broke his oath, he did not set out to become an Underlord himself.

He might have wanted a cult—or perhaps an army of followers—but he did not intend to be worshipped as the other Underlords are worshipped. That is why you found no shrines or altars under the biergarten. We do not hold services to praise the Desecrator's name. It is not how things are done. No, the first Oathbreaker *found* a new Underlord. The ninth Underlord. *That* is who turned him into a demon and gave him horns."

"Shit, that's not in the lore I know," I said. "But you don't praise the Desecrator's name . . . do you know what it is?" I had so many questions! If only I could have a single day without some huge threat looming over my head, I'd be able to sit down with Amethyst and drill her for information.

Online, the Desecrator was simply that. Valiance didn't have a name, either. They were just the two opposing factions. Good guys against bad guys, and that was all any of the players ever really cared about. It was a familiar struggle that everyone could instantly grasp.

"We do not use the name lightly, Steve," Amethyst began.

Please don't tell me his name is Maxkrannar. That'd be too much. All I could remember were the questions Bokta had originally thrown at me from every angle when I'd first been summoned. All the expectations. The hopes and dreams that I had so thoroughly crushed by simply not being a level ninety Oathbreaker demon named Maxkrannar.

"Some people say there is much power held in knowing someone's name, especially when it comes to magic," the Siren went on, her eyes narrowing as the mysteriousness of her words grew. Maybe 'Amethyst' was just a cover name so no one could use her true name to work some sort of evil on her. "If Valiance learns the true name of the

Desecrator, I do not know what would happen. Bad things, I'm sure."

"Could you tell me?" I asked.

Amethyst leaned forward and cupped a hand over the side of her mouth. Her breath was warm against my cheek. "He goes by two names, one that no one understands, and one that we do." Her eyes darted toward the door, then to a window. She was so nervous she actually began sweating along her scalp, her muscles twitching beneath her skin.

"Look, just write it down. In my peasant language so I can read it, ok?" I told her. Clearly, she was beyond unnerved. I half expected whispering the name to summon some unthinkable evil—Mr. Patches came to mind—like Beetlejuice, plaguing and haunting us all in the farmhouse until we died. Hell, maybe that would be a better way to go than being purged by the ascending Torch Bearer.

Amethyst nodded and stood. She got a scrap of parchment from one of the cabinets along with a taper candle and a firesteel. She lit the candle, then set about writing. Her hand moved slowly, obviously struggling to write in my version of English, and she had to stop frequently in order to remember the letters.

When she finished, she covered the name and looked me in the eyes, her expression serious. "I have written both of his names. As I said, I do not understand one of them. You may read them, then immediately burn the paper. It is the only way."

"Maybe I can help you figure out what it means," I offered.

Amethyst let out a long sigh, looked once more to the window, and slid the parchment my way. After so much hype, I almost didn't want to look. If the name wasn't something mind-shattering like Dolly Parton or Adolph

Hitler, if it turned out to just be something impossible to place like Al Jones, I'd be eternally disappointed.

Finally, I looked.

Brayden Applegate.

Strongwarrior43.

"Bokta says she has seen visions—"

"No!" I shouted, turning away. Amethyst snatched the parchment off the table and held it to the flame. It didn't take more than a few seconds to crumble into ash.

"Does the name mean something to you?" the woman asked.

"No, that's bullshit. There's no way that frat boy loser is the Desecrator."

"You know who he is?"

I sighed, then stood to walk around a bit and clear my head. "Yeah, he's a guy I know from work. Kind of an ass hat who still lives with his parents, but he's my friend. And that other name, the one with the numbers you don't understand: that's his character name. When he's in demon form, like when I am called Maxkrannar, that's what the other name means."

"You've met the Desecrator . . ." Amethyst said with awe. "Perhaps you really are the demon Bokta believes you to be."

"Hey, the Desecrator, or anyone like me going by the first name you wrote, they're not here in this world, are they?" I asked, suddenly wondering if Brayden was running around completing quests and grabbing gear, trying to beat me to the level cap. It would be just like him to progress faster than me and then rub it in my face.

Amethyst shook her head. "No, the Desecrator has not been seen in a long time. Hundreds of years. He's gone."

Hopefully she was right, for Brayden's sake if nothing

else. I didn't want one of my friends stuck here as well, though I knew if anyone would absolutely love it, Brayden was the guy. "And who's the ninth Underlord? Who did the Desecrator find that turned him into a badass demon? How'd all that go down?" I asked.

"As the story goes, the Desecrator did not break his oath in Mara, but he did live in Rowane. From there, once he was an exile, he traveled across the Essant Sea to the Shimmering Coast. From Essence, he wandered to a small town at the edge of the world whose name is lost to time. The Desecrator found the Underlord there and leveled the city, making a fortress for the Underlord—a grand temple of sorts, though larger than any puny Valiance lighthouse."

Amethyst seemed to genuinely enjoy explaining the history of her cult, and it was cool to take in all the lore from a real character's perspective. The story lined up decently with what I had known, though there were differences, of course. The differences felt more realistic than the game lore. Of course, if the Desecrator had been human, there had to have been someone who had transformed him into a demon, right? Why hadn't the game writers and devs ever put that into the story? Maybe they had been saving it for a different expansion.

"Does that fortress still exist?" I asked, my mind wandering back to the ascending Torch Bearer who was bound to be scouring Mara for our presence as we spoke. "Maybe we could hide there. Or recruit an army to take down Valiance and overthrow the Dread King. It sounds like a place where we'd pick up some more badass Oathbreakers."

"Citadel Deathgaze is a dangerous place. I'm not sure what is there, but everyone who speaks of seeing it says it is filled with only death. I do not know if going there would be wise," she answered.

Bokta was starting to stir from her magically induced slumber, but I barely noticed. Citadel Deathgaze had been the highest-level raid in Realm of Crafted War's last expansion. That had been the raid I was about to begin when Bokta had ripped me through my floor and wrecked my apartment.

"Correct me if I'm wrong, but the Underlord who lives in Citadel Deathgaze . . . his name's Tom Arnold, right?" I offered, my head in my hands. I could barely even believe the words as they came tumbling out of my mouth. Tom Arnold was a game designer at Snowstorm Entertainment. He was practically a legend among the MMO community, but most of that status was derived from his outright refusal to make appearances at conventions and other real-world Realm events. Now it all made sense. He didn't go to Comic-Con to talk to nerds like me each year with the rest of the devs because he was still *here*. He was trapped in Citadel Deathgaze without any way to get back home.

Amethyst nodded, helping Bokta to her feet at the same time. "He knows the ninth Underlord, Bokta. He even knows the Desecrator's true name."

Hanging onto Amethyst's arm for support, Bokta's eyes went wide. "I told you he was the one we wanted," she said with a smile.

Both of them looked at me, and it didn't take a genius to read their expressions. They beamed. Even if it had taken Amethyst a while to warm up to the idea, it was clear now that both women viewed me as their savior: the next Oathbreaker who would become a legendary demon. *That's why they've kept my useless ass along for so long. Any real Oathbreakers would have kicked me to the curb by now. Bokta had known all along, or she had guessed correctly, that I was like Brayden and Tom.*

Bokta stumbled over to a cabinet and pulled down some food from a shelf. She offered me a chunk of cheese that actually smelled pretty good. "Would you like us to escort you to Citadel Deathgaze so you may acquire your true demon form, my lord?"

'My lord' . . . *Not bad.* I let the honorific ring in my head for a few minutes as I ate some cheese. "Yeah. Let's go pay Uncle Tom a visit. I have a few questions for him."

CHAPTER 17

'd ditched the coin I had stolen back in Mara, so becoming a cool specialized class was no longer possible at the moment. Even so, the next quest was pretty clear. We needed a way to get to the Essant Sea—I still had no idea where that was—find a boat and a crew to take us across, and then figure out how to get to Citadel Deathgaze. Oh yeah, and we needed to make a point of *not dying* while we did it. The ascending Torch Bearer hadn't followed us out of Mara to the farmstead, but that didn't mean other Valiance followers hadn't seen us and reported our location. Information was limited. For all we knew, an outright army could be gathering at the lighthouse in Mara, ready to march on us by nightfall.

Without knowing for sure, we had to assume the worst. Bokta and Amethyst were busy gathering and securing supplies for the journey, and that left me basically on my own. I was still fairly banged up, but no broken bones meant I wouldn't be shot like a lame horse. I decided to do a little exploring around the safe house. Even though I was pretty much the definition of a homebody back on Earth, I still liked to take walks through quiet places every now and then to clear my head. After Amethyst's revelation, it felt like the right time for one of those walks.

The woods around the safe house started a little ways beyond the farmland, and it looked like all the Midwestern states you'd fly over going from one part of the country to another. Thick, old-growth trees wedged between farms with no roads or other buildings to be seen.

Alone in my solitude, my mind first wandered to all my friends back home. I didn't have many, but the friends who played Realm of Crafted War with me were close. We spoke pretty much every single day. A lot of people used to give me shit for playing a game so much—a *child's* game, they'd called it, sneers on their faces—but who else had a dedicated group of friends they talked to every single day? That kind of gamer social network had kept me going. Without them, my life would have been a meaningless shell of a miserable existence.

I wondered what all those guys were doing. Brayden, I knew, would be jealous as fuck. And what the hell was up with him being the original Oathbreaker? I knew he said he'd played the beta back before the game was ever launched, but he never mentioned starting any huge world events or anything like that. Then again, I'd never been too interested in the beta to ask the right questions. Hell, if I was being honest with myself, I had never really bothered to pay attention to Brayden when he had gone on his lengthy diatribes about the 'beta gameplay experience.' Maybe he had tried to explain it all to me, but I had been too stupid to listen. Either way, if I ever made it back to Earth, I planned on getting some answers.

And what about time? I'd slept in both Tamernil and Mara, so I knew beyond a doubt that I was not dreaming. I would not awaken in my bed and scramble out to work. So was time moving at the same rate back home? I'd watched a documentary once that had attempted to explain a bunch of Einstein's space theories to idiots like me. Maybe I was experiencing some sort of time dilation effect, and when I finally made it home, it would be like four seconds after I crushed my desk chair.

And thinking of home, of going back . . . At first, I think I had honestly enjoyed it here. Sure, taking a shit without running water sucked, but the rest of it? Not so bad. And hell, I'd even managed to get laid. Back home, no one would have ever believed a guy like me could get a girl like Amethyst. I wouldn't have believed it myself. Though I still wasn't sure *why* she liked me, other than being the supposed savior, of course. That little idea would have to be a subject for another day with Bokta.

I thought of the handful of girls I had dated on Earth. None of them had been terribly serious, mostly because I never had that much time for a relationship. And I never had time because I played too much Realm. Girls, for whatever reason, *hated* gaming. At least all the ones I had ever brought to my crummy apartment had hated it. If they wanted to talk about my life and interests at all, they'd been interested in my accounting job more than anything else. Granted, I would let them think what they would about my salary, and most of them assumed accountants made good money, but they had to figure it out when they got to my humble abode.

Thinking of my apartment made me wonder what happened to my floor when Bokta had sucked me through the portal. I'd pay all my gibs to see my landlord's expression

when he walked through the door. Portals . . . Doors . . .
with an army chasing us out of Mara, I finally felt like going back.

The fun was over. Sure, getting to Citadel Deathgaze
was bound to be an adventure in its own right, wrought
with plenty of entertaining and new experiences along the
way, but one of those new experiences was likely to be my
death. What would happen then? Would that be the key to
getting home? Maybe. Maybe not.

The only thing I really felt like I knew for sure was the
name of the man who would have the answers: Tom Arnold. I'd read his name about a billion times during login,
and he was a legend in the community and on the forums
for his reclusive nature. People always tried to take guesses
at his net worth. The game was huge, and the guy never
went out, so he presumably didn't spend any money, either. Whenever someone would ask the developer teams
at conventions about Uncle Tom, as he was affectionately
known for whatever reason, they would deflect or just
laugh it off. Never any straightforward answers from that
lot. None at all.

If I could find Tom across the Essant Sea, I'd get my
straightforward answers. I had no doubt of that.

Letting out a long sigh and rubbing my eyes with the
backs of my hands, I realized I didn't quite know where
I was. Checking behind, the farmhouse was out of sight.
I wasn't deep in the woods by any means, not more than
half a mile at the very most, but the notion of getting lost
was deeply troubling.

I turned around to head back, keen on turning *exactly*
enough to follow the correct path, when I noticed something else. There was a cat lounging on a low tree branch
not too far off. I walked closer, and there he was: Mr.

Patches. Thankfully, the little cat was back to normal size. I don't know what I would do had he still been in his demon form. Ha, that probably would have been the end right there.

"Hey, Mr. Patches," I said as I held my hand out for him to casually lick from his tree branch. His tongue was scaly and rough against my skin. I was a bit surprised that he hadn't changed at all as a result of his ridiculous transformation in the street. I kind of expected him to have horns or some other remnant left over. Instead, he was still the cute little house cat who had followed me around before. Oh well.

Apparently finished with my hand, Mr. Patches jumped down from the tree branch, issued a low meow, then began padding along the forest floor. He wasn't going toward the farmhouse, that was for sure. He led me on a winding path which he seemed to know well, and Patches even had the courtesy to stop every now and then and look over his shoulder. Being led into a strange forest was an odd sensation. I knew I should have just let the cat do whatever he wanted to do, but I kept the farmhouse direction on my left the entire time we walked, so I figured getting lost would at least be somewhat unlikely. I needed a compass, but no, that was the wrong tool. I needed a mini-map. Orienteering with a compass required skill. Checking a mini-map was right in my wheelhouse. Sadly, I had neither.

After about fifteen minutes of ducking under branches and scooting around prickly pine needles, we came to our destination. I wiped a sheen of sweat from my forehead, took a few deep breaths, and followed Mr. Patches into a small clearing marked by three stone slabs, each roughly the size of that easel paper teachers loved to write on in kindergarten.

Two of the stone tablets were vertical, and the third rested across the others, creating a makeshift hut or hovel. On the top was a ball of orange yarn. Mr. Patches hopped up on top of the slab and began batting the yarn back and forth.

"Alright, cat, what's the deal? What's your plan?" I asked.

Much to my dismay, Mr. Patches didn't respond. Looking around the rest of the small clearing, there was nothing else of note. The trees were like all the others, and the leaves under my shoes were no different either.

The little ball of yarn tumbled over the side of the table, and Mr. Patches issued an annoyed screech. "I got you, buddy," I said, bending over to grab the yarn.

The underside of the horizontal tablet on which Mr. Patches was contentedly perched was covered in writing. Some of it had been carved in circles like the complex writing Amethyst was so fond of, but other lines had been done in normal English.

Without lying on my back, I couldn't get a good enough look at the tablet to read it, so I shooed Mr. Patches back down to the forest floor and gave the stone a hefty push. It moved, but only a little. I heaved again, really digging my shoulder into it and giving it my all, and the top slab made a hideous noise as it slid from its place to thump into the dirt. Luckily, it landed with the writing face up.

Some of the letters were crusted over with dirt and grime. Digging out the detritus with a fingernail made me feel like a kid on a field trip to an old cemetery. If only I'd had a sheet of translucent paper and a couple crayons, I could have made a legible impression of the stone to take with me. Needless to say, I had none of the supplies—not even my phone to snap a quick picture.

Finally, when the tablet was more or less clean, I took a

step back to get a better look and take it all in. The first four lines were just circles. Trying to memorize them so I could recreate the message for Amethyst would be hopeless. At least I could read the rest, sloppy as it was:

```
       Property of Catsi and Funen,
        Feline Exemplars Extraordinaire
Shrine #34 of 90 - limited edition; erected
   on the fifth of July, month of the Jaguar
            And now, traveler:
   Scratch, scratch, a small wooden door—
      Hatch, hatch, a sudden, loud roar!
```

"What the hell is that shit?" I asked. Not surprisingly, Mr. Patches didn't reply. I read the riddle a couple more times in my head, making sure I committed it to memory in case it turned out to unlock some crazy epic loot room or something. With my luck, it would be some well-known children's rhyme, completely and utterly useless. But whatever. It was still kind of cool knowing I had found a shrine to the cat Underlords. And I was sure if cats on Earth had their way, they'd have some sort of ridiculous title as well. '*Feline Exemplars Extraordinaire*' was pretty cool.

Without much left to do and only a vague sense of where I needed to go in order to find my way back to the farmhouse, I turned back toward what I hoped was the right path. I tried to get Mr. Patches to follow me, but, in stereotypical feline fashion, he didn't really care. He sat next to the little shrine and cleaned his front paws with his rough tongue, a look of contentment on his little whiskered face.

"Fine, be like that," I told him before heading off.

CHAPTER 18

Leaving Mara was a little bittersweet. Mostly sweet since there was a half-ascended Torch Bearer looking to shove my bloody head onto a stake and parade it through the town, but still a little bitter, too. I had grown to appreciate the town during my short stay. It felt almost like home. Not 'home' in the Earth kind of way, but in a way that felt right for Realm. Online, there were seven major capital cities where everyone hung out when they weren't off on a raid or questing. It was where you'd find the most players and relevant NPCs, so everyone made it their daily hangout. Mine had been one of the lesser-used cities, a cool underwater capital introduced in the second expansion. Mara kind of felt like that. I had begun to think of the place as my resting point, my hangout during the downtime hours between dungeon runs.

The three of us stood on a dirt path that led east—a fact I knew only because it was still late morning, and we were walking directly toward the sun—and I looked back at the city of Mara one last time. I could have been mistaken, but I felt like there were more armored men standing around the road than there had been before. I almost expected a parade of steel-clad soldiers to emerge from the gatehouse, shouts and banners mingling with the breeze, and stampede toward us.

Thankfully, the morning was peaceful. We trudged away, each of us carrying a pack of supplies. The design of the common backpack hadn't quite been figured out yet, so our gear had been lumped together without much thought given to organization, and the sacks had the barest of rudimentary shoulder straps. Only ten minutes into the walk, my shoulders and neck were already letting me know how upset they were.

Amethyst took point, staying about twenty feet ahead on the trail just in case the Valiance losers had decided to set up a waypoint or something to keep us from fleeing. She was the fastest, so she'd be the best lookout. Still, I really didn't think it would matter. If we saw a Valiance outpost waiting to capture us, that would mean they had already seen us, and we'd be run down by their mounted knights for sure.

Regardless of our impending doom, I still had so many questions. Honestly, it was hard to figure out where to begin. Watching Amethyst's backside walking in front of us, I decided she would be a good a place to begin.

"Have you two known each other long?" I asked the Blood Witch at my side.

Bokta smiled, though it looked forced. The two women hadn't spoken much at all since the fight in the streets. I assumed their coldness was largely a result of something I wasn't privy to, but that wasn't how women worked. Even I knew that. When three people spent all their time together and only one was a dude, *that* was the conflict. Always.

"She took me in when my parents kicked me out of my home," Bokta answered.

Seemed reasonable enough. "How long ago was that?" I asked. Guessing at her age, I figured she had to be no older than thirty, maybe thirty-two. Though to be fair, I had always been a bad judge of age.

Bokta thought a moment before answering. "It has been nine years," she replied. "Ten years this winter. It doesn't feel that long . . ."

"And Amethyst kind of trained you and taught you how to be an Oathbreaker, right?" I went on.

She nodded. "As a Siren, most of her skills revolve around interacting with other people. Seduction, influence, assassination, persuasion—those sorts of things. She was a good mentor, and she commanded respect."

Well, one of those things wasn't quite like the others! And the way Bokta had just casually thrown in 'assassination' sent a shiver down my spine. I knew they were both dangerous, but Amethyst had an air of unpredictable ruthlessness to her that I didn't really like.

"Anything I should know about her? Any tips to stay on her good side?" I asked, hoping for some inside secrets that would help me stay alive.

Bokta glowered and shot me a sidelong glance that caught me off guard. "Never sleep with a Siren, Maxkrannar," she stated flatly.

For about the millionth time since I had arrived in Realm, I silently cursed myself for being an idiot. Of course you weren't supposed to sleep with a Siren. That was basically an entire trope from classical literature. I didn't remember all the details too well, but I knew one of the heroes from the old stories had been duped by a Siren, or whatever the classical equivalent was, and had spent a decade on an island eating leaves. At least that was all I could recall from reading the Wikipedia page in order to pass my quizzes in high school.

"So . . . what's the deal with sleeping with Sirens?" I tentatively asked.

Again, another sidelong glance shot daggers through me. "Sirens are all about control. They seduce, they persuade, and then they control—assuming they don't just kill you outright first, of course. What greater control is there than sex?"

Damn if she didn't have a point. And I wasn't particularly adept at resisting attractive women, either. Obviously. "Amethyst doesn't have any kind of . . . magic . . . when she . . . you know, sleeps with someone, does she? Like, all the control stuff is just normal, human charisma and influence at work, right? Nothing more?"

A stifled laugh told me I was wrong. Wonderful. "No, Maxkrannar. It is not so simple."

Bokta already knew I had slept with the Siren. No use trying to pussyfoot around it. "How bad is it? Am I screwed?" I asked with a sigh. Ha, technically I *had* been screwed.

"Just wait for the next time she tells you to do something that you do not want to do," Bokta explained. "It will be hard to refuse her. Impossible, perhaps. She has a hold over you that you will find difficult to shake."

"And it only takes one time?"

"Only once," Bokta confirmed. "In fact, subsequent encounters would weaken the effect."

Wasn't that just the icing on the shit cake . . . Not only had I been easily ensnared and essentially mind-controlled, but there weren't even any ancillary benefits. It was like a one-night stand where all I got was herpes and then never saw the chick again. Not saying that scenario had ever happened on Earth, of course. Though . . . Brayden couldn't say the same. Pretty frat boys like him were bound to catch a little itch every now and then.

It took a few hours to reach the next town. Well, it wasn't really a town, more of an outpost with a dozen or so buildings and a large inn off to the side, but it was the first bit of civilization that we had seen since leaving Mara. Amethyst explained that the small village was just a way-point between Mara and Crimson Sands, the next major city on our path toward the coast. A few farms surrounded the outskirts of the waypoint, and they had a well in the center of the street where two older men were busy filling a row of buckets at their feet.

"We won't stay long," Amethyst said. She told us to wait on the other side of town as she went into the general store, the only place of commerce other than the inn, and bought some supplies for the longer journey ahead. Apparently, the distance from the waypoint to Crimson Sands was long. It would take us three days to walk. I thought of my gut and the longest distance I had ever traversed on foot: a six-mile hike back in high school that had nearly been my end. A three-day trek across the countryside to Crimson Sands would be a hell of a lot longer than six measly miles.

Amethyst only took a few minutes in the general store before rejoining us. She had plenty of fresh food and a couple extra waterskins which she loaded in our various packs. Mine was really starting to feel heavy. I didn't think it looked any more weighty than the other two carried by the women, but I was weak compared to them. Compared to almost everyone, actually. A grimace on my face, I hefted my bag and made myself a silent vow to treat the journey as exercise. I needed to erase some of the pudge around my waist if I was going to survive in Realm. A little muscle on my arms wouldn't hurt either.

Without any fanfare or pretense, we set out on our three-day walk to Crimson Sands. As we went, the landscape slowly shifted from deciduous forest to something more befitting the name 'Crimson Sands.' The trees became smaller and smaller until they were only scrub and thorny bushes surrounded by rocky soil and broken boulders. By nightfall, I was beginning to worry that we hadn't brought any tents.

"What's the plan for sleeping?" I asked the others once the sun had finally fallen behind the horizon.

Bokta shrugged. "We will find some rocks to hide us from the path, though we have not seen a single person all day. Not many people take this route."

"Yeah, rocks sound good, but what about sleeping? Do we have tents or something?" I asked. "And why hasn't anyone else been on the road?"

Amethyst still walked a good deal in front of us, but she heard me nonetheless and turned to answer. "We won't sleep long, just enough to get our energy up for tomorrow. The sooner we put some distance between us and Mara, the better," she said.

"Alright, I get that, but *what are we sleeping on?*" I felt like I was begging for an answer. Neither of them seemed to really get it. We didn't have sleeping bags, maybe not even blankets, and we certainly hadn't rented a cabin in the middle of the prairie.

Both women looked confused. Finally, Bokta pointed to the ground. "We'll sleep on the dirt," she said, confirming my fear. "Use your pack to rest your head. Then we leave again at dawn. But we still have a couple hours left before it really gets dark."

I sighed and readjusted the weight on my shoulders. The unrefined straps had dug into my skin, and I knew there would be bruises underneath them. I only hoped that after two more days the bruises wouldn't turn to outright bloody cuts. I didn't piss off the entire Valiance organization just to die of an infection.

We arrived at Crimson Sands not long after dawn on the third day, our feet tired and dirty. More than anything, my shoulders felt like they had carried a couple boulders for a thousand-mile journey. If any other part of our trip to Citadel Deathgaze would require an overland trudging like the one we had just completed, I was determined to spend some of our gibs on proper backpacks and footwear. Or maybe Bokta would be able to learn a spell at some point to ease the struggle of traveling whilst out of shape. Something to summon one of the moving sidewalks from an airport would be fantastic.

The town itself sat on the edge of the sea, an oasis surrounded by glittering red sand on three sides. There weren't many farms, at least as far as I could tell, but the port absolutely brimmed with activity. From our vantage point on the elevated road leading into Crimson Sands, we could see at least a hundred sails poking little white holes in the horizon. Whatever it was that the town had found to trade for food with the other cities along the Essant Sea, business was booming. Sadly, my excitement waned a bit as my gaze found what was likely the tallest structure in the entire city: a big lighthouse built onto a rocky arm that reached into the harbor like a giant giving every ship a hug at the same time.

"So Valiance is here too?" I asked, trying to keep the fear from my voice.

Bokta nodded. "They're everywhere. But if messengers had been dispatched from Mara, we would have seen them on the road. They would have been behind us."

"Or they still are behind us," I said. "We need to get out of here as quickly as possible."

Both women nodded, and I saw Amethyst steal a quick look back in the direction we had come. It was clear that if the ascending Torch Bearer caught up to us, the fight wouldn't last long. The tourmaline die tucked into my waistband didn't give me much comfort. Neither did Mr. Patches circling around my feet.

As we walked down the final stretch of the hardened path, I replayed the cat riddle I had found, trying again in vain to decipher its meaning. Perhaps there would be more cat shrines in Crimson Sands, and perhaps they would shed some light on the cryptic words. More likely than not, any additional shrines I managed to find would probably end up convoluting the riddle even more. Hopefully we wouldn't spend enough time in the brutally hot oasis for me even to find another shrine. I wanted to be gone before nightfall.

Crimson Sands didn't sport any gate or walls, and no guard towers stood watch over the landward approach, either. "Not a lot of people coming in from Mara, it seems," I said, noticing for the first time that the path we had taken had truly been deserted.

"In the fall, great storms of sand have been known to bury entire caravans coming from the west. It is not a safe way to travel," Amethyst told me. She had her shirt rolled up to the top half of her torso, letting her toned abs soak in the brilliant sun.

Sand storms sounded pretty brutal. Perhaps it was the bloody hue of the granules themselves, but I felt like a storm near Crimson Sands would be a lot worse than any back on Earth. "Hey, what season is it, anyway?" In all the time I'd spent here in Realm, I'd never bothered to ask about the time of year.

"Is it this hot in winter where you come from?" Bokta asked in response.

"So it's summer, then?"

She nodded. I felt like an idiot. Nothing ever changes.

"What's our plan in town?" I asked after a moment, grateful to change the subject.

Amethyst pointed east in the direction of the huge docks and warehouses lining the coast. "I'll get us a boat. Passage across the Essant Sea shouldn't be too . . . *difficult* to secure, I think." As she spoke, it looked like she took on an aura of some sort—maybe it was Siren magic—instantly expelling the visible fatigue from her body and adopting a devilish smile that grabbed my eyes and wouldn't let them pull away.

Before I could further embarrass myself, Bokta grabbed me by the shoulder and turned me away toward another street. "I'll get us some food and water for the trip," she said, dropping a handful of gibs into my hand. "You should see if you can find something worthy enough to leave at a shrine to the Shipwright for good luck on the crossing. Nothing too extravagant—we need to save some money."

I took the gibs and turned over my pack to Bokta, thankful to have the weight off my shoulders though at least a little nervous about exploring a new town all on my own. Things hadn't gone well in Mara by any means. I couldn't possibly fathom what made the women so confident that I wouldn't fuck things up here in Crimson Sands. Maybe they really did still view me as some sort of savior, clumsy though I was. It was the only explanation that made sense.

Once we agreed on a meeting place down by the docks and an ambiguous time to be there, Bokta pointed me in the direction of the coastline. Close to the heart of the sprawling desert city, the streets had been built up with boardwalks to protect travelers from the incessant red sand, and it was nice to feel something solid beneath my feet.

By my guess, Crimson Sands was larger than Mara by at least twice. Streets lined with wooden buildings spread out from the coast like half of an enormous pinwheel sprouting out of the ocean waves. Down every street, tall palm trees swayed in a gentle, salty breeze. The whole place reminded me of a vacation I had taken to Miami when I had been little, but without all the rushing people, ridiculously expensive cars racing between red lights, and sleazy club promoters standing on the streets. So it was basically a better Miami. Much better.

First on the agenda was to acquire an artifact that would be worthy enough to leave as an offering to the Shipwright. I had thirteen gibs to my name, a cursed die, and a terribly persistent cat. Not much to work with by any means.

For whatever reason, Crimson Sands had never been planned, and it looked like their governmental body had never taken an interest in building distinct districts to organize their commerce. There was no town square full of traders' stalls, but instead the merchants and mongers were dispersed throughout the entire city, intermingled with houses, public areas, baths, tall buildings that looked official, and noisy taverns full of sailors. The first shop I walked by that looked interesting was full of nautical implements, and something of that nature felt like it would be fitting to leave on one of the Shipwright's altars, so I pushed aside the curtain hanging over the entryway and ducked inside.

Everything from sea chests to large ship wheels and various coils of ropes hung from the walls. The shelves in the center of the room were stacked mostly with clear, cylindrical jars of tobacco and other sweet smelling plants I couldn't readily identify. I only had the idea that everything in the jars was smokable on account of the rows of meerschaum pipes taking up the highest shelves.

Behind the store's counter, a withered husk of a man sat with a book in one hand and a finely crafted pipe in the other. Well, it wasn't exactly a book in the sense I was used to. It was more a collection of loosely held together cuts of parchment—all different sizes—bound with a heavy thread and two pieces of leather. Regardless of the book's quality, I was kind of impressed that the man could read. His eyes looked a little hazy, and the way he sat so motionless on his chair made him almost appear dead.

"Hey," I began, waving and approaching the counter. Behind me, Mr. Patches was busy stretching his claws against the side of one of the shelves.

The old merchant didn't look up from whatever it was that had him so engrossed.

. . . or maybe he *was* dead.

"Hey? You in there?" I said a little louder.

Finally, the man huffed and turned the page, then set his book down on the counter with the pages facing upward. Rather expertly drawn across both sides of the parchment was a topless mermaid, her bronze hair fluttering off one shoulder, her perky nipples pointing right up into the air.

"Sorry to interrupt your . . . book," I said. I looked away, pretending to be inspecting one of the ship wheels mounted behind the counter next to a couple sailcloth patches.

The old man clicked his teeth together and fixed one of his cloudy eyes right on me. "What do you want?"

"Uh, I'm just looking for something to take to the Shipwright. Any recommendations?"

Pushing aside his book, the man leaned forward over the counter, his long beard dragging across the weathered wood.

"Can't just buy something and throw it on an altar, son. Learn some respect."

I guess I could have seen that coming. An old-timey sailor would probably demand that I go out and slay a white whale with my bare hands just by way of an apology for insulting his old-timey sensibilities. Still, I couldn't just leave empty-handed without at least giving it one more try. "Have any suggestions? I'm new here," I said.

Again, that foggy eye seemed to bore into my soul, leering in a way that only a truly ancient, grumpy old man could make it leer. "Have to earn the Shipwright's favor, idiot. Risk something. That's what every sailor does when they go out on the waves. They risk it all. That's what the Shipwright wants."

That, at least, was some useful information. "And it doesn't have to be something sailing related?" I asked, a bit of a plan actually starting to come together in my mind.

The man collapsed back to his chair with a snort and picked up his book. "Does the sea only take the sailing parts of a ship when it claims one for the Shipwright?" he barked.

"Fair point," I replied.

Without giving me a second look, the old man tipped his head back down to the naked mermaid. Trying to be polite, I spent a few more minutes casually browsing the nautical relics before leaving the store.

Outside once more, I knew where I was headed. I needed to risk something, but more importantly, I still needed to steal a relic from Valiance.

For the first time since arriving in Realm, I felt like I had a clear purpose. I was determined. No more hapless jaunting from town to town only a step ahead of disaster.

Before I left Crimson Sands, I would become a Sovereign Magus, one of the Desecrator's chosen.

CHAPTER 19

One thing was for sure: Crimson Sands was hot as hell. The sun beat down relentlessly. Even with the gentle ocean breeze floating off the Essant Sea, the heat was oppressive and unavoidable. Wiping a layer of sweat from my head and flicking it down to the boardwalk, I scanned the skyline for my target. It wasn't hard to find. The Valiance lighthouse stood in the harbor on a little rocky outcropping connected to the city by a line of jagged boulders that would be hard to traverse. And that's exactly where I went.

It turned out that the Valiance people had trampled a little pathway of sorts into the tops of the natural break wall extending to their lighthouse, so it wasn't quite as tricky to cross as I had originally anticipated. The door looked a lot like the one on the lighthouse in Mara. The complete lack of ornamentation was a little off-putting. It made Valiance seem even more confident—as if banners, pennants, and all the other standard temple decoration were beneath them.

Unfortunately, the door was shut. I needed a plan before brazenly knocking and trying to talk myself through a theft—my last attempt via that method hadn't exactly gone well.

Before I made my move, I needed information. And I didn't have much time to gather it.

With the nature of the path leading to the structure, there were certainly plenty of places to hide along the shoreline. I didn't know about the tides in Crimson Sands, but I also didn't plan on wiggling myself down into a crevasse for very long, so it hopefully wouldn't matter anyways. Right as I began to ease myself down the side of the path to a spot that would afford me a decent view of the lighthouse without being seen, the door creaked open, making my heart stop in my chest. My foot slipped as I turned and got wedged between two stones maybe an inch above the lapping waves. Great. I looked like an idiot. And I *clearly* looked like I was up to no good.

The man who exited the lighthouse—thank my lucky stars—did not carry himself with the easy poise and confidence of someone who was used to being in charge. In fact, he looked younger than I was, maybe eighteen at the most. Perhaps that was a good thing.

"What—"

"Can you help me out here?" I asked, cutting him off in as friendly a way as I knew how. I reached out my hand like I had just tripped, and the guy was eager to hoist me back onto the path.

"The rocks are slippery, have to take them slow," the man said.

I nodded and smiled. "Yeah, thanks," I said. "Hey, are you an initiate with Valiance?"

The man returned my smile tenfold like a door-to-door missionary who had just found the long lost member of his flock. "That's right! I'm Rhone. I only joined a couple weeks ago. You're looking to enter Valiance as well?"

Well, it felt like the best plan I'd get. "I'm thinking about it," I replied. Rhone beamed back, his effervescent smile already skirting the border of extreme annoyance. In a way, he kind of reminded me of Brayden at work. Always bubbly and cheerful no matter what kind of shit work was being dumped on him.

"I'll take you in and introduce you to the rest of the house," Rhone went on.

I had to grab his arm to keep him from barging right back in through the front door. "Think I could just ask you some questions? I'm . . . nervous, I guess," I said.

"Oh, that sounds great! I'm on my way to the scrivener to pick up a handful of scrolls. There's a wonderful little tea garden right next to the scrivener. I'd love to take you there and answer your questions!" Rhone already had an arm around my shoulder like we were long-time lacrosse buddies meeting up at our ten-year reunion.

I shrugged away from the eager guy's mitts, heading back toward the town, and he was more than happy to follow. "Let's see the tea place!"

Rhone kept going on and on as we traversed the slick stone path back to the shore. In all honesty, I didn't really pay attention. His voice had just enough persistent monotony to fade into the sounds of the Essant Sea. When we reached the shore, he was still yapping about the merits of joining Valiance and how happy I'd be once I signed my life over to them. He happily took the lead through the streets, his head constantly turned to the side to make sure I didn't miss a word, and he even waited for me to catch up to him, effectively thwarting my attempt to hang back and kill the conversation.

Some incalculable amount of time passed as we traversed the wooden boardwalks toward the tea shop. Mr. Patches had met up with us on the shore, and he dutifully followed at my heels, his orange and white hair now flecked with a sprinkling of red sand. Finally, Rhone had to take a break from his latest boring story in order to switch gears into a Crimson Sands tour guide, pointing out all the antique architecture of the town's premier tea garden. Or maybe it was just his favorite place. I only caught about a third of what he was saying.

No matter which famous designer had hand-carved the store's façade, I did have to admit that it was a pretty cool place. Tall palm trees anchored the five corners of the garden like the points of a pentagon. Between the trunks, an intricate latticework of carved wood and reeds formed the walls. Delicate silks like those that had adorned the dice merchant's stall in Mara wove themselves into a roof of sorts from the high ends of the palms. I guessed, being a desert and all, that Crimson Sands didn't see much rain, so a real roof wasn't necessary.

Inside the rather serene setting were a few low tables, cushions upon which to sit at them, and several differently colored tea services awaiting patrons. The only other guests were a group of four rat men, instantly reminding me of the one I had killed back in Tamernil. I felt bad for the little creatures. Of course, there was a pretty obscure chance that the rats sitting on their cushions a few feet from us would have known the rats in Tamernil, but it still felt shitty to know that I had murdered one of them.

I pulled my attention back to more relevant tasks as a server approached our table. She was a slight woman dressed in silks similar to the store's décor, and her raven-black hair was done in two braids that fell down her back to the top of her ass.

"Do you have a preference for tea, masters?" the woman quietly asked.

Being referred to as a 'master' had a certain ring to it that I enjoyed. Lost in my own thoughts for a moment, Rhone was left to order our tea, and I didn't really care. I had never been a big tea drinker back on Earth. And come to think of it, a cup of hot tea actually seemed like a horrible idea considering the outrageously hot sun beating down on our necks through the silk overhead. Who drinks tea in the desert?

When the server was gone, Rhone scooted his little cushion closer to the table and leaned over, obviously eager to regale me with more of his incessant yammering.

I listened patiently as he carried on, or rather I daydreamed about the waitress' curves while occasionally nodding, and Rhone didn't seem to notice. Finally, the man's story came to a merciful conclusion as the woman returned with a porcelain tea service for two. She set the platter down, bending over to offer me a generous view beneath her silken shirt in the process, then offered a gentle curtsy before departing.

I reached for my cup, but Rhone stopped me. "No, no, not like that!" he interrupted.

"Uh, what do you mean?"

He took his own cup gingerly by the handle, letting only two of his fingers touch the white porcelain. "You have to take it lightly, to not let your skin touch the cup," he explained with a voice that betrayed how upset my faux-pas had made him.

"Won't my skin have to touch it when I take a drink?" I

asked. Apparently drinking tea in Crimson Sands was serious business. I watched the rats at the other table enjoying theirs. Lo and behold, they were barely grasping the little cups, then tilting them back an inch or so above their mouths, seemingly to avoid further contact.

Rhone shook his head and demonstrated the proper tea-drinking etiquette. I followed suit, though a bit of apprehension made my hand shake as I tilted the cup, and a little splash of tea found my chin instead of my mouth.

For all of Rhone's jabbering and generally annoying cheerfulness, the tea was truly exquisite. Much to my delight, it wasn't hot, either. It was stingingly cold, like mint and menthol flavors had produced a tea-flavored offspring, and that child had been cold-brewed and served over ice. "Actually, this stuff is great. Good choice," I said, lowering my cup back to the table. I didn't want to down the whole thing in one go.

Rhone beamed. "The best tea in all of Crimson Sands," he said. "Now, you can't get tea like this inside the lighthouse."

"Ah, speaking of Valiance, do they give you any sort of trinkets or amulets to mark you as an initiate?" I asked, hoping to get my mission back on its tracks.

"What do you mean?" Rhone replied between delicate sips.

"I was just wondering if there's anything that tells other people that you've joined. You know, so other people could see and then ask me about it as well?" I hoped the ploy was good enough to get him to reveal an artifact, something that I could steal later to offer to both the Shipwright and the Desecrator at the same time. Maybe I was nuts, but it felt like a solid plan.

Sadly, Rhone shook his head. "Only the Torch Bearers

get a seal of office," he explained. "The rest of us get to show our devotion to Valiance through the honor with which we live our lives every single day."

Great. I couldn't very well steal his 'honor' and sacrifice that . . .

Or . . . could I? The seeds of a new plan began to worm their way into the soil of my mind. It took a conscious effort to keep my mind at least partially focused on the rest of the conversation throughout the remainder of our stay at the tea garden. The pretty serving girl came back a handful of times, once refilling our tea pot, and then Rhone paid her a handful of gibs before we left.

"Hey, one quick thing before we go back to the light-house," I said as innocuously as I could.

"What is it you need?" the man happily asked.

Nervously, I scratched the back of my neck and looked away. "Where's the nearest temple to the Shipwright?"

"Why would you want to go there?" Rhone said in what I guessed was as close as his cheery voice ever got to a scoff.

"Oh, that was my old deity," I explained, not really knowing the right words to use. "I'd like to pay him one last visit before I convert."

The man nodded happily, then waved me along as he bounded toward the harbor. "There are two temples to the Shipwright, one not far off," he said.

"Perfect." Mr. Patches followed at my side, occasionally diverting his course to investigate a bug or a bird which had landed to hop around in search of a grubby meal.

"You worked on ships in the past?" the man asked me.

Why not? "Yeah, sure," I said. "I was the lookout on a huge ship. Maybe you have heard of it: *The Titanic*. It was pretty cool. We had an artist on board and everything. Lots of pretty girls, too. Some French ones, believe it or not."

"The life of a sailor is often wrought with peril. What happened to your ship?" Rhone had slowed his roll a bit in order to fall into step at my side.

"Wrought with peril is correct," I said. "The ship went down. Not too many survivors, but a handful of us made it back to land. Poor Jack . . . He didn't make it." We were nearing Crimson Sands' extensive system of docks and wharfs. Some of the ships had three or four masts, and they looked like Spanish galleons from old history books, alive with ropes and tackle, sails and sailors covering the decks.

"Well, you won't have to worry about drowning with Valiance," Rhone told me, a smug expression on his face.

"Yeah, I think you're right."

At last, a fresh layer of sweat covering my body—and covering the other layers of sweat that had already accumulated on my swampy skin—we arrived in front of a small temple to the Shipwright. It wasn't really a temple, not in the traditional Realm of Crafted War sense, but rather a shack about the size of a jail cell perched dangerously on the edge of the lapping tide. There was another sailor inside when we arrived, so we got to wait on the shore for a while until the man left. I was starting to get nervous. I didn't know what time it was, and I kind of had the feeling that my 'sacrifice' wouldn't be the fastest thing on the planet.

The inside of the Shipwright's temple was a little different than I had expected. There wasn't an altar or anything like that. Just a wooden hut with bare walls, and half of the floor was missing to reveal the frothy ocean surface underneath. Barnacles covered everything.

"Well, time to say your goodbyes," Rhone said with a sigh.

"Yeah, not a bad way to put it."

Pretending to be absorbed in sentimental memories of a life spent on the sea, I lingered toward the back of the little shack. As planned, Rhone stepped forward up to the water's edge with a disinterested frown tugging at the sides of his near-permanent smile.

In all my years on Earth, I'd never sucker punched anyone. I'd never really *punched* anyone at all, come to think of it. I had been decidedly anti-confrontational. Thinking about the half-ascended Torch Bearer on my tail—wielding magical powers that I would never be able to withstand—made the first punch come pretty easily. I needed a sacrifice if I wanted to power up. And the old man at the nautical shop had told me I needed to take a risk in order to earn the Shipwright's favor.

Rhone, to his credit, kept his balance fairly well after my fist crashed into the back of his skull. When the second hit fell, he let out a yelp and splashed into the water. The ocean in the little temple wasn't deep, so he didn't sink to the bottom and make my grim job any easier. There were, however, lots of large, jagged rocks to keep him from getting his balance and quickly scrambling back to safety.

Bracing myself against the tight walls, I kicked as hard as I could. My foot connected with Rhone's nose. The man slumped back into the ocean, a stream of profanities intermingling with the splashing water. The temple was like a small ice-fishing shack on a frozen lake. The far wall hung down low to the water's edge, and the large boulders making up the shoreline prevented all but the skinniest of people from hoping to swim out to deeper water and safety. The only thing that Rhone could do was struggle to pull himself back into the temple.

All I had to do was continue to kick him every time he got close to extrication. Before long, I knew Rhone's nose was broken. I think I had dislodged a couple of his teeth as well. He was struggling to breathe, likely beginning to truly fatigue as well, and each time his head bobbed under the surface lasted longer than the previous one.

"Why—" he gasped, spitting salt water on my boots.

"Take this annoying dude, Shipwright!" I yelled. I landed another kick to the top of the drowning man's head. "And to the Oathbreaker, I give you whatever Valiance points this guy is worth! Make me a Sovereign Magus!"

Rhone's eyes filled with terror—well, with *more* terror.

The man mounted one last desperate attempt to rid himself of the bloody, briny waters. He screamed, blood and snot running down his battered face, and clawed hand over hand at the stones. I jumped. My foot landed right on one of his hands, crushing the delicate little bones against the jagged surface underneath.

That did it. All the fight left in his body fled. His hand was probably broken in a couple places. There would be no escape. The barnacles were pretty sharp too, and they had done some extreme work.

"Come on, Oathbreaker! Desecrator! Brayden! Give me some awesome skills!"

Rhone drifted back a little, the constant waves splashing over his face and mouth, and cried. His bloody head tapped against the back wall of the shrine. He'd die—probably—but it would take some time. Watching my step to make sure I didn't lose my balance, I got into the water with him. The waves came up over my knees by about a foot.

Rhone was too beaten to fight back as I slowly made my way to his head. All I had to do was hold him under for another minute or so, and it would be over.

Still, drowning a man with my own hands was even

more personal than my only previous kill. Maybe I was a bad person. Likely. Damn likely. But then again, I still wasn't entirely convinced that anyone here was real. If it was a video game, something I would only learn when I reached Tom Arnold in Citadel Deathgaze, then I was only killing a line of code. If not . . .

Rhone stopped kicking before I had time to ponder any further. He was dead, his body limp.

"Alright," I breathed, clambering up out of the water. I thought of maybe pushing Rhone under the back wall where he'd float out to sea, but touching the corpse again wasn't something I really wanted to do.

When I was once more standing upright and brushing some of the algae from my pants, a strange sensation fell over my body, starting at my shoulders and working its way down through my spine until it ended in my feet with a tingling vibration.

I accept, said a familiar voice lodged somewhere in my brain behind my left ear. It was Brayden. I'd know his frat-boy timbre anywhere.

All at once, I simply *knew* I had gained a class. Then it happened. A translucent stat sheet scrolled into my view from the bottom of my vision, displaying all my stats as though I had just logged on to play a new character from the comfort of my desk chair.

Name: Steve Gabbon
Devotion: Desecrator
Class: Sovereign Magus
Level: 1
Experience: 700 / 1000
Favor: 800 / 1000 – Rank 1
Physical: 4
Magic: 1

Defense: 0
Charisma: 1
Commerce: 1
Luck: 6
Current Modifiers: Siren's Call: You are under the influence of a Siren. Your ability to act on your own in the Siren's presence is diminished. Hunted: Powerful members of Valiance have marked you with a bounty. They will pursue you indefinitely. The Shipwright's Favor: The Shipwright has accepted your offering, granting you +10 luck on your next sea voyage.

Thoughts of Rhone's corpse bobbing in the ocean not five feet from me were instantly replaced by sheer joy. I had *finally* done it, and it was time to start powering up. I knew my XP, could see level two practically staring me in the face, and, best of all, video games were my thing. My expertise. My only real skill. I could grind and level like a boss.

I ran from the Shipwright's shack, giving no thought at all to covering the evidence of my crime, and even shouted for Mr. Patches to keep up. The cat obliged, and we scampered back into town toward the designated meeting place.

When I arrived, my two beautiful companions were already waiting for me. Amethyst wore a devilish smile—basically par for the course on her lovely face—and Bokta was busily munching away on a broken loaf of bread covered in dripping honey.

"Guys!" I shouted, running up to them. Amethyst's smile weakened a bit. "Ladies, I mean, you won't believe it."

"Did you complete your task?" Amethyst demanded, her voice as flat and dry as the desert surrounding us.

I nodded vigorously as I caught my breath. Mr. Patches leaned back on his hind legs to playfully claw at Bokta's waist, eager for a snippet of bread and honey.

Leaning in close and shielding my words from anyone who might have been near enough to hear, I told them what I'd done.

As I finished my brief tale, Amethyst's sly grin returned. I had won her approval after all. Bokta, on the other hand, looked crestfallen. "Now we'll be wanted in Crimson Sands," she said with a sigh.

"Not if they don't know who did it," Amethyst said. "But we secured passage across the Essant Sea. We need to get to the boat."

I couldn't agree more. "The faster we leave, the better. Though I wouldn't mind grabbing some more of the tea they sell here."

Bokta's eyebrows raised, her frown still marring her beautiful face. I could tell her fear of being caught by the Crimson Sands authorities wasn't the real reason for her displeasure. For whatever reason, she didn't like traveling with a murderer. Or maybe I was simply bad at reading women. "You spent your gibs on tea?" she asked, obviously displeased.

I pulled all the gibs from my belt. Every single one was still there. "Nah, didn't spend a dime." I jingled the gibs once before returning them to their pouch.

"What's a dime?" Amethyst asked.

"Never mind."

"Well, let's get going. I don't think you have anything to worry about here, but knights from Mara are still on our heels. We need to leave."

"Hey," I said, placing a hand on Bokta's elbow to capture her attention as we walked toward the docks. "The guy I . . . sacrificed . . . was a member of Valiance. When I killed him, I heard the Desecrator's voice in my head. I became a Sovereign Magus. I have a character sheet and everything. Stats, experience, a level, but no skills or cool spells. Any ideas?"

Finally, that bit of information seemed to lift her spirits, though she still appeared confused. Again, being bad at reading women was really hamstringing my progress. "Once we get onboard and away from the city, I'll show you."

A familiar wave of tingling excitement danced up and down my spine.

I had a class. A beautiful Blood Witch was about to teach me how to cast spells. Real. Fucking. Magic. My primary goal was still the same: to find Tom Arnold and figure out what the hell Realm really was, and maybe even go home. But now I had a new calling tugging in my chest. I was a true member of the Oathbreakers, a devoted follower of the Desecrator and owner of one of his damned eyes.

A half-ascended Torch Bearer was coming to kill. Now that I was a Sovereign Magus, I had a chance to fight back. I just needed to get my grubby hands on some experience points as fast as humanly possible.

CHAPTER 20

The ship Amethyst had secured for our journey across the Essant Sea was larger than I had expected. I guess I hadn't seen many wooden sailing ships in my days as an accountant, so my expectations were probably pretty miscalculated to begin with. The ship—christened *Annelista's Glory*—had three huge masts, each sporting multiple square and triangular sails, and four rows of portholes descending from the rail to the waterline on the barnacle-encrusted hull. It looked a little like an old-fashioned ocean liner, perhaps whatever class or type of ship had been the predecessor to steamships, easily capable of carrying over a hundred passengers apart from the extensive crew and cargo.

Needless to say, I was impressed. What I had feared would have turned out to be a rough and bumpy trip seemed like it would actually be a rather relaxing voyage on a ship large enough to not be thrown by the swells of the sea. Perhaps my luck buff was paying off already. I inwardly smiled and recalled my stat sheet just to read the buff again for the thousandth time. Finally, my joy subsided a bit, and it was time to go.

After ascending the steep gangway, the captain met us at the rail. It didn't take me long to figure out just how Amethyst had secured our transport. Her skills as a Siren were certainly persuasive.

"My lady Clarissa, please, I have a meal prepared for you and your companions, if you'd be so kind as to join me behind the mizzenmast," the man said, offering a sweeping bow as he removed his hat and crossed it over his chest, one foot jutting forward like a Shakespearean actor finishing a play.

"Clarissa?" I asked under my breath. Amethyst shot me a sly grin. Bokta only shook her head.

All of us were eager for some food, and we followed the captain to a small table set up on the part of the ship highest above the sea, a little deck behind the rearmost mast, the one I guessed from the jargon was called the mizzen.

Sidling up to the captain's elbow as she walked, Amethyst whispered something into his ear that made him hastily spring into action.

"Cast off! Free us from Crimson Sands!" the man shouted to his crewmen nearby.

One of them scratched his chin and pointed toward one of the gangways leading into the cargo hold at the ship's belly. "Goods aren't properly stowed yet, Cap'n," the man said with a gruff argot born after years on the sea. His voice was one of the first true dialects I had heard since arriving in Realm. The captain and everyone else I'd met in Crimson Sands had spoken English with a clear and discernable vernacular punctuated only by slight nuances here and there. The sailor, though—and I began making an effort to listen to the other men and women of *Annelista's Glory* to see if they shared the trait—had a distinctive accent. Part of me wondered if he had been born on Earth as well. Perhaps he'd been a sailor on a real ship crisscrossing the Atlantic and dodging hurricanes.

"What are the accents like on the other side of the ocean?" I asked Bokta as the two of us took a pair of seats across from the enamored captain and the woman who played with his heartstrings in her fingers.

The Blood Witch looked confused, like she hadn't heard the sailor's accent.

"That guy," I said, pointing, "he has an accent. Do people across the Essant Sea have other accents? Are there other languages in different cities?"

"No other languages, but plenty of accents, of course," she answered.

It made sense. Though, come to think of it, Realm of Crafted War had come out in something like twenty different languages around the world, so finding other tongues spoken here wouldn't be entirely out of the question. For whatever it was worth, it felt good knowing that no matter where our journey led, we wouldn't have to worry about a language barrier.

"Ah, shall we commence?" the captain announced, waving his hand for another of his crew to begin placing trays of food onto the table. I got the feeling the man had been speaking all along, probably divulging important facts about the boat or the trip ahead, but I hadn't heard any of it. Judging by Amethyst's bored expression, the man's soliloquy hadn't been particularly important.

The spread brought forth from the galley was truly impressive. Before long, the small table was covered in an array of tropical fruits—including a watermelon carved in a shockingly accurate miniaturization of the ship—complemented by a host of flaky pastries.

"Is this just the first course?" I asked Bokta quietly, careful not to let my voice reach the captain and potentially insult him.

Bokta grabbed one of the square pastries and poked a hole through it with her index finger. A goopy mixture of braised beef and white cream sauce oozed out onto her nail. "Eat the fruit last if you want to follow proper etiquette, but it doesn't really matter. And I don't think anything else will be coming out. Shipwright's Delight followed by fruits is a traditional meal to celebrate the first day of a voyage. Expensive, but traditional."

"Awesome," I said, grabbing a meat pastry for myself. Much to my obvious enjoyment, it tasted as good as it looked. The cream sauce was somewhere between an oily alfredo and white breakfast gravy while the meat was tender enough to fall apart before I could chew.

"How long do you suspect the journey to last, dear captain?" Amethyst asked. She carefully pushed a bit of cream sauce from the corner of her lips to her tongue after she spoke.

The captain practically swooned out of his chair and into the Siren's lap. "For you, dear Clarissa, we shall put all possible haste into the sails. We'll cross the Essant Sea in less than a week, should the Underlords be so kind."

I finished off four Shipwright's Delights before I noticed that everyone else was still politely working on their first serving. Glancing awkwardly at the captain to try to read his expression for any hint of malice directed toward my breach of decorum, all I found was lusty infatuation. Good enough for me! I plucked two more meaty pillows from the platter and plopped one down on the table to save for later—which of course was only about twenty seconds into the future as I wolfed down pastry number five.

By the time the meal concluded, all that remained of the flaky main course were crumbs. I had enjoyed seven, perhaps eight, of the suckers, and everyone else had slowly consumed their modest pair. Out of sheer willingness to fit in and not break with tradition, I even managed to stuff some sweet fruit down on top of my gluttonous portion of meat, though one of the berries that had been on the top of a watermelon mast was something I knew didn't exist on Earth. It had been all white and puckered like a raspberry or blackberry, and its innards had spilled out in bright orange. All in all, everything the captain had offered had been exquisite. I believed Bokta wholeheartedly when she had said the meal was an expensive one.

Perhaps even more comforting than the veritable feast slowly digesting in my stomach was the feel of the ship moving beneath my feet. *Annelista's Glory* had gotten underway sometime around my sixth meat pastry. Looking out over the aft railing, I watched with a smile as Crimson Sands became smaller and smaller.

Leaving the coast meant safety. No more half-ascended Torch Bearer stalking me across the continent—for now, at least. I knew Valiance well enough to know that their sense of honor would mean they'd never stop. Their followers would be relentless, inexorable. They'd probably offer quests for my head and organize bands of veteran adventurers to set out and claim it. The condition so plainly explaining my predicament was proof enough of the cult's wild determination.

At least for a while, I knew I wouldn't really have to worry about them. In the time we had to cross the ocean,

I could explore my new class. Luckily, Bokta had the exact same plan in mind, and she led me to a dimly illuminated room she identified as the forecastle to begin our training.

"Now," she said, rubbing her hands together. "You've become a Sovereign Magus. That's the arcane class for followers of our order. And don't go slinging Oathbreaker terms around the crew, either. I don't suspect many of the crew would really care about transporting a handful of people like us, but the fewer people who know where we are, the better."

"Yeah, I get it. Don't leave a trail for Valiance to follow." I stretched, feeling the dense food shift around in my stomach, and wondered if I'd be able to train at all without throwing up. If our first session was anything like my brief romp in Tamernil's recruitment center, I wouldn't have a hope of keeping everything down.

Gently showing Mr. Patches out of the forecastle, Bokta took my hand in her palm. Her flesh was warm and comforting beneath my touch. "Sovereign Magi don't really fight, not like Sirens at least, so you won't need to worry about memorizing technique or practicing some sort of form every day."

"Should I just be able to think of some spells, say a couple phrases, and do magic like you?" I asked. Learning abilities and unlocking new spells was always a cinch online. Of course it was. If the developers had made you work for every last thing, the game probably would have flopped. Sadly, there wouldn't be any instant gratification like that aboard *Annelista's Glory* . . . though . . . looking at the way Bokta shirt clung to her curves, a little damp from the heat of the enclosed space . . .

"It doesn't work in such a manner," she said, shattering my thoughts and jolting me back to the present. She held my palm with one hand and lifted a finger to her lips with the other.

After a long silence, she whispered, "Feel your pulse. Try to predict it, to anticipate the heartbeats, and let your mind clear."

I closed my eyes to facilitate immersion. Sadly, I didn't think it worked. Clearing my mind was nearly impossible with the Blood Witch standing so close, her breath tickling the side of my neck.

I pulled away from her touch and turned toward the room's only porthole, letting out a deep sigh and readjusting my pants in the process. "Let me try again," I said quietly.

Finally, after what felt like an embarrassingly long amount of time, I thought I had it somewhat figured out. Perhaps even good enough to move to step two. "Alright, what next?"

Bokta exhaled deeply. "Keep your mind clear of distraction. Try to imagine a physical connection between yourself and the Desecrator, and ask him for an ability."

Well . . . I didn't really have the faintest clue what in the hell that meant. How was I supposed to imagine a physical connection with a demonic, grotesque Underlord? Images of the Desecrator's stitched, twisted face filled my mind. Then, completely unwanted, I imagined him touching me with a single finger like a perverted version of Michelangelo's famous painting. If nothing else, the imagery was certainly an effective method by which my mind was purged of all thoughts of Bokta's ample chest. Silver linings, I guess.

A few moments passed before I gave up and broke the silence. "What's going to be my first spell?" I asked. I hoped for some sort of ridiculous ability at least on par with my cursed die being able to turn a cat into a rampaging demon, but I was level one. Online, the first ten or so abilities were always pretty lame. Maxkrannar's first talent had been *Vicious Strike*, a simple enhanced attack that added twenty percent bonus damage. The developers hadn't even added an animation for it.

A skill tab next to my floating character sheet would have been a huge boon. Maybe I'd unlock one later.

"No, there aren't scrolls where you can look up that sort of thing, not like that," Bokta replied. "Once you've found favor with the Underlord, it just sort of . . . happens, you know?"

"Actually, I have no idea. Things don't operate like that where I'm from." I stepped a little closer to the porthole to take in another deep breath of fresh ocean air. Closing my eyes, I tried again. I pushed everything I could out of my mind, imagining Bokta, the ship, and all my frustration drifting out to sea where they'd sink to the sandy floor, crushed to pieces by the immense pressure.

Slowly, evening out my breath and focusing on my own heartbeat, I began to feel more at ease. It was a subtle change, nearly imperceptible. When I felt like my body and mind were as calmed as they would ever get, I reached out toward the Oathbreaker. I didn't ask for anything—praying for answers had always felt a bit contrived—but rather opened my own relaxed mind to the possibility of accepting a gift.

The feeling that came over me was hard to describe. Some of it was the first stage of seasickness as *Annelista's Glory* began to gain speed and reach stronger swells, but the rest of it was altogether surreal. Beneath the slowly churning waves of my stomach was something new: an ability.

It didn't have a name, and there was no special incantation I would need to mutter in Latin while waving a wand like a damned idiot. Like tying shoelaces or knowing to swallow food after chewing, the skill was simply there in my memory, protected by a layer of years I had not known existed, but there nonetheless.

When I opened my eyes, I held the intangible magical impulse right at the edge of my conscious awareness. I hadn't seen it before, so I had no idea what would happen when I released it.

Bokta let out a little gasp and covered her mouth with a hand.

The more I looked at anything at all, the more I felt the power slipping between my fingertips. If I didn't loose it quickly, the skill would recede to the attic of my mind, presumably unavailable for some length of time—on cooldown, I supposed.

I whirled toward the window and unlatched my hold over the arcane energies I had tentatively captured. About fifty feet from the hull, a spike of black ice jettisoned skyward from the waves, sending a fresh spout of foamy seawater out in all directions. The icy stalagmite propelled itself roughly twenty feet into the air before shattering into mist and floating back down to the surface of the Essant Sea in a shower of reflective, harmless shards.

"Holy. Shit." There were no other words for what I'd done.

A little blinking light in the bottom left corner of my vision told me I had a notification waiting. I focused on it, and it jumped to life in the middle of my vision, plain as day:

New Ability: Doom Spike. Unleash a pillar of frozen ice on your enemies, ripping them to shreds.

Bokta placed a hand on my shoulder as she gazed out over the waves, watching them settle back into their normal pattern of frothy undulations. "Well done," she said, her voice honest and impressed.

"That was real magic."

"Yes, of course it was," she answered.

My mind struggled to comprehend what I'd seen. "But magic doesn't exit . . ." It was one thing seeing the Blood Witch—someone I still kind of viewed as a character in a video game—summon smoke to her fingertips and stun people, but it was something altogether different to witness magic coming from myself.

"So . . . what did I do?" I asked, still thoroughly dumbfounded.

Bokta held out her hands and smiled. "You cast a spell!" she beamed. "Call it whatever you like. There's no manual for Oathbreakers. No codex of approved spells like Valiance has developed over the last few centuries. Just know that you won't be able to activate it again without some rest, ok?"

I barely heard what the woman was saying. All I could do was marvel at my own hands, at the power they had brought forth, and I knew the smile splayed out across my face must have looked insane.

"You're alright?" she asked.

I nodded, still looking at my hands. For as calm as my heartbeat was just a few moments before, now it raced and hammered against my chest, threatening to shred my aorta and flatline my pulse.

I was a Sovereign Magus. Real magic had obeyed my command.

Even though it was a single spell, one that, in the grand scheme of Realm, probably wasn't very impressive—it was still magic. Real fucking magic. Never in my entire life had I felt so powerful.

On top of that, I could now *feel* the presence of a skill list hiding in whatever part of my brain housed my character stats. I called it up and read the details of Doom Spike once again. It wasn't a skill that had existed back in the game, but it felt like it would fit in. And for level one, it was pretty badass.

Life in Realm just got a whole better.

CHAPTER 21

Between the constant rise and fall of *Annelista's Glory* and the churning, relentless excitement dancing through my body, I didn't get any sleep during my first night at sea. In fact, I spent most of the night leaning over the starboard rail and vomiting, then swooning backward and struggling to maintain my balance. Curiously, Amethyst had chosen quarters in the cargo hold, and Mr. Patches had been her only companion—much to the captain's obvious dismay.

When morning broke, the sunlight made me feel a little better, and I managed to eat some of the biscuits and salted meat the crew seemed to enjoy. The worst part of the whole thing was that my newfound magical ability was still on cooldown. As Bokta had said, I would need a rest to reset the spell, so my training would have to wait. Between bouts of seasickness throughout the night, I had constantly called up my stats and skill sheet to read everything. I was in the game for real. I knew that, like everything in life, I'd eventually stop feeling so damn elated, but those kinds of diminishing returns were still a good ways off.

After breakfast, the next item on the agenda was . . . nothing. There was tons of work to be done around the ship, but the passage Amethyst had negotiated for us didn't involve working for our keep, and the large crew appeared to keep everything in tiptop shape without the need for a few extra hands.

For the three of us Oathbreakers, there was nothing to do. I thought about training more with a sword or even my fists, and Bokta offered several times to spar in the forecastle, but I felt weak and uneasy from my restless night, so I turned her down. Instead, I settled on badgering the Blood Witch with questions about my newfound class and ability. She wasn't any help. Right out of the gate, the way Bokta and Amethyst had talked about their skill had been too informal, too casual. To them, their progress and abilities were innate.

I was the only one with a character sheet. I saw my stats as numbers; they saw their progress as muscle growth on their arms, new techniques, and perfecting old talents. Sure, those things all worked for me as well—if I lifted weights, my arms grew, but I had the added advantage of seeing all my information directly displayed in my vision whenever I pleased.

My constant stream of questions finally concluded as the sun was sinking beneath the glittering blue horizon. Though still feeling a bit seasick, I knew I was too tired to do anything but sleep. At the behest of one of the crewmembers, a tanned man with rugged skin like old leather, I made my residence in the deepest part of the cargo hold that was still dry. My bed—if it could be called such a thing—was a heap of wooden boxes contained within a thick net of ropes, and the hold was so hot at night that blankets were far from a necessity.

The next morning, I awoke with a singular thought running through my mind: I could cast Doom Spike again.

I raced up the ladders and emerged into the sunlight, immediately regretting my haste as my eyes clamped shut against the brutal sunlight. Judging by the amount of activity on board, it was past dawn, and the majority of the crew was up and at their tasks.

Amethyst and the captain were standing near the wheel, her right hand on his shoulder. They talked and laughed as the captain made minute adjustments to the steering that I swore did actually nothing to alter our course. After a while, Amethyst left the man to join me by the forward mast. "Did Bokta tell you?" I asked, excited to share my magical news.

The Siren nodded and offered a sly grin. "Just don't get ahead of yourself and destroy the boat," she said.

I nodded. "So the crew really won't mind having an Oathbreaker on board if I practice a little?"

Amethyst thought for a moment before replying. "Sailors typically follow the Shipwright, of course, so I would be surprised if any of them were particularly interested in Valiance and their conflicts."

"Isn't the Desecrator evil?" I asked, keeping my voice low.

"Sure, I suppose," the woman said with a chuckle. "That's what Valiance says. All we want is to be free from rules and constraints. Is that so evil?"

I didn't really have an answer. In tabletop gaming terms, the Underlord's cult would probably be judged somewhere between chaotic neutral and chaotic evil. I mean, we'd killed people and orchestrated a prison break, but it wasn't like there was an army of Oathbreakers gathering somewhere in secret, intent on marching across Realm in the name of world domination. Honestly, that felt more like something Valiance would do.

Mulling over the moral dilemma in my head, I led Amethyst to the bow and prepared to show her what I'd learned. Or rather, I hadn't *learned* the spell so much as I had been given it upon officially reaching level one, so maybe *acquired* was a better way of describing it. Either way, I could practically taste another Doom Spike ready and waiting. It was weird sensing the cooldown with my mind. Online, a little grey spinner would tick down the seconds until a skill reactivated off cooldown. Here, no such luck. I just had a persistent feeling lodged in the very back of my skull that told me the skill was ready once more.

"Wait," Amethyst said when we were at the rail. "Let me see if I can get something for a target."

She darted back toward the captain, whispered a few things into his ear, then smiled as he readily abandoned the wheel on a new task. He returned a few moments later with a pair of his crewmen in tow, an old dinghy and a few coils of battered rope between them.

Amethyst returned to my side to watch them work. "You could basically take over the entire ship, you know," I told her. It was fascinating watching all the men and women of *Annelista's Glory* so readily complying with their captain's orders when I knew where those orders were all originating.

The Siren offered a knowing smile and a wink. "Who's to say that's not *exactly* what I've done?" she cooed. "Maybe when we get to port, I'll find whoever's in charge and take over the city."

The way she said it, I didn't doubt that she'd have the power to do exactly what she described.

A few moments later and the dinghy was floating out behind the ship, attached to the rail by a hundred yards of old, frayed rope. A couple crew members stayed around to watch the display. Chief among them was the captain, standing as close to Amethyst as possible, the sides of their hands bumping one another on the rail.

"Well, I'd like to see that little boat sent to the ocean floor," the woman said.

Having an audience was a little nerve wracking, but it also offered a bit of exhilaration as well. I liked showing off.

Looking at the little boat being thrashed around by the waves, I cleared my mind and latched onto the magic of Doom Spike. I felt it as easily as I felt the wooden rail under my fingers. When I thought I had the spell fully under my grasp and ready to be released, I then moved on to the more difficult task of aiming. When I had cast before in the forecastle, I had simply aimed outside the ship and let fly—now I wasn't sure how to get my spike to burst through the bottom of the dinghy. No translucent pre-image of the Doom Spike appeared for me to move around and perfectly position like it would have if I were sitting at my desk with a keyboard and mouse under my hands.

I closed my eyes against the reflected rays coming off the water and imagined the Doom Spike shredding up from the waves to shatter the little boat. In my mind's eyes, I would release the spell effortlessly, and—

"—Come on, boat out there's sinkin'. Doesn't have but another minute, maybe less," one of the tall sailors standing at the rail said, breaking all my concentration.

A determined grin on my face, I opened my eyes and released. A frozen spike the size of a pillar from the capitol building in D. C. erupted from the waves. It *almost* hit the boat where I had aimed. Thankfully, the front quarter of the dinghy was launched about twenty feet into the air, creating a rain of splintered boards over a much larger area than I had expected. When the black spike reached its zenith, it simply dissipated into the air like a cloud of mist being blown about by the wind.

The sailors clapped and cheered, and a few of them slapped me on the back before returning to their tasks about the ship.

"Not too bad," Amethyst said. It was always hard to tell with her, but I thought her voice sounded genuine, and I couldn't keep my pride from swelling a bit at the praise.

"So having a class and being able to use abilities is really rare enough to warrant a crowd? Or was the Doom Spike just something the sailors hadn't seen before?" I asked. I leaned against the rail with my elbows propped up at my sides, and my heart fluttered a little as the wooden beams gave an inch or two, making me jump back to the safety of the deck.

"Doom Spike?" Amethyst said, an eyebrow raised.

A sheen of red embarrassment flushed through my face. "Hey now, I didn't pick the name. How about the frequency of magic and classes; let's get back to that, shall we?"

Amethyst laughed and shook her head. "Classes are only given to the most devoted of an Underlord's followers. Among the common folk, people like us are rare. Don't let it get to your head, Magus."

Alright, so I was level one. I'd unlocked my class, completed the tutorial, and was poised to advance through the ranks—to continue leveling up and acquiring skills as I made my way to Tom Arnold at Citadel Deathgaze. Hopefully I'd live long enough to learn more about the world. Even though we hadn't seen any sign of Mara's Torch Bearer in hot pursuit, we all knew Valiance would only be a day or two behind. They had their magic, and they certainly had ways of tracking us down.

The city of Essence, our port of call along the Shimmering Coast, made Crimson Sands instantly disappear from my memory. To say the city was large was a gross underestimation. According to Bokta, the entire region of Rowane that we had left back in the west didn't even have half the population of the city of Essence. I didn't know if her census information was exactly accurate, but it felt possible. Essence was the size of Seattle, port and all. Huge wooden ships carrying more cargo that *Annelista's Glory* would see in her lifetime were moored in dozens and dozens of long slips all along the coast. Behind each wharf was an army of warehouses and offices, each bustling with activity.

Dominating the skyline and towering above the two- and three-story warehouses was an absolutely monolithic tower of reflective marble and granite crowned with a flaming wreath that competed with the sun as the city's main source of light. Despite the absolute magnificence of the structure, my heart still dropped down to my heels at the sight. It was a lighthouse, perhaps the largest ever built in either Realm or back on Earth. What it meant was clear: the Valiance presence in Essence would be thorough and oppressive. There would be no avoiding it. If they knew who I was—if they were actively searching for an Oathbreaker toting around a cat—I'd be dead before making it ten steps off the wharf.

As I struggled to come up with ways to remain

undetected, *Annelista's Glory* sailed into a relatively small dock on the southern side of the harbor that the captain assured us was far from the watchful eye of the men in blue and gold tabards patrolling the larger docks. There were other docks, more secretive places frequented by thieves and smugglers where our little band of Oathbreakers would have been able to disembark without any risk of detection, but that kind of subtlety came at a price. We'd have to pay for the entire ship's passage through the smugglers' port, and Amethyst's seduction—impressive though it certainly was—couldn't conjure up the funds.

As we made our way down the gangway and onto solid ground, it took a concerted effort to get my eyes to stop darting to every city official we saw. I just had to keep reminding myself that we were the ones a step ahead. Mara's Torch Bearer was still at least a couple days behind, probably on a ship of his own in the center of the Essant Sea.

"So, Valiance basically serves as the official government here, right?" I asked Amethyst as we detached ourselves from the captain and his crew.

"Not exactly," she answered. "Specifically, Essence is the administrative capital of Realm. We're in the region of Calisx now."

"What do they have, a king? A president?" We walked past the last of the warehouses and entered the city proper, a sprawl of tangled streets and alleyways packed with citizens.

Amethyst shook her head. "A president?" she repeated.

Obviously, democratic lingo hadn't made it to Realm just yet. "Eh, that's what we call a king . . . doesn't matter."

"Well, the Crown Regent lives north of the city, but you are right. Valiance controls Essence, and Essence controls all of Calisx," Amethyst said.

Bokta, a slight sneer on her face, finally added her voice: "And the Dread King ruling Rowane is the Crown Regent's wretched brother," she said.

All in all, the government structure of Realm was starting to take some shape in my head, though I still wasn't exactly positive how Tom Arnold and the rest of the development team from Realm of Crafted War fit into things. "So what's the plan to get to Citadel Deathgaze?" I went on, curious to start learning the geography of the new continent and how we'd finally get some answers. Mr. Patches nipped at my heels and scurried ahead, intent on sniffing behind an open-topped barrel full of salted fish sitting in front of a business.

"No one . . . no one's really sure how to get to Citadel Deathgaze," Bokta answered.

Amethyst, smirking, let out a sigh. "That's our first order of business. We'll need a map, and we'll need supplies. Citadel Deathgaze is dangerous, a constant battlefield whence few return, and so little is known." She looked my outfit up and down, and I could basically feel her negative judgment.

Alright, I needed gear. Honestly, we all did. I was still in my first-level outfit. On Realm Online, that would have meant a cloth shirt with no stats and a pair of "Shoddy Boots," though what exactly those were no one knew for sure. Amethyst and Bokta both had what I suspected was still lower-tier gear. Their outfits were unarguably better than mine, but that wasn't saying much at all. If Citadel Deathgaze was anything like the online version, we'd need some serious armor.

"What exactly *do* you know about the citadel?" I asked.

Following Amethyst, we entered a small building perhaps a half mile from the docks. The sign above the door indicated something that wasn't exactly self-evident. The shield displayed a severed head from some sort of beast that was part dragon and part tropical bird. Inside, there were tables and chairs like a typical medieval inn, and the three of us sat down at one such table near the center of the room.

"There," Amethyst said, pointing to a large oil painting in an elaborate frame that hung to the side of a rack of long spears.

"Oh . . ." I stammered. Though I had expected Citadel Deathgaze to at least be similar to what I had known from several months of raiding online, I hadn't really been prepared to see an exact likeness. Seeing something here in Realm that had been such a large part of my past back on Earth was jarring. But . . . there it was: Citadel Deathgaze. I knew it well.

"You said you recognized the citadel? You know it from somewhere?" Amethyst asked.

Bokta cut in with a smile. "I watched Maxrannar fight through the enemies of the citadel dozens of times. He's been there, remember?"

The same mistiness I had seen when Bokta had first summoned me to Tamernil was present once more in her eyes. She truly believed I was a demon Oathbreaker named Maxrannar. No wonder she'd kept my inept ass around for so long. She had the kind of misguided infatuation that meant nothing would ever change her mind. If I was being true to myself, it didn't bother me at all. What did it matter if she thought I was something so much greater than a sloppy accountant at a dead-end firm? And it didn't hurt that she was downright gorgeous.

"Yeah," I said. "I've been there back on my world more than once."

"How well do you know it?" Amethyst asked. She waved for an employee of the establishment to attend to her, though I still wasn't sure what kind of place we were in. It had the feel of a pub or tavern, but the actual alcohol and food were both distinctly missing. There wasn't even a bar or a wall full of mugs.

Amethyst exchanged a few lines with the employee before sending the young boy on his way. She looked back at me, and I figured it was time to divulge the exact layout of Citadel Deathgaze. I knew its construction better than the floorplan of my own office or apartment building.

"Alright, that painting looks exactly like the Citadel Deathgaze that I know from my home world, but there still might be differences. Obviously, I've never been to the one here. On top of that, things change. Maybe Tom's remodeled the place recently. But do you see the side there, by the purplish flames? That's our way in." Explaining a high-level raid to what essentially amounted to my guild mates brought back a wave of exhilaration.

"What kind of resistance should we expect?" Amethyst asked, leaning in close. "I've heard rumors of giants and deadly swarms of insects. Is any of that true?"

"Oh, that's true, but you've only heard the first wave. Hell, Bokta's probably seen a lot more through her scrying. With my friends, we made it almost to the final boss. The first boss, the giant, is at the end of a long hallway full of mobs," I explained.

"Mobs?" Bokta raised an eyebrow.

"That's what the easy kills are called, just mobs. Or trash pulls. But honestly, nothing in Citadel Deathgaze is 'trash' like the other raids. The mobs are tough. We'll need specialized gear for sure." As I finished speaking, the young male employee returned and dropped off an armful of parchments, each written in the swirly script I still couldn't really read. Amethyst looked them over for a moment before dismissing the boy—without paying, I noticed.

"What kind of equipment will we need?" the Siren asked as she leafed through the loose parchments now scattered across the table.

I had to think back to all the fights I had memorized so well. "There are eight levels to Citadel Deathgaze. Outside, the insect and ground-based traps aren't that bad. Armor is going to be a must, and we'll need something to ward off poison. Do you think we could get a couple Resist Envenomation potions in Essence?"

Amethyst nodded. She organized a couple of the parchments into a purposeful stack to one side, then kept reading through the others.

"Once we're in, we'll need to clear the first hall. At the end is a giant. He's big and dumb, but he hits like a truck." The first boss had been an auto-clear for my group online. We'd killed him so many times that the prospect of potentially losing to him felt ridiculous. But that was at level ninety. Not level one.

"What's a truck?" Bokta asked.

I let out a sigh. "A huge wagon, sort of, but that's not super important. The main thing is the giant has a massive club, and if he hits you with it, you won't stand a chance."

"And the next level?" Amethyst asked. She didn't look up from her work, though I could tell she was still paying close attention.

"We can go one of two ways from the giant. If we kill him close to where he spawns, we can climb up his dead body to a hatch in the ceiling, effectively bypassing the second set of mobs—not the next boss, of course—but saving some time and energy for sure. If not, we'll have to take the tunnel on the right through a mushroom cavern. If you step on one, it'll explode for a ton of fire damage. At the end of that hallway is a group of lizardmen guards. They aren't too tough, but they can take hits. The mob is mostly there to slow you down." As I explained the levels, Amethyst kept sorting her papers into various stacks, and Bokta sat with her head in her hands, elbows on the table, completely enthralled.

"Getting in is task one, and the giant is two, what's three?"

"That's my favorite fight," I said. "You don't need to worry about bashing in skulls or dodging fireballs. The third area is a puzzle room. It changes all the time, or it did in my world, so you'd never know exactly what to expect. The usual stuff involved riddles, deciphering patterns, putting stuff together in unique ways. Lots of non-combat roleplay."

Amethyst looked up from her papers, an eyebrow raised and a smile playing at the edge of her lips. "Role-play?" she asked with a bit of surprise.

"Yeah, the fun stuff that takes you out of the spread sheets and die rolls for—" Then it dawned on me. Damn. Always a sentence too late. "N-not like that," I said a little too quickly. "Not . . . Siren stuff."

Amethyst's hint of a smile evolved into a devilish grin that made my rough pants suddenly feel a little too constrictive. "That's a shame," she said. "I'm *quite* fond of roleplay."

"Well . . . yeah, moving on from area three, we'll have a bit of crumbling ruins to traverse, and then comes one of the hardest bosses. There's a frost troll, and he's protected by a pair of bats that start out sitting on his shoulders. What makes it tough is the mix of elements. The troll

is all frost and ice, but the bats drop fire as they fly around."
As I explained the area, I couldn't keep my gaze from drifting to Amethyst's chest. She was sitting so close, and the
proper posture she exhibited meant her tits were basically
staring me in the face. Plus, I was fairly certain she had
purposely moved her papers a bit higher up and closer to
her eyes specifically to give me a better view. Not that I was
complaining . . .

"These are all scavenge reports from Apostate's Rise,"
Amethyst said, pointedly ignoring my stare or at least
choosing not to bring it up. "That's a city north of here
along the Shimmering Coast and on the way to Citadel
Deathgaze. If there's gear we need, we'll be able to find it
there."

"Holy shit!" I practically gasped. "You mean to tell me
you have dungeons and raids where adventurers go to find
loot? Am I hearing it correctly?"

With a smile, Bokta picked up one of the papers on the
stack nearest her. "This one is a report from the Northern
Quarter of Apostate's Rise. After the Emergence a couple
decades ago, there's been tons of dark activity there. People even pinned it on the Oathbreakers at first, but raising
monsters from the dead isn't the Desecrator's style."

Whatever Apostate's Rise was, it sounded awesome. And
there wasn't a corollary in Realm Online, at least not by
name, so I didn't really know what we were talking about. A
place to test new expansions? An area designated for world
PvP? Realm of Crafted War had both, though neither had
a fancy name like Apostate's Rise. Needless to say, I was
pretty damn eager to get out and scour some dungeons
for gear. Crushing through hordes of undead—power leveling, as we would have called it back home—certainly fell
into my very narrow area of expertise.

"The report says there's a new threat coming from the Northern Quarter: a rogue follower of Miasmara has set up a fortress of sorts, and the official cult leaders want her taken out." Amethyst took the report from Bokta's hand and looked it over one last time before setting it back on the pile with the others. "We'd probably be able to get some armor and a couple enchanted items from the Northern Quarter, maybe enough to sell for some gear that we actually need, but another one looks promising as well." She handed a second report to Bokta.

After a brief moment, the Blood Witch explained what the quest would entail. "There's a deserter from the Crown Regent's army, and he's been seen prowling the wall that separates Apostate's Rise from the wilderness. The report also says Dorian has been in league with someone—maybe some*thing*—from the forest, and the people still living in the ruined city are worried. Plus, the Crown Regent wants his head for desertion, and that will pay in gold."

"What do you think?" Bokta asked me, her gentle eyes looking to me for direction.

"Why do I have to pick?" I answered. Deciding on a quest that could potentially get us killed felt like something for Amethyst, our leader.

But was the Siren still our leader? Had I usurped the role without noticing it? Looking at the two beautiful women sitting across from me at the table, I knew their expressions suggested an obvious answer.

"You know the most about the citadel, right?" Amethyst said.

I nodded.

"Well, then you'll decide what we need first. Potential enchanted items from the Northern Quarter? Or hunting down a deserter for the Crown Regent's bounty?" She gathered the other thirty or so pieces of parchment into a neat stack to stow with her gear.

I didn't really know what to decide. I almost asked if picking correctly meant I'd get to try out Amethyst's idea of roleplay, but I'd never been so forward in my life. Besides, the way Bokta had looked at me while I had regaled them with the first few areas of Citadel Deathgaze was enough to make me at least hold my tongue in front of her.

CHAPTER 22

The thought of golden gibs filling my pockets made the decision a pretty easy one. We'd hit the Wall, find the deserter, and claim the bounty. Plus, going up against one man sounded like it would be a lot easier than hitting an undead raid right out of the gate. That didn't mean the Northern Quarter was entirely off the table, of course . . . just that the three of us had agreed to put zombies on the back burner for the time being.

Wanting to leave Essence as quickly as possible to minimize our risk of detection, we had also decided to set out before nightfall, opting to stay in one of the roadside inns between the huge port city and Apostate's Rise. There wouldn't be any lighthouses in the small outposts before the ruined town, so it felt like as good of a plan as we were likely to get.

As I was given the simple task of lying low and practicing speedily accessing and aiming my newfound magic,

Bokta and Amethyst went into the city to gather supplies. Despite the relative ease of the mission compared to the more complex quests Amethyst had picked up, we were woefully under-geared—a fact that constantly ran through my head as Mr. Patches rubbed up against my legs. He was the only vestige of magic I had besides the tourmaline that summoned him and the solitary ability I had learned. We needed some power leveling and some gear pronto. Luckily, the two women returned in the late afternoon with heavy packs, one of which landed at my feet.

"Let's go," Amethyst said flatly as she stood in the doorway of the room we had rented. The inn—and especially the stables attached to the side—smelled like an open sewer that had been used for centuries by horses raised on Mexican food. I was happy to leave it behind.

As we quietly, inconspicuously left the building, I could tell something was wrong. The two women were more tight-lipped than usual, and Bokta's back was perfectly straight, her eyes on high alert.

"What's up?" I asked quietly, leaning close to the Blood Witch's left ear. Amethyst was a couple steps ahead. Her body language was exactly the same: Defcon One.

Bokta made doubly sure that no one was within earshot before responding. "Amethyst saw your likeness on a wanted poster. We went past the lighthouse just to see, and they're looking for you. High reward, too," she whispered.

"My likeness? They had a picture of me?" I asked. I imagined a Polaroid photo of myself, maybe a little blurry and out of focus like a classic shot of Bigfoot, pinned to a corkboard on the side of a Valiance stronghold. Then I remembered how ridiculous that would have been.

"They have a drawing, and it's fairly accurate. You'll be recognized before long," the woman replied.

Shit. I sighed. Shit again. So I wasn't a few steps ahead of the Torch Bearer and his gang of do-gooders. Not at all. "Should I change my appearance?" I asked, struggling to contain my nervousness. "I could shave my head. Or . . . you could shave it for me, I guess. Never done it myself."

Bokta shook her head, and her long, beautiful hair brushed against my shoulder. "Nothing yet," she answered. "Doing something sudden would only draw attention. You need to act natural."

"Let's just get out of the city."

Mr. Patches purred as he loped along to keep up. We were already moving faster than most of the people we passed, and I could only hope we weren't giving away our trepidation by our speed. Thankfully, we reached the edge of the city without being stopped.

"We need a permit to enter Apostate's Rise lawfully," Amethyst said. We had regrouped in a dusty staging area next to a city wall where a bunch of travelers were either preparing for departure or acquiring their necessary governmental permissions to enter Essence. It reminded me of a border crossing from Earth—not a heavily guarded one like the southern border, but maybe the security level of Niagara Falls. Basically, all the armed guards appeared bored.

"What name was on the wanted poster?" I asked. If we needed official paperwork to get into Apostate's Rise, maybe another change was in order.

Bokta smiled. "The same one you gave the recruiter in Tamernil."

"So they're after Donald J. Trump. Good to know. I'll switch it up again," I said.

"The guards here won't be as naïve as the recruiter in the village. Essence is a huge city. They'll know about the search, and they might be able to recognize you," Amethyst stated, her eyes fixed on the nearest bureaucratic establishment. All the government buildings were easy to spot; each one sported a red banner on its roof's apex, and the shields hanging above their doors were all similarly emblazoned with quills and images of stacked gibs.

"Could we skip the permit? Sneak into Apostate's Rise?" Bokta asked. Her voice told me she wasn't hopeful.

As I expected, Amethyst shot her down. "We'll need to show the permit if we want anywhere to sleep inside the quarantine zone," she explained.

"Could you do some Siren magic to get us through?" I asked.

Amethyst's flat stare curled into an almost imperceptible grin. "Again, the man you must have dealt with in Tamernil was an idiot. The guards here will not be so easily fooled."

Well, I wouldn't consider her Siren magic to be *easy fooling* . . . though she hadn't needed much effort to wrap her spells around me.

As I searched my brain for some scrap of a plan to coming bubbling up to the surface, I watched as a caravan of three covered wagons departed past the government offices. I couldn't see what was contained within the vehicles, and I didn't really care. Instead, I found my eyes attracted to the curious humanoids manning the caravan. They were creatures I had never seen before. Somewhat similar to the rats I had met beneath Tamernil's bar, the little humanoids were covered in fur with long snouts. They were clearly vertebrate mammals, but their lanky arms—all six of them—reminded me more of segmented insects than anything else. All in all, each being sported eight limbs, though they only walked on two, curiously bipedal.

"What are those?" I asked, casually pointing to the end of the three-wagon procession as it departed Essence.

"Grey Tamers," Bokta replied. "They're more common up in the north and to the east. Probably trading spice from the mountains."

"And what other fantasy races might we run into?" I had never seen any Grey Tamers online as either playable choices or NPCs. Maybe they would be introduced in a later expansion. Maybe they had been scrapped in beta.

"What do you mean?" Amethyst asked.

"Uh . . . Oh, fantasy. So non-human. What other non-human, intelligent races are there out there?"

Still, Amethyst and Bokta didn't really understand what I was asking them. To the native residents of Realm, the races weren't anything usual, so I guess it made sense. "Any elves or dwarves?" I asked. "Perhaps orcs?"

"Dwarves, yes," Amethyst said. "Though 'orc' is something I have not heard."

I turned to Bokta. "You watched me in the citadel, right? Remember my companions? One of them was an elf—tall and slender, pointy ears. Anyone like that exist here?"

Bokta smiled as she remembered. Then her expression turned dark. "No, Maxkrannar. All the elves were killed long ago."

"And good riddance," the Siren interjected.

Alright, so elves were a touchy subject. I decided to let it drop. Maybe I would learn more later. For the moment, we still needed a plan to acquire our permit.

Finally, Amethyst sighed and shook her head. "You," she announced, pointing an index finger at my chest, "take the gear outside the city. We'll get a permit for two to enter Apostate's Rise, and then we'll change it to three."

"That's the best we have? Forgery?" I had played a lot

of characters throughout my decade on Realm of Crafted War. Though rogues sometimes had some pickpocketing quests, there were no forgery quests. They probably would have been boring.

"Keep your voice down," Bokta urged. She looked to Amethyst, her eyes large and pleading. "Forging official documents is punishable at the gallows."

"So is harboring a known fugitive." Amethyst jabbed me with her eyes. I had to admit, she had a point. It kind of made me feel like shit, though.

Without further complaint, I grabbed our bags from the ground, hefted them up to my sore shoulders, and began trudging for the northern road along the same path the Grey Tamers had taken just a few moments before. No one stopped me at the gate. In fact, I was fairly thrilled to realize that no one even paid me any special attention. I walked a ways down the road, constantly adjusting the three packs slung over my shoulders, until I came to a gentle bend where I decided to wait. I could still see the city perfectly fine. Above the buildings and the wall, the huge lighthouse in the center of Essence gleamed against the clouds, eternally watching and searching.

I turned from the lighthouse and set down the packs, then plopped on top of one like a particularly lumpy beanbag chair. About fifteen minutes later, the two Oathbreaker women emerged from the government office. Amethyst had a scroll in her hand. Bokta still looked nervous.

When they arrived, they each grabbed a bag and quickly kept moving. "We got the permit, just keep going. Try not to look suspicious."

Having never run from the cops before in my life, I wasn't exactly sure how to blend in. Especially since the road didn't have a crowd or even a generous helping of other travelers. "How long to the inn?" I asked. The prospect of carrying a heavy pack for a couple days like we had done between Mara and Crimson Sands was one I dreaded. My back couldn't take much more of that kind of trekking.

"Only a few hours. Apostate's Rise isn't far," Amethyst said.

I could work with that. We kept up a solid pace, one that made us all rather sweaty under the weight of our gear, and arrived at our destination in the middle of the night. The mosquitos were out in force in the darkness, and Mr. Patches was nowhere to be found. It had only been about four hours of hiking, but I felt miserable.

Up ahead, the little outpost had only a handful of buildings, and the Grey Tamers had parked their three wagons out in front of the largest establishment. "They're going to Apostate's Rise as well?" I asked. We came to a stop to refill our water supply at a well in the center of the outpost.

Amethyst didn't look so sure. "I've never heard of Grey Tamers being adventurers," she said. "Maybe they're here to sell supplies to the inns."

As we were putting the stopper back on our final water skins, two of the Grey Tamers emerged from the big inn with a long bundle of covered items held in their many arms. The three of us watched as the interesting little creatures loaded their rigid bundle into a wagon, and then their caravan set off again, continuing north toward Apostate's Rise.

"No one goes to the ruins at night," Bokta said under her breath.

"Something's not right." The Grey Tamers gave me an uneasy feeling. Though I had to admit, seeing a bipedal, eight-legged rat thing back on Earth would have made me a hell of lot more uneasy than it did in Realm. Somehow, the wonky amalgamation of animal and human designs seemed a little . . . expected.

I shook the notion from my head as we walked toward the inn where the creatures had just exited. We stopped outside in a pool of golden lamplight, and Amethyst produced the scroll she had acquired back in Essence. Unfurling it, I saw it was covered with a bunch of the circular writing I was finally starting to recognize. The official script was, unfortunately, a little more ornate than I was ready to translate.

Bokta fished a quill and tiny ink pot from her own pack. "Give it here," she said. She held the scroll against the side of the inn and began editing. After a few strokes, she dropped the parchment to the dirty ground, and Amethyst immediately stepped on it.

"What the hell?" I nearly shouted.

Bokta, an opened water skin in her hand, ground her heel into the bottom of the parchment. A little bit of the document tore. Then she poured an ounce or two of water on it, further ruining it.

"Uh, guys? Don't we need that?" I implored.

Amethyst bent down and plucked it from the dirt, a devilish smile spread across her face. "The permits are too clear and easily deciphered when they're fresh," she explained. "Now it looks genuine. No one will question a little bit of messed-up writing. Besides, we don't need it yet, remember? We'll only need it to get a room once we're inside the ruins. The few inns still in Apostate's Rise won't let you inside without credentials or a cart full of gibs."

"Ah, that makes more sense, I guess," I said.

"Now we'll have a day for the forgery to set. Best to do it now and wait until then to mess with it on the Wall." With that, Amethyst secured the parchment once more and led the way into the tavern.

Inside, the building was sparsely populated. There were a few rough-looking people who appeared to be employees, and another group of apparent adventurers was seated to the right of the door around a circular wooden table.

"Just two rooms, we have our own food," Amethyst told a pot-bellied man wearing a leather apron. The two haggled over the price for a moment, and then the transaction was concluded. She handed me a key. "We need to leave early to maximize our time. Be up at dawn, you two, and make sure you actually get some rest."

I watched Amethyst carry her bag to the hallway in the rear of the building that housed the small rooms. Sleep sounded great. My back hurt, my feet were sore, and . . .

Wait a second.

Wait a goddamn second. Amethyst had directly said 'you two,' and she had been referring to Bokta, clearly. And I guessed I was the second half of the pair.

Not that I was about to protest . . .

"So, Amethyst grabbed a room to herself, yeah?" I asked, awkwardly stumbling over my own tongue as I spoke. My head was filled with images—glorious images—of fleshy bits rubbing together in the dark.

She let out a sigh. I couldn't exactly tell what the sigh meant. "She doesn't like to be bothered on the night before a raid."

"How many raids have you two been on together?" I asked, eager get my mind off the sudden and somewhat uncomfortable tightness that had appeared in my pants.

The Blood Witch stretched her back, obviously tired as well from the journey. Her shirt was still wet with a little bit of sweat, and it clung to her chest like a tight club dress. "We've been on a few adventures," she said. "Not much beyond the level of the municipal dungeons you saw back in

Mara, but there was one in particular that you would have enjoyed."

I decided to be bold. It was against my entire nature—something I would have never done back on Earth without a copious amount of social lubricant—and my hands shook a little with the buildup of anticipated failure. "Want to head to our room, and you could tell me about the raid?"

The moment of truth. Even though we were *supposed* to be sharing a room, it still felt like I was asking a beautiful stranger from the hotel bar to accompany me back to my private suite. Bokta turned without saying anything, just flashing a smile and heading toward the hallway of rooms. I took my cue and followed, Mr. Patches bringing up the rear as always.

We reached the wooden door for our room. A swoopy, circular word was written on the center in dull paint, but I didn't have the attention span left to try and decipher it. "Hey . . . before, you know . . ."

Bokta turned and placed a gentle hand on my chest. "What's wrong?"

"Nothing," I quickly added, hating myself for opening my mouth at all. Why couldn't I just keep my damn muttering to myself? I had a charisma skill of one, low to be certain, but I shouldn't have been absolutely inept, right?

The woman smiled and turned back to unlock the door. I could have sworn I heard her issue a soft purr as she moved, but it could have been the multi-colored cat rubbing up against my calf. Inside, I wasn't sure if I was pleased or terrified to see that there was only one straw mattress. The solitary bed meant there was no chance to back out. My heart accelerated, and I quickly decided that the room's configuration was a good thing—a *very* good thing.

Bokta went first to the opposite side of the room. It was dark, lit by only a faint spray of light from a pair of candles in a brass sconce outside a small square window.

"How—"

I stopped when Bokta began taking off her shirt. She peeled off the road-worn layer and casually tossed it to the ground. "Three years ago, when the Dread King first came to power in Rowane, Amethyst and I had invaded the provincial governor's palace. We had a dozen or more Oathbreaker initiates with us, and only a handful of them survived."

Beneath her shirt, Bokta opted to keep her black cotton undergarment in place, though it wasn't exactly large enough to cover her ample features. When she started untying her pants, my jaw basically hit the floor. I was still standing awkwardly in front of the door. I turned back and fumbled for the lock, but of course, the medieval door didn't have one in the traditional sense. Instead, the inn offered wooden locking bars to secure the rooms, and ours was leaning against the wall to my right.

It took a painful amount of time for me to figure out how to get the locking bar properly set in place. When I turned back, Bokta was sitting on the side of the low mattress, and what little clothing had previously been on her body was in a pile on the floor. Her dark, gently curled hair hung down to cover the top half of her breasts.

"So . . ." I muttered, struggling to make my voice loud enough to actually be audible.

"Want to know more about the raid?" Bokta asked. Her smile told me she knew exactly what was about to happen.

"Not exactly?" I replied.

She nodded and pat the mattress at her side. "Come here, Maxrannar . . ."

I didn't mind her using my character name. In fact, I preferred it. "Yes, ma'am," I said with a sudden measure of confidence. Despite the darkness, my body's physical enthusiasm was certainly clear to see. I sat on the mattress, feeling the rough straw through my pants and Bokta's hand on my shoulder.

"I've always wanted to be with a demon," she cooed into my ear.

For a second, I thought about bringing up Amethyst, trying to smooth things over and make sure Bokta wasn't jealous or anything like that. The Blood Witch reached for the hem of my pants, and that brief second of thought fled with the rest of my hesitation.

Her lips found their way to my cheek and lingered there a long moment, one of her hands lacing up through my hair. Then she turned my head to initiate a proper kiss. At the same time, her other hand had deftly moved my pants down to a spot just above my knees.

All the tiredness I had so desperately wanted to purge from my mind and body suddenly didn't seem like such a big deal. I could sleep when I was dead.

Tonight would be a good night.

CHAPTER 23

When morning came, Bokta woke me up before any other noise made its way to our room. She was gently shaking my shoulder, leaning close enough for her hair to fall over my face and her nipples to rub against my bare torso. My body, tired as it was from the long night, immediately reacted. Bokta's naked form was better than any cup of coffee I'd ever had in my life. The fog of sleep instantly evaporated. Within the span of a minute or two, we were entwined once more, the Blood Witch's legs wrapped around my waist as she bounced up and down.

I didn't last long. My only consolation was that I had lasted longer the previous night—the second time we had fucked, not the first by any means—and Bokta didn't seem too concerned. When I had finished inside her for what I believed to be the fourth time in less than twelve hours, she collapsed at my side, nuzzling her naked body up against mine.

I had so many questions, so many things my mind wanted me to figure out, but I said nothing. I wanted the morning to last forever. Apostate's Rise could wait. The Wall could wait as well. Lying on a rough straw mattress with a beautiful woman clinging to my chest made the Torch Bearer from Mara feel a thousand light-years away. It was almost like the Torch Bearer was the one stuck in another world, and Realm was where I was meant to be—where I had always been, at least in my own mind.

Then, far too soon for my liking, a knock sounded on our door. "We'll leave in half an hour. Make sure you eat. Breakfast has been paid," Amethyst said with a complete lack of intonation that fit her business-like style.

I extricated myself from Bokta's cloying hands as slowly as I could, savoring the feel of her skin until it was finally gone.

"Thank you," Bokta said softly as I pulled on my shirt from the floor.

Of all the things the woman could have said, a compliment of that magnitude was pretty far down my list. I stumbled around the words slowly forming in my head. "Uh, you're welcome . . . I mean, thank *you*, really . . ."

Bokta laughed. She didn't laugh *at* me—no, she just chuckled softly to herself in the way a satisfied woman might do after achieving some small milestone that brought with it an accompanying burst of dopamine. I took it as a good sign.

"If I may . . . what . . . brought on all that?" I dared to ask, hoping beyond reason that my prying question wouldn't ruin everything in the span of a heartbeat.

Bokta came forward and leaned on her elbows, offering me an absolutely glorious view of her bare back, her hair cascading in soft curls down her spine, and the tightest ass

I'd ever seen outside of the internet. "I've watched you for so long," she said with a glimmer of longing in her soft voice. "Being an outcast, I had never found a suitable companion before. No one I could trust with my secrets. Then I found you, and I knew you would understand, that you wouldn't judge me for being what I am."

"Hell no," I replied honestly. "A Blood Witch is probably the coolest thing I've ever met. Your secrets are perfectly safe with me."

Bokta smiled and rolled to her back, brushing a wave of her dark hair from her face. "I watched you for so long. Now that you're here . . ."

I guess in a way it all made sense. I was the only one Bokta had ever really felt close to, even if she had just been watching my character on a scrying mirror instead of the flesh and bones that composed my body. For her, it must have been like watching a movie star, becoming enamored, and then finally getting to meet the heroic figure in person. Essentially, Bokta was a fan girl. An incredibly hot fan girl with a nigh-insatiable appetite for sex, but a fan girl nonetheless. I couldn't keep myself from smiling as I considered the proposition of what most likely was in store further down the road, so I took one last visual drink of Bokta's naked body and turned, hiking up my pants as I faced the door.

"There's, uh, no chance you get pregnant, is there?" I awkwardly asked as the sudden thought of attempting to raise an infant—in Earth or Realm, it didn't matter—crossed my mind.

I felt Bokta's hand slide playfully around my waist. "Sirens can help prevent such things," she said into my ear. Her teeth grazed the bottom edge of my earlobe before she pulled away. The subtle gesture was enough to make my pants uncomfortably tight once more. With our presence expected in public in just a few moments, I struggled to push my heart rate back into the range of normalcy, thereby calming my own lustful urges.

"She'll take care of it today?" I asked. As soon as the words left my mouth, I felt dirty. And not in a good way. I had essentially asked a woman I had just fucked half a dozen times to go out and find some Plan B. Some boyfriend I was. Hell, I felt more like a customer at a brothel than any kind of boyfriend. I felt sick.

Much to my relief, Bokta laughed off the question. "She cast her spell on me some time ago," she answered.

A burst of relief made its way through my body. "Cool." Admittedly, I still felt like a scumbag for asking.

We made it to the main room of the inn not too much later, and the keeper had provided a spread of warm sausages, various cuts of meat that smelled like they had been roasted in almonds, and several loaves of dark, crusty bread. Amethyst had paid for us each to eat our fill and then take some for the road as well, and she was outside seeing to the gear and final preparations while we did some serious work on the buffet.

Stomachs full, Bokta and I emerged from the warm, smoky inn just as the sun was fully peaking above the horizon, perhaps an hour after dawn. We were behind schedule, I supposed, though not by much.

"The road into Apostate's Rise isn't dangerous, not like the city itself will be, but it sure isn't what anyone would call safe, either," the Siren said, standing in front of three small piles of gear. She and Bokta didn't have much in the way of armor or weapons. Instead, they had general supplies like ropes and climbing hooks, torches, pitons, a lantern, and a few other kits I assumed were related to first aid. My stash, on the other hand, was essentially a spread of gear similar to the one every character received after completing the tutorial in Realm Online.

"Here," Bokta said, noticing my obvious wonder, "I'll show you how to strap it all on."

Over the next ten minutes, Bokta helped me get into a set of leather armor. Most of it fit pretty well, and almost every piece was adjustable, so getting it cinched into place was all that was really required. Wearing it would take some getting used to. I had greaves—or perhaps they'd be called spats—that fastened over my shins and the tops of my boots, a studded leather brigandine with long tassets to cover my thighs, and a pair of hardened bracers that left my elbows and biceps woefully exposed. Still, despite feeling like a squishy mage walking into a high level area without the slightest clue how to survive, the armor brought a distinct feeling of safety that I hadn't experienced since leaving my computer chair. I felt a little more like the demon I was supposed to somehow become.

For weapons, I didn't have much. Amethyst had procured a sturdy short sword in the style of a Roman gladius for me, and my other hand was expected to wield a fairly large wooden kite shield covered in untanned animal hide. Both the gladius and the shield were far heavier than all the games I had played and movies I had seen had led me to believe they would be. For now, I was able to keep the gladius in its sheath on my left hip and the shield slung over my back.

While I felt like a lowly level one character finally getting some relevant gear, the two women were outfitting themselves for actual war. They appeared comfortable as they moved, fastening straps and threading leather strips through brass buckles. Amethyst had her trademark pair of swords in a harness that dangled off both shoulders—a setup I still didn't entirely understand—one of her armored skirts, and a hardened leather breastplate that had been made to accurately encapsulate her generous curves.

To my left, Bokta wore an outfit more befitting her magical nature. She had a small dagger, though it felt more ornamental than practical, and no other weapons that I could see. To protect her from incoming attacks, she wore a long robe made of thick cotton and accented with horizontal bands of reinforced leather. The garment cinched together at the front of her waist, allowing her to move as quickly as the rest of us without sacrificing any potential protective value.

Suited up and ready to venture into Apostate's Rise, no one had any final words. There was no rousing speech, no inspirational quote offered, and no formality at all other than a curt nod from the Siren. The road to the ruined city turned out to be a lot more grim and dismal than it was dangerous. We passed a few 'last chance' vendors selling food, weapons, clothing, and other supplies. Between the occasional merchants hocking their wares was a depressing assortment of discarded items. Clearly, people had died on the road. Amethyst explained that it was often the case that the seriously wounded wouldn't be able to afford healing upon exiting Apostate's Rise, and so they'd have to run as quickly as they could back to the nearest vestiges of normal civilization, sometimes all the way to Essence. Judging by the amount of discarded and forgotten items along the road, most of the wounded never made it. Sadly, all the good loot had already been picked over.

"How many people go into the ruins?" I asked once the huge, jagged skyline of Apostate's Rise was visible over the horizon. We were close. "Will we come across others?"

"There are always bands of adventurers inside the ruins. If we're lucky, we won't run into them. If we're unlucky, we'll have to worry about more than just monsters." Amethyst adjusted the sword on her left side to keep the hilt from bumping into her gear.

At my heels, ever-present as always, was Mr. Patches. I kind of felt bad that the adorable little cat didn't have his own set of armor to protect him. Then again, if he died, I was fairly certain he would come back. Under the armor on my right side and tucked into the belt that held my scabbard was the soft little bag containing the cursed die. Its presence, along with Mr. Patches, was a constant reminder of how I had fucked up. Mistakes back in Mara and Tamernil had been bad, almost catastrophic, but a mistake of that magnitude inside the ruins would certainly get us killed. It was a sobering thought indeed.

The southern gates to Apostate's Rise were, to say the least, intimidating. They had clearly once been a grand structure in their own right. Now, however many years after the city's destruction, they stood on broken hinges, eternally open, their tall iron bars twisted and destroyed. It looked like something massive had broken out of the city . . . Huge claw marks dug into the ground between the two halves of the gate told me I was probably right. I shuddered to think of what it could have been.

We passed through the eeric gates and into the city itself with a quiet air of reverence. The main boulevard through the center of the ruins was lined on either side by decrepit buildings. Most of them had tumbled to the ground. A few still stood higher than one story, and those

in relatively decent condition had barred doors and shut-
tered windows. I assumed they were outposts for those
who still lived in the city, the hardened few who had set
up camp to essentially farm the ruins and plunder the loot
to be had.

Everything in Apostate's Rise was dark. A thick blanket
of haze rested atop every surface. "What's all the dust on
everything?"

"The Emergence brought the dust," Amethyst said.
"When the monsters started coming out of the ground,
great waves of black dust began spewing out of the crater."

"Is it safe?" I asked. There wasn't a gas mask in our gear.

Amethyst only shrugged.

We continued onward toward the very center of the city,
past hundreds of ruined buildings and slimy, algae-covered
fountains. What had once been a fairly well-developed system of gutters paralleling the streets had since been filled
in by horrid refuse. Most of it looked like sloppy, soupy
mud, but some of the protrusions breaking forth from
the clogged gutters certainly weren't branches or pieces of
construction. They were bones.

At the heart of the city was a thriving establishment
Amethyst said was named the Crone. It was a pub of sorts,
but also housed most of the rest of the city's remaining
function, containing everything from a library to a mercenary guild. "Only one rule inside," Amethyst said before
we pushed open the door to enter the noisy interior. "No
fighting. You'll be safe in there, but don't piss off anyone.
The moment you step outside, they'll kill you."

That made me feel better. "Wonderful . . ."

We entered the Crone, and a host of varied smells
and noises instantly assaulted my senses. The building
was huge, far larger than it would have been had the city

retained all of its splendor, since the pub's proprietor had knocked down the walls to expand the main room into a dozen or more of the bordering businesses. The groups of adventurers nearest to us all turned to run some eyes over the newcomers before looking back to whatever they were doing. Most were bent over wooden tables to dissect maps and yell back and forth about the supposed locations of whatever it was they were hunting. The whole atmosphere was one of rugged, violent exploration. Everyone was eager to set out into the ruins and chase their dreams, but they were also a hair's breadth from killing each other at the same time.

Amethyst took a minute to find who she was looking for. She led us to a tall, circular table where two of the most heavily tattooed men I had ever seen were busy arguing over a stack of maps. "Hello, boys," the Siren said as she approached.

Both of the men stopped to eye her up and down, neither taking much care to hide the lust in their eyes. I had to wonder how much magical sway Amethyst held over them. Clearly, her influence was palpable.

The first man, a tall specimen of corded muscles sporting a long black beard and a shaved head, was the first to answer. "Kind of surprised to see you around here, Ammy," he said. His accent was gruff, like a mixture of mountain man and a smoker's cough. His bald head sported several tattoos of large talons clutching at gemstones. I guessed he was the fantasy version of a biker, if such a comparison even made sense.

Amethyst ran a finger down the man's scarred forearm. "Aww, you didn't miss me *that* much, did you?"

"Heh, you're lucky you're safe in here, woman. Lot of people in the Rise that want you dead." The huge man casually gathered up his maps and shifted them to the side of the table, pointedly out of our purview.

"Lot of nerve showing up here," the second, equally large man added. He shook his head and sighed. Though his beard wasn't nearly as long, his head was still decorated by a large black tattoo of a raven with its wings spread wide.

Amethyst turned back to me and Bokta with a smile. "Gideon here is still a little upset over the way our last raid ended," she explained somewhat jovially, a stark contrast to the dour atmosphere of the Crone.

"Used to be three of us! Brothers!" the man named Gideon yelled at her. He raised a fist, but he didn't come close to swinging it. Whatever enforcement procedures were in effect in the Crone, they were serious. Keeping a rugged crowd like the one currently present from devolving into a massive brawl was a commendable feat. Whoever was in charge must have been more feared than anything else, and that fact was terrifying.

"Oh, Val, he brought his own demise down on his own head." Amethyst stepped between the two hulking men, pointedly moving closer to the stack of maps while pretending to only be interested in the brutes and their muscles.

The two men both grunted. One of them pointed at me. "Who's the new guy?"

"Just another merc we're dragging through to the Wall in an hour," Amethyst answered.

More grunting. "Doesn't look like a merc. Scrawny little one, he is."

"Hey, I'm right here, you know," I said, but no one other than Bokta paid any attention to me. Eh, honestly, I didn't really want to get involved in anything. No matter what the prohibition on fighting meant, the two brutes at the table could easily wreck my shit.

Amethyst carried on as though I wasn't even there. "What kind of maps have you two seen from beyond the Wall? Any news on a deserter?"

The one with the raven tattoo put a heavy hand down on top of his stack. "You know the deal. Lay down some gibs, and then we'll talk."

A devilish gleam flickered behind the Siren's eyes. I could practically feel the magic she conjured as it left her mouth and entered the brains of both men at the table. "Give me the map of the Wall," she commanded flatly. *Practically* feeling the magic quickly changed to *actually* feeling it.

I remembered Bokta's words explaining how Sirens operated. I was just as ensnared as the two warriors at the table. My hands moved toward the stack of maps on their accord. I tried to stop them, urged my fingers not to continue their chosen path, but it was no use. Before long I was haplessly fumbling though the maps, my relatively small hands lost amidst twenty pale, tattooed sausages. Well . . . nineteen, I realized. One of them was missing a pointer finger.

A moment later Amethyst had a map in her hand, and the three men around the table—myself included—were standing there dumbfounded. It was already beginning to become difficult to remember how it had happened. The devious Siren didn't wait long to get our little trio out of the Crone. I figured the . . . whatever she had done . . . I couldn't recall . . . wouldn't last long.

Once more standing in the dark, hazy morning light outside the pub, I knew I could finally think clearly, though I wasn't really sure why I felt such a wave of relief. "So . . . we got the map, right?"

Amethyst nodded as she spread out the map against her

thigh for a better look. "Here," she said, pointing to a gap in the darkly drawn battlement. "That hole is new. We'll go through there."

"And once we're on the other side?" Bokta asked.

"The reports said the deserter was bringing things through the Wall. Monsters. We need to find where he's getting them if we're going to track him down." Amethyst rolled the map into a tight cylinder, then tucked it into her pack. "Come on. I don't want to be out overnight if we don't have to be."

The confident woman set her feet toward the west, quickly taking us away from the Crone. Only a few streets later I could see the Wall in all its glory. At one time, it must have been over forty feet tall. Some of the sections still towered to such an incredible height. Most of the structure, however, had crumbled to maybe ten or twelve feet. We got closer, and we could see entire segments of the wall that were missing. Some of the gaps were small, barely wide enough to admit a child, if that. Others were much larger. Amethyst turned us north, silently counting paces in her head.

Perhaps two hundred yards from the main section of the wall was a crumbled bit of stone and mortar that began narrow at the bottom and expanded into a v-shaped chasm that must have been at least fifty feet wide. A slick, fresh-looking layer of slime coated the sides of the fracture.

"What the hell is that?" I asked.

The edges of the break didn't look quite right. Something about them was different from the other breaches.

Amethyst and Bokta both stood close to the bottom of the fracture, and the Siren touched some of the slime with the tip of a single finger. "Anything you recognize?" she asked the Blood Witch.

"Not my kind of magic," Bokta answered. "It looks like . . . saliva, I think."

"Guys, look at the sides," I said. What I was seeing finally clicked in my head. "The stone there wasn't just knocked down. Something *chewed* it apart. Those are teeth marks."

Both the women craned their necks to see. Their following silence told me they were coming to the same conclusion I had.

"If the deserter we're hunting has wrangled something big enough to eat the Wall, we're screwed," I said. *Maybe we should have decided to hit the Northern Quarter . . .*

"We only need the deserter's head, remember?" Bokta moved back to me to get a closer look at the top of the Wall and the distinct marks left by something's enormous mouth.

Technically, she was correct. That minor technicality didn't do much at all to set my mind at ease, though. "So what's the damn plan? Avoid the dinosaur and just hunt the dude who's managed to tame a T-Rex?"

Much to my surprise—no, *horror*—neither woman asked me to explain what a dinosaur was.

Bokta looked at me with fear in her eyes. "You might be right," she said quietly.

"I've never heard of dinosaurs roaming this far north," Amethyst added, fear making her usually stoic voice waver.

"You've actually seen a dinosaur?" I practically demanded. I didn't know how to mime a T-Rex, and I hoped against the odds that we were simply talking about different animals that happened to share a peculiar name.

Amethyst had her hands on her hips. "Big lizard, green skin, more teeth than you can count?" she asked.

Shit. Fucking shit. "Yeah, that's a damned T-Rex."

"You wouldn't know how to kill one, would you?" Bokta asked. "Anything you know from your world?"

The idea of a single person—or even a trained crew with specialized gear—taking down a T-Rex was so absurd it made me laugh in the face of my relentless fear. "If I ever figure out how to get you two back to where I'm from, we're going to sit down and watch *Jurassic Park* together."

CHAPTER 24

"**S**o what do we know about dinosaurs?" Amethyst asked, dropping the question so casually she sounded like a bored professor on the first day of class instructing the students to introduce themselves.

Where could I even begin? "Well, they're all godless killing machines," I started.

Bokta looked confused. "They aren't that bad," she interjected. "Almost all of them only eat plants anyways. They're only dangerous when they're trained to kill."

Amethyst nodded and shot me a look that said I should have known better before opening my mouth.

"Let's start by going over the basics to bring me up to speed. How many kinds of dinosaurs are there, where do they live, and how common is it for someone to tame one and go on a rampage?" I was pacing back and forth in front of the desiccated Wall, a bad habit I had developed back in high school and had never been able to shake. Even when running raids online, I would frequently have to stand and walk back and forth behind my chair, especially if we were about to attempt something we hadn't completed before. I stopped my anxious feet and tried to jam my hands into my pockets—but of course, the armor I was wearing didn't have pockets. Everything I owned was in a small pack hanging from my shoulders under my shield, not in pockets.

At the very bottom of the Wall, Mr. Patches had taken to investigating the saliva-like ooze coating the stones. He pawed at the goop, sniffed it for a while, and then returned to pawing as though the slime was the most fascinating thing he had seen in quite some time. Come to think of it, it probably was.

Bokta apparently knew the most about dinosaurs, so she offered the much-needed explanations. "They only live far to the south. There's another island a long way from the Shimmering Coast. That's where the most experienced adventurers go to train, and sometimes the beasts capable of swimming make it to one of the main continents. I haven't seen any myself, not in the wild. There used to be a group that would haul around cages full of dinosaurs they had captured, and for thirty gibs you could go look at them."

"What happened to the traveling carnival troupe?" In the back of my mind, I felt like I knew the answer already.

"They were eaten when one of the dinosaurs escaped," the Blood Witch answered.

Ha, I was right. Not that I wanted to be right . . .

"So they all eat plants, right? They're herbivores?" I asked.

"As far as I know, that's correct," Bokta replied.

One little thing didn't add up. "But then why did they eat the carnival guys?"

Both the women laughed. "You can't just cage a wild creature like that and expect it to become your friend," Amethyst said.

"Alright, fair enough." I gazed up at the towering rend in the stone and mortar Wall and tried to wrap my head around the idea of fighting something large enough to chew through stone. Herbivore or not, I was having a hard time coming to terms with the looming threat.

"As to how many species exist, I'm not sure anyone knows. I've never seen the island, either," Amethyst said. She looked a little crestfallen, like the prospect of fighting a rampaging T-Rex was finally starting to sink in.

Mr. Patches hopped from the crevasse he was exploring and made a cute little puff of noise as he landed back on the ground.

"Alright," I said, the first flecks of a new plan beginning to come together in my head. "Like you said before, the mission was predicated on the successful capture of the deserter's head, not his towering pets. We just need to figure out where the guy is staying, somehow separate him from his little friends, and then do the deed."

Both the women thought a moment before agreeing to the general parameters of the quest. "First things first: we need to get over the Wall and find where the deserter is hiding." Amethyst went to the split in the stone and easily clambered up to the base of the crevasse. She wasn't quite as lithe and graceful as Mr. Patches, but she was close. And she was certainly more pleasant to watch. She climbed a little ways until the crack widened far enough for her to pull her body through to the other side, and then she turned back to offer a hand to Bokta.

Moving like a slow caterpillar, the three of us eventually plopped down on the other side of the Wall a few minutes later. Maybe it was the armor protecting me from the rougher edges of the split, but I felt a little swell of pride when I realized I had made it through without any scrapes. Sure, the journey had been about four feet in total, but I felt like my jaunt through the caves underneath Mara had paid off.

"How do we track down the deserter?" I asked. I imagined our next side quest would involve a cross-country trek to some obscure hunting lodge where we'd then have to complete tasks for the owner of a pack of dogs in order to be able to purchase a pair of them, then we'd have to head the back to the Wall, and by that time everything would be destroyed, thus triggering a new world event quest . . . at least that's how I imagined it going in Realm of Crafted War.

Luckily, the answer was a lot simpler. "Look," Bokta stated. "Whatever took a bite of the Wall left some pretty big tracks."

It turned out that giant bipedal dinosaurs left divots in the ground roughly the size of smart cars. Even without a pack of bloodhounds, following them through the wilderness would be a fairly simple task.

The tracks wound haphazardly between the trees, heading deeper and deeper into the forest. In the canopy, a bunch of the branches higher up the trunks had recently been broken backward, further adding to the dinosaur's already immense size in my mind. I tried to imagine how my Doom Spike would look bursting up through the ground at the underbelly of a T-Rex. Would it even be relevant? I had no idea.

After what felt like several hours but was more likely than not less than sixty minutes, we found our next clue. The deep tracks, instead of continuing on in a straight-ish line, stopped and became confused for about fifty yards. They clearly circled around a small mound of dirt and sticks, but I got the impression that the T-Rex—if that truly was what we were hunting—had been too large to fit its head inside the small opening. The mound itself was maybe five or six feet high, though the dark tunnel at its base was just large enough to admit an average human torso.

"What do you think—"

A noise came from inside the dark hovel. Whatever had made it was certainly an animal.

All three of us were quiet as the grave as Amethyst gingerly approached the opening. Another sound emanated outward, and she stopped once more, frozen in place.

"What do you think it is?" Bokta asked with a voice so small it was barely audible. We all waited again, straining to not miss the noise.

The only thing that kept me from turning tail was the mere fact that whatever lived in the den had to be smaller than I was. No T-Rex would ever be able to fit in such a place. Or . . .

"Babies?" I guessed. "Could be T-Rex babies."

Amethyst, the closest one to the mound, nodded and waved me forward to join her at her side. I took a hesitant step forward, and a stray twig snapped beneath my boot. I felt like every single noise, every rattle of my pack or jostle of my shield, was amplified tenfold. Whatever was inside would almost certainly be aware of our little band of intruders.

"You'll fit inside if you crawl," Amethyst said.

I didn't really follow what she was saying. Certainly, if anyone was going to venture through the dark hovel, I was the last choice.

"Go! If there are dinosaur babies inside, we need to kill them," she urged.

"Why me?"

Quietly, her eyes wide, Amethyst issued a simple command. "Go into the tunnel and see what's there."

My body began to move without my explicit permission. It felt like being caught in a dream, or maybe the confusing space between dreams and reality where balance was always nonexistent and free will was at an all-time low. I couldn't stop myself from dropping down to my hands and knees. The forest floor poked and prodded at my skin. I got my upper body about halfway into the small space before the shield on my back hit against the low ceiling. Without really thinking, I shrugged off the shield and my pack, eager to continue onward into the suffocating darkness.

My body was fully lost to the lightless hovel before I realized what had happened. Amethyst's exact words were fuzzy in my memory, but I thought she had cast some sort of spell over me. Some mind control, perhaps . . . But I couldn't fully recall what had gone down, or exactly where I was, or the ultimate goal I was hoping to achieve.

With a shrug, I continued onward, one hand after another, until I bumped my head in the lightless passage. Something wet was under my hands. I lifted the fingers of my right hand up to smell whatever it was I was crawling through—blood. *But why was I in the tunnel?*

I felt around the sides of the passageway, but it ended there in something akin to a spherical bowl at the end of a pipe. Then I felt something hairy between my fingers. It wasn't coming for me; I had only bumped into it. "Oh shit, T-Rex babies," I remembered aloud as the record of the events from just a minute before suddenly became clearer.

"T-Rex babies aren't hairy," I muttered. I didn't want

to risk moving my hand forward at all and startling what-ever I had touched. The hair brushing the back of my hand moved in a steady rhythm indicative of breath.

I remembered from high school biology that tons of animals could evolve, or whatever it was called when they advanced from larva to adults and whatnot. Maybe the T-Rex babies were hairy, more like mammals than rep-tiles. It didn't really make sense, but I had to remind my-self that I wasn't on Earth. Anything was possible.

For a brief moment, I considered casting my Doom Spike and ripping apart the hovel. Then a tiny, impossibly sharp claw pricked the skin over the knuckle on my left index finger. I had felt that sensation before. I reached for-ward—slowly—and touched the paw. I counted five little pads with my thumb, one large centric pad surrounded by four little ones.

"Ah, shit," I exclaimed. I reached down and felt the fa-miliar outline of the black tourmaline tucked into my belt. "A goddamned kitten, right?"

I reached under the creature to heft it from the ground, and sure enough, it was the right size and shape for a young kitten. "Alright, time to come with me."

Backing out of the tunnel in reverse was a lot harder than going in had been. Reaching the exit, I heard the tail end of what I suspected had been a brief dispute between Bokta and Amethyst. I didn't catch it all, but I heard the words 'expendable' and 'our salvation' before emerging once more into the hazy light of the forest.

The kitten in my hand was jet black with poofy hair that stuck out in all directions. His—another gender assump-tion like I had done for Mr. Patches—eyes were still closed, and he sleepily stretched out his front paws as he read-justed his weight in my palm.

"Another cat?" Amethyst said flatly.

I didn't pay her any attention. I knew the cat was mine, a gift from Catsi and Funen that I couldn't return. "What's your name, little guy?" I asked. The kitten yawned in reply.

At my feet, Mr. Patches had his paws up on my leg to get a better look at the newest addition to our team. I lowered the kitten down to let Patches have a smell, and the larger cat immediately started licking some of the dirt from the kitten's back.

"I don't know, he looks like a 'Francis' to me," I announced. I looked back up to the two women, but they both wore disinterested frowns. That's when I realized what we had walked directly past without even realizing it.

From the direction of Apostate's Rise, the shrine was impossible to notice. Only after crawling into the hovel and facing the opposite direction would anyone have noticed it, especially considering its position about twenty feet up the side of one of the tall pines.

There, in the space between two parallel branches, was a stone tablet similar to the one I had found before. I held Francis close to my chest to keep him warm, Mr. Patches dutifully trailing only a step behind, and moved under the strange cat shrine to read the inscription:

```
          Property of Catsi and Funen,
          Feline Exemplars Extraordinaire
     Shrine #51 of 90 - limited edition; erected
             on the seventeenth of May,
                  month of the Panther
                  And now, traveler:
             Winding round the way you go—
          Lost if only you follow the flow!
```

"Great," I said. "Another riddle. Either of you have any ideas what it means?"

The two women shook their heads. Amethyst didn't seem particularly interested as she kept up her guard. She was on high alert, listening intently for any sounds of dinosaurs crashing through the forest.

After a moment of contemplation, Francis began to stir in my arms. He needed somewhere to relax and sleep while we journeyed. Eventually he would be large enough to keep up with Mr. Patches constantly nipping at my heels, but until then, I had to rig some sort of kangaroo pouch to keep him safe. I was just glad I hadn't found an entire litter of kittens in the hollow mound of dirt. Protecting a dozen of the little creatures would be impossible. Hell, just keeping myself safe was typically task enough.

I ended up readjusting the leather straps from my pack and my shield to form a makeshift sling over my belly. It wasn't large, but neither was Francis. It would work for now.

We picked up the dino tracks again on the other side of the hovel, following them through broken trees, crushed foliage, and the clinging haze that filled the air. I did notice, much to my relief, that whatever was tainting the air had grown thinner the farther we had trekked from Apostate's Rise. Still, a high priority on my list was to fashion a gas mask as best I could. Spending time in the ruined city was like sitting in one of the smokers' boxes at an airport.

It took another hour or so to finally see our destination. The fruit of our hike turned out to be a wooden fortress built into a hillside, somewhat reminiscent of colonial defenses from the earliest days of American settlers. The walls were crafted from upright, sharpened logs perhaps twenty feet high, and they made a complete circle—at least as far as I could tell—with the exception of the rear wall which abutted directly against the side of a rather sharply rising hill. Everywhere in front of the small compound had been cleared, offering whoever was holed up inside a perfect view of the entire approach.

Not that there was a single door . . .

From our somewhat safe distance several hundred yards away and tucked beneath the coverage of the trees and camouflage of the underbrush, I couldn't see any entrance or exit. There wasn't any drawbridge or sally door for anyone to come or go. If the compound's owner needed supplies, I had no idea how a wagon would ever move beyond the wall. Curiously, the T-Rex footprints went right up to the side of the fortress and then disappeared.

"How does the dinosaur get in?" I asked aloud.

Amethyst looked to our Blood Witch for answers. "Can you tell if the wall is just an illusion?"

Bokta strained to get a better look, then shook her head. "I don't know. Maybe I can test it if we get closer."

"See anyone looking down from the wall?" I asked. There were no guard towers or other lookout posts, not even a crow's nest perched atop the rear hillside. "Looks like the deserter never planned on guests."

"If that's who is inside," Amethyst reminded.

"Good point." Waiting for a person to emerge felt like the right idea, but waiting for a person also meant hanging around for a dinosaur. If I was going to die in Realm, it was *not* going to be by prehistoric consumption. "I don't see anyone. Let's check out the wall first. Maybe there's something around the sides we can't see."

"You just want to rush in?" Bokta asked, her eyebrows raised.

I couldn't really deny that the strategy had worked for me in the past . . . "Sitting around out here won't do much good if the guy we're after is coming and going from the hill out of view. Come on. Let's hurry."

The three of us, two cats in tow, scampered from the trees to the base of the fortress without raising any alarms. The lack of sirens was only mildly comforting. It wouldn't be the wail of a claxon that announced our presence—it would be the brutal roar of a dinosaur as it chomped down on all of our heads for a snack.

"Maybe the dinosaurs don't fit inside," I told myself. It was a long shot, sure, but the idea felt plausible. Then I remembered all the tiny little raptor hatchlings that had devoured the guy at the beginning of one of the *Jurassic Park* movies. Those little buggers were the size of poodles, not construction cranes, and they'd fit anywhere.

The bottom of the wall was just as I had expected. It was hard as it should have been, which I took to mean it wasn't any magical illusion that we could just waltz right through. "Anything special about it?" I asked Bokta.

The woman had a hand against the tall wooden spikes with her eyes closed. She walked slowly forward a few paces, then turned back. "Nothing," she announced. "The wall's real."

Honestly, I had some doubts about the Blood Witch's skills in the 'detect illusion' department. It didn't feel like a school of magic she would be proficient with, and I had never seen her do anything else that felt similar. Regardless, she was the best arcane sleuth we had, so her word was the final word.

"Alright, how do we get in?" I asked, stating the obvious.

Amethyst took a step back to size up the perimeter fortifications. "We might be able to scale it, but it's risky. We don't know what's on the other side."

"Could be a straight drop or a ton of guards," I said.

Sadly, the timbers had been erected too close together to allow a peek of the compound's inner workings. Whoever had made it had known what they were doing.

I stepped back to join in Amethyst's assessment of the wall's height and quickly ruled out climbing as an option. Besides not knowing what was on the other side, there was no way I would have enough traction to get more than a few feet from the ground. The girls might since they were used to that sort of thing, but my untrained ass would not.

Without any of us paying much attention, Mr. Patches had wandered off to the left, happily trotting with his fur brushing along the wall like a giant scratching post. I decided to follow him, more because I had nothing else left to do than on any real hunch, and that's when we finally found the door. Mr. Patches walked right past it before stopping, doing a couple circles, and a curling up in the grass.

"Here's our ticket inside," I announced. The door had been too small and too far around the left side of the fortress for us to have seen it before. In fact, the door really looked too small for humans. Maybe it was a cat door? Another riddle?

"Doesn't feel right," Amethyst said. "If that's the only way inside, there could be all manner of traps and ambushes waiting for us."

She was right. We'd be forced to crawl on our hands and knees. "Well . . . we should at least try to open it, right?"

Bokta approached and tested the door. There wasn't a handle, so she pushed in gently at first, then harder, but it never gave way. "Probably locked from the other side," she said.

That was certainly depressing. "Well, back to square one. Anyone feel like going on a little climb?"

Amethyst had her pack off her shoulders, and she had grabbed a length of rope from within, but she didn't appear to be all that confident. "I don't know if it will work," she said. She tied a loop in one end of the rope and threw it skyward. Her aim was true, and the loop settled around one of the sharpened tops.

"Wait!" Bokta suddenly shouted. There was a rumbling coming from somewhere within the complex. It was deep and low, resonating like Thor hitting a bass drum from atop a cloud.

"Was that—"

"Footsteps!" Amethyst declared. A second boom shook the ground, and then a third quickly followed behind it.

Everything was shaking. The fortress wasn't rattling and threatening to come down like an earthquake might do, but the ground was certainly vibrating with quick bursts of energy. Footsteps. Huge, heavy, mountainous footsteps. "It's still on the other side of the hill, I think," I said, backing off from the fortress. "We can run back to Apostate's Rise, but we have to move now!"

It was too late. A T-Rex, larger than I had thought possible, reared up from the forest on the other side of the wooden compound. I realized then why the footsteps had come to such an abrupt halt with seemingly no explanation. The creature was so large it just walked over the wall. It didn't need a door.

"We're fucked," I stated. There was nothing else to it. The dino had seen us, it was already approaching, and it looked pissed. No matter how fast we ran, we would never be quick enough to make it to safety. We couldn't duck back into the forest and hope to hide, either—the thing would simply crush the forest as it stomped around looking for us. I tried to remember how the T-Rex had been killed in *Jurassic Park*, but it had been far too long since I'd seen the movies. A cliff? An electric fence? A combination of the two? One glance at the forest and the wooden compound and I knew we had neither.

"Inside!" Bokta yelled, pointing at the little door. "Hack it down! Hide!"

She had a dagger in her hand, and she was frantically bashing it against the miniature entrance. Small as her blade was, it didn't deal any noticeable damage. I grabbed my sword and joined her. We chipped away at the outermost layer of the wood . . . far too slowly to be useful.

The T-Rex roared. Its voice mimicked the movies from my childhood: impossibly loud, terrifying beyond reason, and carrying enough force to make me cover my ears.

In stark contrast to the towering insanity quickly bearing down on us, Francis decided to offer a faint mewl as the roar's echo came to an end. It was so preposterously juxtaposed that it made me laugh. The two women stared at me, fear and puzzlement fighting for control of their expressions.

"Wait . . . that's it! Riddle thirty-four! From the cats!" I ran through the old riddle's text in my head, repeating the short lines. It made sense.

Scratch, scratch, a small wooden door—
Hatch, hatch, a sudden, loud roar!

"Guys, we found the small wooden door. Scratch it!" I dropped to my knees next to Bokta, and we both raked our hands across the coarse wood. It hurt like hell, but we didn't stop. The T-Rex was almost on top of us in the most literal sense possible.

Nothing happened.

Well, actually, a shit ton was happening. A gigantic T-Rex was stampeding directly at us, roaring and flinging up clods of dirt larger than minivans. But, unfortunately, nothing happened to the door. Bokta and I only succeeded in bloodying our hands.

"Shit, maybe the cats can do it." I ripped Francis from his leather sling and nearly rammed his tiny body straight through the door. Holding his little paws against the door, I made scratching motions against the wood, and then a new sound joined the cacophony of the rampaging dinosaur. Gears were rattling and clicking behind the door. A wedge of light began to appear as the gap between the left side of the door and the tunnel itself widened.

"Come on, come on!" I urged, begging the door to go faster. I stole a glance over my shoulder. The T-Rex was close enough that I could see the individual teeth filling his mouth, each as long as a sword.

I shoved Francis through the opening first, then Bokta pushed herself into the tunnel, her sides scraping the still-retracting door. Amethyst was the next smallest, so she went second. That left only Mr. Patches and I exposed to the charging beast. We had a couple seconds, maybe five at the most, before we'd be crushed to death.

"Get in there, Patches!" I yelled, scooping up the multicolored cat and diving into the cramped, square passage and landing hard on my elbows. A thunderous dinosaur foot crashed into the ground outside the tunnel right where I'd been standing just a second before.

"Hell yeah," I breathed, the adrenaline still pumping away through my veins. Amethyst's pack of gear had been thoroughly destroyed by the weight of the monster, but the rope and other adventuring supplies were a small price to pay for our lives.

It finally dawned on me that light coming from the tunnel felt odd. It meant there was something close by, and whatever it was needed light. Anything needing light meant there was something sentient there to produce the light. Judging by the smoky smell, there were torches.

"Be on alert," I said once I had regained my breath. There wasn't enough room in the small area to shift our positions, so I was offered a fine view of Amethyst's lightly clothed backside as we crawled along, though my vision was constantly obscured by Mr. Patches walking between.

Only twenty feet into the tunnel, we found the source of the light. The small shaft ended in a square opening a little larger than the one we had come through as we had entered, and the area beyond was rather large. Seeing no overt threats, Bokta was the first to emerge into the inner courtyard of the fortress. There wasn't much there other than grass, sunlight, and a few stinking carcasses that must have been the remnants of whatever the T-Rex had been eating. Speaking of the beast . . .

The T-Rex had stomped along deeper into the woods, but we could still hear it. "We need to be quick," I said. The others agreed. If the dinosaur knew where we were—and I was pretty sure it would be able to smell our collective fear and lack of deodorant—it would easily be able to leap over the wooden palisade and add our corpses to its pile of partially-eaten refuse.

"Only one door," the Siren said, pointing toward the hillside. Around her feet, Mr. Patches was running in excited circles. I had no idea if the cat's display was meaningful or not, and I had no way of finding out.

No matter what, I knew what my plan was: make a run for the door. I didn't wait for the others. If they wanted to get eaten alive, they were both certainly welcome to make that decision.

Unlike the tiny entrance on the outside of the fortress wall, the inner door wasn't locked. It was a simple piece of tree bark—barely even a door by most standards—and I ripped it aside with ease.

"Whoa . . ." The room beyond the shoddy bark door reinforced the *Jurassic Park* image that had already been cultivated in my mind. I was in the inside the hillside, and I had to wonder how the dirt and soil above my head wasn't collapsing. The whole hillside was hollow. Dozens of torches illuminated a rather sizeable cavern complete with a gentle river flowing horizontally through the whole thing. The river wasn't deep by any means, perhaps four or five feet, but the cliff I was standing on certainly went down a ways. The three of us had about forty feet of ground before a thirty-foot drop down to the level that contained the river. On the other side of the water, the ground spiked back up from the shore to a height on par with the entrance. To either side, there were no doors or tunnels or other passages that I could see. The only way forward appeared to be downstream where the river disappeared under a low hanging rock ledge. But the river was thirty feet down, and what little—wholly inadequate—climbing equipment we'd brought had been crushed by an angry T-Rex.

Behind me, I hadn't realized that Bokta and Amethyst had entered the mountain lair as well. They spread out right and left and spent a good amount of time inspecting things, probably trying to analyze the next move just as I was.

"I think we have to get across," Bokta said, her hands on her hips.

"How the hell do we do that?" I asked.

Amethyst went to the very edge of our little cliff and peered over. Then, shaking her head, she returned with a frown on her face. "There's another passage on the other side, but without a bridge, it'll be impossible."

"Well, any ideas?" I gave Francis a little pet, and the adorable kitten mewled in response. I thought of the second riddle Catsi and Funen had delivered to me by way of carved stone. *Lost if only you follow the flow* felt like a hint that we should dive into the river and start swimming.

Diving into the river would mean death at worst, paralysis at best. Five feet of water—and I was truly guessing there, it could easily have been much less and only appeared deeper on account of my elevation—was far too shallow to use it for practicing my swan dive.

Amethyst thought for a moment before returning to the edge of the drop. "There," she said, pointing into the water below. "Platforms."

Obscured by the flow of the water and the inconsistent light provided by the torches mounted all around was a set of six circular stones. Had they been thirty feet higher, they would have formed a perfect bridge we could have used to easily gain the opposite ledge. "I've seen that kind of shit before. It's a dungeon puzzle. We have to figure out the puzzle, and then the platforms will dramatically rise up from the water below. "

Bokta arched an eyebrow. "Think you can do it?" she asked.

"Hell yeah." I hadn't felt such confidence a single time since Bokta had summoned me in a vat of pig guts. "It's a dungeon puzzle. We're in a legit dungeon. And that's probably the best sentence I've ever spoken in my entire life."

CHAPTER 25

"**A**lright, team. Let's figure it out. Bokta, you check the torches on the right. Amethyst, you handle the ones on the left." It felt good to be in charge for once. I had been out of my element for such a damn long time, and now I was finally directing the flow of things, issuing commands and feeling like a badass.

Sadly, neither of the women appeared eager to become my underlings. "Check them for what?" Amethyst asked.

Ah, right. 'Checking' the torches in Realm Online would have simply meant walking up to them, looking for any sparkle or sheen to indicate that the objects could have some interaction, and then pressing the function key: F. Without a keyboard and mouse, the process would be a little different. "Look for levers, notches, loose mountings, hidden buttons or strings, really anything that might give us a clue about how to proceed," I explained.

That got them moving. They split up to either side of

the wide platform we were on, checking each of the many sconces for secrets. I, on the other hand, took a moment to watch their obedience. It was satisfying, and not in just a visceral 'I'm in charge' kind of way. It was nice to feel a little bit of respect for once, almost like I was finally earning my keep.

My reverie was quickly broken when Amethyst glanced back over her shoulder and scowled at my obvious lack of work. Not wanting to shake my tenuous hold on the reins, I set about scouring the ground and the stones for similar pieces to the puzzle.

Bokta was the first to come up with something. She found a gap between a torch and the wall, and the little space revealed a metal panel underneath—a button, I was sure of it.

"Don't try it yet," I said, still wanting to have more information before proceeding. When figuring out some of Realm of Crafted War's more complex and ever-changing dungeon puzzles, I had kept a notebook by my side to draw out everything I knew and get a fresh perspective. Being stuck in a live action version of the game, I had no such luxury. A few sheets of parchment and a pen were high on my priority list to buy when I got back to Essence or wherever we would end up next.

A little while later, Amethyst found another pressure plate hidden behind one of the torches on her side of the room. Much to my personal dismay, I didn't find anything.

"Alright, we have two buttons. Either we need to push them in sequence, or we need to push them at the exact same time." I paced a little in front of the drop, looking down to the water for some kind of reassurance that I was making the right call. "The puzzle should just bring up the pillars from the water to make us a bridge, but there might be hidden traps or something if we don't do it exactly right. Be prepared."

The two gorgeous ladies stood by their respective buttons and waited for my signal. "Alright, we'll try simultaneous activation first." I held up five fingers on my right hand and slowly ticked them down to a fist. "Now!"

Both buttons were depressed, and both of the torches disguising them instantly went dark. From below, down in the depths of the water, there came a long, steady rumble. Then, just as I had predicted, two stone pillars began to lift up toward the ceiling . . . but we needed three pillars, and the two that raised were farthest from our little ledge, so we still couldn't get across.

"What now?" Bokta asked. Unlike Amethyst, she seemed to be enjoying the challenge. The Siren looked like she just wanted it all to be over as soon as possible. I figured that giving up even a modicum of control must have been hell for her.

"We need to find something, another pressure plate or something similar, I bet," I answered. "Stay at the torches. I'll find what we need."

Both women stayed where they were, but the pillars nonetheless began to descend, splashing water all over the riverbank as they moved. "We'll need to figure out the timing," Bokta said with a smile.

She was right. It felt like hanging out with a gamer chick, the all-elusive unicorn of the MMO world. The few women I had let know about my gaming habits back in the real world—and by few I meant less than five—had never even taken a cursory interest. "Games are for kids," they had pretty much all said. But here I was in a dungeon puzzle, running for my life, and Bokta was actively helping me solve it. The Blood Witch didn't just scoff and blow it off.

I scoured the area in the middle of the ledge for another plate. There weren't many leaves or other debris, so I felt kind of ridiculous trying to brush away dirt in search of a clue. Finally, along the inside part of the door we had come through not long before, I found what I had sought: a metallic lever that I could pull down was mounted directly above what would have been the frame had we been in a modern house. The only problem was I couldn't quite reach it to get a good enough grip.

"Amethyst, switch me places," I called, jogging over to the torch where she impatiently stood.

The Siren looked skeptical. "You just want to be first across the stones," she accused.

"Wait, what?" The thought hadn't even crossed my mind. "We're a team. No one gets left behind." I gave Francis a little pat in his sling just to drive home the point. If I was willing to risk my ass *and* try to save a helpless kitten at the same time, that had to show how selfless I was, right?

It seemed to work, and Amethyst took up my position at the door frame, her hand firmly grabbing the hidden handle. "At the same time again?" the woman asked.

"I think so." I hoped it would work. Three triggers for three stone platforms made sense. In a video game, I was almost positive it would work.

I gave the signal again, and we all did our jobs at once. An absolutely delightful rumble of noise, roughly fifty percent louder than the first time, accompanied our button and lever activations.

"Let's watch how much time we have," I said, shooting Bokta a genuine smile. We counted the seconds silently in our heads until the pillars began their loud descent.

"Twenty-four counts," the Blood Witch announced. By my estimation, a 'count' was roughly equally to a second.

Without the quantification of time, knowing for certain would be difficult.

Regardless, we had plenty of time if we moved fast. "Alright. Amethyst, your lever is farthest away, but we all need to move at full speed just in case. Bokta, you go first, and I'll be right behind you. Everyone ready?"

Nods all around.

"Now!" I pushed my button and took off at a sprint for the pillars in the center of the room. I'd have to make about a four foot jump to reach the first hovering platform, but I wasn't too worried. The insane level of adrenaline coursing through my body would easily carry me far enough.

Bokta reached the ledge just as the first pillar was locking into place. I wasn't behind her by much. She leapt for the pillar, landed gracefully—

—and a new sound joined the rushing water thirty feet below. A rumble and scrape came from the other side of the cavern. I didn't have time to figure out what it was. "Keep going!" I yelled.

Bokta didn't hesitate to jump to the next pillar. Following her lead, I vaulted through the air and landed squarely in the middle of the first platform, though my balance was less than ideal, so it took me a moment to gain my bearings enough to stand.

"Hurry it up!" Amethyst yelled, still waiting on the ledge. The first pillar was already beginning to descend, albeit slowly.

I scrambled up, took a single breath to steady my heart, and leapt onto the second pillar. Another success.

A shrill woman's voice, a shriek, pierced my concentration. I jerked my head up, expecting to see Bokta go tumbling down into the water below, and nearly lost my own balance in the process. Bokta had just reached the final platform. In front of her, maybe thirty feet from me, a new door had appeared.

Three angry raptors the size of overgrown mastiffs had emerged from the new door, and they were closing in on Bokta with their dagger-like teeth snapping out for a kill.

Without hesitation, I summoned Doom Spike to the front of my mind, spent a fraction of a second lining it up, and let loose.

Direct fucking hit. In the space of a heartbeat, I shattered the three raptors. With my goddamn mind! The frozen wedge of darkness had been perfect, rushing up from the ground and shattering the poor animals like a glass skylight subjected to a vertically oriented cannon.

The platform beneath my feet began to descend, violently jerking away my victory rush and wrenching me back into reality. Well, back into Realm, which was close enough to reality to count. I stole a glance backward to see Amethyst about to jump onto my platform with me whether I was ready for it or not.

I jumped forward, just barely making it to the next platform, and heard the Siren land on pillar number two a second after. The third platform began to descend as well, and I didn't waste any more time vaulting for the ledge. I made it, then turned to offer a hand to Amethyst, who pointedly ignored the proffered help in favor of jumping even farther just to be out of my range.

Whatever. I didn't need her approval. And besides, I kind of figured she was just jealous that I had saved a member of our party. Speaking of which . . . Bokta wrapped me in her arms, her soft, ample chest pressed against my torso. She kissed me.

It was a good kiss—perhaps a bit awkward with Amethyst, basically a sexual tyrant, watching us—and I felt like

I could have enjoyed it forever. As it turned out, 'forever' lasted all of four seconds before I felt . . . something else. I didn't know how to describe it. In the back of my mind, certain sensations I had never felt before began rushing about and clearing away cobwebs like all the dusty, unused knowledge stored between my ears was suddenly being revived.

I broke away from the kiss, intent to look at absolutely nothing as the overwhelming wave of whatever it was ran its course. A few seconds later, it ended.

Standing there slack-jawed with the taste of Bokta's tongue on my lips, I knew what had happened: I had leveled up. A digital notification ran across my vision:

Level: 2

Experience: 1300 / 2500

Favor: 925 / 1000 – Rank 1

Available Attribute Points: 1

"Shit, guys. I leveled." Had we been playing online and grinding alts through dungeon runs for quick XP, I would have announced the level with a solemn 'Ding!' and the others would have simply grunted their congratulations before quickly losing all interest. Here, in the real-ish world, it was a much, *much* bigger deal.

"Leveled . . . what?" Amethyst asked, her arms crossed and a frown plastered to her face.

"Like, I was level one before. Now I'm level two." It really wasn't that hard to understand, was it? But again, no one else seemed to have a character sheet.

Bokta joined the frowning contest. "Like the level of a house or leveling a surface to make it even?" she asked.

I sighed. Of course they didn't understand it like that. They acquired new abilities as they progressed because that was how life went for them. Hell, unlocking a second skill probably wasn't even that cool.

Speaking of which, the bottom left of my vision showed the notification for my character sheet. For level two, the Desecrator had seen fit to bestow me with something slightly less impressive than Doom Spike. Still, casting *real* magic was pretty damn insane, but I couldn't help but feel at least a little cheated when I read the notification:

New Ability: Fancy Illusions. Create a swirling pattern of illegible runes on a target surface, confusing and distracting your enemies.

The ability was just as lackluster as the name implied. When I called it to the front of my mind, I saw an outline of intricate swirls, whorls, and other nonsensical calligraphy bits hovering over the nearest flat surface large enough to hold it all. That meant the cavern wall. I *knew* what the ability could do without needing to try it. It would make a bunch of confusing shit appear as though it had been carved or painted there—I couldn't quite tell that part— and that would be it. The symbols held no arcane meaning, and they wouldn't serve as any sort of magical canvas upon which other cool stuff could be accomplished. They were simply Fancy Illusions. Oh well.

Time to allocate my attribute point. I still didn't know exactly what the points would modify, but they seemed fairly straightforward. Online, I had never really been a huge fan of the min-maxing strategy so many other players employed. They'd bottom out all but one stat in order to essentially become specialists. It worked well, but only if you had a reliable party to back you up in the areas where you were lacking. Here, my party was small, and I didn't want to spread myself thin. Since staying alive was the top priority, I dropped my point into defense and dismissed my character sheet. I had to admit though, the commerce attribute seemed entertaining. It existed in the game, but

I had never played much with it. That was one area where I had never delved too deeply. Being able to haggle better would certainly come in handy once we got our bounty.

Before we moved on to the next section of the dungeon, I wanted to see if I could get a handle on what levels my two companions were. Knowing our strengths would be critical. "How many abilities do you two know?" I asked both of them. Assuming my 'one skill per level' theory turned out to be true, it would finally put the world's power creep into something I'd have no trouble understanding.

"You've seen two of mine," the Blood Witch said. "I know five others, though they aren't that useful."

Amethyst wore a smirk that told me she was some crazy high level. "Well, you've seen a lot more than two of mine. Twenty different positions at least, though I didn't count. And how many more beyond those you witnessed have I mastered? You'd like to know, wouldn't you?"

Like before at the little hovel in the woods where I'd found Francis, I felt Amethyst's Siren hold playing tricks with my brain. All I could think about was turning the dungeon floor into a vile den of debauchery. I stopped my hand as it hovered over my crotch, then told myself it had been Bokta's kiss that had distracted me, nothing else.

Coming back to my senses, I figured she was about level thirty . . . if she was telling the truth. But what did it really matter? If all of her talents were just different ways to fuck someone into mental slavery, she wouldn't be terribly useful outside the bedroom. Then again, she *did* have the most combat experience in our little party, and I wouldn't mind another . . . No, that was the magic talking. Maybe. Probably.

"One more thing," I said. "What was the last ability you learned, Bokta? And how much have you practiced it?"

I felt like I had gone from level one to level two pretty quickly, or at least after minimal practice, but that could have simply been the design. The first ten or so levels in any game were always designed to be a breeze, right?

Bokta put a hand on my chest. "Summoning," she said. "And I've only practiced it once."

In all honesty, I could have figured that one out on my own. I should have. "Alright, we've spent long enough here. Only a matter of time before we get jumped by more dinosaurs or by the deserter himself. Time to roll out." I decided another hug and quick kiss wouldn't hurt—it wasn't a speed run, after all—and then we were off down the only path available, Mr. Patches scampering along at our heels.

CHAPTER 26

The stench emanating from the next room hit my nostrils before any of us could see what was there. The hallway, carved right into the stone of the hillside, was cramped at best. At worst, the constricting stone brought back unwanted memories of our flight from Mara. Thankfully, the tunnel didn't last long. Coming to the end was a relief as the smokiness generated by the torches finally let up.

The room was dominated by a single corpse, huge and prehistoric, its chalky rib bones sticking up into the air. Judging by the massive skull, the creature had been a woolly mammoth—or whatever the Realm version of a mammoth would be. I had to cover my face with a hand to keep the smell at bay. The mammoth had recently been alive, though all but the bottom flesh resting against the ground had been eaten. Behind it, between the skeleton and the back wall, was a pile of droppings large enough to give me a good idea of what it was that had eaten the mammoth. Another dinosaur, I was certain of that much at least, and it was huge. It would make the raptors I had killed earlier look like nothing.

"Guys, we need to get out of here quick. Whatever ate that mammoth has to be enormous," I said. There was only one problem . . . Well, maybe we had *three* problems.

"Which path?" Amethyst asked. There were three tunnels leading away from the feeding chamber, each spiraling out in a different direction.

A sound coming from one of the pathways made all us stop. I held my breath, listening intently but desperately hoping to hear nothing.

Much to my dismay, the sound repeated, and it was closer. A howl. Or maybe a grunting groan mixed with a howl. Whatever it was, it was certainly unfriendly. And rapidly approaching.

And—

A horn appeared from the path on the left. Before any of us could react, two more horns joined the first. With a rampaging stampede of cloven hooves, a mottled, grey triceratops thundered into the feeding chamber.

"Oh, shit!" I jumped back, angling myself toward the narrow passage that would take us to the first room with the river and the puzzle stones, but I knew retreat would mean suicide. The tunnel would be a death sentence for at least one of us. There wasn't enough room inside even to hope to dodge or evade, so the triceratops would just run us over one by one like a squishy line of blood-filled dominos.

Thinking much faster than I was, Amethyst leapt into action, pulling a blade from her side and getting ready to strike. The charging beast crashed into the wall to my left with its shoulders. The noise was massive, and I had to imagine the shock the creature felt was tremendous. No concussion protocol here in Realm, but it probably needed it.

Amethyst brought her sword down hard on the triceratops' flank.

The beast's dull, thick hide repelled the blow like a foam sword against the side of a building. "Need to get under it!" I yelled. The skin beneath the creature was a lighter color and looked less armored. Stabbing it from beneath would probably be our answer. Probably . . . There was still a pretty solid chance that the skin there was just as hardened as everywhere else, and I was just an idiot for assuming the color made a difference.

Doom Spike was still on cooldown. It would have been the perfect spell, rending the dinosaur apart from the ground up. My second spell, making some fancy runes appear on the walls, felt useless.

Lumbering and taking its time, the triceratops shook off the concussive force of ramming the wall and turned like a bull in an arena to search for another target. In the small feeding chamber, it didn't need to look far or long. It pawed the ground, tensed for a second, then took off again.

The charge was quick and brutal. With three huge horns sticking forward from its armored head-plate-thing, the triceratops was essentially a trident attached to a minivan, and our parking lot was rather small. Bokta, the intended target of the skewering charge, managed to get out of the way of the deadly horns, but the beast's wide, frilled skull knocked her to the ground nonetheless.

Amethyst and I both ran in at the dinosaur's side. The Siren was clearly going in for a clean shot at the creature's belly while I was more concerned with Bokta's health.

Before either of us could do anything effective, the beast turned and bucked, forcing the two of us backward and leaving Bokta on the other side of the chamber. Not ideal.

The triceratops looked at me. It wasn't a casual glance or an accidental passing over of the eyes. No, it stared at me for a second as though it had some advanced intelligence unknown to animals—or maybe I was just scared out my mind and seeing things that weren't really there. No matter what was actually happening in the beast's eyes, I knew for a fact its feet were moving, and I was the next target of its murderous rampage.

My mind flickered back to a YouTube video I'd seen of a spectator getting gored by a loose bull in a Spanish arena. That shit was rough. And bulls only had two horns, not three. In good matador fashion, I waited until the last possible second to jump out of the way. With a brutal grunt, the triceratops rammed its side into the chamber wall, deftly turning at the moment before impact to spare its horns.

I grabbed the gladius from my side and tried to make the most of the handful of seconds I'd have before the dinosaur found its footing once more. Slashing across the back of the creature's legs proved far more effective than Amethyst's overhand chop on its haunch had been. The creature squealed, and my heart instantly sank through my chest.

Sure, I'd drowned a man—a perfectly innocent, good man—with my own foot . . . but hurting an animal was different. The dinosaur didn't know what the hell it was doing. It didn't hate me, and given different circumstance, we probably could have gotten along. Then I saw that man's face struggling for air back in Crimson Sands . . . But an animal!

I couldn't do it.

I tossed my short sword aside and ran for the tunnel that led back to the entrance. Without a cape, I had to use my body to taunt the thing, but after drawing blood from its rear legs, it seemed intent on goring me anyways. The triceratops charged, and I lunged to my right, feeling the air as it whooshed by into the tunnel.

"Run!" I yelled, pointing to the nearest exit with absolutely no idea of where it would lead.

The others shared my sentiment, and we booked it. I scooped up my sword and threw an arm under Bokta's shoulder at the same time. The three of us sprinted down the random passage I had selected, bumping and tripping over each other as we went. I wouldn't gain any experience points from the fight, but so be it. I could live with that.

Seeing a ladder only about thirty feet into the tunnel felt like a miracle. Unless the triceratops was also a circus animal capable of climbing, we'd be safe from its horns—and I tried not to think about the T-Rex likely waiting for us somewhere deeper in the complex. Bokta went first on the ladder, quickly followed by Amethyst, both ladies offering me exquisite views as they climbed.

". . . there," a voice urged.

"What?" I wasn't sure which one of them had spoken.

Amethyst made a weird gesture with her hand behind her back from the next level.

"What's going on?" I called up to them.

Sounds of a new battle, one involving humans instead of dinosaurs, answered my question. The gesture and whatever one of them had tried to tell me had been a warning. And I'd been too engrossed by the beautiful display of legs and ass to realize what had happened. Hand over hand, I scrambled up the ladder as quickly as I could manage, no doubt cutting a much less pleasing figure as I made the ascent.

When I reached the top, the new battle was in full swing. I was only late by maybe thirty seconds, and already there was blood splattered across the ground. Who was bleeding was impossible to know. The tunnel I had so hastily chosen led to what looked like a room for dinosaur handlers with harnesses, nets, ropes, and other equipment hanging from pegs along one wall. Huge chunks of raw meat hung in sacks on the opposite wall, and an overturned set of tables and chairs dominated the middle.

By my count—and the room was small so I figured I hadn't missed anyone—there were three tamers currently giving a hell of beat down to my two lovely companions. Amethyst and Bokta had been separated, the Blood Witch with one tamer to my left and the Siren fighting off a pair of enemies to my right.

No matter how bad I felt about slicing up the triceratops below, my conscience instantly ghosted me at the prospect of killing other humans. Maybe I *was* evil. Perhaps I'd always been that way. But it was us or them, and I fully intended to survive with at least one of my hot new friends intact. Not being horribly disfigured by a sword edge would be an added bonus.

Since Amethyst was outnumbered, I thought to help her first. Whoever said chivalry was dead had never seen me rescue a damsel in distress, that was for sure. The problem was I could easily tell that everyone was *much* more proficient in hand-to-hand combat than I was. Amethyst spun and twirled as she parried an array of jabs, simultaneously keeping herself alive while at least unbalancing the two men she fought. I knew I'd be sorely outclassed. Hell, I'd probably do more harm by getting in the way.

Against my instincts, I waited. The ring of steel continued to fill the small room as I stood by the ladder, gladius in hand, muscles at the ready. Since none of them were apparently keen on coming after me, I decided to keep my shield on my back. That meant Francis got to keep his leather cradle on my stomach too, and I didn't think his chances would be great fending for himself on the ground.

Like a glorious gift being offered to a god, Amethyst shot me a nod and then pushed one of her assailants in my direction. She used the hilt of a sword to make the maneuver which had left her open to attack from the second tamer, but the gambit had paid off. The first attacker stumbled into my reach, and I grabbed him by the collar with both hands. With a heave—struggling to keep my grip on my sword at the same time—I launched the poor bastard over the ladder. He landed with a thud and a cry so full of pain I knew he wouldn't be getting back to his feet any time soon.

The odds back in our favor, I rushed over to Bokta to lend my sword, and together we cornered the female tamer she'd been fighting. The woman blocked an attack from her right, quickly whirled to parry a second, and then my gladius took her in the gut right above her pelvis. I looked into her eyes as they went wild with pain, but I didn't care. Killing humans was something I could tolerate. And based on the pounding of my ribcage, I enjoyed it to some extent. In the middle of telling myself that it was only the self-preservation drive that had filled with body with joyous adrenaline, Bokta ran her blade through the tamer's throat, finishing off the kill that I had begun.

I could feel a chunk of experience points filling my body. It wasn't like before when I had leveled, so I knew I hadn't hit level three just yet, but I was making progress. Quick progress.

We both turned back to help Amethyst, but we were too late. She was on the ground, both legs wrapped around the final tamer, and one of her swords was pressing down on the man's neck. I have to say, it was a little painful watching the two of them essentially in a fucking position. Hell, if the sword had been a knife instead, I'd be more inclined to think Amethyst was simply enjoying some male company.

A spray of blood followed by a weak gurgle dispelled any remaining sexual thoughts from my mind. Amethyst had been rough, but not *that* rough.

"Alright, what's next?" the Siren asked as she stood and brushed some of the gore from her legs and weapons. She was casual and maybe a bit stoic, her body not displaying any of the adrenaline effects clearly visible from Bokta and me.

"Not even a bit of thanks for saving your ass?" I had killed one of her opponents, after all. I felt like the act deserved some recognition.

Bokta, the living embodiment of a fan girl, slid an arm across my back for a side-hug.

A moan came from the bottom of the ladder. Apparently, the guy hadn't died. "Going to finish it?" Amethyst asked coldly.

"Eh, let the triceratops have another meal," I answered. Honestly, for as brief as the fight had been, I was still tired. Going down and back up the ladder would be a pain.

Bokta broke away from my side to investigate our way out. In the back of my mind, I felt the cooldown for Doom Spike expire, unlocking another use of the ability. I still had no clue how cooldowns actually worked, and I guessed I'd need to find another Sovereign Magus before I'd get some definitive answers. Resting was a sure-fire way to refresh the ability, but maybe leveling or earning XP accelerated the process. Oh well. It was an issue for another time.

"One of the paths goes outside," Bokta announced, pointing toward what looked like natural light emanating from a passage. "The other goes deeper. We'll find the deserter down there."

She seemed confident, and that was good enough for me. It made sense for a bunch of dinosaur handlers to have access to both the forest and the boss.

The boss tunnel, as I decided to call it in my head, was a bit larger than all the others we had seen so far. It was wide and worked, supported by thick wooden beams at regular intervals. Whoever the deserter was, he'd had help building the complex. That much was obvious. I got the feeling that we'd find a huge underground lair full of bad guys just waiting to pound our shit the moment we turned a dark corner. We'd been lucky so far.

Luck never lasted, and judging by my previous life as a boring, lonely accountant with a shitty apartment and more debt than I'd ever hope to pay off, luck had never been on my side before. Then again, it *was* my highest stat . . . so maybe there was still hope for our merry little band.

The more I thought about it, the larger the sinking feeling in my gut continued to grow. We were walking head first into Mount Doom without even a pair of plucky hobbits or a gnarly bald gnome to keep us company.

CHAPTER 27

The boss tunnel was basically a mineshaft. It went down nearly vertically at some points, faintly illuminated by the occasional torch mounted on the wall. The lack of noise as we trudged deeper into the mountain was disconcerting. If the deserter—or maybe referring to him just as a dinosaur tamer was better—lived at the end of the passage, he should have been making more noise, right?

"Maybe we're in a waste shaft or something . . ." I said.

Everyone else was quiet for a bit as we continued. "Maybe one of the tamers up above was the deserter we were looking for," Bokta added.

That idea hadn't crossed my mind. We could have already completed the quest and not even known it. "What then?" I asked, looking back over my shoulder at the brutal climb that would await us should we need to make our exit via the same descent. If we had to leave in any kind of a hurry, I wasn't sure we'd make it.

"We'll know the deserter when we find him," Amethyst answered. I hoped she was right. A typical boss would have a big dramatic speech before we killed him online, so maybe it worked that way here as well. Skulls and pentagrams and whatnot hanging from the walls would be a good indication that we'd reached the final chamber. It always worked like that online. Here, I had no idea.

Without saying anything else, our party of murderers continued deeper into the mountainside until the passage ended with a brightly lit opening connected to another chamber. The room beyond the tunnel was everything that video games and movies had taught me to expect for a boss fight: a huge, swirling pool of water surrounded by a stone ledge on all sides, kind of like Mother Nature's version of a toilet made for giants. Bridging the chasm were three pathways, each shaky and narrow. Overhead, a team of small winged dinosaurs circled like vultures.

The weirdest thing about the whole underground lair was the light. It was bright enough to see without much strain, but I had no idea where the light was coming from. Maybe there was a hole in the ceiling up above which allowed the sun to come down, but that would probably require some sort of mirror setup to be useful. Then again, it could have simply been magic.

"Any ideas?" I asked the women. We had fanned out to where I was in the middle again with Bokta on my right and Amethyst on my left. One of us for each of the treacherous paths across the whirlpool. Though after a second look, my feet inching terrifyingly close to the ledge that would certainly mean my doom, I saw another curious development. On the other side of the chasm was a stone staircase. It had been carved right into the rock, and it led down to the water's edge where a small boat was tied against a single wooden pylon.

If the deserter had constructed more pylons, he could have established a whole yacht club down in the underbelly of the mountain and spent his days cruising . . . wherever. Despite the churning waves, the water did lead somewhere, though it was impossible to tell exactly where. "That boat has to be important," I said, pointing to the small craft jostling against its moorings.

Bokta came up to my side and nodded. "It must lead to the deserter, right?"

"Seems like an awful lot of protection for a guy who has an army of dinosaurs to do his bidding," I answered. "Why go through all the trouble? Why bother with the puzzle and the tamers up above as a buffer? Wouldn't a T-Rex be more than enough to dissuade any trouble?"

Whatever the dude was hiding, it must have been intense. The security system was certainly impressive. Hell, it was a lot more than just impressive. Had I not been standing in the middle of it, I would have called in unbelievable.

"It didn't dissuade us, did it?" Amethyst reminded me from the left where she was also peering over the side of the ledge.

"Good point."

Bokta scooted away from the ledge and shook her head. "I bet that's the emergency exit," she said. "The river has to run somewhere. That has to be how the deserter makes an escape in a pinch."

"Alright, makes sense to me," I said. "So where's the deserter? How do we find him?"

It was hard to tell, but it didn't look like there were any more rooms across the chasm. Not that I had any burning desire to test my balance on the precarious stone walkways above the water. The platforms from the first room had been more than enough to sate my appetite for adventure.

Before we could really begin putting together a plan, part of the wall behind us moved. A bunch of dirt and roots—typical cavern detritus—fell to the ground. Behind it, a previously concealed tree bark door appeared, and it quickly swung open.

"Shit." We'd stumbled into the boss room. No fun Zelda theme played from overhead to denote our achievement. There probably wouldn't be a chest of sick loot at the end of the fight, either. No, the more likely outcome would be a dungeon boss standing over three mutilated bodies, feeding them piece by piece to his pet dinosaurs.

I had always kind of figured that poor diet and lack of exercise would have been my demise. It seemed fitting. Or maybe it would have been asbestos poisoning. I was fairly convinced my apartment had some nasty shit filling the walls, and with the windows all painted shut, I was bound to bite the dust sooner rather than later.

Now, staring at the boss, dying of asbestos poisoning at the ripe age of fifty felt optimistic.

Standing with light at his back and a raptor in his arms was the deserter. There was no question in my mind. He wasn't wearing a faded military uniform or anything like that. I just *knew* it was him the way you always know when the guy you're supposed to meet but have never seen before finally walks into the room. That feeling coupled with the pet dinosaur and a host of thin tattoo lines told me the guy was going to be one badass dungeon boss. Beyond that, he didn't look fazed. Three-to-one odds. Sure, I wasn't much to look at, but Amethyst was sure as hell intimidating. The guy smiled.

"Welcome to my lair," the deserter began, his voice steady and cold as ice.

"No one is proud to live in a lair!" I yelled at him. Backing me up, Francis hissed and bared his cute little teeth from the sling at my front. I looked around for Mr. Patches and found him casually weaving through Amethyst's legs. So much for the Siren striking fear into the hearts of our enemies.

The deserter waved me off with one hand, the other still wrapped around the neck of his raptor pet. As far as combat Pokémon went, I had the equivalent of a derpy Rattata while the deserter was about to unleash a max-level Charizard on my ass. Why couldn't I have been cursed by a trailing pack of rhinos or some cool shit like that? Still, the little cube of tourmaline pressed between my belt and my hip gave me a measure of comfort. If everything went tits up—maybe a one percent chance it didn't—I could always give the Desecrator a turn.

"You are intruders!" the deserter yelled. He set down his raptor on its own legs, but thankfully didn't order it to attack . . . yet.

"Well, he got us there," I said under my breath.

Grinning from ear to ear, the deserter snapped his fingers. In the blink of an eye, a form-fitting suit of dark armor appeared over his body, and a huge, fiery sword materialized in his hands. I couldn't tell if the armor was leather or plate, maybe even something else, but what the hell did it matter? We were fucked either way.

"Guys? How about that boat?" A little cave trip on a rickety boat sounded a hell of a lot better than fighting Captain Kickass and his raptor pet.

Bokta and Amethyst both nodded, but they didn't say anything. At least we were all on the same page.

"Hey!" I shouted to the deserter. "What's your name?" I figured that keeping him talking about things that didn't involve killing us would, you know, prolong the 'killing us' part of the deal. Maybe I was reaching.

The deserter spread wide his arms, and his little raptor buddy jumped around anxiously from one clawed foot to the other, spittle flying from between its wicked teeth. "You have entered the domain of Sir Atatarck, Master of Dinosaurs!"

"Shit!" I basically yelled. "I *know* him! I know the boss!"

My mind reeled with memories. I had fought Sir Atatarck hundreds of times, maybe more. He was a low-tier dungeon boss from a mausoleum instance, a run for characters around level thirty. He was a staple for characters to farm over and over as they leveled because the whole dungeon was on the shorter side, and Atatarck had a small chance to drop a key that you needed later for a much harder raid.

"What?" Bokta shouted back, a confused expression on her face.

The dinosaurs were different—they should have been undead creatures, not prehistoric lizards—but I had a sneaking suspicion that the fight would be the same. Online, Atatarck had a horde of gargoyles that protected him, and his personal minion was an undead dog-leopard-hybrid thing. If the fight was scripted in a similar fashion, the fight would be simple.

"Amethyst! Bokta! Get to the tunnel entrance! You'll figure it out," I commanded. I didn't have time to explain anything. All I could do was hope that they'd trust me. Well, that and I had to hope that the fight actually *was* related to the online version, though I had no proof. For all I knew it could have been a simple coincidence. Whatever. No time for second guessing.

Thankfully, the two girls ran toward the tunnel where

we'd emerged, Bokta facing the incline while Amethyst guarded the front, swords raised. Before long, they would get the idea.

As the defacto raid leader, I had to tank. So even if the fight went down the way it did online, we'd *still* be absolutely screwed.

"Fuck it," I growled. Dropping my shoulder and grabbing my sword and shield, I charged forward to meet the raptor just like the tank had to do online. Francis hopped away somewhere in the mix, hopefully running to safety. The raptor was smaller than the undead I was used to, so maybe my brazen charge would work. Maybe.

We crashed together in the center of the cavern with a dizzying rattle of teeth, leathery skin, poor quality armor, and my shitty gear. Somehow, I came away with minimal damage. Sadly, the dinosaur fared about the same. I hadn't landed a strike. Not even a scratch. Not a single ounce of blood.

The creature turned and snapped its jaws at me. I responded in kind, awkwardly waving my sword around by my head. Shit, the gladius was heavier than I had imagined. My adrenaline did little to ease the weight. Maxkrannar had never shown any fatigue online. The weight in my hand was a poignant reminder that I was not a demon Oathbreaker in a video game. I guessed I was pretty close to being one in some sense, but I wasn't really there yet. And even if I were, I was still hopelessly low level.

Just like the online battle, the swarm of dinosaurs overhead plummeted to the ground, heading for Bokta and Amethyst. In the digital dungeon I was used to, the flying gargoyles had always attacked everyone except the main tank, and the entrance to the room was the best place to fend them off. If the group didn't stack up with their backs to the wall or the exit, they would be surrounded, and all the squishy casters would be picked off without much trouble.

It didn't take long for the women to figure out the plan. They set their feet next to each other and dove into the fight, but I couldn't watch. The raptor intent on tasting my innards charged back for round two.

It was kind of like fighting a thinner, more violent version of a golden retriever. If the retriever was a reptile, of course. I met the second rush with a downward strike of my weapon that connected to the beast's skull. I felt like the hit had dealt some damage—at least judging by the vibrating sting in my arm—but I still had to take a flash of teeth against my shield. And thank god for that! The raptor's teeth did a number on the hide shield, but my flesh stayed right where it was supposed to be.

I swung again, catching the raptor on the front shoulder, and was rewarded with a yelp for my efforts. That one drew some blood. Progress.

The raptor stumbled back for only a second before coming on again, gnashing its teeth for my legs. Down below my waist I was far less protected. I got my sword into position at the last possible second, turning a potentially devastating blow into one that just hurt like a bitch. The creature's teeth had done a number on my thigh. Searing pain shot through my side.

"You fucking bitch!" I yelled, swinging my sword with all my might. The blade connected, and the raptor didn't get the chance to yelp before its head separated from its neck. I hadn't made a clean cut, so the head lolled to the side as the beast collapsed, spewing hot blood all over the ground.

No matter the gruesome nature of the kill, it was still

a victory. But that meant phase two was about to begin. I stole a glance at Bokta and Amethyst, and they seemed to be holding their own. The pterodactyls attacking them weren't making much progress, if any at all.

The final phase of the online fight was by far the coolest. After the undead-dog-thing was dead, Sir Atatarck himself had to be eliminated. Luckily, I knew the fight well enough to know the boss's weaknesses. Realm Online featured a bunch of statues and other adornments common to mausoleums that could be pushed over to distract the boss.

Yeah . . . except none of those were present in the cavern. At best I had some rocks I could throw, but that felt even more useless than it was lame.

A flaming great sword came swinging in at my head. The attack was heavy and slow, inexorable, and it would have shorn me off at the waist had I not dropped to the ground and rolled. Still, the heat from the flaming blade was real.

I scrambled to my feet as quickly as I could. I needed to find something to draw the boss's attention. Bokta's tits would work, but she was occupied, and I didn't really feel too good about my own odds when it came to a sexy seduction. Nope, I needed something else.

Another devastating slash arced in for my side. I skipped backward, but the tip of the huge weapon still connected to my shield and sent me flying. The flimsy wood and hide shattered, sending a vicious sting up my arm. I grabbed at my wrist, lucky not to have been set aflame, and clenched my teeth against the new wave of pain wracking my entire being. I remembered a basic psychology class I had taken back in high school when I'd learned that pain was just a mental construct. That rat bastard teacher was a liar. Getting hit by a flaming sword hurt more than I could describe. But hey, I hadn't been immolated, so there was always a silver lining. Losing my shield was a small price to pay to preserve my limb.

Much to my dismay, Sir Atatarck kept coming. He had his sword held high above his head. The pain was so much I could barely move. Despite my own impending doom, all I could think of was Francis cowering not far away. The little kitten wouldn't stand a chance.

I couldn't let that happen. No one hurts my cats.

Accessing my new level two ability with my mind, I cast Fancy Illusions right at the deserter's feet.

Checkmate, bastard. The dungeon boss stopped, fear obvious on his face, and wondered at the mysterious runes I just conjured beneath him. The runes might not have done a single goddamned thing—was I bitter? Yeah, that's fair—but they worked wonderfully as a distraction.

"Help!" I yelled to Bokta, but I saw that I hadn't needed to call for her. Amethyst was handling the diving pterodactyls fine enough on her own, and Bokta was already running to intervene on my behalf. She reached Atatarck right as the towering boss was beginning to shake the stupor from his face, and a thick tendril of magical smoke extended from the Blood Witch's outstretched hand.

In seconds, she had him stunned. I struggled to my feet, trying as hard as possible to at least keep my pain silent. My legs still worked—silver linings everywhere. Thank god for not being crippled at level two. That would have been embarrassing. I could hear Brayden's sarcastic, arrogant sneer echoing through my head if I had died against Sir Atatarck: "Come on, little bitch, that piece of shit got you? I thought you were better than that."

Yeah, well I was showing him, wasn't I? Sure, he'd been here before, apparently, but I was here now. And with a gorgeous fantasy woman on either side. About to find Tom Arnold and get some answers. Well . . . that last one might have been an exaggeration.

Once more with my feet planted firmly underneath my torso, I figured gutting Sir Atatarck where he stood was the most prudent course of action. It wouldn't take much. Just a single stab, assuming I made it through his armor, and he'd go down.

Bokta beat me to it. The callous, beautiful Blood Witch ran her blade across the boss's neck.

"That was quick," I said, somewhat surprised. I wasn't really sure what struck me as odd about the rapid conclusion to the fight, but I couldn't deny the feeling of unease in my stomach. Maybe it was just the pain. Actually, on second thought, it most certainly *was* the pain.

"I'll check the room for loot, you make sure he lives," Bokta commanded to her superior. It took me a moment to realize that I was the male pronoun in her sentence. Amethyst stood amidst a bloody carpet of thrashed dinosaur parts at the entrance to the room. She hadn't killed more than a quarter of the attackers, but the others had all fled back to the safety of the ceiling upon their master's death.

Time for the meager medical supplies Amethyst had purchased to earn their keep. Unlacing the bracer on my left wrist, I couldn't tell how bad it was judging by the woman's facial expression. If anything, she looked like she'd seen worse. A good sign, I guessed.

"Think it's broken?" I asked, only half kidding.

Her face didn't change. "It isn't that bad, all things considered."

"Great."

"The problem is you'll slow us down if you let the pain get to you," the Siren stated flatly.

That sounded an awful lot like the last words of an explorer about to shoot a lame horse because it broke its leg. "Yeah, but . . . I can keep up," I told her.

Again, her expression revealed nothing. She stayed quiet as she worked, wrapping bits of cloth soaked in some sort of herbal remedy around my throbbing forearm. When I finally looked down to see the wound for myself, I breathed a sigh of relief. In all honestly, it wasn't *that* bad. I'd live for sure, the bones hadn't broken through the skin or anything, and I guessed there was even a chance they weren't fractured. If only I could get the damn pain to subside . . .

"There," Amethyst said, slapping my freshly covered wound and offering a faint smile. "Ready to go." She replaced my bracer, stood, and then offered a hand so I could get to my feet without shifting my bandages too much.

"Thanks." I started brushing the dirt and dust from my armor when Bokta came dashing out of the boss's personal chamber.

"Run!" she yelled, her arms full of some loot that I couldn't readily identify.

I didn't ask questions. If something was chasing her, I needed a head start to power through the gripping pain clouding my head. A hand in my armpit, Amethyst pulled me along as fast as my legs could manage. We were headed right for the central path over the swirling water so far below.

Bokta took the path on the right, and I finally saw what was chasing her. A little brood of hatchlings was nipping at her heels. They weren't infant raptors—those would have been much easier to handle—but instead some kind of weird amalgamation resulting in a spritely raptor body topped by a huge, gnashing alligator head. If any of them caught up to her, it would be easy to bring her down.

One of the little buggers had taken the path I was on, and it looked like Amethyst's grim prediction of my speed was about to come true. I wasn't fast enough.

Nearly throwing me off the narrow walkway, the Siren wrenched me in front of her and turned. With a single well-timed, deft strike, she knocked the dino-gator off the stone to the tumultuous waters below.

Holy shit. Amethyst saved me. That was pretty badass. Maybe a little unexpected, but still awesome. Perhaps she was starting to come around to my side. I knew she'd never be as much of a fan girl as Bokta, though I would certainly appreciate her starting to place some higher value on my life, if that indeed had been the root cause of my rescue.

On the other slender catwalk, Bokta wasn't faring as well. Four of the little broodlings had chased her, and she had only managed to knock one of them into the river. One of her hands was leaking blood.

"Do something!" I tried to command the Siren, but she only frowned. She was a martial class, not a caster, and she didn't have a bow or throwing knives, or even a cheesy mall-ninja shuriken to toss across the chasm.

"She's strong," Amethyst said under her breath.

All we could do was watch. Two of the dino-gators latched onto her right forearm, their vicious teeth sinking deep. All the gear the woman had looted from the boss's private chamber had spilled over the edge to be swept away in the waters below. Bokta tried to swing her arm to throw the two dino-gators wide, but the movement made her overbalance. A third broodling snapped at her legs, forcing the woman to kick in response. With two extra creatures hanging over her arm and only one foot planted on the ground, there was simply no possible way she could keep her balance.

"No!" I yelled. My heart sank through the bottom of my chest. All at once, the pain under my bracer didn't hurt any longer. The pain inside my chest was far too strong to let me pay attention to anything else.

Shouting as she fell, Bokta's voice was quickly cut off when she splashed into the water.

"Come on!" Amethyst urged, barely giving the river a second thought. "We can get to the boat. If she's alive, we'll find her. If not, there's nothing we can do."

There wasn't a third option. Either she was alive and waiting to be pulled out of the water by my strong hands, or she was already dead from the fall. I gave a final glance back to the flaming great sword resting on the ground next to Sir Atatarck's corpse with a bit of longing peeking through my despair. There wasn't any time to grab it. There wasn't even enough time to mourn the lost gear. Besides, it probably wouldn't fit in the small boat.

Amethyst dragged me to the other side of the chasm without any regard to decorum or preserving my bandages. I tried to propel myself harder, and I think I actually succeeded in giving us at least a little bit of additional speed.

I strained my ears to pick up any shred of human sound coming from the river that would give me an inkling of hope that Bokta had survived.

Nothing.

CHAPTER 28

T he words of the last shrine I had found flicked into my head.

Winding round the way you go—
Lost if only you follow the flow!

Well, we'd found the flow. We were basically lost. The boat was the next play, and the two cats were telling me exactly what to do.

We reached the boat, and Amethyst kicked the ropes off the pylon with a single quick movement. I leapt onto the only bench, my eyes eagerly searching the tumultuous waves for any sign of the Blood Witch.

A few seconds later and we were adrift. The little boat barely had enough room for Amethyst and me plus two cats, but Francis didn't take up much room. I had scooped him back onto my chest, and his little claws clung to my breastplate, his eyes full of terror.

"Hang in there, buddy," I told him quietly. Silently, the

words were aimed just as much at Bokta as they were at the cat.

We swirled along toward the side of the cavern where the river disappeared underneath a stone ledge—and into complete darkness—and Mr. Patches took up a position on the bow like George Washington leading his troops across the Delaware.

"Bokta!" I shouted. Amethyst joined in the call from my side.

No response came.

The boat raced closer and closer to the darkness of the next passage. We had no oars, so we couldn't stop even if we wanted to. Whatever was lying in wait in the inky blackness of the cavern would have a fresh meal delivered soon enough.

"Bokta!" I yelled one last time before we left Sir Atatarck's domain.

Under the ledge, the river was much more placid and restrained. The boat slowed a little bit as the bow righted itself, though Mr. Patches had fearlessly ridden it without complaint through the tumult of the previous chamber.

"Hello? Bokta?" I called more softly.

Amethyst hung her head over the water to our left. "Bokta?"

More nothing. The crushing darkness was entirely devoid of any human sounds other than my panicked breathing.

At the bow, two paws firmly planted on the gunwale, Mr. Patches issued a soft meow.

"Can you see her?" I asked the cat. Being able to summon Bokta's luminescent butterfly pet would have been a hell of a lot more useful than attempting to converse with a cat, but we didn't have that luxury.

Still, cats could see in the dark, couldn't they? Maybe Mr. Patches could help, though I wasn't exactly sure how.

"See anything?" I asked Amethyst.

"Nothing. There's no light."

Hopefully the cat on our bow was faring a little better. "We need to buy a couple torches or something." If we ever made it back to a major city with enough gibs to buy some gear, I had every intention of finding the medieval version of a headlamp. But damn my luck, we didn't have Atatarck's head. No bounty for us.

A few more quiet moments went by, punctuated only by the occasional shout of the Blood Witch's name. Finally, there was a little light at the end of our tunnel—in a very literal sense. We could begin to see what it was we had been drifting down, and I wasn't terribly happy about it. The ceiling above us was low, maybe five or six feet from the boat, and solid rock. Underneath the boat was a different story. The water, at least, appeared to be normal. We could see all the way down to the bottom, however far that really was, and there were creatures . . .

Deep, black shadows glided through the water. The silhouettes looked to be about the size of dolphins, and they were quick. Instantly, my mind went to a dark place. No matter what they were, there was a good chance they'd already devoured Bokta. Maybe we'd find some of her clothes drifting along further down the current, tattered and bloody . . . but that wasn't where I was going to let my mind wander.

She's alive, I told myself. That was all there was to it. We'd find her alive soon enough.

The light kept growing until we could see pretty much everything around us, and then the river exited its subterranean labyrinth. We were back in the outside world.

"Shit . . . the T-Rex is out here somewhere." I hung my head. "Can't catch any breaks."

"Stay vigilant. Keep your eyes on the forest," Amethyst bade.

A giant, rampaging T-Rex would be a wonderful little addition to our wretched plight.

The river was slowing more and more the farther we got from the underground lair. I could see the edge of the wooden palisade we had gone through to enter the dungeon, though we were on the opposite side from the entrance. Ahead and downstream, the river continued through the forest for as far as I could see. The only shred of a silver lining was the T-Rex's absence. Sadly, I wasn't confident that it would last.

Then, up ahead on the left bank of the river, I saw something vaguely humanoid. "Amethyst, there! Is it her?"

The Siren followed my pointing finger to the heap of *something* huddled up at the edge of the water. "We'll know soon enough," she said.

The current wasn't fast enough to get us there with any kind of speed. I kept my eyes glued to the figure, only searching for the T-Rex for a fraction of a second at a time—but there was no movement anywhere. Nothing told me we had found Bokta, and none of the trees gave away the dinosaur's position, either.

Both of us jumped off the boat as soon as we were close enough to the shore to not be diving into the water and swimming.

My heart fluttered—it was her. Bokta was there, face down on the shore, and covered in a layer of watery debris that was a mix of algae, slime, and some stringy green plant that I assumed was seaweed or whatever the freshwater equivalent was. I wasn't a botanist, and I certainly didn't care enough about the local flora to bother with it any longer than I needed to.

When I rolled Bokta over onto her back, I could tell fairly quickly that she wasn't breathing. The winged dinosaurs from the Atatarck encounter had taken their toll on her . . . but the fall from the ledge might have broken her neck. "What do we do?"

Amethyst dropped down to her knees and immediately set to work. Like a veteran Red Cross volunteer giving a class on water safety, she tilted Bokta's head back, checked her mouth for obstruction, then began breathing into her, stopping after every few breaths to listen.

No matter how dire the situation, all I could think of was the way Bokta's soaking wet shirt clung to her curves, though I guessed that wasn't exactly *all* I was thinking of. No, the contact between Bokta's lips and Amethyst's was certainly a fine spectacle for my attention.

Knowing that I was getting in the way more than I was helping—and that I had another job to do which essentially amounted to being on dinosaur watch duty—I had to peel my eyes away from the glorious girl-on-girl make-out session taking place right before my eyes. Besides, killing Atatarck had brought a fair amount of XP, and I had hit level three. Time to power up. Curiously, my points in favor had also increased to the next rank, though I wasn't sure what that meant. Maybe I'd get luckier with the cursed die, but that was governed by the luck stat, I thought. Still, I beamed at my new stats:

Level: 3
Experience: 2600 / 5000
Favor: 1100 / 2000 – Rank 2
Physical: 4
Magic: 1

Defense: 1
Charisma: 1
Commerce: 1
Luck: 6
Available Attribute Points: 1

If Bokta was going to pull through, we needed more than the medical supplies we had brought with us. I tossed my attribute point into luck, raising the stat to seven, and silently begged the Desecrator to bring her back while I watched the forest for any signs of incoming dinosaurs.

There still wasn't any movement in the forest beyond the normally occurring biological processes. Birds flew between the trees, the wind played with the leaves, and clouds slowly drifted in and out of the bright sunshine.

Bokta gasped a short moment later, and my attention was ripped away from the serenity of the landscape. She was alive. The Siren helped her sit up, and after a minute or two of spastic coughing, she seemed to gather her wits about her once more.

"Get . . . get away from . . . the water," she urged between coughs.

"Not even some thanks or a little recognition?" I said, but there wasn't any strength behind my words. I saw what it was that Bokta was trying to warn us to fear.

An amphibious dinosaur, one of the shadows we had seen beneath the boat, crawled out onto the shore. "Get her back!" I yelled, but Amethyst was already dragging the Blood Witch by her shoulders.

The thing emerging from the water was kind of like a typical raptor from any *Jurassic Park* movie except for the four-foot tall dorsal fin protruding vertically from its back. Its mouth, full of razor sharp teeth the size of kitchen knives, was shaped more or less like an alligator's. Or maybe it was more akin to a crocodile—I'd never learned the difference.

No matter which modern day reptile or amphibian was most analogous to the dinosaur, one thing was beyond certain: it was trying to kill us. Oh, and it would probably succeed.

I dove my consciousness deep into the recesses of my mind and latched onto the Doom Spike spell. I could feel the spell waiting for my command, practically begging to be released. But if the T-Rex showed up again . . . I felt like Doom Spike would be our only hope against a towering T-Rex, so I had to save it.

"I'm out of spells!" I yelled at our martial expert, opting not to try and explain why I was refusing to use Doom Spike. Saving time was paramount.

Amethyst looked over her shoulder with terror on her face. She passed off Bokta to my waiting grasp before springing into a fighting stance and grabbing her swords.

Dragging the battered Blood Witch to safety, a new thought crossed my mind: I had never actually seen Amethyst in action. When we had fought the ascending Torch Bearer back in Mara, Mr. Patches had been our tank, and we had just legged it out of the city. Even in the bowels of the municipal dungeon we had broken into to spring Ta-ros, Amethyst hadn't fought much. She was our leader, the fearless commander, and she had used others—myself included—to do her wet work.

Whatever part of me wasn't busy being absolutely shit-my-pants petrified was actually eager to watch the Si-ren work. She was, after all, a martial class unlike Bokta and myself.

Amethyst set her dual blades in motion without hesitation. She spun from side to side, utilizing her much faster, smaller build against the heftier dinosaur with immediate effect. The creature snapped at her left, and she ducked, then spun on her heel and came up under the beast's head. One of her blades jabbed into the dinosaur's neck. It wasn't a killing blow, but it was progress.

Using its sizable claws instead of its teeth, the dinosaur slashed and caught Amethyst's harness hanging from her torso. The strappy leather arrangement flew from her body. Luckily, the woman's flesh hadn't been caught. She spun again, and then a yellow sheen overtook both her blades, and the speed at which her weapons danced through the air accelerated wildly.

Strike after strike rained down on the dinosaur's head, neck, and upper body. A few pieces of the tall dorsal fin went flying back into the water. The dinosaur shrieked as it tried to back away from the vicious Siren.

Then the yellow aura of magic faded, and Amethyst was suddenly moving more slowly than she had been before the augmentation. Clearly, the woman was gassed. Her endurance had been spent in the furious whirlwind, but the dinosaur had not succumbed to its injuries. The numerous cuts and gashes in its tough hide weren't deep enough to bring it down.

If I had Atatarck's flaming great sword, I'd lop the beast's head off with a single blow! But I didn't have a great sword. No, I had a gladius, and using it would mean getting close enough to those thrashing claws and slicing teeth to lose some fingers or a hand.

Still, I didn't have much choice. The dinosaur snapped at Amethyst's chest, and that time it got some meat instead of just gear.

Using my left hand to cover Francis still clinging to my pecs, I gripped my sword and slashed downward at the dinosaur's right shoulder with all my strength. Hitting the beast's mottled skin felt like swinging against a Kevlar vest, though to be honest I was just guessing. Maybe Kevlar was shit against blades. I'd never even seen a cop wearing a vest in real life.

Regardless of the metaphor, my sword didn't do much. It sank through the dinosaur's resilient hide maybe half an inch. It wasn't enough. The bloodied and enraged beast kept snapping and swiping, its attention fully locked onto Amethyst, and the woman was struggling to block and parry. Still trying to shield Francis from both blood splatter and psychological trauma, I wrenched my gladius away and swung again, aiming for the exact same place like a lumberjack chopping down a tree.

My second hit landed almost perfectly inside the gash left by my first cut. I didn't let up. Two more hits followed, and then the dinosaur started to seriously flag from the gruesome wound. I was about to swing for chop number five when Amethyst found an opening and took it.

The Siren flicked her wrist upward just as the dinosaur made a last-ditch effort to bite open her chest, and her sword caught in the bottom of its mouth. She had the beast effectively skewered. I finally moved my second hand up to the hilt of my gladius and chopped with all my weight and strength combined.

The dinosaur's head dropped down. It didn't come all the way off, but I had severed enough of its critical nervous system parts to achieve a kill.

"Finally . . ." Amethyst said, her hands on her knees to catch her breath.

My experience points moved up to three thousand.

I turned Francis away from the bloody spectacle—eager to avoid it myself—and let the blood run off my blade and onto the shore. A few feet away, Bokta was still struggling to get to her feet.

"Everyone alri—"

Movement caught my eye.

"What's wrong?" Amethyst quickly asked, her blades once more at the ready—though I wasn't confident that she'd be terribly useful.

"Uh, guys . . ." I pointed at a spot off in the forest fairly far away. The tops of the trees were moving in a distinct pattern. Getting closer.

Amethyst saw it too. "The T-Rex."

"We have to run," Bokta added, leaning the majority of her weight on my shoulder.

I looked her over, and she didn't really strike me as fit enough to do a whole lot of walking, much less running. "How well can you move?" I asked.

She slowly took her hand away from my body. Without my shoulder as a support, she nearly fell, and I had to catch her to keep her from pitching over into the dirt.

The movement in the treetops was getting closer. Sure, there was a chance it wouldn't be the T-Rex, but anything else large enough to bend the forest canopy as it moved was bound to be just as dangerous. No matter what, we still needed to run.

"Get her on your shoulders," I told the Siren. The woman's chest was bloodied and obviously in need of care, but there was no time. God, what I would have given for a couple health potions to speed along the healing process. But we had basically nothing.

"Alright," I said, adjusting Bokta's weight on my side. "Back toward Apostate's Rise. We need to get to the wall, or we at least need to get deep enough into the forest that the dinosaurs can't track us."

CHAPTER 29

"I *really* don't want to be eaten by a dinosaur..." I grumbled. Bokta's weight on my shoulder was starting to kill. We were deep into the heat and humidity of the jungle. For the second time, I cursed my luck and thought of the dungeon boss's sword. A flaming great sword would have been able to carve a swath of destruction through the branches and undergrowth, keeping the dew-laden leaves from constantly clinging to my skin. Despite the stat being my highest, my luck hadn't been quite good enough to score the sword *and* rescue Bokta.

After what felt like an eternity but was probably only about twenty minutes, Bokta seemed to have recovered enough to at least be lucid. We stopped to rest—or at least to let *me* rest since Amethyst wasn't yet winded—and Bokta managed to keep herself up on her own two feet.

"What's . . . coming . . . ?" she asked between heavy breaths. All three of us turned toward the impending dinosaur apocalypse. So deep in the trees and underbrush, we couldn't see anything.

"I'm not sure it's following us now," the Siren added.

"Wait," I said quietly. I knelt to the ground and put both palms flat against the dirt. Yup, there it was. I let out a deep sigh as I stood. "Still following us. And that thing must be huge." The vibrations coming through the ground were steady, maybe a little slower than I had anticipated, but they were still certainly there.

"Come on," Amethyst announced, wrapping an arm around Bokta's chest to help her.

I grabbed the Blood Witch's opposite arm and hefted the bulk of her weight back onto my shoulder. "Have to keep going. Once we reach Apostate's Rise . . ." but I didn't know what else to say. What could the ruined, lawless city possibly offer? Sure, there were plenty of mercenaries and other ruffians who made the abandoned metropolis their home, but why would they care about us? They'd all cut and run at the first sign a giant T-Rex stomping through the woods. Every last one of them. But maybe, just maybe . . . the dinosaur would give up the chase.

Somehow I wasn't quite positive that a man-eating beast the size of a theme park attraction was going to run out of endurance or just get bored. Perhaps a distraction, though . . . but the idea would have to wait. We didn't have anything on hand to pull the beast's attention. Apostate's Rise, on the other hand, was bound to be full of things more interesting than three battered and beaten Oathbreakers.

———◦◦————————◦◦———

We managed to stay ahead of the beast for another hour. Bokta being able to plant her feet and run alongside us—never for very long, just short sprints—was a huge help. Unfortunately, all three of us knew something was very wrong when we passed the small burrow where I'd found Francis.

Bokta, resting her weary legs against a tree, let Mr. Patches rub his back along her shins. "Too many tracks," she said, giving voice to the exact thought we had all been thinking. The clearing had been visited, and from the looks of the muddied boot prints, by a ton of people.

"What could it be?" I asked.

Amethyst shook her head. "Bokta, send your butterfly ahead to scout. Think you have enough energy to cast?"

With a sigh full of despair, the Blood Witch said, "Not right now. I'm too tired . . ."

Amethyst gave me a pained look.

"I don't know if I'm the stealthiest person for the job. I mean, I'll try. But if there's some huge ambush waiting for us, don't expect me to just cut down a bunch of brigands on my own." I gave Francis a gentle pat on my stomach. I was worried for the little guy. He'd seen so much in such a short few weeks of life. The therapy bills would be outrageous. Or maybe the kitten would simply see too much violence and his mind would snap. Then we could skip the expensive shrink and just have him committed.

Giving Francis a few more gentle pats to calm him down, I slunk off on the balls of my feet to do a little recon. If I was being honest, I didn't really know where I was going or what I was seeking. We were still a good hour from Apostate's Rise. Wandering off on my own through the wilderness was a great way to get lost. At level three, I didn't have any good stealth or survival skills in case I got into a jam, either.

Thinking of my lacking skills reminded me: I hadn't actually checked out my sheet since hitting level three other than to assign my attribute point. Maybe there *was* a new stealth ability waiting there. I summoned the sheet to my vision. No such luck.

New Ability: Blighted Ground. Three waves of sickening blight emanate from your body, poisoning the ground and any living creatures caught within the radius.

Luckily, the tracks heading away from the kitten hovel were super easy to follow without a tracking talent, even for a novice like me. All I kept thinking was how many people must have been there. It looked like an army had been through, and they hadn't been too concerned about hiding their presence. Had they been hunting us? I thought of Gideon and the other tattooed hulk from the Crone. Sure, Amethyst had stolen a map from them, but they wouldn't have risked a trip beyond the Wall just for that. Discounting them left me with one option. Valiance. I didn't want to think about the possibility.

I followed the tracks for a good ways before giving up. I had kept the path to my right, fighting through the dense undergrowth surrounding the trees, and I was perhaps a little more eager than I should have been to get back on the main path and meet up with the rest of the party, so I cut my venture short with no evidence of an ambush lying ahead.

When I returned, both women appeared a bit put off by my quick arrival.

"What?" I said, shrugging. "The tracks just keep going back to Apostate's Rise. There wasn't anything else to see."

A thundering footstep not far off in the distance interrupted Amethyst before she could scold my general lack of effort. "Alright, let's move," she said instead of whatever had been about to leap from her tongue.

Bokta was ready to run again for a while on her own, so we set off down the path at full speed, Amethyst taking point.

We made record time. It wasn't too surprising that a death-dealing T-Rex hot on our asses had a pretty significant influence on our endurance and speed. Adrenaline was a hell of a drug.

There was only one problem. We reached the end of the tree line that put us in view of Apostate's Rise's damaged Wall, and it was brimming with steel and pennants.

Valiance had arrived.

I had a pretty damn good idea who they were after. We hadn't been seen yet from the trees, but the T-Rex hot on our heels still hadn't decided to give up the chase. What a dick.

"Well . . . that sucks," I stated.

Amethyst shot me a look that said she shared my sentiment and had already assessed blame. Fair enough. I earned it.

"Any ideas?" Bokta asked. She had a hand grasping her side, and a few parts of her chest were still pretty bloody. We'd be down a fighter. Even without her injury, the odds were impossible. I needed some sort of 'ultimate' ability to unleash if we were going to have a chance. Actually, we'd all need an ultimate. A teleportation spell would have been really nice as well. Nothing like dodging the fight and gaining some levels before coming back.

No one offered Bokta any brilliant plan in response to her question. We just kind of stood there looking at each other. "Neither of you can teleport, right?" I asked. It was worth a shot.

Both responses came in the form of quiet head shakes. No dice.

Wait a minute.

I *had* an ultimate. Sort of, but it counted.

I took the little cube of black tourmaline from my belt and held it out on the palm of my hand. "What do you think?" I asked, a touch of optimism returning to my voice.

Amethyst dropped her head into her hands.

"We don't have time," Bokta said. "I . . . need to rest before I bleed out . . ."

"Don't forget the monstrous dinosaur bearing down on us," I added.

Finally, Amethyst peered down at the Eye, though she kept her hands behind her back. "I suppose we don't really have much of a choice," she said.

I was practically oozing with anticipation. Yeah, I knew the risks were supposedly monumental, but it had worked out last time fine enough.

Before tossing the Eye and taking a chance on our lives, I at least had the forethought to extract Francis from my armor just in case he decided to turn into a monstrous werewolf-cat-hybrid like Mr. Patches had done back in the streets of Mara.

"Where should I roll?" I asked. There weren't any dice towers or even flat surfaces around to ensure I avoided a tilt. Honestly, I wasn't positive a tilt would even matter. As long as I rolled the die and didn't just set it down or accidentally drop it, the magic would probably work.

"Here," Amethyst said, clearing away a small patch of leaves to give me a little space.

The T-Rex was getting closer. The leaves and twigs scattered across the ground were jumping with vibration. If I had a Styrofoam cup of water, I'd be able to recreate pretty accurately one of the most recognized *Jurassic Park* scenes of all time.

"Well?" Bokta said, pulling my mind back to the die in my hand.

I took a deep breath. "Come on, we need a six here, Mr. Patches," I told the cat casually scratching at the ground a few feet away.

Francis, still clinging close to my feet as I knelt, gave a short series of meows to let me know he was still there. Maybe the two cats could sense what was about to happen—either a dinosaur stomping us into oblivion or the demonic invocation I was about to attempt—but I was guessing.

"No time like the present," I said. I gave the die a gentle blow for good luck like a hot chick trying to bang the high roller at a Las Vegas craps table. "Alright, kittens. Here we go!"

I gave the die a single shake before rolling it into the little clearing of leaves. It bounced around a few times, rolled forward, and stopped.

"Uh . . ."

"Wh—"

"We should probably run," Amethyst muttered.

"Damn cats let me down." I stared at the single glittering tourmaline skull staring back at me, mocking me.

A few feet away, Mr. Patches screeched. The T-Rex was almost upon us. If we ran, the only way to go would be directly toward all the Valiance soldiers no doubt hiding on the other side of the wall. Staying put . . . felt like a really bad decision.

"Let's run," I stated, summoning my courage. "To the city."

Amethyst gave me a curt nod as she helped Bokta prepare for the sprint. "Right. To the city."

Mr. Patches let out another screech.

CHAPTER 30

G od dammit, a fucking one!

I had no idea what unholy nonsense was about to erupt from the ground. Or come crashing down from the sky. Or maybe burst out of my chest like the xenomorph from *Alien*.

The three of us ran hard for Apostate's Rise. The Wall was within sight and perhaps within easy reach. It gave me a glimmer of hope, but I knew deep down that we weren't running for safety—we were reenacting Pickett's Charge.

Sure enough, we had been watched.

Half way to the wall, the fluttering blue and gold Valiance banners were joined by a dozen or more stoic faces belonging to the Valiance faithful. Behind them, I could hear the awful creaking of chains . . . the ascended Torch Bearer had come along for a little slice of personal vengeance. I had stolen from him, after all, and I was fairly certain he'd lost a bit of street cred after Mr. Patches had sort of kicked his ass in full view of the public.

One of the Valiance bastards had a crossbow balanced on the top of the Wall. There was only one way into the city that didn't involve attempting to scale a rather impressive collection of stones and mortar. The crevice, the tight broken passage we had used to exit the city not long before, was the most heavily guarded section. Three armored soldiers filled the immediate gap, and another four were stationed directly overhead, one of them holding the crossbow.

The weapon thrummed. A bolt the length of my forearm sailed just over Amethyst's head—and something squealed behind her. I turned my head, still running directly at the enemy, and saw a slain raptor with a bolt protruding from the front of its skull. Three more sprinting raptors weren't far behind.

The three of us caught in the middle of no man's land whirled to face the new dinosaur threat, but Bokta lost her balance. She was still too hurt to fight. Amethyst struggled to get her off the ground, leaving me as the only one of our crew free to defend against the incoming dinosaur stampede. More and more raptors were breaking free from the treeline every second, a prelude to the jungle king stomping toward us. Behind them, I could see the T-Rex as well. It was too big to push through with the same speed as the smaller raptors, so I figured we had about ten seconds before facing the full strength of the Jurassic army.

And honestly, I wasn't really sure if the Valiance guys were there to kill me or the dinosaurs. Maybe they had been summoned to defend the people of Apostate's Rise. It felt like something they'd do, all good paladin kind of shit, but it was a stretch. How would they have known about the impending invasion?

No, I told myself, I was just being dangerously optimistic. They'd come for my head. The dinosaurs were just a ridiculous coincidence.

If I could play the dinosaurs against the Torch Bearer and his friends, we'd have a chance.

First, we needed to survive the next ten seconds. I had another activation of Doom Spike ready to go, and it was my only choice. I lined up the spell with the oncoming raptors, latched onto it with my mind, and let it fly. A giant pillar of dark ice rocketed up from the ground and tore through a small trio of raptors. Their shattered bodies landed in a red mist all across the ground. Well, one of them was still barely alive judging by the horrible bleating coming from its mouth.

"Run under the wall. Now. Go!" Amethyst urged. I was already headed that way. At least the bottom of the wall would offer some protection from the crossbow, though I had no idea what kind of brutal magic the Torch Bearer would throw down on us from his half-ascended height.

"Wait," Bokta muttered, pain evident in her voice. She reached toward the still-living raptor like a shipwrecked sailor reaching for the last empty piece of driftwood. "Get it. Bring the raptor."

"What the hell?" I wanted to scream at her to get her head on straight, but we didn't have the time.

"Blood magic," Bokta whispered weakly. "Get the raptor."

Oh.

That kind of made sense. I had my ultimate, rolling the Eye of the Desecrator, and she had hers. Or at least that was my thought process. She could have been delusional from the stress of combat, drowning, and everything else she'd been through. Regardless, I felt like I had to try. And the closer I got to the Valiance Torch Bearer, the worse I felt about hiding against the wall hoping not to die. There were too many variables and too little time left to plan out our course of action.

I went for it. I sprinted back to the bleating raptor and wrapped a hand around one of its two remaining legs. The pair on the front had been blown off, and that was probably a good thing considering how heavy the beast was even in such a crippled state. Magic sailed above my head as I dragged the raptor toward the base of the wall where Bokta waited. At least the Valiance goons were a little concerned with the massive dinosaur about to plow through Apostate's Rise. I guessed they had quickly realized the larger threat. Three renegade Oathbreakers could wait.

"Looks like the do-gooders up top are giving us a pass. Here's your raptor," I said, throwing the mutilated creature at Bokta's feet. "You have like four seconds before we're dead. Do something."

Weakly, her eyes closed and one hand still clutching at her side, Bokta touched the raptor's head. Immediately, the creature calmed. Then a bit of white smoke escaped the woman's mouth. It twirled and danced through the air before darting into the dinosaur's eyes, and the raptor immediately went still.

"Is it dead?" I asked. I kept my back to the Wall partly to prevent the crossbow above from gaining an angle and also to keep my eyes on the T-Rex. The huge beast roared not ten feet away. Luckily, the Torch Bearer was the closest thing to its eye level, and it seemed to have turned its focus in his direction instead of ours.

Why hadn't the Eye done anything! I raged in my mind. I couldn't see the two cats, not that I had any idea what was supposed to happen. Still, the overall lack of action was disconcerting.

The dying raptor twitched. Its scaly, leathery skin rippled, and then it began changing colors. Symbols appeared all over its body in a distinct, circular pattern.

"What's she doing?" I yelled. "What's happening?" More magic—huge spheres of fire and piercing rods of holy light—lanced out from the Torch Bearer and smashed into the T-Rex's body.

A dagger had appeared in Bokta's hand. She moved it to the raptor's neck with a slow, deliberate hand.

"What's she doing?" I shouted again. Neither Bokta nor Amethyst seemed too eager to answer my question, so I all I could do was wait.

In the center of the field separating Apostate's Rise from the wooded wilderness about a hundred yards away, something else was beginning to happen. Under the T-Rex's tail, the ground was starting to break apart. It looked like lava was seeping up from growing fissures all over the dirt and grass.

"Summoning . . ." Bokta finally murmured, her eyes still shut to the chaos right in front of her.

The raptor beneath her hand ruptured. It didn't mewl or roar as it died—it simply split at the seams and spewed a torrent of hot blood into the air. As the putrid red rain fell back to the ground, it landed in the same circular pattern that had appeared on its flesh.

Whatever the Blood Witch was summoning, she was living up to her class moniker. As I watched with a mixture of horror and awe and Bokta collapsed against the wall in unconsciousness, something rose up from the circle of blood and began moving toward the broken, upended ground. Some sort of . . . blood snake, I guessed, was swimming through the air toward the growing chasm.

More and more dirt, rock, and magical debris fell into whatever existed underneath Realm's topsoil. The T-Rex started losing its balance. Its left leg slipped, and then its tail disappeared into the chasm. It clawed for purchase with its other foot, but the creature was so bottom heavy that it never had a chance. A few seconds later, the dinosaur disappeared into the ground.

"That works," I said, though I would have rather seen the fiery hellhole envelope the soldiers on the wall above us rather than the mutual enemy keeping them busy. "We—"

Something was coming *out* of the portal. It had a claw, but it wasn't a dinosaur.

"Summoning . . ." Amethyst stated. "And you rolled a one. She combined the spells."

Combined the spells . . .

A second claw joined the first. I recognized the splotchy-colored fur, a mishmash of white, brown, and orange. Then Mr. Patches' head appeared at the edge of the pit, though it was the size of a horse's head instead of a house cat's. Then, to Patches' right, two more claws dug into the ground. They were jet black, and the nails looked large enough to be swords.

Francis was the first to fully emerge. Behind me and up on top of the wall, the Valiance soldiers had stopped launching their devastating magic. They stood in stunned silence. The Torch Bearer's chains didn't even bother creaking in the wind.

When Mr. Patches, struggling a little compared to his pitch-dark companion, finally emerged, my heart caught in my chest.

He had a rider.

I recognized the rider's armor. I'd know it anywhere.

Strongwarrior43 had joined the game.

If you enjoyed this novel, please consider leaving a review at your favorite book retailer's website. Reviews from enthusiastic readers are vital to authors everywhere. Your support is greatly appreciated!

ABOUT THE AUTHOR

Stuart Thaman is the international best-selling author of tons of books. He began with a little epic fantasy about a goblin, a town in peril, and what happens when the traditional 'bad guys' want to leave their evil ways in the past. Since those long-forgotten days of yore, he has published more than a dozen titles, several of which have gone on to become international successes.

Catch up with Stuart Thaman at www.stuartthamanbooks. com, and be sure to join the mailing list so you never miss a free download or contest.

Want to connect on social media?

Facebook: www.facebook.com/epicfantasylit
Instagram: @stuartthamanbooks
Twitter: @StuartThaman

ACKNOWLEDGMENTS

First and foremost, I would like to thank everyone who read Realm Online when it was in its infancy on Royal Road. You early readers are the best. Without the vital input from all 30,000 (!!!!) of you, the story wouldn't be nearly as good as it is now.

Secondly, a big thank you goes out to all the great folks over at /r/litrpg—the feedback and support I've received there has been extremely useful.

And finally, I thank the readers. Without people like you buying books, there would be no authors.

THE ADVENTURE CONTINUES IN
REALM ONLINE: CITADEL DEATHGAZE

Get a free copy of *The Minotaur King* by joining
the mailing list!
https://dl.bookfunnel.com/lt2mw0eidx